Simon Lazarus

a novel
by

M. A. Kirkwood

Bookman Publishing
Martinsville, Indiana
www.BookmanMarketing.com

Cover art: *"Duo Teste"* (*"Two Heads"*), Leonardo da Vinci, Edizioni D'Arte Nova Lux-Firenze

Cover design: Allen Ketchersid

The author wishes to acknowledge the following:

K. Almgren, M. Mundy, P. Sandstrom, S. Ratcliff, L.L. Evans, G. Golden, D. Gustafson, S. Reuben, L. Smith, A. Sebastian, B. Madrigan, A. D'Angelo, R. Cummings, B. R. Brooker, M. Raphael, the late A.Vaughan and so many remarkable souls who've shared my life's path; all of them not forgotten. I know you are out there!

A note to E. Tolle: In the ten years that I've known you, dear friend, you have always been so true to your word. Thank you for your honesty, integrity, and selfless concern. *Blessings* to *you*, always!

GRATEFUL ACKNOWLEDGEMENT IS MADE FOR USE OF THE FOLLOWING:

"Land": *Horses*, by Patti Smith, 1975, Arista Records

"Slit Skirts", Pete Townshend, 1982, Eel Pie Recording Productions Ltd., Atco Records

"Scary Monsters", from *Scary Monsters, Super Creeps*, David Bowie, 1980

"Downtown Train", T. Waits, Jalma Music ASCAP (Performed by Rod Stewart), 1988, Warner Bros. Records

"Stupid Girl", by Garbage, 1995, Vibecrusher Music/Irving Music Inc. BMI/Deadarm Music ASCAP and Strummers/Jones, Ninder Ltd. EMI Virgin Music, Inc. ASCAP

"Mr Jones", by Adam Duritz 1993 EMI Blackwood Music Inc./ Jones Falls Music, BMI

"Round Here", by Adam Duritz, 1993 EMI Blackwood Music Inc./Jones Falls Music, BMI

"Is There Anybody Out There?", R. Waters, Pink Floyd Music Ltd., 1979, Columbia Records, CBS Inc.

The author wishes to acknowledge Harold Bloom for the following from his book: *Genius*. In his discussion on Miguel Cervantes, Bloom quotes from a curious play written by the late Anthony Burgess entitled *A Meeting in Valladolid*. In it, *Will* Shakespeare and Miguel Cervantes have a discussion. As *Will* brags about his range of talent, asserting that it is in writing *tragedy* where one finds the highest skills of the dramaturge, *Miguel* then says:

"It is not and will never be. God is a comedian. God does not suffer the tragic consequences of a flawed essence. Tragedy is all too human. Comedy is divine."*

****

And not to forget that life is often an exquisite blend of these extremes, the author wishes to dedicate this book to that *Divine Comedian* and the spirits of mirth!

*from the book, *Genius* by Harold Bloom, Copyright 2002, Limited Liability Company, Warner Books

Scratchy Vinyl

Gram and my mother, Nancy, want me to come home for my sister's 16th birthday party when the spring semester ends, which is in about two and a half months. They want to give her a party. I want to tell them both that I've been seeing this head doctor, but I don't. The whole point of my doing this psycho-scrutiny is to free myself from their peculiar form of bondage. I mean to say this with a straight face and not digress into the memory of Nancy telling me about the famous grand-daddy of heavy metal bands, *The Blue Oyster Cult* and their classic record, '*Tyranny & Mutation*', a mock-tribute to things extremist and fascist (and of a more sophisticated ilk than your Ozzy Osbourne variety. After all, Nancy made it clear there was no biting off the heads of bats for these guys!). I also don't want to think much of my dad telling me what I missed as a late 20th Century baby. The famous *CBGB's* nightclub in New York is one of them.

A party back at the house would also mean that Gram will jump into the action along with everybody else. Which is quite a sight. The last time they pulled this birthday bash stuff (when *I* turned 16), Gram was shamelessly swaying around on the carpet to *The Red Hot Chili Peppers*, her fleshy folds rolling and gyrating under a vintage *Goo-Goo Dolls* T-shirt I thought I had left on a boat somewhere at summer camp. Gram is about 64 now and my mom is forty. Andy, My dad, is 46 and has a dent just above his left temple- a considerable scar from a foiled suicide attempt some fifteen years ago when I was three, and he was in the throes of what was to become his last ordeal.

Now to briefly go into *that*. Quite simply, Pops

doesn't drink or amuse himself with drugs anymore, but all he does is talk about it. He goes to these meetings and talks his ass off about the way it was for him and it's going on twenty years now. I was all of about three feet tall when this happened and now I am six foot two inches. I have been shaving my mug for about six years. You'd think that, at this point, he'd be over this. Anyway, my dad's always apologizing to my mother, Gram, the *I.R.S.* He says things like: "I don't mean to do *an inventory* on you, Gladys, (which is Gram's name), but do you think it's appropriate to cheat the Franchise Tax Board on that old apartment building and continue to say you have relatives living in most of those units when clearly they aren't?" Gram just says things like: "I will if I think I'm never going to get the pension money from that bum father of *hers*" (meaning my mom's dad). My therapist actually has names for this kind of stuff. He'll say that this is just another example of some type of *trans-generational transference* or something, and then quickly points out that I can break from the family mode by setting forth my own trend. I say: "How in the hell can that possibly be? I'm saturated with things hip and cool." I remind him that my parents are of the *Woodstock* generation, that my middle name, Elegie, was selected from this song of the same name off Patti Smith's debut album, *'Horses'*. According to the family lore, Patti is the definitive, bad-girl art-rocker who blared: *"Jesus died for somebody's sins but not mine"*. That Patti Smith is so cool she actually barks and howls like a hound onstage before introducing *The Blue Oyster Cult* on one of their now vintage, collectable live albums. *BARKS.*

Sometimes I think that to top all this rebellious legacy of my parents I must retreat and become a bone surgeon dressed in a 19th century greatcoat. Believe me, I tried to put my own spin on things for years. I have a closet full of odds and ends: an 18th century style wig that Mozart might've worn (the Elton John video where he sings *"Candle in the Wind"*, of course, ruined this) a pair of purple lizard cowboy boots, a pince-nez, a Havana cigar box filled with baseball cards, Carl Perkins and Ray Charles LPs, a pair of spats. I also tried doing things in the way of making a statement. Like refusing to drink the bottled water my mom gets delivered to the house. I insisted that the chemicals from the tap water insured some type of immunity from the cancerous nuclear particles that are bound to infiltrate the environment and that I was actually doing my body a big favor by drinking it.

Actually, I've found this inoculation concept to work in some other areas as well. The Strayhorn family legacy seems to indicate that I should avoid alcohol and other such substances. It's been a basic theme throughout my upbringing that I should simply act like I am above such things and actually, I just can't see why I shouldn't have any fun. So I have a whisky every now and again. Well, Boyce, my *hired advisor*, nailed me on this and basically hung me on a cross. My father has indicated that sooner or later the *secret hatch* could fall out. Well, it hasn't happened yet. And if it does; if I do end up blown out with barely a fuse to hold me together then I pretty much know what I'd have to do. Pick up the phone, call a local church and find one of those smoky meetings.

In the meantime, I drink only basic stuff. I have no pretense for liking drinks with umbrellas floating around in them, so it's an uncomplicated thing. I usually know when to stop. I also smoke herb once in a while. Big damned deal. I'm sorry Andy had such a rough and strewn about time of it, but that doesn't mean I have to follow suit. There's nothing worse than having ex-hipsters who still want to groove, but without any chemicals, for parents. At least with other generations, parents were square. At least they had their own separate interests; at least they left your rock music collection alone, so you wouldn't have to go to their bedrooms or glove compartments to fetch your "misplaced" *R.E.M.* CD's.

Andy tried to realistically paint the picture on hallucinogens one afternoon after I came in from spending the day with my old friend Carlin Graves. Andy knew that my friend Carlin smoked grass so he started talking a mile a minute about the kind of potent stuff that's out there on the street today. He sat there looking pensive as he drummed his bony fingers on the drawing table in his living room, architectural drawings strewn all over the place and his usual five or six coffee mugs scattered about. He had *'been there'*; knew people who went on *'bad trips'* and never came back. Even coming from a first-hander like Andy didn't really prevent me from trying. I had my first experiment with drugs at sixteen. According to some, this isn't exactly an early start. A friend of mine concocted a version of what was known as mescaline and it must have had some real bad stuff in it because I never experimented again! The trip lasted for three days. All I remember was this persistent ringing in my ears and laughing my ass off at the old *Star Trek* reruns on late-night TV. There was one unforgettable episode where Mr. Spock, 'Bones' and Captain Kirk get stoned from sprays of pollen emitting from these huge flowers.

I was sitting there with my old, now defunct girlfriend, giggling and thinking: "wow, this is really surreal. *They're stoned. I'm stoned.* Surreal." And then this gauzy sickness fell over me: my parents would've used that word, *surreal.* I remember I picked up the remote and zapped the set off. I told Farrah to go home. She made me sick, too, although I didn't say this to her. It was her slightly protruding teeth. You could say I had these sneaky reasons for getting together with Farrah and it had nothing to do with her looks or her mind. Farrah had about as much depth as one of those puny, seashell soap dishes you come across in road stop diner gift shops along the Jersey shore. Every guy in my high school class had this idea about Farrah and her sensual mouth and I just had to find out for myself. And there really wasn't all that much to the given lore on Farrah, that's all I'm going to say. I have to admit, I enjoyed keeping my friends guessing. They would nod at me and say: "*well*?" when they'd see me departing from her after a class or something and I would just shrug, but always with a look to keep them guessing. But the day came when I had to admit that Farrah wasn't all that intriguing to me, or at least, this is what I told myself. To this day, I try not to think of the way she smiled when I told her things weren't exactly working out. After all, she had odd taste: frosty lipstick and musk perfume. What's in that garbage anyway? The girls love it, but then Gram even told me it's because the perfume manufacturers use sex hormones from male raccoons or muskrats in the fragrance so teenage girls will go *batshit* over the stuff. It attracts the girl consumers, alright, but in the meantime, the stuff repels the guys.

And, well, it dawns on me that's it's almost noon and I'm still lying in my bed. It takes a while for the cloudy residue left from my mother and grandmother breathing down my ear canal to dissipate. I am not going back there. Not for another one of their parties. I will stay here and think of my plan. After all, I'm snugly nestled in the hilly knolls at Grigham College, some hundred miles away from any major city-which is fine by me. It's enough of a distance from my hometown in Connecticut. I can think of better things to do than to run home to hang out with them. It took me eighteen years to finally get away and now I am going to run back there? As soon as I get a break? Are they crazy? I don't want to hear about what my father thinks of the *Counting Crows* and that Adam Duritz is an aspiring Van Morrison. It's been a few years since that song, *"Mr. Jones"* came out and Andy always reminds me that the *"sha la la la la la* is pure Van Morrison." What I can't stand about Andy and his perennial hipster ways, is the man took that song away from me when he said that. And I really don't want to share my generation's music with him. Andy should be acting like a retiring Billy Joel and get over the fact that he was once young like me. It's my turn.

Now there's one thing I've been dreading lately and that's the inevitable talk we'll have on watching out for the danger zones in my time here at school. I don't know when it's actually coming, but the day is going to arrive when we go out to one of the little kitsch restaurants around here to have a little chat. Andy is very nervous about my indecisiveness; he wants to make sure I stick to it and he also wants to make sure I practice safe sex and watch the drugs. I can certainly understand all this, but I know he wants to know what my plans are and I only have one so far and it looks like I will be skipping out of here for a while. He's certainly not going to like the idea.

That's all I'm going to say. And, really, must I endure the man now? Andy and the rest of them? I just spent last week's head session on the *La Leche* thing. I told my hired guy, Boyce, about Gram and my mother going to these weird meetings and how it was such a major decision to discontinue breastfeeding me once my teeth began to show up. A couple of years ago they were still talking about it. Gram sitting there at the kitchen table and Nancy in my *Jane's Addiction* T-shirt talking about how well I weaned. And there I was, with a mouthful of *Wheaties* and this nonfat goat's milk or something, trying to eat my breakfast and the two of them started up a chat about how well I had weaned. Gram was clucking and chuckling away, her arm-flesh jiggling like *Jello* as she scraped her toast. Nancy beamed and smiled as she recalled how pouty I was about the whole thing.

Finally, I flung the spoon into the emptied bowl and flatly told them: "You two are dullard females with nothing better to do than talk about a simple act brain-dead cows and goats do but have the innate class to not make an issue out of. I'm not having anything to do with this vile discussion." I remember I got up from the table and pointed at them both: "So what are you trying to say by telling me this? That I'm a mere calf and you're the big mamma cows? Is this it for you two? Your time in a *lactating* society? Sure looks that way. After all, you now fill your nights chomping away on your *Chex-mix* like cud while glaring at TV-shows like *Cops*. Extra curricular activities? Gram, you're asking me what I'm doing after school these days? Well, I got an idea! I'm going to sign up for membership in this misogynistic society; this backlash chauvinistic group at my school."(I remember Gram just sat there slack-jawed while my mom fingered her permed hair like an aghast *Medusa*). I couldn't believe I was admitting all this to this guy, but my *hired wise man* was laughing and nodding his great bald head. I really had his sympathy. He slid his arms down his great desk and looked right at me. "Yeah. It certainly sounds like you're surrounded by the *All Powerful Great Bosom*. It's what civilization, as we know it, is all about." Yeah? I wasn't so sure I got all of that, but I told him: "My dad ain't much better. In fact, he's one big *nipple*."

My man, Boyce, raised a brow and cocked his head. "Oh yeah?"

I then went into it. "Well, he's a pansy. He's always saying how sorry he is. He and my mom are not divorced, yet they live in separate places. And to look at him makes me sick. When I was last down there, at my mom's house, he comes over one afternoon with a coffee cake from one of his ex-drinker meetings. I wanted to run to the kitchen and grab one of Gram's old aprons and tie it around his waist. He's standing there with his raven black hair, his Jerry Garcia tie, you know, the *Big Architect*, and he's just a pansy. Your garden variety wimp. A joker, really. And he does this volunteer work. When I went out to the car, there was this guy sitting in the passenger seat looking all strung out. I was so embarrassed. My dad picks up drinkers and addicts outa smelly bars and alleys; even leaves the office early on the afternoons he does this. He actually takes these people to emergency rooms. He says he *needs* to do this. Well, it's an embarrassment. I make sure I pop open something alcoholic, like a lousy generic beer or something while I'm standing in the driveway so the neighbors know I'll have absolutely nothing to do with this weirdness. Well, you can't blame me. I come from a family of wimps except for Great Granddad. He had the right idea when he decided to cut them all off when he turned sixty. That was way before I was born. He lives in blissful seclusion in New Orleans; he's about ninety now and something tells me the man is awesomely cool. What I don't understand is, I am named after the guy. His first name, that is. His full name is Simon Forsythe Strayhorn. Mine is Simon *Elegie-excuse-me-while-I-stick-my-fingers-in-my-throat*-Strayhorn. You'd think Andy would be happy to tell me all about the old guy, but he's barely told me anything! Anyway, my dad was standing there in the foyer holding this ridiculous coffee cake and all I could think of was the fact that he couldn't hold a Luger straight. That's the gun he used in his big foiled suicide attempt. Actually, I flashed on the Luger remembering that it belonged to my great grandfather and I now have this urge to return it to the guy before he keels over! And considering that he's ninety, you can see my sense of urgency. "

Boyce sat there in one of his frozen positions. His mouth curled into a slight pout as he fingered the strands of tobacco loosening from the pouch he always has lying atop his desk. For a moment, I felt embarrassed. Then he looked up at me and asked: "Simon, what's your idea of a man?"

Well, I didn't hesitate to bring up my great granddad. So I told him: "He was an adventurer. He's from the old country. Which means, he dropped out of school back in Glasgow, to run the family newspaper. When that went under, he left for America, and he was still in his teens. I think. He was into all this ballsy stuff. Knew the *underground*."

A slight chill rushed up my spine as I bragged, but Boyce only slightly raised his brow and nodded for me to continue. "Well, Boyce, the guy worked for Gig Mastriani, the famous gangster. He amassed a lot of money, and then lost it all during the Depression, then went out west. Lived among Indians." Boyce then rose from his chair to get a notebook off one of the bookshelves and smiled at me. "Well, that's refreshing. No *Wavy Gravies* or tied-dyed sweatshops in Berkeley!"

I resented that. And I told him so. "You don't take me seriously. I don't relate to *them*. When I go back in the family tree I have to bypass all these pansies before I get to someone substantial. At least Great Granddad was a man doing manly things!"

Well, Boyce sat back down in his great chair and tapped his pen on his desk. "I can't say your dad is a pansy. He has a good grasp of himself as far as his past drinking problem. So he doesn't live with your mom. Maybe he needs to be in his *tree-house* until he comes to an understanding of something...although I don't know exactly what that could be."

I couldn't believe the way Boyce was talking. I was on the verge of walking out then and there, but I told him: "That's a real good way to put it, alright. Fifteen years is not exactly an eternity but it's damned close when you're looking at someone's life! After all, my dad doesn't make a decision. He hangs in the shadows of almost-decisions. And it drives me nuts. You know what he said to me the last time we talked? *"Simon, I'm taking you for a walk up to the Belvedere in Florence this summer"*. He then went into this reverie about the time he had apprenticed there in the mid-70's when he was a grad student-blah blah and you know what? He'll bail. He's not going to go through with it."

With that, I slid out of the chair and said: "Next week, I want to continue this." And I shook my *personal shaman's* hand. I don't know why. I just stood up and shook the guy's tobacco-stained paw. And I left and went down to one of the bars on Cromwell Street.

I walked in, ordered a bar scotch straight up and saw my face in the mirror. The eerie thing is, I sort of looked like the old man, my great granddad, that is. The only picture I ever saw of him was taken when he was about thirty-five, and I have the same grayish eyes. Weird. I felt lonely sitting in that depressing stinky bar. I ordered another shot and remembered to hate myself. It's this state I slide into. Every now and again, I'll catch myself writing a graffiti on some loser wall in an alley some-where. And I end up writing these cryptic pleas. I may start out thinking that I want to quote some great philoso-pher or something, but I end up writing things like: T*ake me out of this pain for a life*! And I know it's nuts, but I kind of enjoy doing it.

But on that particular afternoon, I felt like that guy in the book, *The Stranger*, when he goes out into the blaz-ing white streets of Tangiers or whatever and inexplica-bly shoots this guy on a beach. It was a weird, numb feel-ing. And it wigged me to be thinking this way. After all, I thought after so many weeks of seeing Boyce, I'd start figuring out some things, but I feel it's all gotten worse. And now I'm having second thoughts about everything. And I regret catching that episode of the *Hal Ridley Show* that January afternoon when I stopped in the stu-dent lounge to simply sit down and fix my book bag.

There I was, lollygaging about the usual, simpleton things like homework, papers, people I hate, and I sud-

denly found myself engrossed in this program. I could-
n't believe what I was seeing. There were these grown
men on there and this old gizzard poet, this guy who does
these seminars on how messed up adult men are, I forget
his name, anyway, this poet, with wavy, elegant white
hair, is playing a lute and reciting this obscure
Mesopotamian poetry about hunters and lost beauty
while these men are weeping and nodding their heads—
one was even bawling in his hands with his head bent
down—and I'm thinking: what in the *hell is this*?
Anyway, the poet later tells Hal Ridley (whose eyes are
now tearing) that men are in pain. Women seem to have
it pretty much together today. Men, however, seem lost.
Lost little boys inside because of societal taboos. Men
don't express their feelings because they simply don't
know how. And there isn't enough positive masculine
influence in today's world. There's also too much *mother*. Well, that's when my feet snuggling safely inside the
gunboat *Nike's* turned into molten lead. I could barely
move.

Immediately, I zeroed-in on this image of Nancy and
Gram. My dad in an apron and holding a coffee cake. All
like a prophetic dream. My hands actually started to
tremble. I pulled myself off the couch-not caring about
the freakin' book bag-and forced myself out of the building. I trudged the leaded banana boat feet across the
many quads that dot the campus until I finally sat down
near the grove by the river. The ground was snowy and
wet, but I didn't care. I don't know how long I sat there.
After I had bolted out of the student lounge building, I
lost all track of time. I know I missed my last two classes. The sun descended into the horizon and reflected
itself in fingers of light across the water. And I thought

of something else that old gizzard with the lute said: "*Men feel cornered today by women to come out with an expression of feeling they're barely even familiar with and it's not exactly how a man understands feelings; all he knows is that his ability to express himself romantically seems to diminish when a woman expects this*".

It all sounded so weirdly true. This almost inspired me to write the guy and ask if there's some kind of mail-order kit I could have so I could prevent this kind of bull-shit from happening before I get any older. Even in the stuff I had heard Nancy and Gram laugh about like the time Granddad Foley gave Gram a washer and dryer for Valentine's Day. I knew this old guy was hitting on something. Not that I want to think about the sex life of Foley and Gram, but it sure made me wonder. They've been divorced...well, really, since around the time of that Valentine's Day gift. According to what I overheard on the stairs that afternoon back at the house a few years ago, what tipped the scales was the bucket of Kentucky Fried Chicken that came along with the gift. "*It had a cawd that read, Happy Finger Lickin Good Valentine's Day. And it was signed, The Colonel... Well, huny, I can't ever tell ya when the last time wuz that I had a Finger Lickin Valentine's or any other fawr that matta...*"

Gram. She's about one grade above what she calls *white trash* and here she was complaining about Foley. At least he got her out of Huntsville, Alabama and made a decent salary. It embarrassed me to hear Gram shame-lessly talk this way. Especially in front of my mom, who is a class act compared to her. That old man really made me think. I almost wanted to call the number that flashed on the screen so I could maybe personally ask him a bunch of questions, but I figured he'd be too busy for something like that, so my best solution was to seek out someone nearby.

An older man, perhaps, that I could talk to. I really felt that I needed to be given the keys to the kingdom right then and there so I wouldn't get to the point of being a slobbering middle-aged lumberjack crying in my paws on some nationally syndicated TV show. I tried to imagine Andy up there, but somehow, I could only envision him standing behind the stage curtain, slightly trembling. I contemplated things for hours.

My solution was to seek out a type of guide like the old man, but the only thing I could come up with was a therapist. And I didn't really like the idea all that much. I never heard of any guy I know who's actually volunteered himself into therapy. This is probably why I'm keeping everything under wraps. I stash all my bills and stuff under my mattress, I 'm so paranoid, Cory, one of my meathead roommates, will find out. In fact, I 'm now going to insist that the bills do not get sent to me in the mail. That I pay in person.

Anyway, after going through this process at the campus health services office, I managed to get a list of men therapists. I got so scared I couldn't call any of them. Finally, I picked a couple, for starters. Since I also had addresses, I ended up writing a note instead of calling. I'm still not so sure why I wrote this, but I went ahead and scrawled it all out. It read: "I *think I need to talk about some things before I get out the heirloom Luger and finish the suicide job my father could not do for himself.*" I admit, I was trembling. But I wasn't sure if I was in one of my lugubrious spells and looking for some drama. Sometimes, I 'm not so sure. So I signed it: "*Scabrous and all-too-aware of Authur Rimbaud*". I included a line from '*Illuminations*' about the effect of dejected wretchedness in 1870's Paris and waited for some kind of response. I had only written my phone number, and I had my phone in voicemail the next day. Both of these men responded immediately. One simply referred me to an emergency psych-ward. And also left a suicide prevention number. I found this really weird. I mean, the man was devoid of any trace of irony.

The other, almost acting the in opposite extreme, had this understanding, mature tone to his voice and even chuckled. "If you are about the age of Arthur Rimbaud when he stopped writing poetry, then I think you called the right number. Why don't you come by..." That was several weeks ago, and I was pretty curious to see who this Dr. Boyce Donner was. Well, he knew all about the old-goat poet I mentioned when I told him I had caught that program on the *Hal Ridley Show*.

When I walked into his office, he showed me a few of the guy's books sitting on one of his enormous book-shelves. I was so nervous that day, I remember I kept jumping out of the chair as if to leave because I imagined I was being tricked into something. That the large, balding man before me was actually a participant in one of this man's seminars, and the day would come when I'd catch him on a video crying in his sweaty palms along with the lumberjacks, accountants, doctors, plumbers, lab technicians, and all the other lost souls who drag themselves to these things. But he didn't look fazed at my bizarre gestures. In fact, I remember, he got up and watered his plants, mumbling and nodding his huge bald head, as his teeth clenched the smoking pipe sticking out of his jaws.

At one point, he turned around, looked at me and

simply said: "Allow me" and swung the door open. He stood there awhile and finally asked: "You made the first step by coming here, so let's hear it, Simon! I know you want to say something!"

I then asked him if he'd ever attended one of those seminars. He said he hadn't but some of his clients had. I then told him I liked to be seen as a *client* rather than as a patient. He agreed that this would be ok. That he liked the idea that I was looking for a *wise man*, not really a shrink in the usual sense, and actually, I think he felt equipped for the job. His office has all these exotic collectibles, like ancient drums, objects d'art, unusual artifacts, actually, it looked more like Boyce was some sort of anthropologist than a physician. But Boyce corrected me immediately. He was not an M.D. but a Ph.D. and his leanings were Jungian with some variations he'd get into later. He certainly knew about the French Symbolist poets and even quoted Verlaine one afternoon. He was intrigued that I had actually had an interest in such things and wanted to know why I would mention someone like Arthur Rimbaud.

I then told him that my parents were New Age hipsters who trained my sister, Caz, and I, well in such things. My interest, I told him, started with the fact that my mother gave me this unusual middle name. It's Elegy with an '*ie*' instead of the '*y*' ending and it's because I was named after a song by Patti Smith, the original *femme fatale* punk rocker. I was born around the time when Patti was pretty popular.

One night, my mother flopped the old vinyl edition of '*Horses*', Patti's famous debut record, on the turntable and in a song on there, Patti says "*go Rimbaud! Go Rimbaud!*" like some *CBGB*'s cheerleader or something.

And I became intrigued. Nancy then told me that Rimbaud was like a Bob Dylan. He was a teenager who wrote about rebellion and the usual stuff teenagers bitch and moan about but this was back in the 1870's. I came across a biography on Rimbaud in the library one afternoon and I was immediately impressed. The guy refused to do what everybody was telling him. He not only published all this poetry, he basically told the French literary society to kiss his ass. And well, I thought that was cool, too. I was impressed that after he wrote his masterpiece, at the age of 19 or so, he gave it all up. So I started to read his poetry. And his literary outlaw mentors, Baudelaire and Verlaine. All those cats. And I had to keep this private from my hipster parents, lest I endure reminiscences from Andy talking about the first time he had read '*A Season in Hell.*'

I remember Boyce lit his pipe and said, as he was folding his legs across the desk and looking up at the ceiling: "Of course not! He won't let *yours* be *yours*! Understanding generational boundaries is not an exclusion with the hip and cool '*Boomers*. In fact, that is exactly their problem!"

Boyce then swung his legs back to the floor and leaned forward tapping his pipe in the ashtray. "They don't want to lay their *Ozzie and Harriet* stuff from *their* parents onto their offspring, so they try to identify and buddy-buddy with their kids. Wrong!"

Well, I told Boyce that this was exactly the problem. It's what I've been thinking all of my life. Boyce then went into assessing my dad, saying that Andy hadn't completed something, and this is why he lives away from us. That it doesn't so much have anything to do with the usual things couples say that split up their communications. It has to do with Andy's life in general. Boyce stood up and paced around. Smoke was wafting all over the place.

At one point, I opened the window, but I listened intently to everything this man was telling me. "Your dad lives in his *tree-house* because he hasn't finished something. We know his own father had a drinking problem. Which could mean something never developed there. My feeling about your dad is he's the type of man who overly compensates in his work and ambitions. Losers don't exactly end up at M.I.T., a well-known institution for his kind of work. He's what we used to call a *self-made* man. Probably had to figure out a lot of things on his own. Like you, Si."

I was still standing over by the window. Well, actually, I had walked back over there because of the intense smoke pouring out of Boyce's pipe, but it all came unexpectedly. As I was noticing the ice melting on the bare trees outside, I started to cry. Boyce noticed this and shot over in my direction. "Hey! We're going to get there!" I was so unbelievably embarrassed.

That afternoon when I had spilled all this stuff out to Boyce sort of marked a turning point for me. I felt as if a boil that had been festering inside of me had finally popped. And it was strange for me to cry in the first place, but to also identify something that's been sitting inside there for my whole life.

Since I started doing this therapy thing, I've been spending a lot of time walking alone. Sometimes I listen to my lousy *Walkman*. I play the Pete Townshend and Lou Reed music I taped off my dad's vinyl collection. I could've bought CD versions of the stuff, but I find that the scratchy, popping sound from the records have a certain charm.   Anyway, Townshend has this song, "*Slit Skirts*", and it starts out: "*I was just thirty-four years old and I was still wondering in a haze.*" There's this aching beauty to the song that-*and not to sound like Andy*-forgives the bad lyrics, it's so passionate and real. But when I hear it lately, I am thinking: I do not want to be thirty-four years old, like Pete is when he did this song, and still wandering around in a foggy haze. Know what I mean? So in these walks around campus and out to the fields and the river, I think about these things and I'm trying to formulate some plan. A plan of escape, I should say. In the meantime, I have not breathed a word to a single soul as to these ideas. I just find myself watching everyone lately.

Like my roommates Cory Banks and Les Abramson. These guys are alright, I mean, for not knowing them from whatever and being corralled together in a strange dorm room. Cory has a brain about the size of a small chick pea. How he got into this school has to do with connections and his wealthy family lineage. It's obvious. The guy is a wet cell awaiting a battery. Now Les is about as diametrically opposite as you can get from Cory. He is completely absorbed in the world of Artificial Intelligence and hopes to spend the rest of his life holed up in a think-tank. I believe I am somewhere in the middle of the two. At least, I hope I am. I am not a tepid-head like Cory—who, by the way, does seem to snoop around for clues in my personal life by browsing through my things.

And lately, I have just been observing the two of them as they walk in and out between classes. Well, whether Cory is actually attending classes is another thing, but he is rarely in the room. Where he goes, I am

21

not so sure. Probably hangs out in the rec-room or the gym drinking *Gatorade*. Anyway, it all seems weird to me lately. Like they'll be in the room and a conversation gets started about the usual stuff. And Les wants to get cerebral and veer off into some subject like comparing the findings of the English scientist, Stephen Hawkings and heavy tomes like Martin Heidegger's *Being and Time*. So unlike the old days when I'd jump and roll up my sleeves, I now let him run by himself and see how far he gets. And I just have this wry look on my face that says: *"Um, I'm waiting for you to screw this up on your own, Les."*

Well, Cory, bean-head that he is, is just sitting there with his mouth hanging open and checking the Velcro on his book bag and glancing over at the phone, ends up murmuring something about getting his own cell phone so the girls can call more freely or whatever and I'm just sitting back and watching Les' show. The other night, Les brought up the subject of Artificial Intelligence and computing a foul-proof system of Shuttle space flights and he got this real sour look on his face: "Hey, what's with you, Strayhorn? What's with the silent trip? I'm waiting for you to pipe up like *H.A.L.* the *"gay"* computer in *'2001'*, and say 'I *hear you, Dave.'*" Well, that made me laugh. As part of the *Great Film Directors Week* here at school, we had just seen these Stanely Kubrick films, *'A Clockwork Orange'* and *'2001, A Space Odyssey'* the night before at the student theatre. As fascinating and ahead of its time as '2001' is, the gay-sounding voice of *H.A.L. the computer,* broke the place up. And as we sat there in the room, even bean-head Cory joined in the laughter. But I didn't say anything. Les just glared at me: "It looks like you're up to something. Like you have this secret going on. Are you involved with a woman, finally? Are you having an affair?"

I have to admit, Les *is* sharp. Cory piped in: "Dude, I hope you are. I sure hope you are. It 's about time." As much as I hate to say this, Cory is good-looking. He's the *male* version of what they used to call the *dumb blonde*. And to the girls who like him, it doesn't seem to matter.

They could be brain surgeons and it wouldn't matter that they're seeing a lummox. Now there's this girl, Amanda, who regularly comes by the room. She is gorgeous and sparky. Very sharp and talkative, yet mysteriously ga-ga over Cory. I am not bad-looking myself. Some girls say I sort of look like Daniel Day-Lewis. Well, maybe on my better days. I once entertained the idea of luring Amanda my way, and I guess it went by unnoticed by her and I was a bit ticked about the whole subject. So I moved on. Now I have my eye on this intriguing girl in the library where I work. She just started working there at the beginning of the winter semester and I have yet to find out her name. She is quite a beauty. And I think she looks at me from time to time. I call her *Guinevere* in my imagination, of course.

She has very long golden hair and almond-shaped green eyes. She's amazingly beautiful. I am edging a bit closer everyday to simply say something to her and I think that day is coming very soon. Since starting college this past fall, the only girls I've been with have been *one-nighters*. Scoring with no involvement is starting to get weird. I find myself running into one or two of the girls I've been with and there's this immediate understanding between us that we are to keep walking ahead as if we had never laid eyes on each other before.

Boyce tried to venture into the arena of my romantic life one afternoon and I simply didn't want to go there. In fact, I felt like the subject was one of Hawkings' black holes and I told him so. But I ended up going into Thalia anyway. She was my last steady girlfriend. We were together all of about ten months. And we called it quits a little over a year ago. I told Boyce that Thalia was a Greenwich, Connecticut bitch, and he nodded his gleaming bald dome a bit, but then added that I have this weird idea that these girls are doing a number on me when it's really something having to do with what might be missing in me. But almost in the same sentence the guy assures me that I'm *getting there*. Whatever in the hell that means. I hate the guy. I really do. I hate him. Whose side is he on, anyway?

In these past six weeks or so of these head sessions with my *witchdoctor, personal shaman,* Boyce, I've had many a disturbing moment when I wanted to fold and bail. Sometimes I think the guy is too smart and quick at identifying these things that I don't see any of my friends worrying about. I can't imagine Les or bean-brain Cory having to explore the intricacies of how they feel about some chick. Well, maybe Les could wax philosophic a bit, but Cory? If you ask me, the guy's doing something right. After all, there's barely a night when Cory isn't out there in the hall yapping on the horn with Amanda, Jasmine, Tanya, and this other one, I forget her name. Apparently, Cory doesn't have to rise much above his jock-itch consciousness in order to impress these babes.

And it looks like I am basically a crab. I'm the gigantic crab crawling on the beach in a low-tech 1950's movie. Actually, I'm Kafka's miserable little *dweeb* that wakes up as the giant cockroach. That's what I am.

This scabby big thing that crawls among the coeds, sometimes even offering to carry their book bags as I contemplate scaling my tentacles under their delicious skirts. I can even look dashing and clever in my penciled-legged limbs. The lovelies look at me, and I grin but sooner or later, I feel like the biggest imposter of 'em all. I am nothing but a crab inside. Actually, there are times where I want to run and hide and shrink myself into the ground and become hollow like a sandy, dried-up cocoon. And I was reminded of this when I walked into cafeteria the other day and sat down next to the old jukebox. Someone must've had a thing for David Bowie because all these old Bowie tunes were playing. Songs like *"Alladin Sane"* (which I think should've been called *A Lad Insane*), "Ashes to Ashes". Anyway, someone had the poor taste to select *"Scary Monsters"*, an amazingly bad song with lousy lyrics save for the one line: *"She asked for my love and I gave her a dangerous mind. Now she's stupid in the street and she can't socialize."* Well, this all took me back to the time when I wanted to mess with Thalia's Greenwich, Connecticut brain. And it really didn't take all that much to do this. All I had to do, really, was go through my dad's old LP Collection and put on Lou Reed's *'Metal Machine Music'* or drive her around with only my right speaker on because I wanted to hear the pure, grinding, guitar riff of *The Velvet's "The Gift"*. I knew this would curdle her blood like the sound of a hundred fingernails screeching down a chalkboard. And this was fine and well, until I told Thalia that I loved her one night. We were at her stately home while her parents and her brother were away. Now a lot of people would say, "hey, that's really great." But

I'm a weirdo. I dimmed the lights and all, and there she was, lounging on the chintz sofa and we had candles glowing here and there, and I tell her this, and place the vinyl version of Lou Reed's *'Herion'* on the old turntable; I then blew out a couple of the candles and left her there. Alone and in the dark. Now *'Herion'* is about as romantic and charming as swallowing a fistful of horse tranquilizers with your *Krispie Kremes* on your way to school or something. I don't know why I did this. I wanted to wig her out, I guess. It was lame, but I had to find a way to get rid of her, even though my statement was sort of true. And I really shouldn't be talking about all this stuff I'd rather forget about.

It seems that a lot of people seem to spend their lives subsisting on the brain energy of a toaster oven and why should I be any different? Just blissfully drive through life and don't bother with all the nonsensical cross signals. I've tried to express this to the *witchdoctor*, Boyce, but he just laughs and says something like: "It's called a feeling, Si. *Feelings*. That's all *that* is."

And he'll grin and light another bowl of tobacco like I just slid into a booth at a diner and asked what's on the menu. I try to think of Boyce's down-playing this stuff and sometimes it calms me. "Normal. All very normal stuff to be feeling when you're 18 and living away from the folks back home. It's exciting, really. I envy you." Boyce is about 57 years old and the only hair he has is the graying patches near his ears. He's a tall man, about my height, and his bald head reflects well under the track lighting in his office. I remember when he told me this one day, I kind of felt sorry for the guy—best years behind him and all, but I also felt like he was humoring me. I mean, to envy me is like envying a young *Bomb*

Stalker. And I have to remember I even dressed as the *Bomb Stalker* for Halloween. I'm not sure where that puts me.

The door to my room suddenly swings open. Just when I'm gathering my things for the shower here's Cory in his black gear; his boots shining like a state trooper's on his first day on the job. He gingerly walks over to his closet and digs through his piles of stuff. Bending over, he yells: "Strayhorn! What in the hell are you doin' in here, dude? It's like practically noon and you're not even dressed." Cory seems to have a need to keep tabs on my routines. I walk over to him, "What brings you back here, man?" He stuffs the pile of dirty laundry back into his closet. "I gotta get my *Ray Bans*. Amanda gave them to me and I'm going to be seeing her." I can't stand this guy. I decide to ignore *Battery Acid Brain* and walk over to the shower. Now he's knocking on the door. I turn the faucets on full blast and step in. In the meantime, Cory's hanging around at the door, talking away like a lunatic. I'm oblivious to what he's yapping away about. There's no rule book that says that just because I share a living space with this guy I have to talk to him, much less listen.

****

That's what I love about this job. Never a dull moment when it comes to the babes. This fawnish creature looks up at me as she approaches the desk. She's stroking her downy cheek as she furrows her brows; she wants to know if I've read the lugubrious tomes of this sad Dane, the 19th century philosopher, Soren Kierkegaard. I tell her not exactly, but I wouldn't mind helping her with her homework. I could write her essays for her. She looks at me as if I just stuck my hand up her sweater and Ron, my boss, is now leaning over the counter, telling me that our computers are down.

As he yaks away, I spot my *Guinevere* sailing by with a stack of magazines to place on the racks out front. All attention of what this other girl is saying is lost by me and now a small group is beginning to form at the desk. The girl steps back a bit and looks me over, pointing at me, "You were the one dressed like the *Bomb Stalker* for Halloween weren't you? You were at the party at *Frank's* sitting in the corner, not talking to anyone. Right?" The crowd now seems to be interested in this sudden inquiry. I shrug my shoulders and tell her I have no idea what she's talking about. My *Repunzel*-beauty, my *Guinevere*, walks over to the desk, and I'm thumbing through a huge *Reference Guide* for this graduate student bozo who's sliding his wire-framed glasses up his snout as he waits, and right behind him is my *Lovely*. She's sweeping the glossy golden tresses away from her cheek; her dimples are exquisitely in place and right before me she lays an *Ultra Bright* on the guy, leans over and gives the *dweeb* a big wet kiss. I swiftly move from behind the counter, my body now much quicker than my brain, and I drop the lunk-volumned tome on the guy's foot. And I walk out. That's right. I sail through the swooshing doors as if there's a sudden fire drill or something. Without even a thought of looking back, I march forward, right down the hall, to the elevator bank and, well, out into the quad, the many multifaceted quads, and right down to my little grove area, my solemn place down here by the river and I sit down and become very emotional.

I'm freaking over *Guinevere* and her kiss on the

toad's cheek, and I'm thinking up all these crazy excuses as to why I walked out on the job. I mean, I have no intention of quitting. Actually, I'm hardly in a position to quit. So I'm tripping and thinking up a *good one* at the same time. I mean a *good* one, and I'm trying to pull myself together down at my little private grove. These two vaguely recognizable figures standing there in the distance, waving and flapping their hands at me, are growing a bit more recognizable. It's Cory and Amanda. As if I just came to, I finally get up and flap my hand back at them. I tell them: "Taking a break! Gotta go back to work! See ya!" And I high tail it back to the library, drumming my brains for some reason why I did the bail number. *Well, you see, Ron (my boss), I'm on this medication and I am still adjusting to it and I get these waves of vertigo, especially when I strain my eyes to read such fine print under the fluorescent lights and the only solution is to go out and get a breath of fresh air. In fact, that's doctor's orders until I adjust.* Ok. . That could work. Then I start musing as to what possible medication I'm taking and for what. *Shingles*! I heard Gram say something about scratching her *shingles*. But I don't exactly know what *that* is. I mean, what if it's a woman's problem or something? So I finally decide that it's an eye exam that I had had earlier in the day, and my eyes were still dilated.

I whip out the sunglasses spending the rest of the afternoon with them on and glued to the computer typing away like a lunatic. To make things worse, to really compound the insanity of my emotions, Lisa (*Guinevere's* real name, by the way) plops down at the screen next to mine and tells me that she and her cousin, Graham, were very concerned about me. Her *cousin*!

I tell her: "You're snowing me."
She grins. This marvelously delectable grin.
"Nope. And guess what else?"
"He's gay!"
She roars at this.
"Bingo!"
"Spare me the cousin bit. How do you really know that *dweeb*?."

Apparently, she's not going to bother with my remark. Instead, she stands up and hangs her tresses in front of her face. As she brushes her golden locks, I nervously type away like a fool as I stare, not bothering to glance at the screen. She flips her mane back and sashays her butt as she leaves. "See you tomorrow, Simon."

I have never been so nervous around a girl since I was thirteen. Lisa. I like that. Just plain Lisa. Not *Thalia* or *Farrah*, or *Aspen*, or whatever trendy names have spawned from the post *Jefferson Starship-Fleetwood Mac* era of yesteryear. None of that for *this* gal. Just *Lisa*. Gorgeous and unattainable. Now what in the hell do I do?

I spend the rest of the evening pacing around the shadows of the quad in front of the dorm. And I find myself stumbling on a memory I have. I only get a glimpse of this when I have a rare micro moment of perception that I can only call a twin or multi-viewed experience where I can see myself as I experience myself. I'm involved yet detached at the same time. And I'm remembering a time when I was about twelve years old and at the beach with my sister, Caz, and my dad. And we are in the water and the waves are lapping and rolling and my body is small and shiny as it glistens in the noon-day sun screaming in the sky and it is rich, this experience, this soul-feeling that slinks around in my skin and I'm looking at the people around me wading and snorkeling and swimming and like a thunderclap in my head I'm seeing it all in front of me: I'm aware that I am aware and involved in the sea, in the rippling sea and all these people are swimming around except *I see*: *we are infinite beings swimming in the sea*. And I recall feeling that *I am not my childhood self, I am not my childhood self, why I am not my childhood self at all.* This bird's-eye knowing and scooping up the view below of humans in their silky wet skins dipping and bobbing and somehow the ever-knowingness is right there. *Reality within a reality.* And I'm remembering this as I'm walking and puffing away at a cigarette and thinking of this girl. And I am watching myself while I'm involved with myself. Like that day at the beach. And as I walk up the stairs to the dorm I look up at the night sky and I fold this up, this memory, and I place it somewhere inside of myself where I may not even be able to find it later, it is so special to me. I tuck it all away somewhere inside myself. It is a secret I want to stow away for later. An illuminating treasure I keep preserved and away from the drabness of *'Headline News'* and Les' penchant for dissecting the latest scientific breakthrough. I think this as I glide into the room. Les is sitting on his bed tapping away at his laptop and Cory's sitting on the bathroom floor talking on the phone. This gives him a sense of privacy. Quite a homestead we have here.

"Have you been running, Strayhorn?" Les asks me this as he types away.

"Naw. Just walking."

I *am* breathing a bit heavily and I have no idea as to

why. And to myself I say: *I'm whirling about in my own orbit tonight, Abramson. And I don't want to talk about it.*

I shimmy out of my jeans and pull off my sweaters and jump in my bed, with my headset and blissfully doze off to *R.E.M.'s 'Out of Time'.*

****

"Ask her out, Simon." Boyce is going pipe-free today and I'm raising my brows. He gives me one of his blank looks and finally says, " I just want to give my mouth a break. Fever blisters... You do what any normal guy would do. You ask her out. Nothing big. Just: "Hey, would you like to tool around campus and see a flick? Or whatever the kids say today."

"I'm not very good at that."

"It isn't a matter of being good at it, Si. It's a matter of doing things in a non-impulsive way. Which I think is what's the usual thing with your generation and also, considering your pattern. I mean, jumping in the sack and wham 'bamin it and then never having a conversation with the girl is well..."

"Neanderthal-land."

"Yeah. Good. There's no need to feel like you have a handicap because you see me. All the better to handle your life and it's on-going sagas. Right?"

Boyce slaps his knee before getting up to walk me to the door. "You kids! We never had it *that* good! Back in the '50's, when I was a teenager, we had to work our butts off just to get a smooch and a *feel*. I remember all kinds of rituals I had to go through. Dates, dances, movies, opening the car doors, walking her to the front door, struggling with the petticoats, poodle skirts, bra straps. *Jeezum Pete's*! You kids have all the fun! But none of the romance!"

None of the romance. As much as I hate to admit this, Cory looks like he could teach me a few things. I watch him when one of the girls come to the door. I occasionally eavesdrop on his conversations. The guy's got so many girls around him, he's got to be doing something right. And it looks like he and Amanda are becoming a pair, and I'm intrigued as to how this can be so. He's majoring in volley-ball or something and she's a pre-med. Okay, so last Halloween I *did* dress like the exact depiction of the *Bomb Stalker* that ran in every newspaper around the country. Perhaps, that should be a clue. But the girls actually loved it when I walked into *Frank's*, among other places, wearing the French beret, *Captain Bly* patch, moustache, and fake curls flying past my shoulders. I retreated to the corners of the rooms because I felt like that's what psycho-bombers would do. But that didn't stop the *babes* from coming over to me, asking me if I wanted a drink or a clove cigarette- clove cigarettes being the one thing detectives knew the 'B*omb Stalker'* liked because butts were always found around the sites after the explosions. Now if I could only turn my gross tendencies into an asset.

The electric doors magically swoosh open as I walk through the familiar marbled hallway that leads to my work station back at the library. I have given a lot of thought as to trying out a new way of approaching Lisa, who should be arriving soon. Ron eyes me as I settle into my desk; a stack of documents that need to be scanned into the computer awaits me. My hands are now flying across the keyboard. I'm resisting an urge to explore some chat rooms on the Internet. Ron has caught me doing this from time to time, and lately, I find it weird. I was invited to join a vampire cult thing once while I was researching something and became intrigued by this little "group" chatting. At first, I was sort of flattered. But then this weirdo wanted to "chat" with me alone.

I backed out of that by telling him something pretty bizarre and I think it worked. Now I want to see if I can find him just to mess with his head. Out of nowhere, I hear this sonorous voice coming from behind me.

"Surfing the *'Net*?"

My *Guinevere* leans over, a tress or two dangling over the partition that divides my desk from the floor. I'm typing, pretending I've gone deaf. I have no idea what to say to her, so I finally grunt.

"Sounds like you're busy, Si. Come by the desk later if you want to." She is now walking away.

"Lisa! Sorry, I just have to finish something!" I lie. My brains scramble for some kind of approach for later but it all sounds so fake to me. *You know, I ended up seeing '2001' the other week with my geek-head 'roomies, and well, would you like to see 'Elephant Man' this week*? Or something. Fake! I shrink to the size of a mouse and spend the rest of my time glued to the computer, and upon leaving, I smile at Lisa rather sheepishly, and say: "Busy! Lots of stuff I had to enter. Sorry I couldn't come over and talk!"

But she's just nodding her head without looking at me and digging around in the desk drawer at the counter.

She furrows her brow and says: "I lost my bathroom key! I have to run upstairs, Si. Ron will be here soon. I'll see you tomorrow."

I leave, shrugging my shoulders; I feel like I'm the

lowest of crabs scratching around in its miserable sand dune existence. I find comfort in saying that I need to think of my plan. I guiltily go out to the grove after catching the news in the rec-room and talking briefly with some guys I know. It's very beautiful and serenely barren of humanoids out here. And I derive a delicious solitary pleasure in doing this.

Except for that one afternoon where I saw Cory and Amanda, I rarely run into anyone. It's as if no one knows about this spot but me. But then again, I am thinking: No one is as screwed up as I am and in such dire need for this isolation trip among the pines and maples. Most guys I know are hanging out and having a good time, or on the horn drumming up some female action. Not walking like a monk on break from a day of scrubbing floors and meditating. I find my spot and settle in to think things over. The sky is all aglow in soft golden colors. The river is quiet and all is tranquil. I want to stay here and muse about things; I want to believe that I shouldn't have this problem approaching this girl. Whatever it is, it doesn't belong to me. For years, I believed that Andy had some kind of castration problem, but that was only because he was living away from my mother. Andy has no problem with women. There were times I remembered seeing indications here and there that he was definitely getting some female action but never really wanted my sister and I to know about it. What I don't understand is his apparent attraction to my mother to this day. For some reason, he just doesn't live with her. And he didn't want to live with us. At least that's how I saw things. But there's something weirder about it. It's more like Andy moved out , alright, but he left some *luggag*e behind, and that stuff happens to be with me. The problem is, I have it all here with me at school. And I don't know what in the hell to do with it all because it's all in the way. In the way of everything.

I rise from my spot, noticing that the sun is beginning to sink into the horizon and remember my appointment with *Baldo Boyce*. I run over to Cromwell Street and run up the stairs practically tripping over the *gunboaters*. I tell him about the latest episode with Lisa. After listening to this stuff pouring out of me for about ten minutes running, Boyce looks up.

"I think we should explore feminine and masculine energies today. There's a lot of talk nowadays that says: *hey, there's no big difference between guys and gals*, but there is. It's a basic law of energy dynamics. Why there is a positive and negative charge in batteries, for instance. Males being the more active, directive force, females, the lesser active force. Now because there is this seemingly inherent difference in men and women, men are a bit slow at catching up to women on an emotional level. They are slower in moving around in that arena. Now why is this so? We begin the study of civilization by saying the Greeks had this great culture that sprung up. What is commonly known as *Great Age of Greece*. In fact, we identify this as the hub of Western culture. Well, what really constituted this so-called greatness was a very aggressive usurpation of the 30,000 years' tradition of agricultural, or you could say, *Matriarchal* culture."

He leans his shoulders forward and begins to finger the strands of tobacco in his pouch. Boyce continues: "Now what was *Matriarchy*? It was not as if the women had the reigns of control or anything. It was nothing like that at all. Although some may disagree with me, that very tendency is usually, a predominately male trait. Instead of something like what you might think, it was a culture that was more reverential to the feminine, as being the true essence of power because it is not only *life-generating*, but *life-sustaining*. It was a *quiet* kind of power. Sort of like water running over a rock. Today, and actually, since about four or five thousand years ago, men know, deep down, that the *life-power* is really with the *women* and they are, in part, actually, almost born with a guilt trip. Somehow, men feel they must conquer that. Ah, yes, to control and contain! That's always our basic agenda! I remember little *Tigger*, that's what we called my son, who's now 28, would always pee right in his mom's eye just as she was changing his diaper."

Boyce emits a guffaw and, of course, I laugh a bit nervously, and I go along with him even though I think he's nuts.

Boyce puffs away as he continues: "But whenever *I* had to change the diaper, he'd just remain dry and, well, there was a barely perceptible grin there beaming right back at me. *Lot of hard work being a man, Si!* All this power we have to strap down and conquer! And your basic masculine sense doesn't like it that your father, at least, in part, is somewhat reverential to this dynamic by bringing..."

He looks up at me.."...*the old lady*..."

I interject, "Gram!"

"Yes! Gram and Nancy...coffee cakes. There's a wisdom in that, Simon, and I am trying to bring some attention to it. Your dad is no dumb-dumb. I rather think he's wise."

I'm taking in what Boyce is telling me but with much skepticism. I think he's just impressed that my dad has accomplished some things in his life and he wants me to see that. I know better. Andy is a wimp. Pure and simple. If he is so delicately in touch with the *feminine power* in Nancy and Gram then he stops there. He loses it. *It* being the thing that really makes a guy a guy. So he stays in limbo-land never making a real decision.

I hold up a traffic-stop hand. "Boyce! That's real nice for you to say, but I can't really buy it. He's a wimp. Sorry. I'm the one who's sorry. I have a plan that I'm formulating and when I'm ready I will tell you about it."

I rise from my chair and this time, Boyce is growing a bit impatient and he's shaking his bald dome.

"We aren't done, Si."

I sit down, glancing at the clock. Ten minutes left.

"Ok. Shoot."

Old Boyce starts in: " Just when I am about to get to the main drag of this thing, you want to interrupt and bail. That's very normal, Si."

I hate when he starts this.

"But you might want to consider your situation with *Goldilocks.*"

He stops cold. And he looks up at the ceiling as if he is asking: *Now what in the world did I see up there?*

I plainly ask: "What about her?"

That's his cue. But this time, he is flinging it back at me.

"What about her, Si. You tell me."

" I had bad role models? I was stuck in a house with three females. While I realize that my dad never really lost his attraction for my mom, he continued to live away from us. I have no idea what that's about... I have cancelled dates with girls."

I can't believe I admit this. Old Baldy is loving

every second of this. His eyes are flashing and grinning as he stares at me, puffing like a steam engine, teeth clenched on the gnawed-marked pipe stem hanging out of his mouth. I continue this confession by saying that it was always when I was about to enter a more serious stage of a relationship that I would bail. Like the time I put on '*Herion*' and left the room and Thalia sitting there baffled and groping, literally, in the dark. Not so much that she couldn't find a comfortable spot in which to take in what I had just said or the scratchy, squeaky music for that matter, but to probably grab her coat and run the hell away from me! Which is, actually, what she ended up doing.

Boyce is grinning and waiting. Finally he blares: "So. Tell me about your plan. Sounds like it all came together handily. Right when you are seeing me, and meeting *Golden Girl.* A new bail strategy, Si?"

I shout back,

"Yes!"

I rise up from the chair pointing my finger at him. I can't believe how the man is pissing me off. I continue,

"You're damned right!"

I settle back in my chair. All is quiet for a moment. And Boyce is busily tapping the dead remains of his pipe into the ashtray. Finally, he says:

"Sounds like a good idea, Si."

I shoot back,

"You're damned right, it's a good idea."

I fold my arms and stay that way for the remaining minutes of our session. And I leave without saying a word. I shake my head as I'm exiting the building, feeling Boyce's inevitable smile as he most likely leans back in his great big chair raising his eyebrows. The man will say anything. Anything to hook me in enough so that I'll come back by next appointment. And he knows this. He knows I'm hooked! It's those cliff-hanging, one-liners that just keeps me coming back for more. Jeez! How did I get myself caught up in all this?

There are swarms of people rushing down Cromwell Street. As I approach the campus, I run into Les. The last person I want to see right now. He tells me he's going to see '*Eraserhead*' tonight with this girl, Pony (I am not lying; that is her name). I grin when he says, "Her name's really Persephony. Which I think is gross". I'm grinning even more at this.

Les asks, "Do you know who *Persephony* was?" I recall, as Greek legion has it, that she was the wife of *Hades*. I remind Les that my middle name, Elegie, is the name of a song, true; but it's a type of poem written for a dead person. Les ponders this and says: "Your mom probably didn't realize it, Si. She was thinking of how she liked the song. "

And I reply: "Yeah, but I have to go into that kind of explanation whenever I tell people my full name. It always follows the blank stare I get."

Les walks along, squinting up at me, "So where have you been? Out seeing your *secret sweetie*?"

This bull is really starting to bother me. About a couple of weeks ago, Cory and Les started calling my late afternoon disappearances as the *secret sweetie*. At first, it was ok. But now it's getting a bit ridiculous. We'll be in the cafeteria or walking across a quad or something and Les will look at Cory as a woman or a girl saunters by, and says: "*secret sweetie*, Si?" These guys need more recreational activity than keeping tabs on me, and Cory being that he is such a colossal geek head would have the audacity to follow me someday as I walk down there and lately, I'm looking over my shoulder. I'm super paranoid I'll be found out. Lately, though, it does feel like this thing is a kind of secret affair. And my little dilemma with this new girl, a sort of *secret sweetie*. But it's kind of sick when I look at it this way. In fact, I think I make myself sick all the time. Like I am stuck in this six-foot, two-inch lanky body and I have to cart it around like a side of beef for the rest of my life. It's a sentence, actually, and I'm stuck with it.

Les pokes me in the arm as this jock-lummox, Barry, hobbles by.

"Hey, Strayhorn. Look who's here."

The guy hisses as he edges away from us. Les shakes his head.

"Dude, you really pounced the hell out of that jerk the other day! The whole floor loves ya, man. I don't know why you get so geeky. You're a hero!"

Well, it's sort of true. Cory, Les and I were out on the Rugby field a few days ago and Barry—a guy I barely know—started in on Cory. Normally, I don't really get myself involved with someone else's stuff, much less an idiot like Cory, but the guy was so obnoxious I leapt on top of the jerk and pummeled him.

As I was doing this, someone kicked a ball onto the field and Cory and Les started kicking the thing toward myself and this yo-yo. Pretty soon the ball was bouncing in this guy's face. And all the while I'm remembering my *side of beef* burden of a life. Les shouted: "Maim the sucker, Strayhorn!"

And, well, I pretty much took care of the guy, alright, but all I could think of was myself and my *dweeb* existence! And for a slice of a moment, I wanted to step back and look at the guy all writhing in pain and say , *"nice job"* to myself, but I couldn't shake these creepy, snarly, slippery feelings I have around Lisa. In fact, the truly pathetic thing about all of this is, I don't even do anything in the way of *capturing* Lisa.

Les tells me that he needs to run up to the room. As he departs, I stop off at the student lounge and make a few phone calls. I pop in the money and dial Lisa's number at work. I well-know she isn't there, I just like to listen to her voice. I don't leave a message or anything; in fact, I hang up before the beep so she doesn't know that I call just to listen to her sexy voice.

****

I should realize something's up when I turn the doorknob to my room and it's unlocked. Les is a stickler for keeping us under tight security around here. I fling the door open, the late afternoon sun is pouring in, practically blinding me as I notice the familiar figure sitting on the edge of my bed. He's talking to Les. For a moment, my stomach jumps. It's Andy, and as usual, he's arrived unannounced. He's looking over at me, wearing this ridiculous headgear, some *virtual reality* device. He's yaking away as he pulls it off, allowing Les to try the thing on.

He walks over to me, shaking his great mane of black hair, which now has a few strands of gray in the front. He's pointing his thumb back in Les' direction.

"Friend of mine gave that to me. He's chairing the department now. You should see the stuff they're doing. It's amazing." Andy grins. He's all spiffed out in one of his designer suits, telling me he was a speaker that morn-

ing at a conference in Boston and decided to drive the extra three hours or so to see me.

"Sorry, I decided to do this last minute, Si."

I can't stand it when he does this bullshit. He knows damn well and good I hate surprises, especially coming from him. Les is waving for me to come over and try the device on. I say in my perkiest voice,

"Hey, no, Dad, it's great to see you!"

He asks me if I want to join him for dinner, and really, only as a diversion from the usual garbage I eat here at school, I enthusiastically reply,

"Ya think I'm nuts?"

I walk over to Les and try the headgear on.

"Wow, this is something!" I whip the thing off, handing it back to Les. "Dad, let me change and shower and all!"

I grab some clothes and a towel, and step into the bathroom. I hear Andy at the door.

"Son?"

"Yeah?"

"I'm going to be outside strolling around. Take your time. I'll meet you in front of the building."

I hear him talking to Les. Something about research and technology or the like and the always sociable Andy is giving the usual Southern well-wishes and leaves. I open the bathroom door. Les is still wearing the device on his head. I tell him,

"I am not prepared for all this. He comes over like it's nothing. I haven't talked to him in almost two months! He does this kind of thing. He's going to drill me about my plans for the summer, and all I can think is: I want to get the hell away from everything."

Les stands there, this thing on his head; the "visor"

portion aiming straight at me, which is absurd since I know he can't see me. Finally he takes the thing off, and shrugs his shoulders.

"Si, he's your Pop. Just grin, nod your head and agree with everything he says. He seems like a pretty interesting guy."

Les looks down at the virtual reality device. " Hey, I'm going to run down there and give this back to him, okay?"

What can I say? I agree with Les and decide to take it easy. I shut the door and proceed to shower and get dressed.

I notice Andy walking around the trees out front as I'm running down the stairs to meet him. He's holding this apparatus in his hands and grinding his shoe in the gravel. He's looking quite pensive. For a second, I'm thinking there might be some news he's come to tell me about. Gram electrocuted herself with her curling iron or something. In fact, that might be good news.

"Hey Dad."

"Simon, you look well. You must be keeping fit and eating right. When I was in school I looked pretty scrawny; actually, I was malnourished. The stuff they served in the cafeteria was something out of *Oliver Twist* or something. *Gruel.* That's what we used to call it."

We climb into what looks like a rental car. Andy must've flown into Boston from New York City. I inform him, "Yeah, well, it isn't much better here. I only eat uncooked vegetables, cereal, fruit; you know, *monkey food.* I usually avoid the meat. Especially if it's this scary looking stuff in a casserole."

We both laugh. Andy says, "Yeah, I had my share of the *shepherd's pie surprise.*"

We are driving past the campus and through the trees. The sun is still shining and it's after six. It is definitely the beginning of spring. We end up riding around the main area outside of the campus looking for a parking place. There are dozens of restaurants and my dad is eyeing some of them. He likes places where he can talk freely, and he hates it if they are too crowded. We finally find one that looks rather elegant and good. A French restaurant. Since it is still early we get a table in the corner, a perfect place to eat and have a chat. A pleasant chat and not a heavy, lugubrious ordeal. He can say all his stuff and I can nod and wolf down some real food and leave.

"Well, I hope this didn't freak you out or anything. I should've called."

I hate when he's nice like this; I assure him, "Naw, it's ok, Dad. I just have some tests coming up and it just surprised me."

The waiter comes over and we order something to drink as we peruse the menu. I order a soda and Andy, of course, orders a *de-caf*. Andy adjusts his crazy tie. It's a rather unusual abstract design in these vivid tones of sapphire blue, emerald green and bronze. I have to admit, it's a piece of work.

Andy asks me about my ideas as to a major. He's really concerned about this so I tell him,

"Dad, I'm fascinated by philosophy, and I have some crazy ideas, but I think I'm leaning toward med-school."

The tension is like having a jackhammer hang over my head, but I smile anyway.

Andy looks over at me, his eyes resting where I'm holding the menu.

"Yes, I know. You have the hands that would make a

gifted doctor. I can see it in your hands. I just want to know how you're really doing."

I'm at a loss as to how to answer. Slowly, I tell him, "I'm okay.   I'm studying, hanging out, making friends, doing things, and…"

I pause and I want to scream or cry or do something crazy, but I just finish the sentence by saying everything couldn't be better. Andy shuts the menu and starts to drum the table with his bony fingers. The drinks arrive. Andy and I order. I want the steak and order lyonnaise potatoes, broccoli, an entree-sized salad . I'm famished and, actually, grateful to be getting some decent grub. This lightens me up a bit.

Finally, Andy announces: "Well, I don't know how to go into this, but I have some news about your sister, Si, and to tell you truthfully, I decided not to call, but to drive up and tell you in person."

The hairs in my back are tingling. Andy continues, "There's something going on with her; she's not too communicative these days and we're basically in the dark; some—the headmistress— are saying she's into drugs. I also think this older guy she got herself involved with has messed her up. Your mother and I are flying down there tomorrow afternoon".

For only the past school year, Caz has attended this fancy *horse and pony* school outside Charlottesville, Virginia. It's her first time away from home, and now I understand why Gram and Nancy called me the other day. But still, I'm stunned at hearing the news. It simply does not sound like Caz. Not to me. I don't buy it. I ask:

"So what is she doing?"

"Well, it's an array of stuff they found stashed in her room. These women have the right to inspect the girls'

rooms, you know. They are *minors*. Plus, her behavior has been odd. Her grades started to reflect that something was going on. And now we have to do something about it."

I'm now beginning to lose my appetite. Andy seems to be reading my mind. He tells me that Caz seems to think she's the exception to the rule; that she could never become addicted to anything is typical of her rebellious ways. He can't be talking about Caz. The idea of her being strung out just doesn't make sense. I just can't really believe it. Our food arrives. I'm salivating and practically grabbing the trays out of the waiter's hands. Andy looks at me with his usual raised brow.

"Si, I'm going to give you a couple of hundred bucks for you to buy yourself a decent dinner or two every week. You're devouring that thing as if I just picked you up off the streets of Bombay."

I crack up at this. And so does Andy.

He leans in, " You know, Caz is a lot more like me than you are."

I nod.

"I know. She's got your head."

Andy grins, "Yeah, poor girl. The kids today, though, scare me. They know too much too soon. Gram is always telling me that I laid too much of the *heavy lumber* on you two when you were young when you needed to just have fun. But wasn't some of it fun?"

For a moment, I feel sorry for my dad. I'm sure he got a lot of this from the both of them. I reply,

"Of course, it was fun!"

Andy always took us to the very best places; He showed us all the glorious architectural sites, brought us to the best restaurants and museums. I say:

"Remember that day in the *Cloisters* when we decided to hang out and pretend we were actors on break after giving a performance of one of those ancient Greek dramas? And the year was 200 bc? We had to think of things that people might have talked about back then?"

Andy lights up, "Yeah, you and Layla really got into that"—Andy always calls my sister by her first name, which is Layla. *Caz* is my personal nickname for her; it's derived from her middle name, Caspian.

I assure him, "Yeah, Dad, it was always an adventure being with you."

And it's true. While most of my friends were dragged to corn like *'Honey, I Shrunk The Kids'* or Saturday afternoon drives through *Ronald MacDonald Land,* Andy was taking us to the Metropolitan Museum of Art, or the planetarium at the Museum of Natural History.

Andy beams, "This escargot is pretty good. You want to order some?"

I shake my head, "Salad's plenty, Dad."

Now I feel a tinge of guilt as to how I was thinking earlier. In fact, I'm now kind of glad to be sitting here instead of the cafeteria or something. Andy loosens his bodacious tie. "Well, I shouldn't be surprised at all this stuff about your sister. I have to remember that kids will do what they want to do. But forgive me if I over-do it, Si. I am just especially concerned about all that hell I went through in my young life and I'd like to spare my kids of that. It took a while for the problem to set in. I was in my mid-twenties when things started to get out of control. Before then, I could have a six pack a night and be fine. It all crept up on me. It was a nightmare."

Our main courses are arriving. Dad ordered the bouillabaisse, steamed vegetables . My steak is gargantu-

an. I am in heaven.

" Dad, are you telling me that you just drank like a regular guy and then it all changed or something."

"Yup."

"And that could possibly happen to me."

Andy tells me I have a *fifty-fifty* chance. "If you can drive a car better than most after five drinks, then you are definitely on the road to becoming *one of us*. In the beginning it does for *us* what it simply does not do for other people. So pay attention. I cannot tell you what to do. Drinking age is 21 here, and I know you pass for older than 18. Let's talk about something else. Just keep in mind what I said."

"Ok. What's going to happen with Caz?"

"We don't know what to do yet. We'll be there tomorrow to talk this all out with the principal and of course, we'll talk to Layla. Your mom is very upset."

I then inform him, "They called a week or so ago, Dad. They said they were going to give her a 'Sweet 16' birthday party."

Andy's really getting into the bouillabaisse. He has this huge napkin tied around his neck like a bib to protect his work-of-art tie. And I'm glad for it, too, because he's splattering the thing like crazy.

Andy pipes up, "They still may. But this stuff all came up late last week. I know they want to see you. They find you to be very aloof. I tell them that you need a break and that you probably won't be coming home. In fact, something tells me you want to hang out here or do something different for the summer."

I feel this grin formulating on my face. I know I look like a complete idiot. I'm definitely giving myself away or I am about to. But I regain my composure. I tell him,

"Dad, you must have some kind of radar detector in your head. You're right. I don't want to be in Connecticut this summer."

Andy quickly replies, " And I don't blame you."

I rather appreciate hearing this. For a moment, I want to delve in and ask questions about Great Grand Dad, but I don't want to give him any ideas.

Things seem to be going so smoothly tonight. The last time I alluded to the old man, Andy got shaky and nervous. He kept saying he was in an old folk's home and practically comatose with senility. God knows, I don't want to rock any boats. I just don't understand why Andy's always fidgety when I ask about the ancient Scottish bastard.   So I keep the trap shut. And Andy isn't prying any further. I shake my head, looking pensive.

"I'm sad about Caz."

Andy looks up. His "bib" practically soaked from the bouillabaisse. Andy shrugs his shoulders, "She has to learn for herself, apparently. She doesn't like to listen, you know that."

It's sort of true; Caz is sort of different from me. There's something about her that's too private. I used to think it was because she is so intelligent, but there's something else about it that I can't put my finger on. I sit here in the silence that hangs between my dad and me, eating every bit of food on my plates. I look up and briskly sauntering by, with a rather attractive woman in front of him, is none other than Boyce. There's just a tiny wink in his eye as he catches mine while the maitre d' escorts him down the aisle to the back. The very back, I hope. I gulp my potatoes and glance to the wall. My dad seems impervious to this little moment of recogni-

tion and I'm grateful. *That's my new secret friend. My helper. My advisor.* And he's totally cool. He knows that it's my dad I am with. He just knows. The man didn't utter a word. Now that's professionalism.

Andy looks up, "What are you thinking about, Si? You look very preoccupied all of a sudden."

"Well, I'm rummaging through the memory bank and remembering Caz. How she is a bit different from me. "

Andy wipes his mouth and tosses the napkin and "bib" in his emptied bowl. He looks directly at me, "You're right We've got to give this serious attention now, because she may just decide to mess up her life."

"She wouldn't do that, though."

Andy shakes his head. "Don't be too sure. Listen, I want you to do what you want this summer. I want to take you to Italy and maybe France. So think about it. We don't have a lot of time to do these things. Before you know it, you'll be in your twenties. Pap came from a different generation. He came from rather unfortunate circumstances and he had a limited education. He really couldn't offer me much. I want you to not feel that we can't do these things."

It impresses me to hear Andy say this. In fact, I'm mildly shocked. Maybe he's trying to break out of his mold. Maybe he has been seeing a shrink or something, or maybe he's changing. I am not sure as to what I should say. I feel like it's weird that he is saying such things when, for years, I always found him to be so preoccupied. Foggy. Not all there, but here he is, telling me this. I want to say: *It's kind of late in the game.*

For some reason, I ask him, "Did you ever just bag everything and go out on your own?"

Andy purses his lips. "Yeah, I did. Certainly I did, but it was either basically structured or crazy. When it had something to do with studying or something, like when I did an apprenticeship in Florence, it was good. But the thing I regret was being *pissed* most of the time. I sort of did some meandering things. Never planned."

I sit back, relaxing a bit after devouring my food.

I ask him, " Can you go into that a bit?"

"Go into what?"

"Your lack of planning."

"Well, I just…let's see, it was the late 60's, and I remember I ended up at *Woodstock* and I just did spontaneous, crazy things. I worked on a farm one summer in California. It was ok. But it was stupid. It was just an impulsive decision. Nothing so bad about that, but when I look back, I could've at least chosen better places, or better things. Why?"

I tell him, "Well, I am wondering about some things, that's all. I would love the trip, but I may do something else. Something I've been planning."

I want to add: *Like contacting Great Granddad down in New Orleans before he croaks*! But, of course, I don't. Besides, Andy looks a bit pale. Well, he's always pale, but right now, he's ashen. What little blood there is circulating beneath his smooth white skin looks drained. Siphoned. Maybe this was not the exact moment to say something like this.

Finally, Andy speaks, "Well, ok. Si. It's good. We can do it another time. Next year or something. Just let me know by May. I want to do this in August."

Andy is now looking at the bill and takes out one of his gold cards.

"I hate these things. Banks really make a fortune off

the interest. Hey, how's the job at the library?"

It's pretty obvious he's nervous. He knows something's up with me. I tell him it's great. I tell him everything he wants to hear. I tell him that it's a great place to meet girls. And yes, I tell him about *Guinevere*. Not in full detail or anything, I just say she's a cute, nice girl I like. He seems pleased.

As we leave, I tell Andy I need to quickly run to the men's room. I step into the back area and spot Boyce sitting at a small table in the corner of the room; the soft glow of the candles give his smooth, bald head a warm sheen as he holds the hand of the woman he's with. He looks over at me and smiles. I retreat to the front of the restaurant to join Andy.

As we ride back to the dorm, I am thinking of how strange it was to have Boyce there in the restaurant. That it was fated or something, that it was a sign. Yet Andy is being real cool tonight. We aren't really talking much. Just more questions about the school, the grounds, the sports, the girls, the professors. He thinks it's good I backed off from the frat thing.

Andy muses: "It certainly wasn't my style. It's the kind of mentality you have in those things! Doesn't mean I didn't like to go to a keg party here and there; but these are the guys who... "

I jump in: "...are now taking the kids for adventures in *K-Mart* or the latest suburban theme park!" We both laugh.

Andy continues, "Yeah, Gram told me off one night-throwing a book or two at my head because she thought I needed to take you two to see kiddy movies instead of, well, wherever in the hell we ended up going."

I ask, "She threw books at you?"

Andy grins: "Yeah, and she almost caused an avalanche in the living room. That old bookcase had a loose shelf. Your mom actually found this antic of hers to be hilarious. I don't know where you were. Maybe spending the night at one of your friends'. I think you were about twelve at the time. Tell me, what did you *really* do when you went to your friends'?"

We are now pulling up the drive to the dorm.

"Well, Dad, that's a good question. Usually, we'd build camp fires, smoke cigarettes, maybe share some girlie magazines, and tell ghost stories."

Andy continues, "Sounds like me. Except we'd run around the *French Quarter* pretending we were runaways. Sometimes we'd panhandle, getting sympathy from the tourists. I don't think we made much from it, but we found it entertaining enough. Well, Si, I'll let you know about Layla".

Andy's holding onto my arm. As I am about to get out of the car, he swings his left arm around me. It feels weird when he does this.

"Ok, Dad. Great."

I pull away from him slightly. I don't want to embarrass him or anything.

I step out and wave as the car gradually disappears down the drive. It's going to be some heavy night, that's all I'm going to say. I run upstairs to my room; the door swings open; the room seems hollow and empty. I step over to the drawer where Les keeps a tidy stash of herb, and help myself to some of it. I remember that this is ultra potent stuff. And I don't seem to mind taking it. After all, Les owes me ten bucks! Here Andy and I chatted for nearly three hours about how Caz is all messed up and his usual litany about his own drinking failures, and

I'm gingerly going about as if the conversation had never happened. There comes a time when you just have to do what you need to do. Sermons, warnings, lectures and all. In fact, a brandy or two sounds like a good idea right now. After all, the bottle I keep stashed in the closet is only brought out on occasion. Cutting myself away from the clan sounds like an aim I want to achieve. *Sorry, Dad, but that's just the way it goes.* I am the next generation. I am the one who will live well into the new century and damn it, I don't need the excess baggage.

****

The wooded area that lies some distance from the cluster of dormitories where I live, seems dense and thick this time of night. I can barely see and branches are slapping me in the face, left and right. I'm like a blind man walking and forging ahead as if caught in a thunderous rainstorm. I check my pockets to see if the *herb* is still there. It is. And I trudge through the forest until I get to a quiet, moonlit clearance where I can sit, smoke and think; where I can embalm myself in a more *real* reality. I find a spot. It's not exactly what I envisioned, but it will do. There isn't the slightest sound. The ground is mossy and dry.

I plop down, dig around in the pocket and pull the joint out. I ardently light up, leaning my head against a pine tree. I am ready for the show. The panoramic display of things unrecognized in the trap of three-dimensional consciousness. The sound between sounds? Isn't that what the '60's were all about? To get *in touch*? It's all really bourgeois when you think about it. My dad's generation is now leaning toward old age, really, and

they think they are so totally *in the know*. Like what they passed off for higher consciousness is something we're supposed to drool over and envy. If you ask me, they were failures. Whenever I think about cats like the true peyote-takers, the true marijuana-*imbibers*, there's a basic respect there. Those guys were seriously seeking spirituality and they didn't run when the going got rough. They stuck it out and initiated themselves through to the other side. Something our president and his little boy scout generation completely failed to do. The '60's hipsters just can't stop patting themselves on their backs for dipping their toes in what was an idea of outsider modes of experimentation when the actuality was simply wanting to have a good time. And they seem to remain in this mode of nostalgia around what really was recreational activity and now they have dominated the airwaves with all this bs. *Remember when?* stuff. Like top forty tunes they want every beer-bellied 50-year-old to scan their memories of when they show that stuff on these TV docu-drama programs. I wanna simply say: Hey, grooves, remember *The Doors' "The End"*? This could make them squirm a bit. After all, there might've been a time in all those hashish sessions, when they might have thought. Might have thought deeply. And just when they were about to really get going somewhere they freak and bail only to wind up at the 'fridge popping a *Budweiser*. Like stick to the plan, dudes. Stick to the god-forsaken, blasted, whatever...plan. Andy. Andy and his spontaneous abortions in consciousness. Andy plowing the land. Now I laugh. I can't help it. I'm imagining my dad, pre-dent days, with a band around his head, and his raven black locks dripping sweat off his bare back as he is stupidly working with a bunch of underpaid Mexicans

in California. *De Profundis* . I am thinking of *De Profundis* . Who wrote *De Profundis*? Was it Pascal? Dad is plowing the earth while a dog eared paperback of *De Profundis* slips out of his back jeans' pocket and plops into the earth. Your thoughts are mud. Your thoughts are mud. My, but your thoughts are reduced to mud when you're in the blazing mid-day California sun and raisins are now drying out in heaps and massive sheets containing thousands upon thousands of raisins baking in the California sun.

There is a man now approaching, and he is old. He is witheringly old and his skin is parchment red. And he knows who the author of *De Profundis* is, and he has invited him into his cave for lunch. He has invited him in for a lunch of oily seeds, and muffin bread, and Jim Morrison is being skewered on a pit. And his hair is dangling and flopping and dragging on the ground, as his body is being spun slowly over the smoky pit. Oscar Wilde is the author of *De Profundis* , the old man says. *Pensees* is the famous work of Pascal. Have you studied your *pensees*?

I once read a group of poems by Rainer Rilke and they were about reality and experience, and how a zoo animal experiences reality and how it looks at humans who are looking at it. All day long. All day long. Sadness abounds in animals when others peer at them in cages. The moon is a giant silver pregnant disk of light. It is only reflected light from a greater light. Nothing more. The old man wants to talk to me. He gets up from his comfortable position on the cave floor. Oscar Wilde has gone to count the raisins that are lying and baking in the sun, and now the old man approaches me. I hide in the back of the cave. I'm not ready. His eyes are chalky

blue, yet his skin is bronze. He is ancient. He grins. Great old teeth. His body is adorned in miniature paintings like tattoos over his chest and arms. He's the walking museum man and every picture tells a story.

He approaches and I slip through a hole in the earth. I'm in a field now of ripening olive trees and it is dusk and there is a sea in the horizon. A beautiful blue and green sea. And I am alone. I have no shoes on my feet and my clothes are torn. The walk is long to the sea. And there, in the slightest distance, is the old man in a tattered suit and his skin is now pale and his hair is white and long and he is shouting something to me. He's delivering a message to me and I am deaf to the sound. As I approach, I notice that I'm deaf to the language. It is ancient and gravelly sounding, this language.

My body is as heavy as a great stone, an unmovable boulder. I can feel the discomfort in my tailbone as I sit against this tree. What in the hell is in this stuff? Les said it was extra special. I reach down and feel for my watch. It's nearly midnight. I light the joint again and take a couple of deep drags. In the scene with the old man, I caught a glimpse of something like a diaphanous something fleeting the scene.

I feel like I'm a character in *Alice in Wonderland* chasing a delicate, white...a veil. *Thalia.* A scene with her at the ballet. Well, we went to several ballets. She was a freak for the stuff. She had these girl friends who were all into the ballet, modern choreography, anything to do with dance. And when they would run into each other at City Center or one of the famous dance arenas, or auditoriums I should say, they would giggle and chat about how horrible some principle dancer's feet were and then upon departing one of them would say some-

thing like: "See you at ' Don Q.' !" and then they'd wave their arms at each other as a way of saying *'toodle-loo'* in the exact dying swan fashion in Swan Lake. I stood there rolling my eyes at Thalia and shaking my head: "You guys are really something else. What's *'Don Q'?"* And Thalia would smirk and roll her eyes and say: "*Don Quixote*, stupid. You know the famous book? Well, it also happens to be a ballet." And she'd saunter off to the women's room, her butt wiggling ever so slightly under her black tights and mini skirt. The ever-elusive, bitchy Thalia! I was a bit slack-jawed while I stood there thinking of how beautiful she looked and that I didn't have to like her silly ballet or her ballet friends, for that matter, and I think I went home. I left her there. And it was only a few weeks after that incident where we got together and I did the dark living room number and the *'Herion'* bit on the stereo. You can't blame me. I'm freaking. I can feel the warm tears run down my face. The old man is back. He is calling me to come with him to the sea. Into the sea. He is wading his bony shins in the cold blue-green sea and there is a ship, an old clipper ship bouncing on the glistening waves of blue and green and he is now walking on the water to the ship and he is beckoning me to come with him.

I run down the grassy hills that lead to the dunes, and I am panting, trying to catch up with them, with this mystery crew of the parchment paper-faced old man and his ship. Ship of what? Fools? Wise men? My feet are smacking against the smooth wet sand of the beach and the ship is now growing more distant. I am cutting my feet on rocks and broken glass and I stop and wave. "Meet with us later, at the horn!" some one shouts from the departing ship. And then, a shrieking sound, a mes-

sage in my head that says: "You're not done. Not done with *her*." And I'm seeing Gram and Nancy, and Thalia, and *Guinevere* and Pony and all the girls I know on campus, and even Caz. Andy is plowing the fields again. His hair mangled and wet with sweat from the California sun. Oscar Wilde is brushing off his frock and the old man has gone to sea. Everything I have brought up with Boyce is now here and magnified. And still a question, only it feels more foreboding and pressing.

I flick the lighter and look at my watch. It is now twenty minutes after one. The moon is still huge and mirror-like. It's freezing cold. My body no longer feels as heavy, but I'm exhausted. I hear voices. Real voices. There are people actually hanging out here in the woods drinking and smoking as if it's eight in the evening or something. The more I walk through the woods back to the dorm, to my safe little place away from the precarious unknown of such cerebral exploits, the more I feel grounded. Like I'm returning to palpable everydayness.

I creep back into the room. No one is here. Lover Boy is probably shacking out somewhere with Amanda and maybe Les got lucky and scored with *Wife of Hades*. I pull out my headset, slip in *Nirvana*'s '*Nevermind*' and note the song "*Come As You* Are", anticipating my favorite, "*Lithium*", and appreciating the basic appropriateness of it all as I quietly lull myself to numb-out land, not bothering to take off my clothes or get under the covers.

****

The sunlight is screaming through the room as Cory

vigorously raises the shade all the way up. My heart is pounding fast. The foggy stupor lifts with the blaring reminder that I have an exam this morning in which I barely read the several chapters or so pertaining to the Pre-Socratics. This is supposed to be an area I am interested in and well, the only recall I have of the subject is Andy's references to Pythagorian theory. I grab my books, thumbing through the chapters like a lunatic. I have about an hour to absorb this stuff. Cory's looking at me: "Hey, dude, where in the hell were you last night? Les told me you swiped some of his hallucinogenic grass."

Immediately, I snap, "I don't believe that's any of your business. He owes me money. Did he tell you that?" I am in no mood for this kind of garbage, especially from cerebrum-voided Cory.

"Where were you?" I ask.

"Dude, I was with Amanda. We ended up camping out. It was an awesome evening. Didja see the moon?" I ignore him, busying myself with gathering my clothes, towels and stuff to take a shower. Cory follows me. I turn around to close the door, his face just inches away. He informs me, "Si, there's really something wrong with you, man. You're always copping an attitude about something. You need to get laid. Badly." I shut the door in his face. He's right, you know. He's absolutely right.

The moron may actually have some brain activity after all. Afterwards, I walk out, flapping the towels and Cory is still sitting on his bed. I tell him, "Sorry. I just remembered I have a test today, and I got pretty loaded last night." Cory looks up, a bit surprised. "Hey, it's ok, Strayhorn. It must've been heavy seeing your dad and all, too."

What is this? Are they now taking notes? Can't I ever have some privacy? Les reports to him my every move. He must! I ask, " How did you know about that? You're never here."

Cory shrugs his shoulders. "I dunno. Les said he had this cool virtual reality device and he was showing it to him. My dad's an old bag. He's like 67. You should consider yourself lucky."

I ask, "Were you an "*accident*" or something? Why's your dad so old?"

Cory scratches his bean-head, "I dunno. My mom is his third wife! He was rich and wise. And she was young and scared. She's only 38!" I gather my books and stuff them into my bag.

Cory continues, "Your dad is this cool guy and you're embarrassed about him. Didn't he used to go to *CBGB*'s and stuff? Les said he had on this Jerry Garcia tie."

I kind of feel sorry for this geek-head. But to go into it with him would take a lot of exhaustive jaw work. And it just simply isn't worth it to try to explain how that very thing about my dad really rakes on my nerves.

I tell him, "Well, Cory, I gotta go corral myself in the library and pour over this stuff so I don't flunk out. He'd kill me. I mean it. The guy is such an intellectual. He'd consider it more noble if I volunteered as a mercenary before letting my GPA slink down to the dreaded mediocre level of a low B or C-plus average".

Cory is counting some loose change on the bed.

"Man, that's kind of cool. My dad just wants me to be a jock. He excelled in everything but that. So he'd like me to fill in that gap for him. Lame, huh?"

I listen to this with much reservation. It seems it's

more like his old man saw that his son didn't have much
up there early-on and as a consequence, encouraged his
darling Cory to be a jock.

I smile and say, "Well, you should rebel and become
a raging mad scientist or something. Les will help you!"

I collect my things and high tail it out of the room,
relieved that I wasn't born Cory Banks. The one thing
I'm grateful for. Amanda is swinging her hips down the
hall. I recognize her walk and hair anywhere. I know he
has this babe as he's had probably many others, but I still
wouldn't want to be Cory.

Amanda greets me,

"Hey, Si. Is he in there?"

I nod and continue to walk past her. I have this very
important flight to catch and it is leaving very soon to the
library. I don't want to hang out and get into a chat with
Amanda. She'd probably start asking questions since
Cory probably tells her about my little rendezvous afternoons with the 'secret sweetie' and I don't want to
encourage any further speculation.

I race through the main doors of the library and run
right into Lisa.

"Si!"

Great. What perfection in the timing. Now I'm really in a hurry to crack open these books, and she's standing right in front of me. Just looking as beautiful as ever
and I'm watching myself as if I'm a bird perched atop my
head, and I'm saying that I have this test. That, no, I'm
not working early today but will be there later, and I am
watching myself suddenly say: "Hey, what are you doing
after work? Wanna grab something to eat or something?"

She's nodding her head and giving me this gorgeous
dimple-dewy smile and I feel like I am thirteen and talk-

ing to a girl for the first time. Actually, it's a miracle. And as soon as I get into the elevator, I'm drumming up a way I can get out of this test.

I have about a half hour to cram. It's going to be impossible. I slide into one of the carrels. My fingers are flying over the books like crazy. Finally, I check my jeans' pocket for change and I head for the phone bank in the lobby. I'm getting out of this test. I'll write a ten-page essay to make up for it. I know precisely how I am going to do this. I call my prof's department and I immediately hang up. What if he's there? What do I say? I call again, I am put on hold. He is there. I drum up my best cracked voiced act. I tell him with extreme effort in my voice that something has come up. That it concerns a family member, that I was not able to properly prepare to take the test. He tells me to come see him tomorrow afternoon or Monday. I tell him Monday as I may have to go out of town today. I hang up the phone absolutely joyous and relieved. I practically don't know what to do with myself.   I want to run upstairs and talk to *Goldielocks*, but I hesitate. I don't think it would be a good idea to just go up there and hang out when I'm not slated to work. I feel like I can practically go on a picnic or something.

I waltz out of the main doors and head for my spot by the river. I slip in my *Nirvana* CD and groove along to "*Lounge Act*", an essentially cool number. (If I were John Lydon, aka Johnny Rotten, or *The Ramones*, I'd say, these guys do one better. You can't argue with the superior, grinding, guitar sounds. It's the essence of rock; that and the *monster-outsider-don't-touch-me* sensibility. It's the Phantom in the '*Phantom of the Opera* ' who would've flourished in the medium had rock music been available. It's actually, *Melmoth the Wanderer* with a set of lousy lyrics and a steely guitar.)

I find my spot by the water and pull out my things from the book bag. I spread everything out on the ground. I have about two hours to write about these ancient minds. The headset is now shut off.

****

There's this kid sitting across from me and he has this nervous tick. He fidgets and squirms in his chair. He'll pretend he doesn't talk to himself by propping one of the kiddy magazines in front of his face, but I know better. Kid doesn't fool me. Kind of makes me wonder, though, these shrinks look like they have a hard time of it. And I know this kid is a patient of the other therapist who shares the quarters next to Boyce's.

I hear the front door open. Boyce is now entering the building. His bald dome begins to appear as he climbs the stairs.

"Simon! You're actually a bit early today. Come in!"

I follow him into the room like a spindly spider and slide into the chair. I grin. Boyce shakes his head at me,

"Well, looks like something's up! What's happening?"

I tell Boyce about my little encounter with Lisa and our getting together tonight. I go into the whole thing. I tell him about Thalia and how I had these heavy thoughts about her the other night, that I am concerned because I am ashamed to admit how I handled everything with her. That I was an idiot and that I am scared I will screw everything up all over again. I tell him about the conversation with Andy and my sister and my observations about Andy still being the pansy that he basically is, but also the good things I had thought about him and I end up confessing that I toked on some amazingly profound weed the other night and ended up crying and hallucinating.

Boyce's mouth is slightly open. His pipe has hung there unlit for about ten minutes or more. He tells me to go on if I want and I do. I tell him that I am glad I *toked* the other night, that I do not do these things as occasionally as I do in order to get revved up so I can screw some girl, that I am actively on a *search* and it is all driving me slightly nuts. After a long spell of silence—something that happens with Boyce from time to time—he emits a wide grin and says:

" I think we are about to go through a new door, Si. This is good. Thanks for telling me this."

I have no idea what this man is talking about. I'm expecting this guy to go into a lecture about drugs and cannabis and the usual stuff I've gotten from *authority* figures all my life, but *new door*?

Boyce continues: "Oh absolutely. In just these past six weeks or so you have transformed. You probably don't even see it. You are about to enter a real stage of growth and this is good. Now, the last time you told me that you had this plan. Well?"

I tell him that I want to bag out of school entirely for the next year. That I could leave at the end of the summer or even earlier, depending on how much I can save. That I need to get the hell away from everything I know. A summer really wouldn't be enough. Boyce is stroking his chin and looking up at the ceiling.

He asks, "Where does that leave us, Si?"

"Well, I just think we can take a break for a few

months and when I return, we'll just continue. Can I do that?"

Boyce shrugs his shoulders and asks, "Of course. Now how much longer would you like to work with me? Can you commit til mid-summer?"

I feel very uncomfortable about this. I tell him that that would probably be so. But I can't really promise anything.

Boyce interrupts. "Aha! Promises, promises, like Andy, Si?"

I must be flushing crimson. I hate when this man pulls stunts like this. I simply hate it. I'm caught in his trap!

Boyce now leans forward, lighting his pipe he tells me, "I'm going to be direct with you here, Si. Bail now. Because the longer you do this with me, the harder it will be to cut it off later. Unless we come up with something. You can choose to work with me, but there are other ways. You can go out into the world and find things out on your own. Which is a hard way. But beneficial because nothing teaches like experience or you can stay here and we hash things out and get clear on some things first, so you can handle things better as you go off on your adventure. Where are you going, by the way?"

I tell him that I have some ideas of driving down south. That I have some friends here and there. One in Virginia and one in North Carolina. Then I would go on to New Orleans. I want to work an oil rig job. Boyce smiles when I tell him this.

I say, "I know. I know. It's hard work. I know all about it, Boyce. But the idea is to make money so I can eventually end up in Europe".

The man arches his brows and begins to puff his pipe

fast, emitting tiny jets of smoke like a little steam engine, as if this will push our session forward somewhere. Really. He always gets puffing when he wants to push something.

"And *Goldengirl*? Gonna try to take her with you?"

Here he goes. I tell him that that idea is totally absurd. I haven't even gone out with her yet and already he's asking something like this. Boyce is now getting out of his chair and walks to the front of his great desk. He's leaning against it, his face practically right in mine. I'm really feeling squirmy. He's never done this before.

He asks: "Can we think about an agreement? I have a proposal I am going to offer you. I am all for your adventure, but I am going to ask you to-and I don't know of any other way to put this but do you remember when we had our first appointment? You had indicated that you were looking for an older man to convey... some *guidance*, as in a wise-man sort of way? Remember that?"

I nod my head vigorously.

Boyce continues, "Well, here I am!"

I'm not so sure what old Boyce is driving at, but my mind goes blank. I shake my head. The man rolls his eyes a bit "You may want a little guidance while you are out there on your adventure; no, I won't be accompanying you or anything, I just want to offer some suggestions. We'll get into it next session, hmm?"

I'm really feeling weird about this. Like, what does he mean, *guide* me through it? I am sitting here frozen in this chair. Boyce goes into it:

"In much simpler times, and actually, in more indigenous cultures, the older men in the tribes would take over the teenage boys and guide them through things. Not their fathers! Sometimes, the grandfathers, but the mothers, especially the mothers. were completely kept out of this and the fathers had to bag out, too. You see, sometimes you need another man to walk you through something. The only equivalent we have in today's society with something like this is maybe a coach and a budding athlete or a one-on-one tutorialship of some kind."

The hairs on my head are tingling, my palms are now defrosting rapidly, my heart flutters. I practically lunge out of the chair, not exactly realizing what I am about to say, but I say it anyway. I say "yes".

I leave our session shaking Boyce's clammy paw. I tell him I'm open to it. I'll take anything, I'm so desperate. And that's probably good news for him. Boyce grins and says something about the grateful beggar in front of the well or whatever and I say to please save it for next week.

As I walk out of the office, he wishes me luck with Lisa. Of course, I'm still kind of curious about the woman I saw him with the other night. Had he scored with her? Does he still struggle with bra straps and dating rituals? I highly doubt it. Not old smooth-boy Boyce. I can imagine him with the ladies. He's probably something else. Bald head and all. There's something about this guy that is so confident, that if he had acne (and I knew a guy like this in high school), he could take out a medicated pad and wipe his mug with it and not skip a beat in what he's saying while some dewy-eyed girl is standing there, hanging on to his every word, oblivious to the craters on his face. Now that's power. Something I sure could use.

****

I've spent most of my afternoon here at the library, thumbing through some anthropology books I gathered from the shelves. I even grabbed one by that wavy haired old man I saw on TV several weeks ago. And it's all fine and well, except my Lovely is upstairs doing some cataloguing. I think Ron knows I've got something for her because he keeps sending her all over the place. It just occurs to me that maybe he has something for her, too. Guy's got a lot of nerve; he's like 32 or something. And he's one of those perennial grad students. They're worse than drop outs! I've looked up at the clock nearly a dozen times and the afternoon isn't going any faster. I've reviewed the dozen or so pages I've already written for my philosophy class.

I've resisted the urge to leap up the back stairs so I could at least take a peek at my Guinevere as she goes through the stacks. I don't want to seem overly excited about our date tonight. She might think I'm a real bozo especially since I can't take her any place fancy. Like the restaurant Andy and I were in the other night.

"Strayhorn!"

Jeez! I leap up like a loon. Lisa's just pouring an armload of books all over the counter top. I watch her and ask,

"What's up? Whaddya doin., *Gorgeous*?"

She's looking at me askance.

"Silly. You're supposed to help me, and isn't that bit

premature? I haven't even arm-wrestled you yet."

With that, she sashays over to the other side of the counter and starts pulling out the file drawers. Well, I can tell, already, this is going to be some date. I walk over to her, saying,

" Put her up. Come on! Ron is probably buying lottery tickets somewhere right now. Put her up. Let's get this over with."

She's looking at me and grinning like a cheetah. I tell her, "Come on! You started it!"

She shushes me. "I was just kidding. I only came down to keep you company and to find out where we're going tonight."

I tell her nothing fancy. That we can stop off at *Frank's* and then on to some of the dance places around Cromwell Street.

She says:" The gay clubs have no-cover tonight "

Jeez. I dunno. "Lisa, I'm not gay. Now why would I be taking you on our first night out together to dance at a gay bar?"

She gives me this incredulous look; shrugs her shoulders and says, "Cuz *I* am!... Nah...just couldn't resist saying that...um...well...they're great to dance in, Si. And it'll save you some dough.."

I decide that money is now not a problem. I tell her, "Hey, let me worry about the money. I've got plenty of money, *Babycakes*. Let's skip out. Come on. Put that stuff away, let's leave it for candy-ass Ron. He'll freak. It'll be good for him! Let's go!"

I honestly don't know what's gotten into me. It's like I've known this girl all my life. I take her by the arm and swirl her around the carpet. Some people are beginning to look over our way. Lisa's laughing all over the place and we're being shushed.

I tell her, "Aren't you sick of this place? Always having to be so damned quiet. . Let's go." I walk her over to the counter and we gather our things. I assure her, " Ok. So we're leaving a bit early. About a half hour. Big deal. Ron'll have his cow and then get over it."

I sling my book bag over my shoulder and gently usher Lisa to the door. Lisa's eyeing me up and down as we walk. She giggles and points at me. As we approach the marbled hallway, she says "Si, Please check your shoe. You've got a *little friend* there." A wha...I look down and there's this ream of toilet paper dragging behind me. Great. I really know how to impress 'em! Lisa is just coochy-cooing me as I shamelessly pull the thing off and proceed to the elevators. I bet Cory Banks never had this happen to him. Of all the nimble, cortex-voided lame excuses of brains there are out there, Cory would be spared this kind of embarrassment. And that makes me sick. And mad enough that I'd start an Anti-Ayran movement and rally all the big nosed, Jewish guys I know to spearhead it. I'm sorry, somebody's got to take care of guys like Cory Banks.

Lisa is looking at me with those green doe eyes. We step out of the elevator and there's Ron in the lobby. We greet him and say that everything's taken care of; that it's been a slow night. Of course, I'm lying; Lisa and I literally crammed the pile of stuff that needed cataloguing in a storage area. But old Ron here is just nodding and grinning at us. As Lisa and I walk into the parking lot, we both realize that Ron looked preoccupied with something. Lisa asks, "I've never seen him so...mellow.

Have you?"

We get into my car. It's a pathetic oyster white Ford *Escort*. About as basic as it gets. I point to the seat belt and tell Lisa that this is what you call a generic, no frills machine. She tells me I should see hers. I'm glad we're off on an even start. All the more to have an equal opportunity affair.

We drive out of the campus and head into town. Actually, the parking seems so bad, we decide to spin around the neighborhood. Lisa points out the two gay bars, (*Marlowe's Muscle*, and *Stiff's)* in all of Bryant county. I tell her that I remember being in one of them one afternoon and wondered why there were no chicks in the place. Of course, had I noticed the name of the place, I might've understood why, but I blindly walked in without noticing. She laughs.

I tell her, "Seriously. I had no idea. Nobody tried to pick me up or anything; it was in the afternoon and most of these guys were sitting around chatting about interior decorating, chintz slip covers and Martha Stewart, you know, the usual macho garbage. How wuz I to know?" Lisa keeps a straight face as she eyes a parking spot. We decide to walk over to *Frank's*.

As we enter, we recognize some people we both happen to know. Craig Wheeler and Bern Bischoff. Their dates wave at us as they beeline for the ladies room. Bern and Craig both happen to live in my dorm. We chat for a while about the local happenings. Bern reminds Craig that I'm the one who took care of that jock, Barry *Whats-his-name*.

Bern says: "You shoulda seen our guy here. The creep is nothin' but a *wuss*, huh, Strayhorn? A big pussy willow wuss. You should see this guy. He's a jock and Strayhorn pummeled him. Way ta go, dude!"

Lisa's looking up at me and I am... like, wait a minute, I'm not really like this. I have no idea of even why I did this to the guy in the first place. I don't even know him. I just happened to mosey along on a day when I wasn't all that happy about things, that's all. Bern asks: "What was that whole matter about anyway, Strayhorn? Something to do with Cory Banks? ...Never mind. You don't have to say. Everybody hates the guy." Craig asks me how I know Cory.

Bern answers for me, " He's his roommate. Isn't that right?"

We all wish each other well, and Lisa and I are finally seated at a table. A cozy tiny table with a burgundy candle burning in the center. After we settle a bit, I casually ask Lisa how she knows Craig and Bern. She looks at me briefly and lowers her eyes on the menu. "I forget, actually. I think I originally met Bern at the library when I used to work in Government Documents. Why?"

Ok. Those guys both happen to be good-looking. And they seem to be popular with the babes. I'm curious about Lisa's past relationships, dates, and the like. I know I can't ask her any questions like this, at least not right off the bat, but I'm a little curious. Who wouldn't be? She's my...*Guinevere*. I barely realize it, but my hand is gently stroking her lovely , glossy, nail-tips.

Lisa's still looking at the menu as she speaks "Stop it, Strayhorn! We haven't even ordered yet!"

I interject, "Nor have we arm-wrestled, my sweet."

Lisa grins, shutting the menu and before setting it down she swats me with it. Isn't she just lovely, now?

I look down at my watch and tell Lisa, "Ok. Gimme the bio. You have about three minutes."

"Strayhorn, that's not fair."

"Come on. whaddya think this is? You have three minutes. Just see what you can cover in this amount of time. Shoot."

Lisa rolls her eyes and reluctantly begins her spiel: "Ok. birthplace is Flint, Michigan and don't gimme one of your smirks. It's the place where '*Roger and Me*' was filmed. No, I wasn't in it, but we know a few people who were. I was born during a snowstorm. Actually, the worst blizzard in the last twenty-five years. I'm a February baby. An altruistic Aquarian. My mom is a manager at one of the auto plants. She worked her way up and all that stuff. After she got out of the mental institution. My dad put her there. He was a roadie for a famous English rock band. We don't talk to him anymore. And mom now tells us that she pretended to be nuts because she got all these benefits and grants so she could earn a Masters at Wayne State, a no-nonsense school in inner city Detroit. Why she elected to go there, we never quite understood. In the meantime, my Aunt Bonnie and Uncle Bill helped out in raising us. Uncle Bill was friends with Mitch Rider, you know of the *Detroit Wheels*. Well, it was Mitch that got my dad into the music biz. I have two sisters. I'm the youngest. I'm here on a National Merit Scholarship. Beckwith wanted me. Brown wanted me. And Grigham wanted me. So here I am! I first had sex when I was 16. It was something I felt I had to get out of the way. I wasn't all that crazy about the guy I was dating, either. I know I'll regret admitting this; actually, I don't think I've ever been this honest on a first date before… Anyway, it's not that…Strayhorn, are you keeping time? What are you doing? Stop smiling at me. You're ridiculous."

I am. I check my mouth for anything that might be dribbling there. Lisa looks embarrassed. She changes the subject. And fast. She adds: " You know something? You look a bit like that actor…Daniel Day-Lewis? Did you know that?"

Our waiter comes back to our table serving our desserts. I can't believe I ordered a piece of pie. I never do that. But Lisa insisted. Now she's ladling my pie with mounds of ice cream. "Ya gotta try this, Strayhorn. You'll love it. It reminds me of my Aunt Veronica's. She's another one. I come from a big family, Si" *I bet you do, old girl.*

She perks up. "Ok, hand over the watch. It's your turn and *you* have all of two minutes!"

I marathon it and tell her everything covering the basics of my life. I was born in Stamford, Connecticut, and raised in Astor just outside Darien. Not as uppity as Darien, but not as humble as New Haven or Norwalk. My dad is an up and coming architect and he thinks he's hot stuff cuz he works in New York City and has a funky office in SOHO. My mom is a graphic designer, and my grandmother is an embarrassment. I briefly tell her that everyone in my family thinks they're hip and cool. I'm considering going in the direction of medicine. I've always done well in the sciences and it looks like being a doctor may be my calling. I'm not totally sure. Lisa interrupts, asking me who Andy is. I tell her I call my dad by his first name. It's a Southern affectation. Like in that movie, *To Kill A Mockingbird*. Andy loves Atticus.

So he basically likes it when my sister, Caz and I call him by his first name. My whole family is Southern. They all happened to meet here in New England. It's weird. Oh, Beckwith definitely did not want me, Georgetown did and Grigham wanted me but with no scholarship. It's the neighborhood I'm from. Really, let's face it. A hard-working girl from Flint, Michigan is definitely going to stand better than a guy from well...Ow!"

She's now swatting me again, but not with the menu. Girl's got a frisky little slap. I tell her it's time. We should get this over with now. I prop my arm on the table. "Let's go!"

Lisa looks me up and down and informs me, " No, Strayhorn. I'm the one who decides when we should..." and now she's grinning like a cheetah again.... "do it ! Okay?" The waiter is looking right down on us as he slides the check my way. I look up at him, trying not to laugh, " It's not what you think. Honestly."

Lisa and I step out into the night and decide to check out some of these dance spots. We walk into one of them and the music is *Euro-Industrial*. Lisa says she likes dancing to that kind of stuff so we spend an hour or so spinning and gyrating around the dance floor, which has a pretty cool light show. Finally, I tell her I need to get some air, so we step outside, stroll around a bit and decide to check out this other place that plays everything but what we've been dancing to, which leaves us with rock music and perhaps, R&B. We step into this place, *The Loft* and end up staying a few hours. I mean, we rock, we boogie woogie, we laugh and we spill drinks all over the floor, not because we're drunk or anything, in fact, I only ordered sodas, but because Lisa is just a rowdy girl. I guess. She sure has a lot of energy, that's all I'm going to say. Just as soon as we stop dancing and both want to take a breather, another song comes on that she must dance to. So we do this until the place closes. It's now after 2 am. Lisa wants to take a walk. I decide that we should head back to school and I ask her if she would like to take a walk with me in the woods.

We arrive at one of my favorite spots. I'm pretty worn out. Actually, I'm glad I'm pooped because I have no energy to make any moves. I wouldn't want to make her uncomfortable. So we continue to talk. Lisa tells me she is off to Europe in the fall. That she'll be studying in Switzerland as part of an exchange program. She's majoring in psychology and feels it's a good move to study there. I have only spent a few hours with this girl and already, I feel a slight pang of jealousy as she tells me about this jaunt she'll be taking next semester. I'm transfixed by her lovely face in the moonlight. I could watch her for hours. She tells me she'll be working at a real nuthouse for the summer. A place in central Connecticut. My heart sinks as she tells me this and suggests that I'll visit her at some point. I am like, what? The one time I'm avoiding home like the bubonic plague and she's going to be like 100 miles or so away from there. I could just ride up the highway and see her. And now I'm wondering about everything. I'm very tempted to bag this idea of dropping out and wandering around, yet I feel that if I do that, I'm betraying a deal I've made with myself and Boyce wouldn't approve. I can't bail, I know this. Yet I can't entirely go without wondering about her. It's nuts. My first date with her and I'm head-tripping.

Lisa gets up from her squatting position and arches

her lovely body in the moonlight. I do likewise. Man, I must look really obvious. I gather my wits, walk over to her and tap her on the shoulder, "It's time for me to take you...back." She slings her sexy arms around my neck and kisses me. Damn! This one is full of surprises. We kiss a little more and finally I tell her that we must be heading back. That people will talk, that Ron will be jealous; somehow, he'll find out. She cracks up at this. Besides, she needs to arm-wrestle me before we go any further. And she must win.

"Deal?"

She hi-fives me. "Deal, Strayhorn! And thanks! It was great!"

I leave her standing in the foyer of her dorm and wave as she enters the building.

****

I wake up today and Andy is looming over my head. Like his soul is breathing down my back. And there's this foreboding sense I may end up liking Lisa more than I expected. And this could lead to some problems. Like an unwanted marriage preceded by an unwanted pregnancy. Or something. We've spent some time together since our first night out a week or so ago. In fact, almost every evening we do something like take a stroll out to the river bank or have lunch or dinner together chatting about this and that. And I am trying to play it safe. But I'm getting to like her more and more.

Even Les and Cory have seen her with me and they mouthed "*secret sweetie* " as they passed. It was ridiculous, but I was actually relieved to finally have them see me with her. And I can tell they're impressed as hell. Lisa is a rock aficionado. She's lent me *Iggy and the Stooges' 'Funhouse'*, a superbly vintage classic from about thirty years ago. She also has some great Hendrix stuff, along with collectors' items like rare stuff from the rocksters of yesteryear. I hate to say it, but I think my parents would be impressed. Anyway, when I told Les and Cory about her rock collection, I'm sure they were expecting to see a leather-clad babe with spiked purple hair. But she's got the wholesome appearance of *Rebecca of Sunnybrook Farm* and they were a bit taken aback by this.

Anyway, when Lisa and I were in the woods the other night, I told her all this horse manure about my wanting to explore the Old South and visiting Great Granddad; even made up some stories. That I had a mission in mind. Of course, I had no idea what I was talking about. The old man is probably feeble-minded and has tubes running in and out of his orifices; For all I know, he's in a rest home and very senile. And I want to find out for sure. But I know I was saying all this because I'm scared that I could end up liking her too much and forget my plans.

I pull out my laptop and e-mail a message to the Derbigny Clinic down in New Orleans, a facility where I understand he's had some medical treatment in the recent past. So far, they have not been able to determine his current living situation. The address they have for him has not worked for me so far. I had sent a note and received it back with "return to sender" stamped by the post office. I shower, dress and head out the door for my appointment with Boyce. As I walk over to Cromwell Street, I decide that everything is feeling too good. Too damned good. That sooner or later, Lisa is going to see the crab crawling around in my head and actually, maybe

I'll even see that she won't be so fresh as farm milk anymore, either. That, really, it's silly for me to be doing this, and we will part ways simply because in a matter of weeks we will have poured too much of our guts out to one another and it will be time for the inevitable end.

I slide into my chair as Boyce lights up his mushy bowl of tobacco and while he's puffing away, I decide that I'm not going to make this into any big damned deal. I let him know that we have not had sex yet. He seems relieved at hearing this. And I agree that it would be disaster if I carried on with my usual pattern of jumping in the sack before really establishing anything. It's good practice for me. Boyce nods his domed head and says he wants to get back to the area where we left off in our last session. He further explains that it's important that I set out this summer and carry through with my ideas. That I have a task to do and that it is a good thing that Lisa will be going away. Boyce taps his pipe against the ashtray, eyeing me directly.

Slowly, he says, "It will add a healthy tension. You see, men and women-and it doesn't matter about the age-need tension. It makes for a good relationship."

Old pro, Boyce.... I know it's probably totally out of line of me, but I ask it anyway. I ask him about the attractive woman I had seen him with the other night.

He cocks his head, sticking his pipe between his cherry lips, "That, dear Simon, is my wife of 30 years!"

My mouth drops. She must be 50 years old, but I swear, she looked a lot younger. Boyce grins, informing me, "She's all *natural*, too. She's had no cosmetic surgery. She just takes care of herself!"

He then rubs his smooth, shiny dome of a head, "I can't believe she actually still *likes* me!"

There's this sparkly little twinkle in old Boyce's eye that really gets my attention. Here's this old guy who's still *turned on* by the woman he married about twelve years before I was born. Andy was probably still in high school. It sort of blows me away. I apologize if he thinks I'm being out of line or something; certainly we can resume my telling him about where things are for me. But I feel compelled to ask,

"When I came by the table and saw you in the candlelight, weren't you *wooing* her?"

Boyce puffs and grins.

"Well, yeah. Maybe I'll tell you about that later...You see, we made an agreement a long time ago, that I would take her out once a week as if I were courting her. And it does something. I take her to a romantic place, bring her flowers, the whole bit, and I woo her as if we were dating. I recommend this for all marriages. It's odd. But when I do that, I feel like I am re-establishing my masculine position."

I'm sitting there thinking: *can you come again, please*? The bit about the-? I had never heard of anything like this. That married people could actually do that. But what was with the masculine position part? That guys are such basic lunk heads that we have to do these things because otherwise we'd drop our morality down to the level of geek-ville, forgetting to appreciate the women in our lives. I bet it is something like this. I'm especially absorbing these things Boyce says because I badly need instruction. I don't want to mess any of this up with Lisa.

As we end our session , I tell Boyce that I feel like I can relate to these gushy lyrics about love and *batshit* emotions like the fear that runs through me when Lisa doesn't call me back in thirty minutes. I know that sounds like I was never a teenager in love before, but I don't really remember feeling this way about any other girl. It's so insane. Whenever I see Lisa walking through the breezeway as she approaches the library, my heart literally flutters and bounces around in my chest. And I simply don't sleep much anymore. I lie there just looking at the stars. While my roommates are *zz-eeing* off, I'm staring at the moon. Thinking of her. Thinking of a cottage we can live in someday. After my travels, and explorations and whirlwind adventures, we'll meet, marry, have a baby and promise that our kids will never see the insides of a *Pack 'n Pork* or the dreaded, sickly colored jungle gyms and slide tubes of any *Ronald MacDonald Land* suburbia has to offer. I mean this. I imagine myself taking my brilliant children to the Museum of Natural History to hang out with the dinosaur bones. In that way, I'd say I'd be like my dad. Speaking of which...I have about three messages-one from Nancy and two from Andy- on my voicemail and I haven't completely listened to any of them. It's been three days and I know I have to hear the news about Caz. I just had no idea I was going to really fall in with this girl, and I can't believe it's only been a week or so since we first went out.

I arrive back at the room and Cory and Amanda are sitting on his bed talking away. I'm not in the most social mood. I feel like I'm in a real butterfly place. I get real emotional at the weirdest moments. And right now, I could start *tripping* right in front of them. I was in the shower this morning, and all of a sudden, I started crying. For no reason. And I had to stay in there until I felt like my eyes were ok and not bloodshot. It's so weird. Cory was staring right at me as I walked out of the shower. He does this. And I could tell he noticed that something's going on with me.

Amanda asks me if I would like to go with them to buy things for a party she and Cory are throwing Saturday night. They're asking me to come along because they want to drill me about Lisa, but also, they know something is up with this stuff with Caz. Cory had overheard me talking to Lisa on the phone the other day where I had mentioned that there was something going on with her. It was rather stupid of me. I hardly wish to go into the whole family skeleton bit with these guys. I immediately think of the other night when my dad was here. I know Les noticed the dent in my father's head. When Andy was sitting on my bed showing him this whatever that thing was, he was taking these quick glances at his left temple. It's not that noticeable, but Les is observant as it is. Cory isn't at all observant, he's just a staring fool. He's like the kind of people who stare at you with their mouths slightly hung open even when the topic isn't exactly intellectually challenging.

So like a nimble skull I go to the mall with these guys and we're running around the supermarket with shopping carts and there's this song; a Rod Stewart song, playing on the PA system, and it is, I think it's called "*Downtown Train*". I always change the station whenever this gooey, syrupy, kind of music comes on the radio or whatever, but here we are, walking down the aisles in different sections of the store, and I'm glad I'm alone, because I find myself, like my guts, my very insides are just soaking up this song like a sponge and I find myself really relating to what this guy is saying in the song. He's all worked up and freaking out about this girl that he sees on a subway and he is asking himself over and over again: "*Will I see you tonight? On the downtown train?*" Well, it's like I'm having a heart attack or something, and I'm tossing things into the cart and getting all fluttery. My eyes are tearing up and I'm practically sobbing by the time the song ends with Rod whimpering that she's left him lonely yet again. And I know this is ridiculous, but I leave the store. I leave Cory and Amanda in the *Pack 'n Pork* to fend for themselves, my cart abandoned with all this food in it. Corn chips, huge boxes of pretzels, gargantuan-size blocks of cheese and stuff. And I'm watching myself as I'm doing this.

As I walk right through the automatic doors and in the midst of feeling all this emotional garbage, I notice this absurd, cartoon-like electronic pig on the wall, his curly little tail wiggling back and forth, pushing a *cart* as I exit the store. It's this puerile stuff that really makes me sick about suburbia. Anyway, I walk around the building to the side and I gasp for air. You'd think someone died or something. " *All my dreams fall like rain on a downtown train*". I stand here watching people, mostly young women with small children, walk by. I have this insane foreboding sense that Lisa is simply not going to last. It will be over soon. And this is ok, but if I'm going to go crazy or something, let it please happen when I'm away, in some insignificant town where no one knows me. Just not here.

After I stand in this spot a while longer, I force myself to get back to a level of normalcy and I waltz back into the store. Cory and Amanda are standing with the carts at one of the registers. They look at me as if they are the proverbial deer startled by the night flash of headlights.

"Whereja go, man?" Cory stares.

I tell him, "I had to take a whiz and a smoke. I got a lot on my mind".

This seems to work. I retrieve the cart of goodies I had abandoned and bring it up to the register. We remain basically silent during the drive back. That is, until Amanda perks up and starts saying things about Lisa. She happens to be in a couple of her classes. She thinks Lisa's real nice and real smart. Amanda is just chattering away about how great Lisa is. She seems friendly, she says and she'd like to get to know her better. I can't believe I 'm listening to this.

I reach under the seat as if there's something I can *heave* into, and of course, I find nothing, not even an old crumpled paper bag. How can I respond to such vile refuse? Lisa just can't wait to get to know her, too? Like they are going to get together for sex or something and Cory and I can watch. Maybe Lisa *is* gay. I can't believe my own mind. It's a crazy, scary thing, this mind. And well, maybe she is. I don't know. I know she looks at me. She does look at me. The old steal-a-quick-look - eye-bit never lies. That's always the test. And the kissing is real. It's real kissing. It's like great anticipatory kissing. It's sexy, sloppy, creative kissing, is what it is. But you just never know. Maybe I am smarter than I will ever know. And there is a part of me going: *She's bi, Simon*...she's *both*. Underneath those wet, sexy kisses is a dyke dying to surface. That explains the heavy metal, *Lita Ford* thing. But we'll see. Nothing shocks me anymore. Well, I shock myself more than anyone I know. And I've never been sucked in by a song like that before. Not that I was sucked in. It kind of felt that way at the time because it caught me off-guard and I sort of slid into the emotions of it unexpectedly. Dangerous! I'm never going to let a gooey song like that do it to me again.

Amanda is staring at me. "Si? Where are you? Hello? Well, don't answer me!"

I honestly don't recall Amanda say anything to me, but I apologize anyway. I say: "Amanda! hey, I'm sorry. I'm a mess! Don't take me so seriously."

Cory horns in, "Yeah, Amanda. Why don't you just shut up? Why are you giving him the tenth degree? They've only been seeing each other here and there. You act like they're married or something. Lay off."

Amanda asks Cory to stop the car. Geek head is just driving ahead, ignoring her. Amanda shouts at him, "I mean it! You're not going to talk to me like that. Screw your party. Stop. I mean it. I'm walking back. Don't touch me. Don't touch me!" Amanda's freaking. Cory shifts gears and begins to pour on the charm. *Coochy cooing* her like crazy. Making little *kissy* movements with his bee stung lips. Amanda begins to simmer down, cooing a bit to Cory's sickly *kissy* number. This is ridiculous. I was hoping she'd jump for it, but as the car slows down at one of the major intersections, I'm the one leaping out of the car. They both look at me, a bit embarrassed. I tell them, "No big deal, guys. I think I need to walk anyway. Sorry for everything."

I gently shut the door so they'd know I'm not pissed or anything and proceed to walk the highway back to the campus. It's the best idea I've had all day. I remember there's an old dirt road I like that actually leads to the dorms and I take that instead. It's more private. And being that this is my mode, well, I should say, my newfound *modus operandi*, to be somber and solitary, I'm discovering all these secluded little places. I feel like leaving. I want to leave now, to tell you the truth. I want

to leave tomorrow. I don't want to see Lisa too much.
This is all going to turn sour anyway. She'll realize that
I'm basically boring. That I see a shrink and that I really don't know anything. To accompany these murky feelings, the sky is now clouding over and thick pellets of
rain are falling over me. Now the rain is really starting
to pour, and I'm passing the little place where I sat a couple of weeks ago smoking the weed. As I run past the
spot, I feel a twinge of guilt, as if I betrayed something
in what I was thinking that night. That I skipped over
some sacred territory; the old man, or something having
to do with what Boyce was telling me about going on my
trip and having him have a part in this little adventure.

When I was in Boyce's office earlier today, I noticed
this drum sitting on the floor and a voodoo-looking mask
laying on the coffee table. After I stared at the things for
a while, he went ahead and explained that he might be
wearing the headgear from time to time to make a point.
And I got a bit squirmy about the whole thing. I thought
it was a bit ridiculous, actually. And here's the rain. Wet
and real, all to go along with the emotions which are
going full blast right now. I make my way further in the
woods, and in the corner of my eye I see her.

Like a prophecy, she is standing to the side of me,
about fifteen feet away and she is talking and laughing
with one of her friends and they are sharing an umbrella
and I hear her calling my name as I leap over branches.
I halt and turn around. She approaches me with that
beautifully dimpled smile. And I hear the words falling
out of my mouth, "Tell your friend you'll see her later,
Lisa. Can you tell her we have to talk or something?"

She turns around and her friend is nodding her head
as she grins and walks away and I take this beautiful girl

in my arms and I give her this sexy, passionate kiss, but
to me, it feels like the kiss of a drowning man. A man
with no legs, a man who cannot jump aboard the ship and
join the men of old. The man with no wisdom, and so I
plunge myself into the abyss of her beautiful mouth and
I force myself to discover the missing link, the missing
know-how, the missing page, or whatever you want to
call it, by taking this girl and holding her, possessing her
if for only these three minutes-the longest three minutes
I ever kissed a girl and we are now kissing our faces like
we're about to depart, as if I'm going on this journey
somewhere of which we may never see each other again
and she's pulling away a bit as she cries.

I hold her lovely wet head to my soaked chest as I
mildly freak over what I should do. She tugs my jacket
and kisses my face. She wants to go somewhere off campus. She wants to go to a motel. I check my pockets for
the *ATM* card, and she assures me that her car's running
fine (mine is screwed up and in the shop again) and while
she tugs me along, I recall the things Boyce and I had
spent hours discussing.

Could I consider this an improvement?   After all,
Lisa and I have known each other for almost two weeks.
Well, actually, I have known her and liked her from afar
for about two months, and yet, we only actually dated for
about eight nights and my, have they been long ones,
with both of us restraining ourselves and screw it. I'm
going for the motel idea. I just can't see myself putting
all of this off, and staying scared, and picking at it under
a microscope with Boyce breathing down my neck in his
African ritual mask while thumping his drums. Cory was
right. I need to get laid. I need to get laid. I really need to
get laid. Badly. But she isn't a *lay*. She is unlike any *lay*

I will ever have and even though this is going to end
soon, I am going for it anyway. I better. I'd be a fool.

My face is being slapped left and right by branches
and the like as we walk through the saturated woods to
her car. She gently snuggles up to my chest as we walk.

I ask her: "Are you on the pill, or do I need to buy
condoms?"

Crinkling her cute forehead, she quips: "Yeah...but
how do I know you're not an IV user, Strayhorn?"

Jeez. Of course, being that *jeez* is a word Boyce
would use, I'm thinking this is a Boyce moment. And it
is I who is envying the innocence of Boyce's poodle skirt
generation. I have to smile at this. Lisa is watching me.
I tell her that I'm smiling because I am so delighted to
see her. That my morning sucked without her. That I'd
like to, next time I walk back in the *Pack 'n Pork* , tear
that pig's curly tail off his little butt and give it to her; to
save for our children. To save for a time when our children will ask why they have never seen the insides of a
Pack 'n Pork or a *"Mickey D's"*, and I'd take it out and
simply *show* them why.

We get to her little Volkswagon. It's kind of a sad little car. Grey and old looking. And we get in and start
kissing again. We are steaming up the pathetic little windows and we don't really seem too interested in starting
the car. We're just smooching and slobbering our mouths
like lunatics and finally I pull away and tell her to get the
freaking thing to the *Motel Six* up the road. She's shaking her head. She wants something more romantic. I
don't care. Whatever in the hell she wants. So we drive.
And we drive. We wind our way up country roads, and
she's getting out at truck stops and asking directions, and
telling me about this place a friend told her about and that

it has cabins. And the owners are real cool. Aging hippies. And so, we load up the car with all kinds of snacks and goodies. I am depleting the *ATM* card as if I'm never coming back to civilization or something. We even buy a flashlight. And we have logs for a fire and all, and we end up -almost an hour and a half drive later-at this little place in the hills.

"It's a weekday afternoon. Don't you think they are going to ask questions and stuff? Look at us funny?" I ask as we walk up to the main cabin.

Lisa rolls her eyes and deadpans: "Not if you act nonchalant".

We both walk through the little screen door. A young woman is sitting behind the wooden counter. We were expecting gray haired hippies in granny glasses and love beads, but she seems perky and friendly. "You guys from the university?" she asks. Naw, we're travelers, I'm ready to say. But we ignore the question and ask for the best cabin in a more remote area.

She raises her brow, scrunching her face as she speaks: "Well, that would be cabin six, but it has some slight plumbing problems, if you don't mind."

I'm practically busting out of my seams with anticipation and Lisa blares, "Oh, we don't care. Long as the shower works and the mattress is friendly."

Such charm, Lisa. Really, did you pick that up back in genteel Flint by any chance? The woman behind the counter eyes me up and down and says, "Oh, I think *he* can handle it."

I sign the papers, give her the *ATM* number and walk back out to the car, shaking my head. As the screen door is slamming, I hear the woman say: "Cute!" And I mutter: *yeah, you're cute, too, babe. How do you do that crazy hair?*

I know Boyce is not going to like this, but now I'm thinking, after all the fun, I may not like it, either. What if we get too attached? Like the inseparable *Velcro twins* of all time? And, of course, I am referring to Cory and Amanda-who are now starting to fight and he is treating her differently, actually, more harshly than he did a couple of months ago. Because they are getting too *in to* each other. When that happens, couples become pure cannibals. Cannibals of the soul. Before it ever gets to that point, I'm going to do Lisa the favor of departing. I'm going to do what Boyce is suggesting, only I feel guilty when I keep all this to myself. Like I'm cheating.

And here she is, flouncing down the moist little hill in her neo-Nazi bomber boots and short-shorts and I am like going mad with desire and she has no idea I'm plotting an escape at the same time. I dunno. Maybe she's thinking the same thing. My *Guinevere* throws her silky arms around my neck.

She tells me, "You're gorgeous! You're too much!" She kisses me again.

This is so weird. A girl telling me this. Gram once told me I looked gorgeous. I was so embarrassed but secretly flattered when she said this. I think it was when I was leaving the house for my high school prom. I had on a tuxedo for the second time in my life. Andy and I spent the whole afternoon trying to find one that had style. And I have to admit, my dad has good taste in clothes. Unusually good taste. He's almost like one of those old European tailors or something. He touches fabric first, then tells you if it's lousy or not. Then he pulls the things out and examines the stitching and lining. Then he microscopically goes about finding right colors and designs. I swear, he's like a scientist or something when it comes to clothes. But what's with these girls today? Before I can tell Lisa I think she is a delectable morsel of heaven, she is telling me how *gorgeous* I am.

I say: "Don't take words out of my mouth, my love-ly *Guinevere*."

I told her about my earlier, private wooings that seemed to have gone on for decades before we finally started seeing each other. She blushes. And this is all so *vomit inducing*, I know. It's the kind of sickly sweet stuff that makes you want to smash the head of a doe-eyed, snow pup because it is so undeservedly cute.

I tell her, as we trudge our way to the cabin carrying armloads of stuff, "I think we need to get into a fight, first. Don't you? It's like we're the poster children of squeaky-clean, non-*Clearasil* complected love."

She replies, "We can always listen to some Iggy Stooge, first, Si. I think that might inspire... a different kind of tone to the afternoon? I once knew a guy from inner city Detroit who told me that his fantasy was wearing his girlfriend's fishnets. It was sort of shocking coming from him. He was a biker. Weird, though. I think that was the last time I had a conversation with the guy. But he was so into the *Stooges*. Do you feel like barfing now?"

We flop our stuff on the little bed and immediately, we begin to undress. I haven't even checked to see if there's a fireplace so I have somewhere to put these logs we bought, and I am pulling off the turtleneck. And she is just standing there, slowly teasing me with her little tank top. I'm like going completely nuts.

I stop her. "Don't! *I* want to do that and I don't know if I want to jump in just yet"

I pull her closer, "Let me look at you."

She moves toward me and I start to lunch on her beautiful torso. As I nip away at her, my entire head practically crawling underneath her sexy top, I briefly recall my previous sexual escapades. None had this sort of rapture to it. It was all too fast, too matter-of-fact and I want to do this differently. I pop my head out, asking her, ever so gently, "My precious, cooing *Lovely Creature*, could we jump in the shower?"

I can't believe I'm talking like this. Where is that *snow pup*?

My gal suggests: "Si, let's just lie down for a while. Can't we take our time? Aren't you tired?"

We both stretch out on the bed, holding each other, our underwear still intact. I imagine that she's wearing a chastity belt; and that I've been away at sea, or something, for a very long time. After all, she is my *Guinevere*. I just love listening to her breathe. It's a beautiful sound, breathing. And I feel her silky hair fly across my shoulder as she turns her sweet lovely head to settle next to mine. I am in heaven and it is wonderful. She coos in my ear and strokes my chest with her soft hand. And we are both enjoying this heaven.

And I'm slowly drifting into this serene place of beauty and tranquility and I'm falling into a flowing waterfall amid lush greens. Foamy sprays of mauvish water splash over me as I land on a raft that takes me further into this enchanting wilderness of unexplored territory. And I'm wandering now afoot on a mysterious land and as I explore, I spot an encampment of men gathering around in a circle and Andy stands in the center. And these other men are listening to him intently.

The old goat poet is standing there in the background

playing his lyre. And I pass them by, walking to another part of the forest. I look back and wave to Andy and he doesn't even recognize me. There is a thin wispy veil of blue smoke emitting from a group of trees and as I approach it, I notice the old parchment-faced man sitting by a tree and he is offering me his pipe. I sit down in front of him and stare at his many tattoos adorning his shriveled ancient skin and I'm not afraid of him at all. I tell him that he can ask me anything. That I am soon to depart, and that I will be in the Mediterranean Sea some-day and that I may meet him and we could possibly explore the ocean floors together. I ask about my father, and I ask if he knows-and as I attempt to look at him more closely, his face vanishes. For just a fraction of a second, I thought I had recognized that face. There was something vaguely familiar in the features laying under-neath the many folds of aging skin. There was a youth-ful man I had seen in sepia-toned photographs from the 1800's, and I was going to ask if he were my great, great grandfather. Where there was once a face is now tree bark sprouting bright green leaves.

I look around and there are the men from the encampment walking toward me. They hoist me up and haul me back to the circle and they place me in the cen-ter and Andy is standing on the sidelines and he is hold-ing an ancient looking manuscript of yellowed pages and he wants to read me something and I'm feeling nauseat-ed. And I wake up sweating. I bolt up as if a shock wave ran through me, and Lisa is lying on top of me, kissing me all over the freaking place, and I am tearing my clothes off and practically rolling on top of her and we are on fire. And she's pulling her top off and her breasts are the most beautiful I have ever seen. And we are both sweating and panting and the bed is grinding away and for a moment, I almost laugh at the scratchy, squeaky sound of the springs, but we proceed to have sex. A shadow of this dream looms over the moment where my *Lovely* wraps her velvety legs around my body and it's all too weird, too real.

****

It's got to be like 10:00 in the evening. We are both lying here in the dark like small furry animals, hugging to keep each other warm. It seems like we spent hours devouring each other. I lie here thinking about the prophylaxis of birth control pills and if we might have broken some kind of threshold. I ask Lisa if her doctor had ever told her that such a thing could happen if you have sex too many times in one evening. She looks at me incredulously, although I can barely read her features. She laughs.

I tell her: "I'm serious. There are women who can still get pregnant. Your body isn't all that predictable. It's capable of side-stepping things".

She kisses me all over my face. "Then we'll have to abort, Si. That's all."

The fact that we all started out as little *tadpoles* swimming around makes me feel sad about such things. I get up and scrounge around for my underwear. I also look around for the logs we bought. As I'm trying to ignite one of the things, Lisa comes over and squats next to me.

"Si, I won't get pregnant. It would be awful, though, if I did. But we'd both ruin our lives, you know, if we did have a kid."

This is the kind of price I am paying for going along with my impulses and not sticking to the plan. I shouldn't have allowed myself to get so involved with this lovely angel and, the fact of the matter is, I feel *married* to her now. Lisa is just looking at me with those almond-shaped eyes. My little *snow pup*. I want to tell her that I almost feel married to her, but I don't. It seems so unhip to say. Especially for a guy. But I do feel this way. I even understand why, in the old days, they saved sex for the wedding night.

So I mutter, "Go put on your chastity belt, *Guinevere*."

She looks up and replies, "You don't trust me."

I tell her, "Weird, huh? I feel so *medieval* when I'm with you."

The Detroit rocker. Now she's staring at me.

I explain: "Ok. When we were lying there this afternoon I had this thought about my being some kind of knight who had just returned from being out at sea, and you were my lovely *Guinevere* and you had your chastity belt on. And I was imagining this and it was turning me on like crazy. Like I was freaking out because I had left the key somewhere, but forgot where I had put it. So as I was thinking this, I fell into this deep sleep and I had another one of my *quest for power* -dreams. It's like I am Carlos Castencda or something and my *Don Juan* is this very Anglo-looking old man with wrinkly, withering skin. And every time I have one of my bouts with this guy he is about to teach me something and it never comes about. Something always happens that interferes. Either I say something stupid or I freak because he is about to ask me something that's too real for me to handle. This time, it was my dad standing there wanting to tell me something. So I run. I can't believe I am telling you this. You are the only person other than"-and for a minute I pause remembering my secrecy around Boyce-"this certain friend of mine who knows."

The fire is jumping around nicely and we are both now eating some of the stuff we bought at the store on the way here. She is still looking at me, beautiful as ever and she is not saying a word. I can't believe she isn't grilling me. She is just studying my face. Finally, she says: "If you didn't look so much like Daniel Day-Lewis, I would've insisted on arm-wrestling with you first, Strayhorn."

I tell her, "In the least! Come on, put her up, it's never too late. In fact, let's do it in the nude!"

Lisa laughs, "Oh, that could get kinky, Strayhorn! It could lead to something nasty."

I quip, "Like pig-wrestling in the mud outside?"

Lisa is now laughing herself silly. After a while, we snuggle and cuddle closer to the fire, a blanket now wrapped around us. Lisa's musing about the subject of reincarnation. I am *like...wow, I knew you in another life. I swear! I knew her.*

So I ask, "Do you think we were lovers in another life? Like I was maybe this adventurer and I went *batshit* or something because I would be gone for near-decades before I'd see you again and you'd be all locked up in your chastity belt? Do you think..." and I reach out, touching her lovely swan neck, "maybe that's why I couldn't stop plunging into your mysterious layers tonight, my *Lovely*?"

She shrugs me off and laughs, "Stop!"

I insist, "Oh, come on, another round to cap off the

evening."

She play-punches my chest. "Lisa, Lisa. I think you really were *Guinevere*."

She gives me a look that says we should either seriously discuss the topic or move on to something else.

So I tell her, "Frankly, I have never really given much thought to the idea of reincarnation. I always found the Hindus to be a fascinating culture, and I was intrigued learning about the concept. But the idea that we come back and do it again and again sort of sickens me. Like the movie *'Groundhog Day'*. What if life really is like that? We're just one big cycle of reincarnated lives going in and going out until we get the damned thing right. I'd hate to think where I was when I started out. As a new soul. I must have been some miserable *cro-magnon* mess".

Lisa grins and burrows her face in one of the pillows we have sprawled out on the floor. Her shoulders are jiggling away, so that must mean she's amused. She pops her head back up and asks me to continue as she beams at me, her mug flushing red.

Gladly, my *Guinevere*. I continue: "Alright. Then somewhere along the line, some 600 years bc or so, I must have progressed to the level of a street-beggar in the smelly alleys of Alexandria or something, and one day, a roaming scholar dropped a tablet on the side of the road and this was the beginning of my quest for knowledge."

Lisa nods. I tell her Andy had been our-Caz and I-personal scholar in this life, and hey, maybe the *roadside scholar* was Andy. That was our first connection. Then we must have met up again in a pub somewhere in remote Ireland. Which is all pretty remote when you think about it. Or maybe it was Scotland, since my name is Scottish. I tell her we had to have met up in a pub because Andy is an ex-drunkard. And perhaps it took a few ins and outs on the *reincarnational run* for him to work up to that label. She seems to want me to continue, so I go into the whole family mess. I tell her that I believe my genes out washed the trait, but that I live with the notion that I could be wrong. It's just a matter of time. And with that, I gingerly uncork the inexpensive wine I brought along. I take out the plastic, fake wine glasses and start to pour. She taps my arm,

"Simon!"

I tell her even Andy admitted that it took some bending of the elbows to get to the level where he left off, which of course, we all know, landed him in an emergency room, a hunk of flesh hanging from his forehead. I skip this part. I'm probably freaking her out enough as it is. She's being mighty quiet. Now she's looking at me again. This time, it's pensive.

"Well, figures we'd meet."

Jeeeez. I don't think this is going to be good. She sighs heavily and looks up at me with those snow-pup eyes, "At least your dad is alive and doing well, Si. I mean, he quit drinking. I have no idea where my dad is. And last time we saw him, he was a real partying kind of guy. That was when I was seven years old."

And sure enough, here they come. Right now, the *waterworks* are going at a steady stream, but she's going to start howling any minute, and I reach my arms over her shoulders and lock her in a long hug. Like I did with Caz when she was little and discovered that a spider had crawled up her pant leg. But of course, this is different. And I feel really awkward holding her as she cries.

Like-it was no problem to make love to her, but holding her like a rag doll is...well, something else. Like-I'm a real guy now, comforting a gal in pain. And *I swear*... I feel like I can't do this too well, but I'm trying. I rock her like a baby and it feels right that I do this, but what if she later throws it in my face and says I insulted her by treating her like a baby or something? She moves her arms around and slightly pulls herself away. "I'm so embarrassed! I haven't thought about this stuff in a long time, and when you were talking...it just came out. You're so sweet. You're such a nice guy. Your dad must really be a nice guy."

I am thinking, he is. He is definitely a nice, wimpy guy. Nice guy, but a wimpy nice guy. I'm so sick of hearing about how darned nice Andy is.

She tells me, "My dad started out as a *roadie*, you know. And then he managed a very famous rock band. He made a fortune, left my mom in the nuthouse, then I had to be taken care of by my relatives, along with my two sisters, while he drove around England in a Rolls. Si, he was not a nice guy."

So I ask her, "Do you hate all males because of *that*?"

And she says, "I did....for a while. But you're great!"

Well, *gee whiz*. I nuzzle my snout in her soft lovely neck, and we kiss and as she's telling me about one of her sisters, and how much of a mess her life is and I suddenly bolt from the bed.

"I forgot to listen to my messages. It's been about six days. My parents are dealing with something and I have to at least hear what they have to say. Damn!"

I tell Lisa that I'm just running down to the main area to find a pay phone.

After rummaging for quarters and stuff, I step into the dark wooded area, quietly closing the door behind me. It is pitch black out here and I am feeling my way down the little hill, grabbing onto branches as I slowly edge my way down. I'm not sure I particularly care what they have to say about Caz; unless, she's in the hospital or something, or dead. Really, anything other than this, I will just do my diligent duty as a son and move on. I'm serious. I also think I know my sister. And she is not into any addiction; they are all just hyper-vigilant around this kind of stuff, and quite frankly, it's this kind of thing that could drive her in that direction. That's what I think. And I know what's bugging me. I know what it is now. I simply want to be more fascinating, more knowledgeable, and more courageous-which really wouldn't take that much-than Andy. That's what it is.

Here's the lousy phone. There is absolutely no one around here and I just want to do this quickly. There are now about six messages. I listen to all of them. My mom's just says that everything is alright. The second is more severe. Andy is saying that they are going to go along with what the director of the school is suggesting and that is some outside counseling; that she is not going to be suspended because some other girls came to her defense. He doesn't exactly go into this. But says that Caz seems to be depressed over some guy she got involved with over at the college. Great. The third is Nancy again, saying and she is crying, that my sister was seeing a *rat* from the college and he's older that she is, and he is robbing the cradle and that her intellect belies her emotional intelligence. I had to just save this one for later. I can't listen to three minutes of it. The fourth is from Gram. "Suga. It's Grammaw. Your sister is a good girl, but she's got herself in a mess, and she's just walkin a tightrope. Your momma is worried 'bout yew, too. Why havencha called her back? Call me, hun. Anytime. We jus are so proud of yew. I'm thinkin yew must have yourself a little sweetheart or somethin cuz it just seems so unlike yew—" I had to put that in limbo to listen to some other time. The other messages were from a couple of friends of mine. I will call them later.

The faint beginnings of a new day is slowly formulating on the horizon. I decide to stroll around a bit before heading back to the cabin. I walk around the plank-wooden porch that surrounds the office cabin. I barely notice a sign affixed to one of the posts. It reads: "*Drum Circle. A Men's Gathering.* All welcomed. Friday nights at *Hunter Field* in *Westwood Park.* Sundown 'til."

I once played the drums, in fact, I was pretty good at it. It would be about an hour and a half's drive from school, but maybe I should check this thing out. I jot down the phone number, and walk around a bit more thinking about what it would be like if I just flat-out bailed. If I just bypassed giving any explanation, got *Incompletes* in everything and took off. Well, Andy would probably flip out. I have to take this seriously because he could do something scary. He could fetch the Luger or he could start drinking. So there's that possibility, then I'd have to think of new things I could do for Christmas and stuff. It's a funny thing about holidays; as soon as they're over, I don't think about them until they come around again the next year. And what if I ever get in a bad way? Then what could I do?

As I notice the sun filtering through the trees, I realize that I must get back to Lisa. I've been out here for about an hour and if she isn't sleeping, she may be a bit worried about me. I trudge back up the hill and quietly open the door to the cabin. At first, it looks like my Lovely is in the bathroom. So I sit on the bed, looking out the window smoking a lousy cigarette. While I don't hear anything, I get up and walk to the can and back into the little room. On the pillow, where she lay only an hour or so ago, is a note.

Si, I remembered I had to get back this morning. Early. I know you might be ticked. But there's a bus that runs through here and will take you back to campus. Sorry. But I had to go!

I don't like this. Maybe the panic attack I had in the parking lot that afternoon was real. Maybe she *is* seeing someone else. She's definitely a biker chick... All that leather, and she's a-why in the hell didn't she come tell me in person? I have to remember that I had spent almost an hour walking around the woods some few hundred feet away from the main center of the place. But I think it's pretty cold. Pretty cold when a girl just revs up the ancient gun-metal Volkswagon and rolls her way back to her independent little life after all that affection. After all that cuddly, snow-puppy love. It makes me sick. It really does. I don't care to know her anymore. I don't want to know her name. I will go back now, too. I will walk through the hills until the bus shows up, and I will hop on and go back, ready and willing to dump Lisa forever. I will not listen to anything romantic anymore, either. It is now pure, angry, blood-letting rock 'n roll from now on. Actually, that may not work since she's *batshit* over the stuff. Well, this might be a bit challenging. But I'll figure out something.

In the meantime, all the love songs I've been allowing myself to be sucked into are now banned. And I'm not looking at the stars anymore from the dorm window before trailing off to sleep. I need to get into something cold and analytical. I'll ask Les if he could give me a quick course in computer repair or something.

I put the remaining things in a plastic bag and walk back to the main cabin. I give the keys up at the desk and the little ancient hippie couple I had heard about is sitting there. The woman has her back facing the counter. She looks like she's counting money or something. The man looks up at me, a *Greenpeace* sweatshirt adorning his old chest. He says, "Well, it's unusual to have someone check out on a Friday mornin'. But I guess you have your school work to do, eh?"

I'm thinking, *yeah, gramps, I guess so. Why else would I be checking out?*

He continues, "Hear the young gal left earlier. You two getting along ok?"

I shake my head. What is this? A grand inquisition or something? Don't these people have anything better to do than keep tabs on what some stranger's doing in one of their rooms?

Anyway, the old guy grins at me, with his badly capped hippie teeth and I'm thinking, *I am outa here*. I ask him about the bus that comes through and he wrinkles his face, saying, "Well, they don't come by too often, you know. Here, I have a schedule."

I look the thing over. I have almost an hour before I catch the next one. Great. The old man is now telling me about the trail and a little diner I can go to before catching the bus. He is going to be walking down there himself in a little while. Great. Like, all I really need is to get into a little warm and fuzzy chat with this guy. He probably wants to reminisce about the old hippie commune days and the chicks he once *nailed*.

I thank the guy and pop out my headset slipping in Lisa's *Garbage* CD.   Lisa's just your average, 21st Century, *freewheelin* babe. Not a *Middle Ages* damsel in distress. You wouldn't have known this eight hours ago. Not when she was all sappy and wailing about her bum roadie dad. Deep down, I know she wants me to *rescue* her. But this will probably mean I'll have to dismantle her trust issues, first. And that could take forever. I pop out the CD. It reminds me too much of her. In fact, I can tell this singer has an influence on her. Take this song, *"Stupid Girl"*. Old Shirley Manson is telling the gals that it's pretty bad news to "believe in anything that you can break."

Yeah, like some nice guy's heart. And some nice guy's affectionate feelings, and caring and all that good stuff chicks are constantly saying no guy possesses anyway! My advice? Stay away from girls who actually dig Iggy Stooge. Examine their CD collections with extreme care. And if they're wholesome looking, better, better beware! It's one thing if their purple hair is matted and partially shaved on one side of their skulls and if they have a thousand earrings hanging through their noses, but when they're *Buffy-the-Vampire-Slayer*-looking-cute, run!

The old dude passes me as I walk down the main road. He actually waves at me. I wave back. His calves are smooth and muscular for an old guy. I pop in the *Counting Crows* CD. It's the only other CD I have with me. Old Adam Duritz. Well, it's fine and good to listen, but when he says "round here, we talk just like lions; but we sacrifice like lambs, Round here, she's slipping through my hands", I wanna say, *man, tell me about it.*

And here I go! Imagining Lisa has a guy somewhere who has some kind of hold on her. A sugar daddy biker or something. And she needs to cover her tracks. I imagine she has some heavy metal roadie dude somewhere that does her favors. Like gives her free tickets to rock concerts or something. And of course, she gives him all this sex in return, she's such a shameless rock junkie. I must be cool about this. No more going nuts like I did a little while ago up at the cabin. Today is the anniversary of two full weeks of being with Lisa. Well, who would have ever thought all this would happen?

I reach the bottom of the hill and find a pay phone near this old gas station. I pop in a quarter and dial the number I memorized. There's a voicemail message giving all the details about the drum circle. It gives instructions to the park, and the location. I'll go into the job this afternoon and I'm going to be very nonchalant. I have emails to get out. I have my trip coming up. What in the hell do I need some crazy, leather chick from depressing Flint, Michigan for? She's got things to do? Well, hell, so do I!

There's nothing more depressing than a whining old bus out in the middle of nowhere. It sort of reminds me of that scene in '*North by Northwest*' where Cary Grant goes out to the sticks and this is desolate, flatland, sticks, to meet these people and finds himself in the middle of nowhere and this loser comes by in an old truck, gets out and waits for this depressing bus to show up. And. well, I feel like that guy right now. I step inside and find a cozy spot and slide next to the window. There isn't a single soul saying anything to anybody. It's just the whine of the engine running through the forest. Grinding its way down a lonely country road.

****

I arrive back at the dorm looking pretty shabby. Les is sitting on his bed talking on the phone. I'm assuming with Pony. He's chatting away while raising his brows at me as I get out of my muddy old clothes. He ends his call as I'm about to go into the shower.

"Hey, where have you been? It seems like ages. Where's your '*sweetie*'?"

I wave him off.

"She's shamelessly licking the boots of some biker dude."

He grins, "Oh, yeah?"

I shake my head. "I dunno. We were together all day yesterday and we both had to do things this morning. Then she told me the news about a dude she likes better. Hey, do you have any time today to show me how to repair computers?"

Of course, Les is looking at me funny, with his head cocked.

"Sure. But why?"

I tell him I wouldn't mind learning, that I may want to get a different type of job for the summer before I go off on my journey. I then go into it. My plans, my ideas about European travel, my dropping out of school for a year.

Les looks at me, " Yeah? I'll miss you, dude. But, everyone I know of who does something like that, they don't come back to school. They stay out forever and when they're like 22 or something or older, they finally go back to school, but by then, it's night school or something."

I tell him about how important it is for me to just break free for a while and that I have no intention of doing this for any longer than a semester or two. I'm not about to have Andy withdraw his paying for my education and I most definitely will be taking advantage of that. I feel rather sober-minded, as if the freak out over Lisa had never happened.

As I gather my things, Les perks up. "Is that really true about the other guy an all?" I hesitate on this one.

I say, "Well, I dunno. Girls are so unpredictable. And I think it's a good idea to tell myself that she's free to do what she wants. If I don't do this, I may end up nuts or something. Know what I mean?"

Les informs me, "Pony's a two-timer. She was just telling me that she's not completely broken up with her other guy. This *dweeb* at Dartmouth. So, I was wondering if you're snowing me, or you are especially neurotic, which is what I honestly believe you are. And, in fact, I know you're snowing me. But what are friends for, right? Cory told me you were in bad shape yesterday. Is that when you were having these suspicions?"

I have someone I talk to about all this stuff. I don't need another Boyce. A Boyce-junior. Especially, if he is dealing with the same thing. Or something similar. But for some inexplicable reason, I'm slipping. I can't believe I'm feeling this, but before I can stop myself, I hear myself say, "No, it was just this realization that I love her. That I really love her and I honestly have no idea why; it's just there. And it takes over. It totally leads me into a spooky unfamiliar territory of which I have no sense of direction or idea of where I am. And there's just nothing I can do about it. Nothing."

Les is now leaning back on his bed, looking over at

me as I say this. He's scrunching his furry black brows and shaking his head,

"Wow. That sounds *serious*. Maybe I should be glad that I've been spared of all that because Pony isn't that *heavy* to me. Actually, I like her a lot but I only realized it when she told me about the *dweeb*. But you...you sound like you have it bad...*bad* for that girl!" He laughs, telling me I'm like the guy in that old Springsteen song.

Well, if I immerse myself any more in the depths of love and emotions of love, I will not be able to make my journey. I will end up in a nuthouse, instead, and she-being that she aspires to this ghastly profession of caring for the mentally ill-will probably end up being my *rehabilitationist*. That would be my nightmare, alright. And of course, she- having no idea of this-would bring me further into the abyss of madness as she attempts to make me well.

Les offers: "You need to write stories, Strayhorn. You have the most warped of imaginations. You're a Stephen King. And you don't even know it. I love the one about the Greenwich girl. How you got rid of her by playing that old *Velvet Underground* record. But you know what? Girls love spooky, weird guys. Look at the *Phantom of the Opera*! Guy's all screwed up and scary-looking, and the chicks really dig him. Or the *Hunchback of Notre Dame*."

I nod my head in rigorous agreement and say, "It's the *monstrous-looking-guy-but-with-the-noble-heart*-thing. That's the whole point. Girls are supposed to *love* that. A guy's ability to swoon and also make the girls feel sorry for him. Doesn't matter what the guy looks like, either. They can be uglier than hell. Actually, they can even be mean. As long as the chicks believe that their love is real and true. But that's not what the babes want anymore. Girls today want to be tough and resilient and not end up as wet noodles on the wall."

Les gives me a quizzical look. I then go on and explain to him that women typically cave in to love and all that swooning and once the guy has them, marries them and loses his grip on love and becomes a suburban bore, they're done for.

I tell him, "They not only watch that stuff on the *Lifetime* channel, they watch those old flicks, too. You know, the ones with Barbara Stanwick, Greta Garbo, Rita Hayworth. *Film Noir* babes. They've *studied* them, man. And they aren't going *there*. Especially when their mothers get around to lecturing them on their bum fathers who walked out and never paid any child support! By the way, I didn't *intend* to get rid of Thalia. My intention was to freak her out, yes, but also to slip in the fact that I simply couldn't handle the emotions I felt. That I was strongly attracted to her, and wanted to be chivalrous with her, but didn't quite know how. I know that's an old-fashioned word, but I have no other way to put it. So I ended up freaking her out. But I did feel a certain satisfaction from it, because of the way she was, well, she didn't deserve any chivalry."

Les is looking extremely thoughtful and says, "Yeah, I think I know what you mean. But it sounds really mixed up, dude. Like you're a compass that's been smashed and the arrow is pointing all over the place."

For a moment, a weird notion flashes through my brain, the guy thinks I'm nuts. My old buddy, old pal here thinks I'm a freakin' loon! I calmly tell him:

"With Lisa, I feel clear and real. There is no doubt about how real I feel when I'm with her; with the other girl, it was like I was railroaded by her slippery manner. She was hot in body, but cold in mind. See what I mean?"

I'm relieved to see Les' face muscles relax as he informs me: "Yeah. I hear you, all right. But you sure have a lot of thunderous passion going on with you. You should apply your imagination and write horror stories. I mean, what are you going to do if this doesn't work out?"

I don't know about horror stories, but I have this idea about a guy who crawls the earth searching for great revelations, but ends up working at a *Pack 'n Pork*. And there's no hope for the guy. Not even the promise of a mid-management spot. Because he thought too much, and is now brain-damaged, the only job left for him is one where he swirls wisps of pink cotton candy on paper cones all day long. I tell Les that whether things work out or not, I'll survive. We laugh.

Les adds: "I know that. I was just joshin' you, dude."

****

I spend most of the afternoon on the computer at work. I also check out some books, travel-related things and briefly acknowledge Lisa as she's entering stuff at the main desk. I keep my cool, and well, it seems like she's keeping hers. Finally, I pass a note to her, asking if we could meet outside. I take the elevator down and wait for her. She finally comes sauntering out and throws her arms around me. We kiss a little when we get over to the side of the building where no one can see us, and then she starts asking me a lot of questions about Caz and my parents. I tell her that everything was ok, but I have to ask her why she just left like that. If she's snowing me, she really has it down pat.

"Oh", she tells me, "I had to get these very important notes for a class from..." this brain she knows who records classes and takes sharp notes. She had missed a couple of the classes and had to get to her room early to retrieve them because the girl was going on a weekend trip early this morning. It all sounds so smooth and plausible as hell. She had meant to get them yesterday afternoon when she saw me running through the woods. But of course, we were swept away and all. Well, Lisa, that sounds good, but I don't exactly buy the whole thing. And I will keep my mouth shut, I promise myself. I have to. I love her. I want to leave this place entirely and go build a nest with her somewhere. Settle down, get a job, drop out of school. Just live and breathe with her. She is chirping her cute little mouth like crazy as the sun is blaring all over her golden hair, and I'm barely able to take in her words. Only the sonorous sound of her voice as it lilts into little questions. I'm a zombie.

She asks, "So do you understand?"

I can barely recall the two-minute spiel she just went into. Something about cramming for finals and all, and I remember, of course, my own studying that must be done and I nod my head like an idiot and rub her soft little tummy with my knuckles as I stand there thinking.

"Sure." I finally say. "In fact, I'm doing something with some guys tonight, then, yeah, I have to finish some work and study for tests next week".

It dawns on me that school is going to be ending in about three weeks. And she will be going away. All summer. And then I will be going away for the summer and then next year. And she will be gone, too. In Switzerland. All year. For a moment, I feel real pressured. Like should we cram in more time together somehow? So that when we depart we will have enough juice to keep the engines running while we are away from each other, or is this all going to come to a complete end? Anyway, I spend the rest of the afternoon quietly working and occasionally looking over at Lisa. As I leave I tell her that I'll be calling her Sunday night, and I make a promise to myself that I will keep my paws off the phone if it kills me. I'm not going to look like a drooling fool and give her any ideas that I'm hung up on her or anything. Even though I know I am.

I leave the library this afternoon with shreds of my dignity in tact. It's a little after four-thirty and I have a lot of time to tool around. A couple of the guys asked if I wanted to play pool, but I declined. I decide to go over to the garage to pick up my car. From there, I drive up to that little place in the woods where Lisa and I had been just the day before. When I arrive at the park, I can hear the sound of the drums. As I approach the entrance there are two men standing there, waving these sage branches over my body, saying welcome and all this stuff. One is Native American. In fact, there seem to be several Native Americans in a circle of about sixty men of every possible race. Some old, some young like me, some about my dad's age. They sound pretty awesome. These guys seem to be professional percussionists. And the sound is mesmerizing. I find myself just standing by a tree looking at them. I'm hesitant to actually jump in and help myself to a spare drum-which they have on a table nearby. As the sun slowly descends, the sound seems to grow more rich and complex. I don't know if this is deliberate or not. The forest seems to resonate with a pulsating, vibrating rhythm that extends for miles around. It's as if all these sixty or so drums are talking to each other, then rolling along separately here and there, then talking together. It's pretty cool. The only thing missing is a bit of herb. But maybe that's not so. My spirit slips into the womb-like sound while my body remains on the sidelines. It's hard to describe, but I feel scared and drawn to this thing at the same time. Like there's this craving deep inside of me that's being satisfied, but I find myself surprised to see it manifested in this sound.

Now I find myself staring at what looks like the master drummer of the circle. He's about middle aged and has the strong features you find in a lot of Native American men: hawk nose, high cheekbones, long, glossy black hair with prodigious streaks of gray on the sides, a model for the buffalo coin par excellence. And he has the kind of presence you wouldn't want to mess with. Anyway, he's just slapping away at his drums. And now he's giving out a siren-like call. Others siren back to him. Soon, the whole group chants and sirens back and forth on top of the gyrating drum sound. It's an amazing sound. After this dies down a bit, several of the men stop drumming and the chief guy goes into the awesomely cool drum solo. Others begin to howl, making groaning, chirping sounds, and the drumming is so crazy and good I begin to dance.

I know I must look like an obvious fool over here by the trees in my little corner, as I shamelessly shimmy like a loon. But I figure I'll never see these bozos again, so what the hell? It reminds me of the footage I had seen once of rock concerts from the '70's where you'd have a crowd of people standing in the mud and rain bobbing their wet heads to *Fleetwood Mac* or something and there in the midst of this sea of legs and arms would be one or two fools dancing around like idiots by themselves.

The chief drummer's hands are flapping and flying and his accompanying crew— about eight of them— are just grinding along, creating a complexity of multi-leveled vibrations, each individual and distinct, building layers upon layers of sound. This seems to go on forever, until suddenly, everything stops. Now everyone lights sticks and branches and brings them to a pile of logs in center of the circle, igniting a small bonfire. There are a few people standing around waving branches of smoke in the air. Some kind of herb or sage brush. Everything is still and quiet save the popping and crackling sound from the bonfire.

The sky is turning all kinds of wild purple and orange colors. And it is not quite dark. The head guy, old *Hawk Nose*, begins to chant and after about ten minutes of doing this solo, all of the other men join in by humming in these deep, low tones. Then this groaning and wailing starts up and goes on for a good while. I have no idea what this is all about. Suddenly, a man leaps from the crowd and dances his way to the bonfire. With outstretched arms, he circles the fire in great, forceful spurts and the long, sinewy fringe from his jacket are swirling and spinning in the air along with his long black tresses. This is some show, that's all I'm going to say. Two other men now join him with these scary-looking masks covering their mugs. All three are now bounding around the fire, chanting and squawking. As they swerve and move around, they pick up speed until they almost look like a giant mythical creature circling the fire.

A faint drumming begins to slowly resound, building a momentum as about twenty or thirty drummers pick up their drums again and slowly begin to thump.   The sun has just about gone down, and the soft hint of violet and pink light swirls into the dark folds of the oncoming night sky. The dancers have gone back to their places and now everything is quiet again.   I stand here probably looking a bit dumbstruck and there's this light tap on my shoulder. The hairs are tingling on my back and immediately, I think of Boyce. As soon as I turn around, I recognize that it's one of the guys from the dorm. I don't know him too well, in fact, I forgot his name. He picks up on this and immediately announces himself.

"Hey! Trent Chisolm. Is this your first time here?"

I nod and tell the guy my name.

He says, "Oh, I've seen you around. You're the one who pummeled that jock, Barry. I happened to see you in action. It was a crack, alright. Where'd'ya learn to kick like that? "

I'm a bit speechless.   Actually, I feel a little suspicious. I look down a bit and notice he's holding a drum.

I ask, "Were you part of this group or did you just get here?"

He responds, "I've been here for a while. I've been coming here a few months now. I'm from New Mexico. I'm pretty familiar with them. You think I'm up to something, don't you?"

I almost jump when he says this. The guy's a *freakin* mind-reader. I look at him more closely. He has light brown hair and his complexion seems fair but something about the dark eyes and about the mouth made me think Native American.

He says, "The group is going to break in about five minutes. Wanna walk over to the river for a minute? I have some herb".

I hear myself telling him that I was so transfixed by the entire thing, I feel I don't need any hallucinogenic assistance. He calmly shrugs his shoulders. He's right. The group's now breaking up, the men now standing, stretching and talking to each other.

Trent looks over at me, "I'm part Pueblo Indian, on my mother's side. My dad's a musicologist and went west to study indigenous people's music and met my mom and settled there. He's a professor at the University of New Mexico in Albuquerque. Ever been out west?"

I tell him that I had been to Colorado skiing once, and that I had been to California. But not the Southwest.

"It's a trip out there. Mirage country. Vision quests. Ever heard of that? Vision Quests? "

We arrive at a little spot near the river. He pulls out a small joint and begins to puff away. I answer, "No. But it sounds like something in the books by Castenda. Am I right?" I sit and watch the streams of smoke whirling around, feeling pretty satisfied in my decision.

Trent smiles: "Yeah. Only it's solitary. No Don Juan or teacher to meet you as you return; your head burning like parchment in the midday sun."

As he slowly exhales, he casually says, "Man, you look uneasy. What's on your mind?" I'm not sure how to answer such a direct question. Especially coming from this stranger. It's like he sees through me and I know he's older, about 21 years old or so, but there's a directness about this guy that you don't see in most guys I know.

"I just don't know who you are, dude. Are you who I think you might be? Or are you putting on some act? I've never talked to you before."

Well, Trent here wants me to be at ease. He tells me that he thinks it's limiting to be at Grigham all these years and he really looks forward to finishing up his studies in the next week or so. And that he's looking forward to going off to med school next year. This relaxes me a bit. I tell him I may be going in that direction. I ask him if he had ever taken time off from school. He says he had when he was in his third year. Since he had started college a bit early, he figured it wouldn't hurt to take a semester off.

He says, "I traveled with a friend-a Native American- to a reservation in British Columbia. His family's from there. Well, I can tell you about healers that'd make these assholes in their white coats look like blubbering fools, man. It was scary as hell, and maybe I'll tell you about it one day. You wouldn't believe this stuff. It was one of the most important things I will ever do, that much I know. Johns Hopkins —that's where I'm headed—won't know what to do with me. I'm going to freak that establishment; maybe give them some demonstrations. I have it all planned. This shaman showed me some things that would eliminate all notions of corporate medicine. That's all I'll say." I feel a bit tingly when this guy tells me this and I find myself reaching for a toke on his joint.

I take a long drag, " Ok. You're on. Tell me one of your Shaman stories. Just one."

Trent rubs his hands together, " Ok. There was this old guy, sick and messed up and all. Had a huge tumor in his neck. We walk in his little room, with this healer, and he proceeded to do this elaborate ritual. We had all kinds of herbs and smoke was pouring all over the place. And at one point, the healer chanted for like an hour and when he was done, he dragged the old guy from his cot and took him down to a sweat lodge. He put him in it. And then he pulled the guy out after an hour or two and placed him in nearby lake. Dunked him in the water. Afterwards, he dragged the guy out and laid him on the grass. He waved his hands over the man's body and pulling the air around his neck, hence, the energy out of the tumor—which was the size of an orange and the thing was gone by morning. Gone. I mean nothing there".

I take another toke. "Wow." I mean, what else could I say?

Trent continues, " Yeah, come by my room. I have one to myself, on the first floor. Anytime, dude. I'll show you some of my stuff. I leave in a week or two. I'm not graduating and all that. I'm just taking off. So come by. Good talkin with you. I need to go now."

We can hear the drumming start up again and I find myself wondering why I had never paid any attention to this guy before. "Hey, I'll catch you later?" He turns around "No, I'm staying in this area for the weekend. Come by next week." He waves at me, and I take a final puff of the herb.

Grunge Soul

I arrive here back at the room around one a.m. It's mighty quiet in here. After I flick on the lamp, I find myself staring at the phone. For about eight hours I had managed to void Lisa from my mind. It was a relief, but here I am staring at this stupid hunk of plastic. It's a mild torture, but I'm managing to avoid it. Les is gone, Cory is probably married to Amanda and never coming back.

The quad outside seems suspiciously still and barren for a Friday night. The dread is descending upon me. I pull out my black box where I keep my treasured music.

Being that things seem a bit bereft, it definitely feels like a night for *'Imperial Bedroom'*,   Ian MacManus, a.k.a. Elvis Costello.   I pop in the CD and after a few minutes, I find myself extremely bummed. It's too profound. Too heavy. The odd thing is, if I listen to *Nirvana* or something more hard-core rock, I'd end up desiring her all the more. "*Smells Like Teen Spirit*" seems to be our song, anyway. Hardly your *boy-meets-girl-boy-desperately-desires-girl* variety.   But knowing me, it'll spawn all these crazy desires. Especially when I think of the famous video with those hot, sexy, high school cheerleaders devilishly waving their pom-poms. I'd imagine Lisa in there, her golden tresses whipping around. Unbearable on a night like this.

It occurs to me that there was a brief moment, as those guys were slapping their crazy drums, where I thought: hey, where are the girls? It might've added a nice touch to have some Native American babe get out there and do a fire walk or something. But I suppose that would've been beside the point.

It was an all-guys kind of thing where the men are supposed to bond and all I did was watch. No wonder I was thinking this way. At least I wasn't imagining Lisa up there. She better be studying, that's all I am going to say. There she was, looking luscious as ever this afternoon, and she was into all these heavy explanations as to how badly she needs to cram and study and well, underneath all that she was saying, there was the rising suspicion that she sure picked a ripe time in our liaison, our little rendezvous, ok, our *affair*, to begin this staunch crusade to become scholarly. I know this is nuts, but I am going over there. Her room is on the ground floor. I'll just see if the lights are on, or if my Lovely is sound asleep. Just to check up on her. I'm not a weirdo, or anything. I am not a pervert. I am just curious to see if she is ok and studying, cramming like she said she was going to do. I walk over to the closet and pick out some black clothes. I reach for my hooded parka and flashlight, I tell myself I just have to see if Lady *Guinevere* needs any rescuing tonight; that this is sort of a courtesy call.

I rush down the stairs and race through the quads. It's a perfectly beautiful spring night and there are stars shining all over the place. I tiptoe around the dorm, hoping I don't run into anyone I know. Watching out for security guards, I loosen my stride so I can appear more casual as I approach the side of the building. Shrill laughter is coming from one of the upstairs rooms, otherwise all seems quiet as I approach Lisa's window. Everything is astoundingly quiet and I'm wondering if she's asleep. Her window is open, but I don't hear any breathing. I would be able to hear something. Rustling of the bedcovers, a cough here and there, something. But all is suspiciously quiet. If she's in there, she's been mummified.

Ok! Time to check the parking lot. I know I shouldn't be doing this, but I walk to the nearby lot and as I survey the cars, I don't see the *gun metal wonder* anywhere. She's a free girl, with loads of guys to choose from. She's probably rockin out at some concert; or swilling beer with some biker roadie dude backstage with all the groupies. Looking sexy as hell. My little *Rebecca of Sunny Brook Farm* girl gone bad! She's supposed to be sound asleep after a long night of studying. In a long, conservative night shirt. Her hair smoothly laying across clean, cotton sheets. Alone. In her twin bed. I walk back to her building and sit on the stoop outside the emergency exit, wondering if I should wait a while. I can still hear the laughter coming from upstairs along with some music playing in the background. I wonder if maybe she's up there and get this crazy idea to go back to her window, slide it wide-open and crawl through, but I can't risk having the security guards haul me in. Knowing my glorious luck, I'd get caught. I decide to walk back to my dorm. It's getting very late and I am beginning to worry about the studying I have to do tomorrow. As I breeze along past the dorm adjacent to Lisa's, I notice this tiny car putter its way into the parking lot. I don't recognize it and continue to walk toward the figures getting out of the car.

For a minute, my heart flutters like crazy. Slowly emerging from the backseat door is the wispy, flowing hair of my *Lovely*. She's giggling and chatting away with these two people. A guy and another girl. They're all holding books, notebooks, thermoses. And I freak. There's nothing to hide me from them. No tree or street lamp, or convenient bush or shrub. And it's nearly two in the morning and I'm just waltzing by as if this is exactly where I belong. And it isn't. It simply isn't. My dorm is clearly across campus and Lisa knows I really don't come to this side of the campus anyway. So I am strutting away, like it's nobody's business.

And sure enough I hear: "Si? Si? Is—what are you doing over here?"

The other two are standing there looking tired and inquisitive along with her. I shrug my shoulders. As I am nonchalantly looking at her, I notice she's dressed pretty raggedy and looking rather studious. I'm relieved. So I smile, "I was out in the woods. Can't sleep. Had an interesting night. I'll call you Sunday, Love". I can't believe I'm saying this. Lisa knows that I walk the woods in the northern part of the campus, and that there is nothing but thistles and brush on her end. We both know this because we tried to pick some berries back there one afternoon. I'm an idiot. I walk away with my tail between the spindly legs and I really feel like a spider. Actually, I am a crab; a creepy crawling crustacean *dweeb* crawling back to his little hole in the sand. Well that's what I get. *I'll call you Sunday, Love.* Like I'm *Agent 007* or something. I wouldn't have anything to do with me. If I had my druthers, I'd drop myself. What an idiot. They're laughing. My *Lovely's* most likely telling them that I was freaking out because I didn't see her car in the parking lot. Well, I'll get over it. But damned, did she have to look so good? Even when disheveled and raggedy? And holding a bozo thermos?

****

Back at the dorm, the lumpy shape I see before me— usually identified as *Les*— is sound asleep. I don't know how he does it. He just comes in, tears his clothes off, dives into bed, and actually falls asleep as soon as his head hits the pillow. I spend some time reviewing my notes and writing an essay I need to have done by next week. After about an hour, I plop my notebooks on the floor and reach into my black box for a tape to listen to while I fall asleep. I pop in the vintage '*Metal Machine Music*' into my headset. It's about five am. I plunge myself under the covers thinking back on the day, beginning with my solitary walk to the woods, my reluctant bus ride back to town and everything after. I close my eyes and submerge myself in the wailing drone of the music. The drumming circle and that guy, Trent, keep popping in my head. And the droning lull of Lou Reed's metallic ode is pulling me, pulling me into a vortex. And I'm falling again. There are shafts of bright light surrounding me. I arrive at a place that feels very familiar. It is a place of soft green grass and a wispy view of a very old building. As I scan the area, I realize that it's a place I somehow have visited before. It's one of those dreams where I'm an observer of my own experiences. I've had these kinds of dreams before and they are frighteningly profound. There's a voice in back of me telling me to pay attention and it is scaring me. I'm paralyzed with fear. And it is misty, this view of a stone gray castle amid a lush lawn of green.

There is a beautiful river running alongside of the ancient building of which I now enter. The voice is telling me that I'm in the lower chambers and as I look there are these elaborately detailed stain-glassed windows reaching up a circular tower of some kind. And dazzling colors of light are shining all over the place. Up and down this tube-like tower. *You're not looking at it* the voice is telling me. *You're not looking at it*. My eyes are suddenly riveted to the top of the ceiling of the tower and there is a depiction of a dove, a sculpture, looking right down at me. And there are tiny pinpricks of light encircling this dove-like sculpture, giving it a heavenly aura. I'm transfixed by this sight. A shock is running through me as I observe this.

I'm floating up the shaft of dazzling rays of light and I 'm now looking down on a very small figure, a very small boy sitting on a cold floor of stone and slate. I can see this almost microscopically. And I wave to the boy. And the feeling is exhilarating. I am that bird again out at the sea. In the incident of my twelve-year old self, out at the beach and *aware*. And I'm flying over everyone, and I'm racing to the sun as it slowly burns through another June day. I know this place. I definitely know this place. For it is a place within me, it is a place I've known about through time. It is a place that holds my truth. I'm now plummeting back to the earth and walking along a seashore. I see a small figure approaching, and my walk is apprehensive.

For a second, I want to turn away and walk back, to where I do not know. I'm regretting my abandoned place in the tower- like room of colored light. I want to be the dove again. I want to soar but my feet are trudging slowly, sinking into the wet sand of this beach and I see this cloaked figure. He stands before me and his eyes radiate an incandescent glow. His gaze is powerful and the fear that is lodged in me is weighing me down like lead in the presence of this mysterious figure, this man; this holy man is staring me right through with such an awesome but loving power that I am now buried completely in the sand standing straight up with my eyes peeping out giving a parallel view as I slowly descend into the ground and the loving powerful voice is telling me to go there, to completely go there and not come up until it is time. It is a journey I must take.

And I'm sinking into the earth, into this hollow, darkened space, cavernous and cold, and there is barely any light except these faint pale yellow rays emitting from somewhere above. And I'm standing in what feels like a domed cave and there is this echoing sound and I'm covered in what feels like ashes and I feel my bones crying for the tower-space I had seen and its dazzling colored lights and I'm shaken awake and lying in my small bed in a room bathed in the morning light.

I attempt to gather my stir-fried thoughts as Cory stands over me asking me if I'm sick or something. "It's 1:30 in the afternoon, dude. Hey, are you alright? Where's my razor? Hey, are you comin' to the party tonight?"

I duck my head under the covers, allowing my memory of the dream to settle. I know this is something I will want to think about later. Cory continues to talk to me as I lay here buried under the blankets and all I can hope for is that he finishes what he's saying and that he leaves the room soon. Very soon. But I see that I shall have no such blessed luck. Now he's fumbling through my notebooks.

"Hey, this is pretty weird. The-what in the hell... You sure are warped, Strayhorn, but this is. . ."

I lunge out of the bed, snatching my stuff out of his arms. For a moment, I want to kill this idiot. This…this rat-*scabetic*-brained idiot! I leap over to my chest of drawers and pull out his razor and point it at him.

"I've had to put up with your bullshit for an entire year, *Wet-cell*. And I am warning you, stay away from my business. Here's your lousy razor!"

And I throw it at him as he ducks his amazingly stupid head. And for some equally idiotic reason, I start laughing. It just comes over me. I stand here laughing like a fool and Cory looks at me, with this impish smile beginning to form on his peachy lips.

He shakes his ox head, "I dunno, man. Ever since you got together with that *Detroit* babe, you just aren't the same".

I tell him that I may not come to the party and he doesn't look too disappointed. I thumb through the notebooks, checking to see if Cory removed anything, gather my stuff and head for the shower.

****

I spend most of the day-what's left of it-at the library, reading and writing. I don't get out of here til 10 pm. Towards the end of the night, I stop by a phone and check my messages. There's nothing from Lisa, of course, but there is a grave and serious one from Andy. This is the one thing that brings everything back down to every-day reality. I had e-mailed him a letter late yesterday afternoon telling him that I had given it a lot of thought and would like to take a year off from school. It was a mad-dashed effort, and I feel pretty guilty about how I had so casually stated that while I had loved learning and everything, I had to give myself a year off to work on an oil rig in the Gulf of Mexico and then hopefully having enough dough to travel in Europe for a few months. But there was one bit in his message that got under my skin. He wants to fine me a couple thousand bucks! For my decision. As a penalty. He then goes into this harangue about expenses and sacrifices. And that it is not an entirely ok idea for him to go ahead and continue paying for my education a *forgoed* year. That if I do this, I better have a clear-cut major when I come back and that I had better commit myself to finishing school.

He really regrets his long-gone youth and that he can't have the fun he used to have. His whole generation knows they look like fools with their badly graying hair and having to stoop to the realization that *Jerry* is now dead, well it's apparently too much for them. The rocker -hipster himself just can't admit it. It's clearly about power. He knows I barely have any dough. He'll wipe me out so I'll have to phone him at some point to have him wire me money so we'll both know who's really in charge. And he'll just grin and go into his mistakes and that they weren't all so bad because he did graduate and moved on to M.I.T. Well, I'm not going to do it. If it kills me, I'm not calling Andy even if I have to beg on the streets of the *Fauberg Marigny*—his old neighborhood in New Orleans. And he's not going to know where I'm going, either.

That's it. I am not calling him back. I'm going to write a check tonight and *Fed Ex* it to his glass-dome-wonder office Monday morning. And I am not talking to him. Not for a long time. The cheap, new-age, bony-fingered creep! In fact, I think I will stop by the party and swill down a couple of beers in honor of Dad. Hell, I'm going to stop by the dorm to pull out my bottle of *Remy Martin* and get drunk. Why not? Why the hell not? All of my life, I have tried to be a good guy like Andy. And all I really am is this monster dragging around a body that feels like a side of beef. And I live with the unshakable knowledge that something dire is missing.

I get a lot of solace from a dream like I had the other night. That at least, I soar somewhere. But of course, I left off by plummeting down into some kind of cave and of course, this is irking the hell out of me. Sitting there in a cavern covered with ashes. Is this some kind of omen? Is Andy's request just the beginning of a big mistake? Well, it is a mistake I must make, then. I won't let fear keep me in the *'burbs* this summer working some lame job with little sprints up to the madhouse in Storrs so I can drool over the candy-caned outfit my *Lovely* will most likely be wearing while I try to cop a feel of her newly *Naired* leg. I simply won't settle for it. However, the leg bit doesn't sound so bad. It's a temptation. It's a lure, a tease. I won't do it. She'll dump me anyway because she's off to Switzerland in September. And now that I am hopelessly in love with her, I have to leave! It's the only noble and decent thing to do. Leave now. It looks better. Especially after my meandering number last night. And I can't see myself listening to Nancy and Gram chatter away about all this bs.

There have been times when I've overheard their hushed chatter at the kitchen table and found myself thinking of a couple of old, withered douche bags gurgling down the insides of an old fashioned, claw-footed porcelain tub. In fact, I was thinking that very thought as I was walking out of the kitchen door with my luggage in tow last September when I headed out for this place. Needless to say, it was a timely exit. I say, it feels like a good night to get drunk. I'm done with most of my studying. Why not fry a few brain cells?

I stumble into the room like a blind idiot. The place is completely dark. Everyone on the floor seems like they are at Cory and Amanda's party over on the other side of the campus. The territory, I should say, I should avoid, if I'm to not think of my Lovely. I'm at peace with the idea of staying in and having the room to myself. I can listen to some non-threatening, unromantic, not-too-heavy-metal*ish* music (of course, this leaves me with some classical or instrumental stuff that has no affiliation with *Guinevere*), pour the brandy and get mildly intoxicated. I'll have fuzzy, unmemorable dreams and lay in a stupor of ignorance for a few hours, and as I'm pilfering through the garbage in my closet I see that my treasured brandy is simply...nowhere to be found! That Cory! It's already after midnight and I can't go out and buy another bottle. This leaves me with one choice. I now must crash the party—well, I was invited—but I will go over there with my laundry bag and I will take everything alcoholic and put it in this sack and taking it all back here. Cory. The guy has no concept of other people's property.

I walk out into the quads and head over to the site carrying the sack over my shoulder like some unemployed Santa Claus looking for a cot to rest his aging bones in, not caring whether I run into Lisa. In fact, I hope I do see her. I think we need to drive out to our little place again and pick up where we left off the other night. I'm so tempted to just call her. And well, I do.

I pop over to the pay phone and dial her number. And I hang it up before the call goes through. If I do this, she'll think I'm a drooling fool. I'm supposed to call her tomorrow night and if I have to sit on my hands I will wait til then. I'm not doing it. God, I hate myself right now. I really need to get blasted. I can hear the music now. It's screaming all over the place. They're playing *Garbage* and that song, "*Stupid Girl*" is just blaring all over the field. It's already got a haunting sound as it is, and out here, it's practically ominous. She really shouldn't have anything to do with a guy like me and well, actually, she looks like she's doing just fine. With songs like that, what do you expect?

It's too late for me. I'm already in it. In it thick. And here's idiot-head Cory swilling his beer and chatting away with these *dweebs* from the dorm. I recognize a few of the girls, but no one resembling Lisa. I guess I am halfway expecting to see her here. I bypass Cory and head for the table and tubs of iced beer. I start filling the sack like a brazen thief, and of course, no one is paying any attention to me, so I go all the way. I grab a couple of bottles of whiskey and a bottle of vodka, about a dozen beers and drag the sack on the grass behind me as I clear away from the scene, not bothering to say a word to anyone.

And it looks like I'm back in the *Melmoth* mode, in my isolated, dejected, no-one-bother-me-don't -touch-me-*scab*-mode and I'm heading for my private place near the river. I need to look at the moon and review my plans. As I attempt to make my getaway from this scene of amateur *party-ers*, I hear a shrill cry of my name. I freeze in my tracks. I want to proceed, pretending I don't hear anything, but it doesn't work. It's Lisa. I halfway turn around. She's looking as beautiful as ever. And she's a mess. She has on torn jeans and a sloppy sweatshirt. I love her when she looks like this. My Lovely's pointing at the sack and giggling at me.

"Si! What are you doing?"

She's so cute when she wrinkles her forehead. I could just kiss her all over when she does this.

"Why..."I bend down like the *Grinch Who Stole Christmas* as he is gently bs-ing little *Cindly Loo Who* or whatever, and I paraphrase on the bit about fixing the lights on the broken tree, but she doesn't seem to register. Ok. So it's not the best joke. She rolls her eyes around. I can see the whites shining in the dimly lit yard. I say, "Cory decided to help himself to my only bottle of brandy; actually, the only thing alcoholic I had in my closet. So I thought I'd help myself to a few of his bottles and go over to the grove. I have a lot on my mind, my *Lovely*. Wanna come?"

"Si, you're crazy! You practically took the whole bar!" Taking her by the hand, we run, the sack dragging on the ground behind us. I tell her that we'll just go over there for a while. Let them wonder what happened, then later, we'll bring it all back. The song, "*As Heaven is Wide*" is blaring through the quads and it echoes as we run down to the river. My little temptress breaks her hand away and looks up at me with those doe-fawn, snow-pup eyes. Now she frowns and scratches her arms.

"Si, Can we just drink a soda and enjoy the evening? We can have fun and not drink. I had this whisky and I feel sick. Did you remember to take a few sodas, too?" I tell her, "Coming right up, my Lovely."

I dig through the sack praying I have a something in there to please my gorgeous lady and, well, there are two cans of club soda. I hand one over to her. She's smiling. That's good. I'm now smiling. I pop open the other can and sit at her feet. She collapses beside me. This is wonderful. As it should be. We need to be together. I'm going to just hang onto my paltry dough and live here at school and follow her when she leaves for her nuthouse job. I'll find a place to live near her work and visit her every day. This babe is intoxicating. Who needs the alcohol?

But then I hear myself say, "I wanted to get shit faced because I'm mad at my father who hasn't had a

drink in nearly fifteen years. I don't mind getting mildly high here and there, but it's like this big moral question whenever I walk past the liquor section in the *Pack
'n Pork*. Oh, by the way, when we marry, I'll have something for you to show our brilliant children. It's a neon
day-glow glob of plastic that adorns the behind of the
plastic pig in the window...it's supposed to be a tail. I'm
going to give it to you; it will be a symbol of the non-pol-
lution effort we will make on behalf of the minds and
sensibilities of our future offspring."

I unscrew the cap off the whiskey bottle. Lisa's actually laughing. "You're so weird, Simon! The things you
come out with. You should be a philosopher or something. Si, the *Pack 'n Porks* are here to stay. You can't
raise children and shield them from what's out there. I
mean, not entirely. Unless you want to live in *Amish*
country."

I tell her that she has a good point, but we can make
strident efforts to discard social pollutants by not having
TV's; maybe even computers. Children should be out in
the woods creating games and playing in nature. Not
amusing themselves with violent video games.   They
need coloring books, and fairy tales. I say, "Actually, not
coloring books, because they're so trite. It's better to give
them plain brown paper and crayons and paints and stuff.
And they need to have meager resources for toys. I mean,
so meager that they have to make them and create them.
Can you imagine Frank Lloyd Wright as a child watching *Barney and Friends*? He probably spent most of his
childhood playing with sticks in mounds of dirt".

She looks at me. I tell her about Frank Lloyd Wright.
How great he was. I then describe a time when Andy got
into a tirade about Ayn Rand. Andy ended his spiel by

saying that Ayn Rand contradicted her idealistic visions of humankind by modeling her protagonist on someone like Frank Lloyd Wright.

"'In fact,'" Andy quipped amid the lush flora near The Boathouse Cafe in Central Park one sunny summer afternoon, " ' Frank Lloyd Wright had too much of a celestial sensibility to have aligned himself to such nonsense. When you enter the very spaces he created, it's like being in the waiting rooms of God. He didn't do these things out of a sense of humanitarianism or integrity, he did them out of a sense of well...holy space. As if he were building cathedrals. No difference, really, from a Michaelangelo." And of course, Andy threw his napkin down in disgust and walked away from me to gasp some air. I had to remember what Gram and Nancy said: *"Don't let him talk too seriously about stuff he's passionate about and you'll have a great day!"* But, of course, I forgot I had been carrying *The Fountainhead* around with me. If anyone knows Andy, that's like carrying a bomb. I rather enjoyed the book, but told Andy otherwise to shut him up so we could leisurely toss the crusts from our sandwiches to the ducks or whatever and have a pleasant afternoon. Well, he eyed it immediately and proceeded to argue Rand's philosophy. He's too much. He left a message telling me to cough up a wad of cash for my wanting to travel and work next year."

My *Lovely* replies, "You're too smart to drop out, Si."

She's so pretty and so sweet. I love her hair. It's glowing in the moonlight. I nuzzle my snout in it and kiss her neck. And I feel myself wanting to cry, but I hold it back. I then remind her that I'm definitely going to finish college. That I just need to break away for a while.

We promise each other that we'll write letters and vow to save plebian e-mails for our buddies. There's something charming about writing in your own hand and waiting for the mailman to deliver a letter on what is carefully chosen stationery.

She asks, "Promise you will tell me where you are and where you're going?"

I do. I promise her that. So she won't worry. She is asking me why I was walking around the other night. I tell her that I had thought of her and wanted to leave something on her windowsill, but I forgot it back at my room. She looks at me, a bit miffed.

I tell her I'll give it to her when we see each other next, and add, " I was going to call you on Sunday night to tell you that I had something there for you. I'm kind of weird when I give presents."

I tell her that I think people should leave presents in unexpected places. People should go on something like an Easter egg hunt whenever there's a birthday, even Christmas. It would make it more pleasurable and maybe more fun. I know I try to have fun.

That is, if I can only shut my head off once in a while. I confess: "In fact, I want to chop my head off sometimes. You know. Just leave it somewhere. On the bed or in the shower, so I can go about doing things without having to worry and think all the time. It wouldn't be gory or anything. It would just be nice to gently remove your head like taking off your socks or something."

She snuggles closer and I kiss her. She says she thinks it was thoughtful that I bought something for her. This is just too much for me to handle. I'm weakening. And there is a tear falling from my eye. She is the only girl I have ever felt so emotional with, and it's ridiculous.

I must stop myself from doing this.

"Si, don't get up!"

I can't let her see me. I have to go back to the dorm. I walk over to the group of pine trees and Lisa remains seated on the ground, picking at blades of grass, looking over at me here and there.   I stare at the moon like a transfixed idiot and gather my thoughts. This isn't supposed to be happening. I'm supposed to be getting mildly drunk and bragging about my trip and talking about the drumming circle and other things than doing this.

I walk back over to where she's sitting; I kneel in front of her. I take her by the delicate chin and kiss her. And we kiss for a while. It seems like a long time. And I want to be with her but I know we need to cool it. I have to prepare for when I leave. And I want her so badly, but it wouldn't be the thing to do. She kisses my face as if she's searching for the tears with her lips. But they are gone. I am already dry-eyed. I want to believe that it didn't happen. That I'm more in control of things than that. I tell her I'm just tired. And freaked about money for my trip. And I feel like a big baby. Actually, I must be a big baby to her because I can't handle it if anything upsets my idea of how things are supposed to be. I have a two-hour session coming up with Boyce on Monday and it's like I can't wait to see the guy to tell him that I think I should just cancel everything and continue on staying here. I'm not ready. Not really ready for anything. Her, school, a trip away. Time abroad.

So here we are, lying in each other's arms, kissing like crazy and of course, we're oblivious to the party that's going on a few hundred yards away and there's this brushing sound coming up from behind us. As I stroke my *Lovely*'s hair I hear this heavy breathing, and the

sound of someone running on the grass. A thought immediately flashes through my mind: *it's Cory!* And I imagine he's pissed as all hell.

I turn around and just when I'm about to tell the idiot
(and it's him, alright) that I'll be returning all the stuff to
the party, his trooper-boot kicks me in the face. There's
blood running from my nose, and all I can do is lunge
myself on the guy. And when I do, we immediately
begin to wrestle. I try to fight the geek off, but he's like
a wildcat. He's so drunk and angry. I attempt to tell the
guy that he can take all the liquor back. And now Lisa is
saying something about the brandy Cory took from my
closet and that we were just doing a prank to get him to
stop helping himself to my stuff, but it is no use.

The guy is going for it. I ram him into the ground and
pound his ears a few times before I tell him that I will
destroy his limbs if he doesn't stop clawing me. So now
Lisa, the Detroit rocker, is jumping around, playing ref-
eree. As Cory wails about the bottles, Lisa points to the
sack and assures him that we only opened a couple of
cans of soda and I only had a shot or two of the whiskey.
That this is only fair.

Finally, Cory breaks away a bit and paces back and
forth as he says to me, "You're really a sick bastard, man.
I didn't touch your brandy. Les and Pony took it and told
me to leave you a twenty dollar bill for it, which I did,
nimble-head. It's under your pillow along with a note
from the lovebirds. By the way, they're staying together.
She ditched *Dartmouth.* And she's up for an award for
this A. I. competition. Les is now in love with her *mind.*
Figures."

Lisa and I look at each other in sheer disbelief.
Maybe Cory is gaining in the brain department after all.

I wipe my bleeding nose on my sleeve.

"You're a lummox , Banks. A real nimble-brained, cortex-voided, pig-knuckled head gnarled in the vilest of brines, but —what can I say? Here's your stuff."

I kick the laundry bag and Cory leans down and grabs it. As he is about to leave, I remind him,

"Is it still there? The *twenty*? Under my pillow?"

He tells me,

" No, Strayhorn! The *tooth-fairy* took it!"

He bobs his head like a yo-yo and bending down to grab the laundry sack, we watch as he vomits all over the thing. Lisa and I are so shocked that we laugh. I tell him,

"Hey, Banks. Sure you want more of that shit? That's the way you do it back home?"

Cory's still puking as Lisa dabs my snout with wads of tissue. It's gross, watching this, and Lisa and I decide to walk away from him for a few minutes. Lisa and I walk closer to the river bank. I turn around to see if Cory's ok. He stands there, shaking his head as he pours club soda all over his face and hair. He tells us,

" I'm an asshole! I'm sorry. I'm so sorry, you guys. I feel like such a scum sucking idiot."

I walk over to the guy and slightly nudge him in the arm.

"Dude, it happens to the best of us." I can't believe I say something so corny. But I sincerely confess, "I shouldn't have done that. I'm sorry I ruined the party. If I did, man, I apologize."

Lisa and I take the bottles out of the vomit-drenched laundry bag and walk with Cory back to the party, carrying the stuff with us. We're not really saying much as we approach the tables outside. They're still a lot of people hanging around and Lisa and I place the bottles and cans back on the tables. People are coming up to us and asking where in the hell we've been. Les is dancing around with Pony to the classic, "*This is Not a Love Song*", by the *Sex Pistols*.

Lisa begins to rock back and forth in her bomber boots. I have to remember that around Lisa, this music can be dangerous. I shake my head and tell her no, no dancing in front of these guys. Now she's giving me that doe-eyed look as she cuffs her hands like puppy paws in front of her. She cocks her head to the side and smiles. "No!" I tell her. She continues to rock around anyway and these girls from her dorm join her. I'm standing there watching them. They are beautiful, these girls accompanying my *Guinevere* with their silky arms; their tight little butts wriggling away. There's something about girls dancing together that really *floors* me. One is a *Nubian* babe with wild, fluffy hair and the other is flaxen blonde and well, *Nordic*-beautiful. And they spin and entwine themselves as if they are dancing around an invisible Maypole

I can't help but think of that famous painting by Boticelli. The famous panel of these wispy-haired Renaissance babes dancing by a tree in these see-through gowns, and these lovelies remind me of them. *The Three Graces*. Perhaps a more updated version of Th*e Three Graces*. And in my girl's case, a leather-clad, Detroit rock version. Their hair is flying in the air and their hips are rolling around and I put on my best indifferent front while my hands stay glued to the insides of my pockets. It is beckoning me, alright. And my indifferent front is melting. Fast. Well, what the heck! My feet start to spin and slide as I part the sea of girls with my swerving hips. And my ladies shriek and squeal.

One of them says, "Lisa told us about your dancing. She's *right*!"

I turn crimson at this, but continue to prance around like an idiot amid these beautiful creatures. I swear, I don't know what comes over me sometimes. Lisa looks over at me but I can't help it. I know she's thinking I'm especially turned on by these girls, but it's not entirely so. The music has now possessed me and I'm dancing around like the devil himself. It should be banned, the way I dance. Actually, there's this black couple over in the corner and the guy, if I'm seeing correctly, raises his brow as his girl emits a big grin. I'm nothing but a shameless exhibitionist trying to impress the hell out of everyone with my bodily antics. Lisa shimmies up to me. She's trying to tell me something, but I can barely hear her. I lean closer to her and she shouts in my ear.

"Is this going to be the last time I see you dance, Si? Or are you going to meet up with me in London next fall? Hey, let's do that! Meet me in London at Christmas! I bob head like a complete deaf fool.

She chirps, "You will?"

Oh, of course. I wiggle and spin as continue to bob my head up and down like a fool. Where in the hell am I going to get the dough together to meet up with her in London? I tell her, "Well, it might be a low-budget Christmas. But we'll do it after I go on my Scottish expedition. " She snuggles up to me just when I'm about to do my swirling number with these accompanying beauties, their arms now held in an arc for me to dip my body under so I can nestle between them. Lisa says, " Si, write to me. Hey! Maybe I'll join you in Edinburgh!"

I'm trying not to wince at myself. Me and my huge mouth. Edinburgh! I don't know anybody in Edinburgh!

"Lisa!"

I want to tell her, but I don't. I just pray that I end up making the money somehow. Cory's now dancing with Amanda. He actually looks revitalized. They're now playing this band, *Matchbox Twenty* and the music is kinda rock-acoustic, which suits me because I need a break. I take Lisa by the hand and we walk away from the dance scene. We're walking toward the middle of the field, and I'm holding her dewy moist hand. So soft and petal-like. I tell her I am nervous about everything. That I will miss her and I will be thinking of her. That I know we are young and free to do what we want, but that I don't really want to know anything if she meets other guys. To keep that business to herself. She's making little sounds. Little chirp-like sounds and it's driving me nuts. I tell her,

"Stop it! You like me now, Lisa. But things are going to change. You're a beautiful girl. And I know there's not going to be much happening in the nuthouse in Storrs. But when you go abroad, you will be meeting a lot of guys. Charming guys with polyglot abilities and God knows what else I don't possess. Face it."

Lisa purses her lips, biting them in little intervals. She informs me,

"Si, you are going to be meeting girls, too. And I just don't see why we can't just say to each other and admit that most people aren't like us. They may look real good and know some interesting things, but so what. Chemistry doesn't happen everyday, you know. As long as we stay in touch, we'll still be together, right?"

There's something so pure about what my *Lovely* is saying to me. I take her in my arms and pull her into the folds of my chest, my arms encasing her slim body. I just love this. I simply love it and I just don't know if I want to leave her just yet. Maybe I should just stay put for a while and visit her during the summer and we'll separate more slowly, gradually, and gently, we'll depart by September like summer grass slowly fading, and leaves slowly turning. Like nature. The way things should be. Why should I pass up any more opportunity to be with her when clearly I can?   My trip can wait. What's the rush anyway?

****

"Absolutely, positively not". Boyce is barely audible. But audible enough beneath his African war mask. I can't believe he's sitting here today with this thing on. And I can't believe he's telling me this. So I point-blank ask him,

"Why the hell not?"

He pulls the thing off and looks directly at me, his pipe slowly dying in his ashtray.

"Because it is the classic thing that young guys in the position you're in should not do. The biggest temptation for you is to cancel your journey-let's just call it that because of a girl! You need to do a few things on your own, first. Stay here and postpone things and you may live to regret it later."

My *side of beef* body is slowly sliding off the chair as he says this. Isn't this all my fault? Aren't I the one who enlisted this guy a few months back because of a temporary spell of weakness? Who is this man anyway? How does he know these things? What makes him so damned sure?

I ask him, "So what's with the rig here? I mean, what

are you trying to tell me by wearing this stupid thing today, Boyce?"

He tells me, in his patient and calm manner, that he's glad I asked him this. That, in fact, he's surprised it took me this long to finally inquire and well, he had the thing on because we're going to talk about initiations. About something vital that I'm most likely headed out for and that once done, I would then be able to harbor myself more readily and securely in not only my life to come, but in the relationships I will have later.

I'm trying not to yawn. I really am. I then decide to talk. I tell him that of all the girls I have ever met nothing has made me feel more manly and more *initiated* than this relationship. That it seems that he and Andy are almost conspiring to frustrate me. Andy with his petulant fine and he with his insistence that I go forward and leave my *Lovely* behind. And as I say this Boyce's nostrils are actually beginning to flare. He rises from his big leather swivel chair and walks over to the front of his enormous desk.

I know what it means when he does this so I promptly shut my beak. He's fishing the dead pipe from the ashtray and re-lighting the thing. Here it comes. I remain bolted to the chair with my mouth sealed shut.

"Si?"

He's arching his fuzzy brows, his bald head shines like *Mr. Clean's.* I'm fully prepared for what he has to say. He slowly tells me, actually, he is questioning me. Reminding me that we had made an agreement. That I really can't renege on something we had earlier agreed to.

He sourly asks, "Long before you got together with *Golden Girl.* Remember? We both sat here and determined that you wanted to do this and I was going to see that you go through with things. Remember? Well, I must say things have a way of changing once Simon here gets together with a member of the opposite sex. And Si, I think this is all fine and well, but you well know that if you decide to postpone this you will hang out here indefinitely, and while she is skiing in the Alps, you will be saddled back here-or worse, she will have you talk her into staying with you and then where will you be? And I am talking about the both of you. Things start to calm down, and lapse into ordinariness and well, your problem with Andy remains, and you remain unraveled-forever bound to women-let's see-Gram, Nancy, Caz, *Andy* and now *Goldielocks* and this will contribute to a growing frustration and an inevitable fiery break up and your ultimately being angry with yourself for letting pleasure get in the way of your convictions. Welcome to *manhood*."

Boyce walks back over to his chair and reaches for his mask. He places it over his huge head once again. And I grin. I can't help it. The guy is something else. It's quite a work of art. And scary-looking at that.

I tell him, "Ok, Boyce. I get it. Do you have to get so....*Smithsonian* about it? Jeez!"

He tells me,

"Hey! That's my word!"

I continue to grin as I tell him,

"Oh, I say it all the time now. *Jeez. Jeezum Pete's. Jeezum!* I kinda like it."

He still has this ritual mask on and he's comically placing his pipe in the mouth part and puffing away. Whew...he's really something else, this guy. But, of course, Boyce is totally serious when he says,

"I need to hear you say that you are bound to your

commitment with me, young man."

I nod my head, saying, "Yes. I said what I said. And I won't back out. I'm leaving by June. I'm off to Virginia. I will stay a few nights on my friend's farm. I already e-mailed him and everything's going to be just great. We'll hang out a while, then I'll be passing through the Carolinas and then down to Louisiana. I have the rig job waiting for me to start sometime in July ".

Boyce still leans against the desk with the puffing mask on. And he's nodding as I yak my jaws off telling him of my plans.

He interrupts to inform me, "There's something I may send your way before you leave, as for your gal...when she skidaddles back to wherever she is going, tell her, *hey, this is our last time*! Shut the door for now, Si. I promise, it is for the best. Make it sweet and simple. Be lighthearted about it. Don't go lugubrious on her; put the breaks on your weepy stuff. At least in front of her. Jeez! What do you see me for?"

I inform Boyce that I wanted to call him last Friday morning when I was out in the sticks. That I should have told him all my stuff out there, but I was hesitant to do so. That I thought he would make fun of me, or worse, tell me a bunch of "I told you so's". He shrugs his shoulders when I say this. I continue,

"See what I mean? To you, it's no big deal, but I don't want to have to deal with sarcasm when I feel this stuff, and every man I've ever known is sarcastic around emotions."

I pause right here. The dreams I had had the other night are coming back to me and I'm wavering as to whether I should delve into the subject. I know he is sensing this and he's still sitting there on his perch, looking faux-casual with his mask on. I decide to pass for now. I know I'm not going to be seeing him much after this session. And I'm too unclear as to the importance of my dreams. Are they indicative of something to come? Maybe I should keep it to myself. I realize that I'm remaining silent because I really feel that there is a part of myself that is wiser than what these sessions are all about, and if I say this, it will lose its power. Boyce shifts his weight to his other leg.

I should just say it. And I do.

"I'm having vivid and real dreams and they frighten and excite me. The other night I was in another realm of knowing. It had to do with vision, and I was soaring and I ended up meeting up with a figure that was wise and it was a man, but that's all I can say about him. He was like this higher being, an advanced, illumined man. Wise and whole. He had these powerful, incandescent eyes. And the next thing I knew I was being plummeted to the insides of the earth and I was slammed back into…well, what I call a desultory, pedestrian state of existence. It all felt laborious and troublesome and yet the wise man told me that it was vital that I be in this cavernous, underground place. Maybe it was a higher version of you in that dream, but the thing I want to say about it is, I felt that I already knew all this stuff. And my question is, why is it that I seem to know these things on that dream level and yet in my waking state I'm a basic *dweeb*?"

Boyce is sitting still. In fact, he is as still as a statue. He's barely moving his bald head, which he usually nods when I talk. Finally, he takes the mask off and puts it on the table. Slowly, he says, "Dreams, at times, are the openings to what metaphysical thinkers call: the *fourth dimension*. Jung knew it, but he was bound to a dedication to scientific thought, so he hesitated to really go out there on a limb, even though he's considered unconventional in this regard by established psychiatric circles. You might want to explore metaphysics, Si. Yeah, I agree, there is a part of us that seems all wise and knowing, but the dream you told me has an essential lesson. Did you understand the lesson, Si?"

I tell him that I think it had something to do with being prepared for something. Something that may be out of the ordinary. He's nodding his head. As far as a lesson, I am not sure. So I tell him I do not know.

"Good."

"Why is that good, Boyce?"

"Because it will take a series of experiences before you understand the lesson. Perhaps, your dreams to come will process that as you go along. Is this all or are there any other ones you want to talk about?"

I tell him about the one I had had about Andy and the men. That I thought I had seen the face of my Great, Great Granddad. And that I only recognized him from some old photographs that were taken in the 19th century, but then when he saw that I recognized him, his face vanished.

Boyce seems more interested in this one than the other. He's now nodding his head vigorously. He says, "So you see, something in your development must take place in order for an integrated sense of self—and that may have some reference to the ancestral tie there, or maybe, for your more actualized self, I should say, to take shape. Do you follow me here? Because that may be what the dream is all about. Think about it. That's why the figure, who is enlightened, instructs you to take it *underground* for a while. You may not be ready to handle the higher perceptions. Not yet. It's rather poetic, the life of dreams. And often they're dead center accurate. And so, you see, you are about to…"

I can't believe he's doing this. Boyce takes out his drum, and slowly bangs it as he continues, "...take your first steps into your adventure. Although, I would say the journey has been taking place all along. You're just taking it out into the world. Right?"

I sense that he feels I'm discouraged about taking off and I tell him so. I'm only hesitant because I wonder what the big deal is anyway. I have a nice girl who likes me and I'm simply being honest in saying I wouldn't mind postponing things a bit. Boyce reminds me about the story of *Odysseus* when he's tempted as he approaches the Isle of Circe. That a little *girl-action* can stymie the hero's journey. I rack my brain trying to remember the story, which I liked a great deal, but was only 15 when I read it.

Boyce quips, "Well, you might want to re-read it."

Old, smoking, *baldie.* His arms are folded behind his neck as he leans back and puffs away, his teeth clenching the plastic stem of his pipe as he talks. I'm going to miss this guy. And I tell him so. He shrugs me off, saying,

"Nonsense! You'll be in touch. In fact, you may feel my shadow lurking here and there! And just when you least expect it!"

I can only ask,

"Why do you say that? You're scaring me."

He lets out a cackle. The kind of wild cackle a mad scientist would make.

He shakes his head and says,

"Good! Now get going! And we'll meet again next week!"

****

I walk out into the busy intersection and decide to cross Cromwell Street and take the car to the Pack 'n Pork. That stupid electric pig has been on my mind and I have this insane idea as to how I might go about snatching its tail. I want to leave it for Lisa on her windowsill along with a poetic note about our future offspring. But there's this *lum-lum* security guard that stands right in front of the thing. And I'm wondering what goes on in the late shift. Whether the security guards doze off or preoccupy themselves with small electronic equipment or something.

I enter the store and sure enough, the security guard is standing there. The pig is a pretty simple device. But I need to look at it more closely to see if its tail actually comes off. So I walk around the guy and pretend I am looking at something through the window that faces the parking lot. I attempt to focus on the tail by looking through the corner of my eye.

And it seems like the thing wouldn't be hard to take off in a hurry, which, of course, is what I'll have to do if I am not to be caught, but it wiggles back and forth and it's not so easy to tell. For a split second, a thought flashes in my head. It doesn't even belong to me, this thought. It feels like an Andy thought. *Why don't you just ask the store manager if you can actually order a pig from a factory or a warehouse or something?* Simple. It's definitely something Andy would think. So proper.

There's a pair of shoes approaching me. It's the guard. He's standing right in back of me. I shake my head, as if I just can't, for the life of me, remember what my car looks like.

His voice speaks to me from behind,

"Looking for someone?"

I remain staring through the window. I put on my best faux casual pose,

"Yeah. She's a real nut." I turn and look at him. "She was supposed to stay in the car to watch my things, but I saw her taking off to the beauty supply store over there."

The guy shrugs his shoulders and stares at me for a minute. I spin on my heel (something I picked up from Andy) and walk to the aisles shaking my head, hoping I don't look totally stupid. I don't think my idea is going to work. Maybe I will ask the store manager about ordering a pig for my girlfriend. I'll just say that she thinks they're really cute and wants one for her dorm window. After all, it'll be some publicity for the store. Free advertising. Maybe they could give me a discount.

As I am browsing the bread section, I notice that guy, Trent Chisolm, whizzing by carrying a basket-load of stuff. I walk to the next aisle and tell him hello. He's like really glad to see me.

"Hey, Simon! How's it going?"

I tell him that I'll be leaving in a few weeks and he's stroking his chin, listening to me, his basket resting on the floor.

"Oh, drop me a line. Here..." he writes his address along with an e-mail address on a small notepad. Trent continues, "It might be easier. I'm going to be traveling, too. Mostly out west. I'll be at the drum circle next week. Let me know if you're going."

The electric pig beckons me as it swooshes its stupid tail back and forth. If I don't give Lisa the tail or the pig itself, she'll simply have nothing to remember me by. The bracelet, any guy can give her that. But not the pig. The woman at the register looks at me funny. I lean over and ask her where the manager is. She asks me if there's a problem. Why do service people always ask things like that? I tell her, no, she's great , the store is my favorite. Better than *Wal-Mart*. She calls for the manager to show up at the counter over the PA. Trent is standing at the next counter, and I hope he leaves before the manager shows up. And he does, waving at me as he walks through the electronic door.

A small, wiry, guy with sleepy-looking eyes shows up. I ask if there's any way I could order one of those cute little pigs on the wall. It's for my baby sister. She has leukemia and is dying. She wants to put it on her wall in the hospital room. The man furrows his bushy brows and shakes his head. He then says it's a store policy, I can only order one from a vendor in Pennsylvania or something.

The guy shakes his head, and there's a tiny bead of sweat formulating on his crinkled forehead. I'm almost about to bow out and leave, but now the guy is looking very grave about the matter. He says, "takes a couple of weeks to get those things… it's a shame".

His eyes suddenly perk up, " Hey! What hospital is the little girl in? We'll have one sent over. Compliments of the store! In fact, we'll just have the guys take that one down."

He turns toward a guy packing a bag of groceries and points to the pig. I'm partially in shock. I can't believe what the man's saying.

"Hey, that's so nice of you"…and I read his name tag, "Mr. Lomax" *Grant Lomax,* that's what the tag says."...but I better bring it to her myself".

I wince as I say this. I then ask, " Can I please pay you for it?"

Grant immediately says, "Don't be ridiculous! Poor girl! We would never!"

I'm really wincing now. The kid hands me the pig, and the manager is telling him to put it in a box from the back of the store. As I leave, the security guard is looking over at me. He informs me:

"Hey! I've been watching over here. She never came back! But who's the kid sitting in the backseat?"

So I am weird. I know it. That streetwise security guard knows it. He saw me looking at the stupid thing. He knew I was snowing him. He probably read my mind. He knew I wanted to steal the thing. I really am a worm. I really am. I'm also a bald faced liar. The worst kind! I place the pig in the backseat along with my other goodies. I'll probably end up a used car salesman for doing this.

Two notches down the *reincarnational scale* for this one. Andy would shake his head. He'd say it was sniveling and conniving, what I just did. Ingratiating lies of the worst kind. Grant Lomax. What a nice guy! It sickens me how I stooped so low for this stupid little thing! I must remember to send old Grant a thank-you note.

I'll sign a phony name and say that sis has had a remarkable recovery since receiving the thing! In fact, the whole floor is now visiting her room to witness the pig's power. Like Lourdes, or something. Soon, we'll be in a segment on *Miracles Happen*. I suppose the only comfort I have is that I did not steal the thing. But to deceive is probably worse.

Andy once went into the degrees of sin with me one

night. We were sitting on the porch in back of the house
and I must've been around thirteen years old. I was sitting on the old swing eating ice cream and Andy was sipping away at his de-caf. Nancy and Gram had gone shopping and we were talking about the subtle art of deception. We had recently learned of the murder of Mr.
Crawford and how shocked the entire neighborhood was
that it was *Mrs. Crawford* who committed the ghastly act.
My father kept shaking his head. "She always sent us
Christmas cards too early in the season, if you ask me.
Something a little too perfect there. They're always the
ones. The ones who do things so perfectly; *without a
hitch*, as they say. You could see it in her signature. And
her kids are *rotten*. Remember the trampoline?"

When we were little kids, the Crawford children
were the envy of the neighborhood. And all of us would
gather near the fence that surrounded their great home
and drool over the famous trampoline as the Crawford
kids bounced and leapt in the air. Never did they invite
any of us to join them. "She was like that. Selfish." Andy
sipped his de-caf and mused at the moon. "Fitting end,
I'd say, when you really stop and think about it."

"Yeah, but Dad, he was a real creep." Andy added,
"They were a pair, alright," and followed this by going
into a diatribe about character and fate. That the evil that
roam the earth are full of deceptive guises. That the
Crawfords were *Protestant* and *perfectionistic*. That the
murder wasn't even passionate. It was clean and simple.
Swift and cunning. Mr. Crawford was poisoned.

Andy elaborated: "The degree of lying. That's what
it's all about. That's what the nuns and the Benedictines
and the Jesuits were trying to tell us when I was in school.
That evil comes in layers and so, contrition is appropriat-

ed to the degree of one's awareness of the wrongful deed."

So in Andy's terms, I am a grave sinner for using deception and cunning in obtaining the pig. That, actually, it would've been better if I had just randomly stolen the thing while drunk or something. Well, sober, it would've been better. I had flat out lied to get what I wanted and I manipulated the good emotions of Grant Lomax in order to get it.

I steer into the parking lot near my dorm and notice the tiny steeple of a small church peeking out of the trees. I have this urge to walk over to the chapel and pray.

I approach the tiny steps that lead into the church and notice a sweet sound coming from inside. These lovely string instruments, a cello and a violin or two, are playing a somber tune of which my emotions at the moment seem grateful to hear. I step inside and there are two women and a bearded man playing at the front near the alter.

I sit in the very back of what looks like a rather paltry and sparsely furnished church. For a moment I want to kneel , but I change my mind. Maybe I'm getting a bit carried away. So I absorb the sweet sound of the music as I dream of a way to wipe the mental slate clean, and well, all suffering blanched out. No more emotional creditors of soul or conscience. But of course, it may all go on my record; the soul ledger sheet that's drawn up once you croak and depart from this life. I look up and note that the musicians are taking a pause and are talking among themselves. I think it's my signal to depart and I do so, practically forgetting why I had originally come in here.

****

I wake up this morning to the sound of Cory's non-stop laughter as he chats on his new cell phone. You'd think the guy would take the thing outside or into his car as most people do when they have cell phones, but no, he decides to park his butt on his bed and call everyone he knows on the thing. There's an overnight envelope sitting atop my blankets and immediately I think of Andy. I entertain the sad fantasy that in the past week or so he had second thoughts and decided to send my check back. For a minute, I'm all excited. I lunge for the thing and tear it open. To my dismay, naturally, I should have known, really, it is not a returned check or a newly written check from Andy's florid hand, but a three-page handwritten letter from Boyce.

For a minute my heart bounces around in my chest and my stomach sinks at the same time. Cory looks over at me, dumbstruck. "Dude! You're so bizarre. I can't wait til you get the hell out of here, Strayhorn. You look like a sick junkie or somethin'."

What can I say to such drivel? I sadly tuck the envelope under my arm and take it with me to the shower, tossing it on the bathroom floor in a corner where I know it'll remain dry. This is the kind of thing I'm reduced to in maintaining a level of privacy around here. The cocky, jock-plebe. I turn the faucets on full blast. I need to prepare my head for this one and I hope I am ready.

When I step back into the room, dripping wet with a couple of towels thrown about my body and my envelope concealed under one of the towels, I quietly tell Cory that I need to show him something in the shower. And I'm putting on my best horror-struck look, hoping it works. I abruptly walk out of the bathroom, pointing to the door. "I'm real freaked, Cory. I've never seen anything like this. You gotta come in and see this.. I dunno, it's weird." For a minute, the *lum-lum* looks like he's about to get off the bed to check out what I'm saying. But he abruptly stops, lies back and continues his conversation, ignoring me. This sort of stuff obviously isn't working anymore and it makes me sad. It sure does.

My, my, how things can evolve over the course of a school year. All I can do is smile to myself. Cory Banks. I should put out a headline on the '*Net* or something saying, *What was Once Thought Lost*, in reference to the sudden appearance of Cory's brain. The room remains quiet except for Cory's telephone chatter. I quickly dress and saunter out of the room, envelope neatly tucked under the armpit.

Before heading out to the grove, my little sacred sanctum which I will profoundly miss, I walk over to some of the buildings where I have my classes to check my grades. I also want to pick up my essay which will be waiting in a stack by the door where I have my Satirical Fiction class. Of course, I am nervously perusing the list of names on the boards and I am mildly relieved when I see that I will leave this place with a possible 3.7 average. I run up the stairs to the stacks of essays waiting by the door and there is all this writing in red ink all over the thing. At first, I am expecting to see a poor grade—which will be on the last page and I am perusing the comments which are all amazingly favorable. Before I get to the last page I shut the thing. I decide I need to see the final result when I walk out to the grove.

My heart is thumping away as I kneel down on the grass which is sprouting like crazy all over the place. In fact, it's hot today, so I take off my shirt and resume my perusal of the thing. I face the music. And the result is a mere B+. Well, I am not going to complain. I see his pointers. Some of it was excessive and off the track a bit.

But he loves the idea and thinks it is splendid the way I wove the whole thing together. Well, hell, what should I expect? Some kind of prize?

Now for Boyce's letter. I tear the thing open and begin to read:

Simon,

> *The road to wisdom awaits you! Here are my recommendations to you. From the day you set out on your trip, you are not to contact any immediate family member by phone, fax, letter, paper or electronic. Only write a simple post-card here and there—about four to six weeks apart—and always in a cheerful, "wish you were here" (Ha!) tone. NO EMERGENCY calls to any family member. That is, any other related fami-ly member that may be scattered about the earth as you sojourn along. The letters to Golden Girl must be brief. And they, too, must be fairly spaced apart. One or two a month. Here's the deal: NO letters from Lisa! You are on the road and busy. You are out on the rigs working with the guys. You are always moving so, she can't really write to you anywhere.*

I pause right there. I mean, who does this guy think he is? I specifically told Boyce that were are to write letters to each other. What will I do without a perfumed note from my Lovely? Reluctantly, I decide to read on.

It's very important that you keep your end of the bargain in this, Simon. OK. Next section. You will be allowed to call me only three times over the next six months.

I have to take a breather. Who does this bald-headed, *practically-ready-for-a-Geriatrics-telethon-host-spot-on-some-lousy-second-rate-PBS-station-one-foot-already-in-the-grave* guy thinks he is? Talk about self-flattery! Jeeeeez. I mean, jeeeeezum ! The guy's crazy if he thinks I can't do this. I continue:

Now this, of course, pertains to emergencies. Normally, I would like to hear from you, too, by emailing or whatever, as much as you want, really. Just a report on the general goings on. And keep a daily journal! Write about everything. I will reply to your letters. Somewhere along the line we may meet. We will review things.

I expect to read the part where it says: "No sex. No *babe-action* of any kind. Wear a monk's cloth to bed". I fold the thing up and gather my things. I want to just forget this entire idea. A year ago, I never heard of Boyce. I want to betray the deal I made with him. I could bail. I always have that option. But something inside of me is nudging me forward, and all I wish to do right now is walk the length of the riverbank . I want to tell Lisa everything that is going on and I know I can't. It's this dream that I had last night that is now pestering the hell out of me.   I can't really remember all the details, only it was Boyce who was in the central part of it and he was telling me things like the voice that was talking to me from behind in the dream I had before. Only this time I was a school kid. Or I felt like a school kid and I was at a backyard children's party and I was blindfolded and I was groping around like an idiot and I kept bumping into these people who are in my life today like Lisa and Caz, and I felt their hair in my hands and I walked along until I fell what seemed like a hundred feet into a batch of weeds landing flat on my back. That was when I woke up to Cory's obnoxious chatter on his cell phone. It's probably why I looked so freaked when I woke up.

I'm going to take Lisa out for a memorable occasion. There are like two really fancy restaurants in this lousy town and there's one bed and breakfast I know about that's not too far from here. And now that I've walked about a mile away from the campus, I high tail it back to the dorm. I have this brilliant idea. As I walk back, I call Lisa from a payphone. Her voicemail is on, so I leave this message announcing that we are living in a most dull environment and what this town needs is real romance, so I tell her to put on her best evening wear-a long gown if she has one- and that I will be walking over to her dorm at nine p.m. to take her out.   I rush into the room and pull out my crazy clothes. The tails jacket, a blue satin cummerbund that Andy had left in the attic, the pince-nez, the Mozart wig, and I put this wild ensemble together and after a few shots of the whiskey I took from

Cory,

I walk over to Lisa's dorm nonplussed and well, perfectly at home in my get-up. The girls giggle at me, and the guys I run into are just smirking their asses off. I'm carrying the pig in its gift wrapped box as I balance the glowing candelabra that rests on top of it. I feel like a weirdo butler of some kind, with the tails jacket and my wig, but what the hell. I get to her dorm and her light is off. I wait around the front doors like an idiot, so I decide to walk over to the side of the building near the emergency exit door and sit on the stoop. The candelabra is still burning and I'm beginning to feel like a complete *baffo*-idiot when I hear this tiny *eeeeeee* ing sound coming from one of the upstairs windows.

I look up and see wisps of long hair sweeping out of view. Now there's all this giggling. There must be about five girls up there looking at me down below. One of them suddenly shouts, "She's coming, Si!" I'm so relieved I practically blow out the candles. I stand up and proceed to walk back to the front doors and my *Lovely* comes out in this incredibly beautiful creamy white gown. It's all shiny. It must be made of satin. And she looks really cool. Well, beautifully cool. She has on elbow length gloves and she has a bunch of flowers woven into her gorgeous hair. I am like, man, I feel like a real bozo with my stupid get up and she's smiling and laughing and there are these other girls standing behind her laughing and pointing at the wig.

I move toward her, the candelabra now becoming an outright fire hazard as the flames are beginning to leap in the air. I tell her to blow them out. That I have a special gift for her. She looks touched. In fact, there's a tear peeking out of the corner of her lovely eye. Well, I better tell her the gift has nothing to do with romance, but maybe it will have some significance in our future. I tell her:

"When you open it later, you'll understand. I ask that you only open it when I'm gone." She gives me a dimpled smile,

"Oh, Si!"

Now I am beginning to think she's going to be a bit disappointed. So I tell her we have a reservation for 10 pm at *The Glass Pheasant*, a restaurant Cory told me about. He said all the girls love this place because there's violin music and of course, candlelight, and the decor is warm and cozy. The food isn't all that great, but it's the place to be romantic.

Especially when you're about to blow town for a year or so. Not that it's a such a big deal to her, but I know I will not be hearing from her. She, of course, doesn't know, but I sure as hell know. So I guess I need to be doing this for my own sentimental reasons. Lisa hands the wrapped box to one of her friends and asks her to put it on her bed.

We walk out, arm in arm, while my other hand carries the candelabra. We walk over to my miserable little car and drive it to the car rental place where I have this pretty nice looking rental car waiting for me. It's new. And it's better than that piece of trash I'm stuck with day in day out. The sales guy is looking at my wig and smiling at Lisa. He asks us if we are going to the prom. Lisa clearly doesn't like the wig; she's hinting that my natural hair is so much better. I pull the thing off. And we drive away. After the restaurant we have a room at the *Lavender Inn*. A far cry from the little homely cabin we shacked up in the one time we slept together. I guess it was ok, when I see it in this light, but I think an improvement is in order. It may very well be the last time we spend together.

I don't go into all the details, and I hint at whether she's going to have a forwarding address and who would have it. She tells me, "Si, I'll give it to you before I leave school. Or I'll just write to you and give it to you then."

I tell her that I will be out at sea. On the rigs. And it gets messy there. Since we are both adamant about not e-mailing, I tell her that the only other choice is to send a letter to the business I'll be working for. From there, I may get her letters.

The violinists are gathering around the table in front of us. It's obviously somebody's anniversary or something. And I immediately recognize the bearded man that was playing in the church the week before. These guys seem to get around. I lean my face next to my Lovely's and ask if I should request her favorite *Nirvana* tune. "Seriously. Is there anything you'd like to hear?"

Her eyes suddenly light up.

"*Somewhere My Love*" from '*Dr. Zhivago*'?!" I vaguely remember the song. Although I had seen the movie. I ask her why she wants to hear that song. Her eyes tear up.

"It reminds me of my grandmother! She loved that song."

Jeez. This is the first time she's mentioned *granny*. The violinists are waltzing toward our table. I tell the bearded guy the song we want to hear and they look very pleased. It must be an old song they rarely perform. In fact, they looked relieved as I request it. I later ask the guys what are the most requested songs; they say, almost in unison, "Disney! All the Disney songs!"   Well, that makes sense.. What else are you going to request, Igor Stravinsky? A little Aaron Copland? A little *Pearl Jam*?

Lisa and I walk arm in arm out into the night air. It must be around 12:30 and we walk along the tree-lined street that runs alongside the park. Lisa wants to walk in the grass. So we take off our shoes and stroll for a while. We decide to drive over to the *Lavender Inn* and right when we get in the car, Lisa starts crying. It comes rather unexpectedly and I want to say: *Why are you putting on the waterworks now, Lisa*? But I don't. I slide next to her and put my arms around her smooth shaking body. I try joking around with her.

"Jeez. Was the food that lousy?"

She slightly lets out one of her *eeeeee*'s and shakes her head. Now she's looking at me.

"Strayhorn! I knew we should've done this all differently". She's sobbing. "And if we just wouldn't have run into each other in the woods that rainy afternoon, then maybe we would've had a chance."

I ask her, "What are you talking about?"

My *Lovely* hoists up her arm and parks it on the dashboard.

She gives me this puzzled look, saying,   "*C'mon!*" as she urges me to put up my arm, too.

I can't help it, I have to laugh.

"It's too late for arm-wrestling, Lisa."

And now she's crying even more.

" I know! I know! And I hate you for getting involved with me! You know why?"

She's now play-punching my chest. Ow! Actually, she's ramming her fist pretty hard. I gently grab her by the sweet wrist and kiss it.

I scold, "Now stop this! You think you're so tough! Tough *Detroit LeatherBabe* ! Well, you're not! You're a pussy willow!"

And I kiss her face all over.

She purrs in my ear; a golden tress tickling my neck. She says, " Si, Will you let me finish what I want to say? Or should I just go?"

I let her talk.

"Well...it's just that...if we would've actually arm-wrestled on it, and agreed that we really shouldn't get too involved, then, I wouldn't be thinking that you're going to do a number on me and leave. We made a mistake. Or at least, *I* did. Men abandon. That's just what guys do. They leave you and forget everything. Like my dad. That's what you're going to do, isn't it?"

Right now, I want to kill Boyce. I do. I must remember to strangle the guy before I leave. What in the hell do I say now?

I sit here frozen a bit and slowly I say, "Lisa, it's not what you think. I need to do something. I can't explain it all to you, but just trust that I will be in contact. I promise."

I'm practically clawing the inside of my hand as I keep my fist clenched. I finally say that I hope she won't freak if I can't really receive anything from her. She blinks her doe eyes at me, a bit baffled as I yak away about how I will constantly be on the go.

"My friend keeps telling me that it's a real rough life out there in the Gulf of Mexico. It's like a removed place in the middle of nowhere. Nobody gets mail."

Lisa's being very quiet. We sit here awhile in the silence. Finally she says, "Doesn't your grandmother still live down there?"

And she's referring to Andy's mother.

I tell her, "Yeah but she's real nuts. She's on all this anti-vertigo medication and rarely steps out of the house. And I don't even know if I am going to visit her. She's real weird. And I don't want her getting on the horn and calling Andy. She'll probably open your letters and read them. And Great Granddad, well, he's ninety-something and I think he's in an old folk's home."

I tell her I will keep her posted and will meet her in Europe somewhere, at Christmas. I'll have a specific place in mind. I'm totally serious about this. So serious, I kiss her and look into her eyes. I start up the engine, telling her that we're getting out of here and going over to the Lavender Inn. Lisa looks at me as if she has something better in mind. She's scratching her arms and chest; she wants to go back to the dorm to change. She wants to put on jeans and go back to the dump we stayed in last time. And she wants to be casual. She's not in the mood for the *Lavander Inn*. She kisses my face as I drive this ridiculous Buick.

She wants to take the rental car back, get in the *gun metal wonder* and go back to the cabins in the woods. Whatever. The radio is blaring this old song, *"Bette Davis Eyes"*. Lisa turns up the volume. I tell her a story Andy told me about Kim Carnes; legend has it that she elected to have her vocal chords surgically scraped to give it that sultry, raspy sound. I turn the corner of my eye toward her to see if she's shuddering, but as usual, she spreads a wide grin. Jeeeeez, she's some weird babe. I love her, but when you think about it, she's weird.

She says, "That's dedication for ya."

I reply, "That's exactly what Andy said."

Lisa looks over at me and says something. I'm too

absorbed in this song to answer her. She's talking about dancing. She pops one of the CD's I brought along with me. Now she wants to go some place where we can open the doors and blast the car speakers so we can dance the night away in our impromptu *prom* gear. I have just the right idea. I drive onto the field on the outskirts of the campus and park the car. We turn the music on full blast and we start dancing around like a couple of idiots. Lisa is swirling around, her hair flying in the moonlight, and I'm leaping around like the biggest goon. But I don't care.

I shimmy and shake as I watch Lisa twirl around like a marionette as she dances in the night air, and some heavy thoughts are hovering over my head; my eyes are tearing because I hate whatever this is inside of me and it must have something to do with the stupid things I allowed myself to believe. At one time or another. Like competitiveness and how important that was to me. I actually relished a time where people lost at my expense. I mean, all of my teachers told me it was about winning at all costs. But at one point, I saw something. It simply wasn't *it* at all. It was why I let myself slide down the scale a bit in high school and I think, basically why I need to get the hell out of here and finally, hopefully, allow myself to dissolve this thing that sits there. Although I don't feel as angry, especially as I once was, at the babes, and all these bothersome, smothering, elusive-as-hell, females in my life, but it is still there. Like a small tumor.

Lisa's looking at me funny. She knows when I'm thinking about something deep. We roll along right into the next tune. And I am relieved to get the other song over with. It's too much. Lisa wiggles her cute little nose to mine, kisses me, and suddenly turns around, prances a foot or so away from me and tail-feathers her satin-draped butt in my face.

Well. I think it's time we get on over to the *Lavender Inn*. I have no interest in returning to that dump with those homely country people. But she sure looks like she's in no hurry, that's for sure. So I snatch her from behind and kiss her neck all over. She's giggling. I spin her around and we decide to do the limbo. You know, like there isn't a worry in the world. Like the moon and stars are shining down just for us, and the silvery glow amid the trees and green fields is a sign of blessing from some indescribably poetic, divine source and that I am not that scrawny childhood self nor the gangly version I am now, but a blessed being of something extraordinarily wondrous, whole and simply wise.

For a moment, I'm slipping into the memory I have of those dreams, of the wisdom that somehow drapes my deformed wakened self like an invisible halo, and she— well, she simply is the basic heaven I seek, and her satin body, as it slides against my fingers, is reminding me of that. And I am going to be leaving her, but we will meet up in a few months. And I will be seeing her, and there's a vague wish I have that somehow, when I do meet up with her, my eyes will be different.

****

I have spent most of my drive back to Connecticut thinking about that last night with Lisa. We danced like fools the entire night before cuddling together in the back seat of the car I had rented. We never made it back to our place in the woods nor to the quaint Lavender Inn.

We fell asleep in each other's arms after dancing all night and in the morning, a campus security guard lightly tapped on the window. We had lunch together one time after that and the night before last, we spent a few hours talking by the grove. Much to her disapproval, I toked a bit on some herb. She declined from smoking and at one point, I trailed off into mystical things. She rolled her eyes a bit as I skirted away from getting into my feelings about leaving, and kept emphasizing how we were going to meet up by the Christmas holidays. I felt like a real idiot the next day, and of course, I hoped she didn't think too much about my poor choice in smoking the grass. I was just so damned nervous.

My last meeting with Boyce was a bit atypical. He spared me the African ritual mask and drum as we convened in the private garden in back of his office. He thought that would be a pleasant way to end things for now. He made it clear that everything he recommended in the letter were suggestions; that I was free to do what I wished. Boyce reassured me that he only wants me to do what I originally wanted to do for myself and putting too much energy into Lisa would divert that. Okay, I nodded, trying not to stare at Boyce who was dressed as if he were going on a picnic rather than having a session with me. So we agreed that I would keep journals and not involve Lisa in this. Whatever. The way I am feeling right now, I really don't care. I talked about doing this for so long that I simply don't care anymore.

I pull into the driveway of the house where I grew up. It's an old cream and blue Italianate Victorian with charming shutters and huge windows. There are flowers everywhere and the trees in front are sprouting green all over the place. Andy's vintage Mercedes is in the driveway. Of course, I am not ready for any of this. I've got all my stuff from school crammed in the back and I have to unload and re-pack by Sunday afternoon. I aim to keep the mouth shut and basically stay stupid during this visit.

Here he is. Coming out of the front door, squinting his eyes at me. He grins. And every resolve I've made is beginning to melt. I actually want to strangle him. Boyce said that this is to be expected, with all the stuff we talked about. So I plaster a fake smile back and wave like a fool. He eyes my car as I lumber out of the thing. "Simon! You made it!" He looks at me and says, "I'm going to have my mechanic look that over before you go. It's on me!"

Oh, yeah, with some of the money I forked over to you? Boyce is right. I've been overprotected most of my life. I'm basically embarrassed. Andy. Andy being chum-chummy. He's throwing his arms around me. I try my best not to flinch. I honestly can't deal with this. During my last session, I told Boyce that I look forward to the day I sock the guy in the jaw for not telling me what it is in him that makes him a completely paralyzed eunuch sitting in his tree house for nearly all the years I grew up. And here he is, congratulating me.

"3.7! Well, that's more like it, Simon."

I'm trying my best not to sneer. So I busy myself with fishing my things out of the backseat and I try to distract myself from the image I'm entertaining of Andy laying flat out cold on the sidewalk. I'm fussing with these boxes and smile at the memory of my last chat with Boyce. He kept grinning and gnawing on the pipe clenched in his teeth out there in our sunny session. The only comic relief I had at that moment was noticing how white his legs looked. Since it was hot, he had on a pair of huaraches or whatever you call those things and some madras Bermuda shorts. He slapped me on the back as I stared, and said: *You'll be seeing things differently. That's my hunch. You're doing the right thing.*

I am holding onto these words as Andy is talking about the goings on at his firm. He's saying something about an article *Architectural Form & Leisure* is doing on his work. Andy chimes, "They're featuring our work on the Burlington Museum restoration, and a complete profile on Clive Rodgers, Biff Mulhew and Andy Strayhorn. Ever heard of those guys?!"

Ha-Ha-Ha. Aren't we droll, now?

Andy continues, "... I was so nervous I ended up walking up to the roof, forgetting they needed a photograph of the three of us. They had to come get me. Reminded me of when I first stopped drinking. I was scared of everything."

"*Still are.* " I mutter under my breath as I heave the stuff into his bony hands. I know he's going to say it. Soon as he's through bragging about the magazine spread. He's going to say it right now.

"I know you want to spend some time with Caz, but I want you to come over to the house tomorrow night".

See!

Andy continues, as he wipes his brow: "We'll drive into Westport and have dinner and I'll show you the spreads. Just so happens I wouldn't have been able to go to Italy anyway, because I'm absolutely swamped with this project. You should see what we're doing, Simon. It is some job. But we've got to talk, son, about this oil rig business. Those guys are going to..."

Boyce is now in my head, taking over. I want to start

arguing, but the looming ghost of Boyce is telling me to *shut up*. To let him talk. And I do. He's saying all this stuff about the competition to get out there on the rigs in the first place. That they are union-controlled, and very tough to work with. Very seniority-oriented.

"...the money is pretty good! People fight for those jobs. It's your business, son, but be flexible."

I want to blurt out: *then why did you fine me*? *You know I need that money*! But I don't. All the more reason for me to punch him out. I mean, why the hell not?

"Where's Caz, Dad?"

"She's with your mother and Gram. They went shopping."

"Good."

I spin around and punch him in the jaw. He snatches my hand and stares at me with those coal black eyes. Which are now tearing. He's holding my arm in the air as he clenches his teeth at me.

"I don't want you to leave school next year. Okay? A semester, fine. But not two. It's stupid, Simon, and you punch me like that again I'll punch you back. I don't know what's going on with you, and maybe you're pissed at me for a lot of things, but I'm not a normal man. You understand me? If I'm not what your idea is of what a father should be, I can't do anything about it. Sometimes I think it takes all my energy just to drive into New York everyday and hash out a living."

I can't believe what he's saying. After all that bragging. He's trying to pull off this bs?

Andy continues, " My father was a loser! A stupid, loser-nothing, and I spent my high school and college years studying my ass off so I wouldn't end up an oaf like him. It's all I have. My brains. A little talent. That's it! You're going away. I say, *fine*. I just hope you don't blow it, like I almost did."

Andy spins on his heel and walks back up to the house, rubbing his jaw. I'm completely shocked at what the man just told me. I don't know what to do exactly. I had never done this before and I am trying to understand why I did this. Andy knows I'm thinking about something, but he's not saying it. He's not saying what it really is. I leap up the front steps and find him in the kitchen opening a can of soda. He's shaking his head. And I know he's going to start apologizing. Here he goes!

" I must really need a...*meeting*. I'm sorry if I tick you off. But if I didn't ask you to take some responsibility I'd regret it later."

I clench my fists, ready to land one in the wall.

"No, no, Dad. That doesn't sound like it to me. Unless you're going to let out the real truth of what's going on with you and what's been sitting inside of you all of your life. Because, you know something? Somehow, I'm in on it. I've been in on it probably more than you are for all of *my* life! And when you find out what it is I have of yours that I am walking around with, then let me know. Until then, I'm here to get my things, see Caz, have fun at the party and not reduce myself to begging you to give the money back to me."

My knees are trembling like crazy as I say this. And for a minute, I feel like I'm going to vomit. I have never spoken to Andy like this in my entire life and my mouth is beginning to feel like a wad of cotton is hanging out of it. Andy is still standing at the sink with his back to me.

And he starts to speak, "Simon, okay. I'm not going to do it. It isn't worth it. I just don't want you to drift around. I'll put the money back into your account on

175

Monday."

I can hardly believe my ears. He's gathering his things off the kitchen table and grabbing his keys. He's actually leaving.

He says, "As for this crazy bullshit you're talking about, I think you *do* need to get away. What in the hell are you talking about? This crazy stuff?"

He's staring right at me, with this incredulous look on his face. This is pretty amazing. The man doesn't have a clue as to what I am talking about. But it sure is pissing him off! His nostrils are flaring. And I want to laugh. I really do. It's useless. Totally and completely a waste of my time!

"Dad! Wait!" I run after him as he saunters out the door.

I'm feeling sorry for this miserable...

"Dad!"

He stops at his car and turns around. I tell him I'm sorry. That I'm not thinking too clearly. He bends down and proceeds to toss his stuff into the backseat.

"You gotta good punch, Si. A lot of men would say that's a good thing, and I suppose if it weren't me that you chopped, well, maybe I'd agree with them. As far as your spiel on...*carrying* my whatever you call it, do yourself a favor. Don't!"

And with that he slides into the car, politely shuts the door, and starts up the engine. I knock my knuckles on the glass. He rolls the window down without looking at me.

I lean my face toward his, "Dad, I'm sorry. I hope this doesn't mean you're going to drink, Dad."

He shakes his head and grins without turning to look at me. " Simon. I have my days of feeling like a drink, but for fifteen years, I haven't. I have my moments and they pass. That's not something I ever want you to fret over. It's my responsibility. It's the thing *I* carry. And it's not yours. It never was, it never will be. I'll be back tonight to see you and Sis. I have to go now, son."

And with that he rolls up the window and puts the car in reverse. There he goes, right down the drive, and I am standing here baffled. Completely stumped. For a moment, I want to crack open a couple of brews myself. *Jeeez*. I'm not handling this well. In fact, I'm leaving tomorrow morning. At the crack of dawn. And I don't know what I'm feeling right now. I want to give Boyce a call and tell him about it, and now that I'm thinking of the absurdity of this whole *agreement* thing I made with the guy, I think I'm beginning to see what that old balding gizzard is talking about. *"Be careful in confronting him. He seems to be good at shutting things out. Maybe because he needs to bar certain things from himself."*

****

I walk upstairs to my old bedroom with my new notebook and start writing. It looks like my trip has begun. I am scribbling away in my little schoolboy notebook, when I hear a couple of car doors slam. I peek out of the window and recognize the three figures below. My ladies have arrived. Time to put the plaster-smile back on and proceed with the show. You can hear Gram a mile away. She's ranting about the prices they just paid for the usual junk they buy every week at the mall. Detestable environments, malls. Already I hear Layla Caspian running up the stairs. She shouts, "He's here!" And Gram is saying something about Andy and me going off for lunch or something. That's why he was waiting for me here at the house. Oh, well. I run to meet Caz at the top of the stairs. I can hardly believe my eyes. She is such a cute girl. I love Caz. She has on these real baggy pants and her black hair is a stringy mess. But she is a lot thinner.

I race down the old wooden stairs and hug her. Gram and Nancy are beaming at the bottom of the stairs. Gram strokes my back, "Better have one of those for me, you rascal!"

I try not to roll my eyes at the old woman in my vintage: *U-2: ' Rattle & Hum,' The World Tour* T-shirt. But when I glance down at the faux leopard-skin leggings and the way her frosted pink toes slightly hang out of her gold-toned sandals, I can't help but smile.

"Gram!" I put my arms around her while my mom shakes her head at me. She walks over to me and strokes my long hair.

"Look at you!" And I hug her, too.

I can't wait to get this bullshit out of the way and quietly get the hell out of here. So I grin and beam back at them. Gram immediately starts talking about the melting ice-cream and that she always has that problem when she shops at the neighborhood market whereas if she would've gone to the other place, she would not have had that problem.

She tells us: "They just have betta refrigeration thaya."

Caz and I look like we're about to laugh but we contain ourselves. Immediately, Caz wants to go for a spin and stop at the coffeehouse downtown. Gram gets all excited and tells us about all the stuff she bought so we could have some coffee and food here at the house. She

178

looks at us as if we're crazy. "We jus got here!"

Caz and I file into the living room and sit on the couch while Nancy and Gram chat away about the goings on in the neighborhood. Mrs. Crawford was found dead in her cell at the women's state penitentiary. The relatives pitched in, helping the kids get out of town and sold the house. The old trampoline, along with other items, were auctioned off.

Gram informs us, "It was a reeel mess. I tell ya, that family is doomed. The eldest son is —what does he have, Nancy? *Lupis*? No, it's sum obscure bone disorder and he's constantly in the hospital. And he's what? Twenty-three. Now ain't that somethin'? The girl, she run off with that—Mr. well, he's an executive living in Westport—and he must be forty-somthin'. The whole family...*shambles*. I tell ya, I haven't seen a family fall apart as much as Bubba Randall's kin back in Hunstville. Now that was somthin'."

The woman never shuts up. Now she's telling us about this Bubba character. "...He then went over thaya to this shabby nuthouse outside of Montgomry and they were all havin' themselves a social occasion of sum kind. Can yew imagine? A buncha nuts havin' a *social* ? And there she was....yung *Velma Rose*. In this greasy make-up I suppose the orderlies and such let 'em play with. Her lipstick wuz all wrong. A crookcd line in some ghastly plum wine cullah runnin' down clear to her chin and she was standin' next to this gurl with long, frizzy black hayer that jus covered her face completely, and all she did was inch reeeeel slow up the floor holdin onto a raggedy fake mink stole like it wuz the last thing on earth she possessed. And there wuz one lady—she must've been from way out thaya in the country; we awe talkin' *sticks*, hunny. In fact, she wuz from Acadiana down thaya in Luweeziana. A French speakin' woman. She kept swayin' her hips back 'n forth while she clutched onto this very Cathlic—I mean only a Cathlic culda possessed such a ghastly lookin' crucifix cuz it had a Jesus that was just too real lookin'. I mean nuthin spared with the details and I swear, aftah Bubba found Velma thaya with all these crazy people he never wuz the same. "

We all nervously laugh. I say, " Wow! Are we done, Gram? Can we talk about something more *up beat*?"

Gram continues, "Well. I jus' wantchew to know what goes on in those places, Layla, hunny! The thought of us ever sendin' yew to sumthin' ghastly like that place!"

Caz's name is *Layla Caspian*. Andy named her after this Eric Clapton song and the Caspian Sea. None of us knows why he named her this. Anyway, everyone calls Caz *Layla* except for moi. My mother shakes her head at Gram.

"Okay, Momma. We said we weren't going to go into any of that today. It's Layla's 16th birthday and we are going to keep things simple. "

My mother is a beautiful woman. Slim, auburn-haired-which is still past her shoulders-she's a stark contrast to Gram, I mean, she's got style, something Gram is clearly without. Caz stares at her lap. She looks mawkish and depressed. Now she's picking at the lint in her shirt and biting her lip. I lean over to her and tell her that in a few minutes, we'll take a spin and check out CD's at the music store. That I want her to pick out what she wants. She smiles up at me and for a second I freeze. She looks glassy-eyed and afraid. I have no idea what is going on with all this and I'm starting to fidget with my jeans' pockets while Gram and Nancy get into another one of their arguments. Gram announces: "Kids! We have some Swiss cheese—git that ham out now, so the kids can have sum, honey!"

Gram struggles out of the *Lazyboy*. All 250 pounds of her, and I reach my hand out to pull her up. Caz giggles. And for a minute, I'm relieved. She's scaring the hell out of me. My mother is bringing in trays of food and politely, I grab a couple of the sandwiches. I feel that if I stay too much longer, Gram is going to launch a grand inquisition. Nancy passes the tray to Caz and she grabs a couple of the sandwiches, too.

My mom asks: "Where's your father, Simon? Wasn't he here to greet you?"

A fog settles over my thoughts, but I tell her, "Yeah, he had some things to do. So, I don't know."

Gram pitches in, "Call him, Nancy. I can't imagine why he would jus not be here to have some lunch with the kids. Now what on earth does that man have to do when his son is here for only a short while and he knows..." She looks right over at me. "Goin' away, arencha?"

But Nancy interferes, "Momma, we aren't going to start asking all those questions. Si just got here. We'll chat about that later."

The room suddenly falls silent and we're all munching away like a bunch of strangers. Actually, if you ask me, we are like random people in a diner when you think about it. I have about as much in common with Gram as I do with the mail man or something. As usual, all of the windows are open and a mild breeze is running through the house. Andy had given them a lecture some years ago about the dangers of Freon in air-conditioning, so the house is natural now. Natural and hot. Suddenly, we all perk our ears to the sound of a truck pulling up in the driveway and another car pulling up in front. It sounds like a diesel engine. It's Andy, alright. And he's stepping into the atrium.

"Nancy? Kids? I have my friend from the service station here. He's going to look over Simon's car. We're out front, okay?"

He quietly shuts the front door. He's a real trip. Full of surprises, old Andy is. Nancy and Gram look at me.

"Something wrong with the car, Simon?"

This is so achingly boring.

"No, Ma. He offered to have it checked out before I hit the road. He's paying for it. What am I going to say?"

I get up and walk out of the house. Andy and the mechanic are looking over the insides of my car, beads of sweat emitting from the foreheads of both of them. Andy is telling the guy a joke and while the mechanic pokes his hairy fingers in the carburetor, he spreads a wide grin. Andy. He's really something else. You'd think nothing on earth happened an hour or so ago. I smile. I really do. The guy is too much.

"Dad! I thought you gave up on me!"

Andy's head is still stuck under the hood.

"Now, son, would I do something like that?"

He looks up at me, smiling like a cheetah. I dunno. I want to like the way the guy just gets it out his system and resumes to normal speed. He's just fussing away under that hood like it's the most important task of his life. I ask,

"So Pap was an oaf, huh?"

And he quickly replies,

"Oh, yeah. A dense fool. But he was my dad. What

can I say?"

I shrug the shoulders. I ask:

"Was that Great Granddad's fault?"

Andy quips: "He wasn't around. I think it might have been that and the fact that my grandmother's money ran out. Yeah. Great Granddad was shacking up with the psychiatrist at that time. Park Avenue office and everything."

The mechanic tells my dad something, as he points his beefy fingers at the insides of the car. Andy's head pops up,

"You need new hoses, and a belt. He's also going to give you a tune-up. He's going to haul it in. He has the truck. Or do you want to drive it there?"

I shake my head and have the guy haul it in.

"I'm going to take Caz for a spin in Gram's car. Is that okay with you?"

Andy looks very relieved. And so am I. It doesn't interest me to probe his head anymore. It's a waste of time. We'll just keep it down to the level of "how 'bout them '*Mets*?" or in Andy's case, "how 'bout that *Temple of Dandur* over there in the Metropolitan Museum?"

****

Later in the car, I try to get Caz to speak as we drive around the old neighborhood looking for things to do other than our trip to the record store. She just doesn't feel like the old Caz to me at all and I can't roll with it. I don't know what it is. I can only ask her questions as she stares out of the window bobbing her head to the radio. Finally, I abruptly stop the car by the old park we used to play in as kids. I turn directly to her and point-blank ask her,

"Who is he? And what did he do to you?"

I remind her that I'm not Gram or Mom. That I am not Andy or the school principal. She just stares at me lifeless. And rolls her eyes.

"It's not really him. It's me. He's just a guy."

I continue, "And he's in college. How old is this guy?"

"Twenty-one."

"Jeez. Caz! That's a five-year age difference! I don't even hang around guys that age. Or women! I can't even handle the nineteen-year olds."

Caz emits the first smile I've seen on her face since we left the house a half-hour ago. But it soon vanishes and the old silent-number returns. She's definitely not telling me much. Finally, I ask,

"What's this stuff I've been hearing about you and drugs?"

Caz shrugs her shoulders: "The school said my behavior was screwy so they sent me for this psychiatric evaluation. At first, they thought I was into drugs. I am not into drugs, Simon. Some girls down the hall from me planted some stuff in my room because they think I'm weird. Well, I'm not weird. They were just jealous of me and him."

I lean over: "Does he have a name? And can I please have your permission to give him a hard time when I'm down there in Virginia?"

Caz immediately becomes defensive, " Don't be an idiot, Si. He's a lot bigger than you. About five inches taller, actually. He's a major basketball player for the school. He'd cream you! Besides, I'm the one who got myself involved."

I then tell her that that is complete bullshit. That he knew better. Still, she remains silent. She will not go into it with me. Finally, I ask her if she got pregnant. And she swiftly shakes her head. Okay. Then why all the sulky behavior? Why the weight loss and unkempt appearance. She shrugs her shoulders. The relationship is over because everyone stepped in and ended it. So now she wants to just forget about it. Okay. Well, I am out of here. Boyce is right. I have to just let the family do for themselves. Including Caz. But I'm worried about her.

"Caz. What's going on?"

She just stares at me and nervously starts fidgeting with her shirt and rolls her eyes and fixes her gaze on the floor of the car . Tears begin to pool. This doesn't throw me. "What really happened while you were at school, Caz?"

She won't tell me. She just bows her head down and cries into her oversized T-shirt. And they're giving her a party? Are they crazy?

"Caz. Do you really feel like a party tonight? Do you really want it? Or are you just going along with it because of Gram and Mom?"

She blurts out, "You're here! I don't care, Si. What am I going to do? Ask them to drive me to the psych ward? Gram's basically right, you know. They treat people like drivel in those places. They just give you drugs."

And I tell her, "Well, you know, in some circles, Caz, that wouldn't sound like such a bad idea!"

We both laugh a bit. I lean over and give her a hug and brush her back with my paws. I want to tell her to see a shrink. I even want to tell her that I'm doing that, but I veer away. It hurts to do this. It really does, because I want to help her out. But I can't do this. No involvement. Not right now anyway.

"Caz, go talk to somebody about all this. Just get it all out of your system."

She bobs her head and sniffles. I spend the rest of the afternoon cracking jokes, laughing about the old days and she seems better spirited. We go to the record store and what does she want but *The Smashing Pumpkins' 'Mellon Collie and the Infinite Sadness*'? Whatever.

We return to the house and Andy, Gram and my mom are decorating and cleaning everything out for the party. We pitch in and decorate the tables and help Gram in the kitchen. By 8 p.m. the place looks spectacular. A lot of the kids we grew up with are beginning to show up, many home from college like me. And they're all asking me about the fancy school I attend and what my major is and crap like that. Andy brought along his collection of dance music. Mostly R&B stuff and some favorites of Caz. She happens to like a lot of the music Andy likes and beams when he gives her all this collectors' item stuff. Old LPs of R&B cats like Clarence 'Frogman" Henry, a famous 50's crooner from New Orleans. The whole time we've been back at the house, Andy has been upbeat and unusually relaxed. I find this weird. But I ignore it as best as I can and busy myself with chatting with my old friends. Every now and again I look over to Caz who is all dressed now and looking pretty amazingly good compared to the crumpled mess she was back in the car. As the night grows dark, I begin to think about the strangeness of it all.

I quietly sneak upstairs while the party becomes fuller and as more guests-mostly Caz's old friends-arrive. While they're calling everybody to sing *Happy Birthday*, I quietly slide back into the room. I stand here in the corner singing and watching them, and I love watching the room grow dark and the glowing candles standing there on the cake. And I really am wishing my sister a happy birthday, but I also say something to myself at this moment, and that I would remember to fetch the Luger up there in the attic and remember to hide it in a rolled-up sleeping bag or something and sneak it into the car by morning. That I have to at least try to find Great Granddad. Even if he has half-blown eardrums, and tubes running out of his major orifices, I don't care. I must try to do this before he croaks, and hopefully, that won't take place until after I see him. And I'm becoming so emotional that I have to go outside. I'm relieved that everybody is gathering around Caz with all these terrifically wrapped presents and I take the opportunity to escape while I wouldn't be noticed.

I walk out into the yard in back of our house and stroll around the carefully planted garden my mother and Gram have worked on for years. It's a lush wonder of flowers, shrubs and massive trees. As a kid I used to spend a lot of time back here mulling in my head and usually climbing the huge oak tree where I actually once had a tree house. I climb it and sit up here for a while watching everyone through the picture window that Andy insisted on installing years ago so we could enjoy the garden more.

They're all passing the opened gifts around and laughing and Caz seems pretty happy. People got her clothes, CD's, handbags, jewelry. I can hear some of the guys saying: "Where's Si?" "What happened to Si?" And I'm enjoying watching them looking around the room. But my sister, Andy , Gram and Nancy look oblivious as Caz opens another box of goodies. I avert my eyes to the night sky and observe the stars. They always seem to shimmer more brightly in summer. I want to lose myself in them. I lean back on the huge branch and muse at the night sky remembering growing up here and the tranquil feeling of just being right with the world. That the world was good and simple.

The music has started up again and I suppose everyone is dancing. They seem to be having a good time without me, and I say that's just fine with me. I have important things to think about. It's dark and warm out here, and I feel at home. I remember that I have a stash of herb in my room and I have this crazy desire to go over to the playground across the street and get high. I crawl down from the tree and walk back into the house. As I pass through the living room, I notice that the few friends that I invited are dancing with some of Caz's friends, and I swiftly weave my way through the crowd and leap up the stairs to my room. I grab my stuff and head out of the front door, cross the street and walk to the cluster of trees near the swing sets. I only take a couple of hits because I know this stuff is potent. Within a few minutes I'm floating around in my head. Hello, *floaters*... what are you going to bring me tonight?

I feel around on the ground for a comfortable spot to sit. And I plunk myself hard on the grass, and already, I'm feeling an amplification of everything bouncing around in my head. For a second, it feels like this might not have been a very good idea because I immediately focus on the talk I had earlier with Caz. Waves of black dread encircle me. I'm bummed. The glassy-eyed look on Caz' face in the living room when we were all sitting there. The fear that rose up in me. I want to divert my thoughts and think on more pleasant things, but I am not able to pry myself away from these thoughts around Caz. That she's not safe. I remember to focus my attention on something outside myself, my head, and I stare out at the trees, the jungle gym, the swing sets, the garbage cans, anything to divert my fixation on these morbid thoughts, but nothing seems to work. I must be nuts. It's probably something Casteneda's *Don Juan* would say is an example of my *folly* . It doesn't work here. There's too much tension. I should've known. But I'm high. I decide to get up and walk around. My sense of time is getting screwed up. I feel it. I walk and walk and it seems like every thing's in slow-motion. I have no real idea what exactly is in this stuff, but it's scaring me a bit. I run over to the merry-go-round and I spin the thing around. This amuses me, so I continue to whirl the thing like crazy. Of course, it isn't even occurring to me that the neighbors could be watching.

There must be some suburban goon out here walking his dog. *Blind-man's-bluff.* For a second, I'm remembering that dream I had of being at what seemed like a children's party and there were all these people from my life and my God, was that a premonition...look at where I am ? And what was it that happened in the dream at the end before Cory's unnerving voice jolted me out of bed? Oh...my. .gosh.. I was trying to find my way around the people in my life and I ended up falling into a ravine, a ditch, a pit. Well, heck. What the heck? Huh? Story of my life, that one, a lifetime of being in the dark and falling into pits and ravines, and Andy. Andy. Always Andy. And something is touching my back.

"Jesus Christ!" I hear myself shout.

I turn around and Andy is standing there talking to me.

"Simon! What are you doing out here? Something wrong with your hearing?"

For a second, I want to say, *No asshole, I'm stoned.* But a calmness inside of me tells me to shut up. Andy has never seen me stoned, drunk, tipsy, unnerved, unbal-anced, un-cooperative, unwilling, non-compliant (except for maybe this afternoon and a couple of other rare instances). I'm a *goody-goody-two-shoes* in front of this guy. Why? Because, deep down, I'm never so sure that he will lose it and do something stupid. All those years where I had eavesdropped on the hen-sessions coming from the kitchen where Nancy and Gram would congregate night after night has made its mark on my brain. And now he's talking. Actually, yacking away. I bob my head and shrug the shoulders. I honestly don't know what to do. I feel if I talk, my words will come out in slow motion. He asks me to sit next to him on a bench.

He says: "I gave some things a lot of thought this afternoon. Maybe I haven't been fair with you."

The guy has no idea that I am stoned. No clue.

Andy continues: "But I want you to know that I hope you make a lot of money down there, and get over to Europe. It's a good idea, Si. I know you don't want to drop out. I hope you have everything in order with the school."

I'm bobbing my head like a puppet or something. Andy tells me about his travels and how he had the same desires. That it did him a lot of good when he did those trips. He wants to show me that he is my dad and that he cares about me. It really is all the guy knows how to do. As he talks, I'm beginning to gain more clarity. I'm not feeling as I did before and some of the reverberation in my head has quieted down. I think my high is wearing off. And I'm relieved.

Andy gets up to arch and stretch his long lean body. I rise from the bench and as I'm about to say something, he swings his arm in my direction and punches me right in the jaw. I'm stunned. I don't know whether to burst out crying from the sheer unexpected shock of it or crack up laughing. Andy's black hair is flying in his face, and for a second I notice a slight smile beginning to formulate there.

"That's for this afternoon! I grew up in the *Fauberg* before it became hip. Believe me, I know how to fight. When you feel like it, come have some birthday cake."

With that, Andy briskly struts down the pathway and back over to the house.

I walk down the block rubbing my jaw. Somewhere in a back corner of my head I hear old Boyce tapping his pipe-stem, leaning forward, giving me the old eagle-eye, saying something like: *Sounds like he's getting ready to tell you something. But let him feel it out first. That, of course, could take months, maybe years. He might be slow with this sort of thing. Things we'd rather forget.*

****

When I walk back inside the house I remember this is the perfect time to go to the attic while everyone seems to be at the height of having a good time. I leap up the three flights of stairs and enter the stuffy old room. All of our toys are up here. A rocking horse, game sets, dolls, books and records, my drum set, and in the far end, near the front attic window, sits the cedar chest. I open it and it is filled with lace things, blankets, a couple of table clothes and there at the bottom lies the ancient Luger. I had noticed it before many years ago. I have no idea why Nancy kept it. But I always suspected that my dad hasn't the foggiest that it's been tucked away in here all these years. Weird. I nervously wrap it in one of the linen napkins and stealthily walk back to my bedroom and quietly shut the door. The thing is ancient. It feels heavy with age. I'm trembling as I slide it between the folds of the sleeping bag . As soon as I do this, I get this insane idea to go into Caz's room and look around. For what, I'm not certain.

I gently walk back down the hall and into her little room. It's filled with boxes and paraphernalia, I would assume, from school. I check out her desk area for clues as to the *Mystery Guy* and I dig through some letters and notes lying in a small box by her bed. A small note slips out of the fray and gets my attention. In a scrawled hand, it reads, *"Layla, I want you to remember, if I had to do it again, I would. You're worth it. You were great the other night. And , again, I'm sorry for all the interruptions the time before. If I have to escape from this place to see you, I will. You're the best! Wishing I were there with you, and you know I'd tell you to break. a....oh-no...any-*thing but *that*, right? *I wish curses on no one. Especially you, Beautiful! ! Affectionately, Jeff "*

Well. Okay. The name *Jeffrey A. Dabney* is embossed at the top of the note.... *"Escape from this place"*...Guy must be married or something. Either that or he's in prison...hmm... *"you were great last night."* Jeez, that really irks me. Well, I'm sure I can find out some more info on this big guy. *Big hunk* with the fancy stationery. I lift some papers, looking for an address book, something, and hearing someone walking in the hallway, I grab a small stack of notebooks and papers, along with the note and quietly tiptoe over to the door.

I peek out of the tiny opening and notice this kid stepping out of my room. It's one of Caz's friends. Noah...something. I stop him as he approaches the top of the stairway. " What's up?" He turns around and grins, " Hey, where's Caz?" I ask him, "What were you doin' in my room, Noah?"

He grins a bit wider. "Nuthin', man. I got confused. I just went in there for a second and I noticed all your things. Sorry".

He looks down at me, and points to the stuff I'm carrying.

"What's up with all that? Weren't you in Layla's room?"

I politely tell him to shut up and mind his own business and watch as he struts down the stairs. I quickly run back to my room and tuck the stuff I took from Caz's in one of my suitcases. I'm boiling in here. I run to the bathroom and throw water on my face. I lay back on the bed and prepare my head to go downstairs and clamp on the social front. As much as I don't want to, I must. I have to act like everything is peachy cool. As I walk down the creaky stairs, the music is starting up again.

They're now playing this old song, *"Ain't Got a Home"* by the *Frogman* guy, Clarence Henry. I walk into the crowd-filled living room and sneak up on Andy and Caz who are dancing together. My mother taps me on the shoulder and joins in. Andy glances at my face, and leans over to me,

"Go put some ice on that. It's still red."

His eyes spark up a bit as he says this. I smile. This is so weird. I just have to laugh. My mom is dancing with me again and she's trying to tell me something. I lean closer to her, but she waves me off. I then move in closer and ask her,

"Does my face look ok to you?" She gives me a blank stare, "Of course! What are you talking about?" I again ask, "Is there any red there? You know, like someone chopped me?"

She spins and looks closer at my mug, shaking her head, "Si, what in the world are you talking about?"

I look up and Andy is swiveling his hips, staring straight at me- a strand of hair hanging in his face- grinning, naturally. That demon! Andy and Caz are playing all of their favorite oldies songs tonight. She's the birthday gal, alright. Andy's spinning around like it's nobody's business. I want to stick my leg out and trip the guy on his butt. I'm about take a few steps over there and shove him on his ass, but I hold myself back. It would absolutely ruin the party and I think Andy might break out into an unexpected rage. I dunno. It scares me. Let him win. You know? Let it go. I dance around a bit to the next tune, *"Fortune Teller"*, and tell myself that I am going to tell everyone goodnight, go upstairs and shower and quietly slip into bed. No scenes. No talks afterwards. No chitchat about everybody from the old neighborhood. I'm just tired, dead tired.

When I get back to my old room, I lock the door and pull out the Luger. I just want to hold the thing and look at it. Great Granddad supposedly brought this over with him from Scotland when he was a young guy; he lugged the thing all over the country. Out west. Down south. It's about all I know. Somehow Andy's father got it and later it was given to Andy or maybe Andy just took the thing. They're still dancing down there. I can hear them bopping around to Lee Dorsey's "*Ya Ya*". I put the gun on the bed and hide it under a pillow while I look through my notebook that lists the information I've gathered about Great Granddad. I have a number of addresses and the names of some of his doctors. I have no real idea if he's in some nursing home or in a hospital. I only know that he is still alive. At least as of last week. With old goats like Great Granddad, you just don't know when they're going to finally keel over. I put the gun back into the folds of the sleeping bag, take a shower, climb back into bed and spread the maps and travel books on my lap. I look through my stuff and notice the house is quieting down now. In fact, I can only faintly hear the music.

It's about twelve-thirty in the morning. I guess the rockers have fizzled out. Soon, they'll be wondering where I am. I toss my stuff on the floor and click the lamp off. The lights from the backyard are shining through my window and I can hear Andy and Caz talking. He's telling her goodnight and talking with Gram and Nancy as he walks out to the driveway. I can hear him saying that I must be upstairs sleeping. It's weird when you hear your parents talking about you.

I leap out of bed and grab the electric fan I have stored in the closet. I plug it in and nestle back into bed. My mind is reeling; perhaps the droning sound of the fan will lull me to sleep.

****

You could say I stole away in the night like a thief, which I did. I couldn't handle it anymore. Instead of cleverly weaving my way out of staying with Andy a few nights ago, Caz finagled on me. This guy she used to know stopped by the house and she ended up staying out with him and some other kids from the neighborhood. We spent the next day, Friday, driving around, talking and eating lunch at some lousy fast food place in the mall. I managed to jot down some information from Caz's address book. At least, I got Dabney's address. I couldn't seem to find much else in the way of evidence. But that note irked me. Guy's probably married. All these inferences about him wanting to get away, and crap like that. Anyway, I put all the stuff back, but I did help myself to a couple of the notebooks. They looked practically new and I figured she wouldn't be any worse off without them.

Andy and I did end up going to dinner in Westport and later at his house, I noticed the drawings for the Burlington Museum renovation project spread over several areas of his living room. Andy showed me some of the details and actually, I found them fascinating. Luckily, we talked about his work and his concern about my being away and stuff like that.   We even laughed a bit about the party and we both seemed to be polite around the fact that we both took a whack at each other. There was nothing said about it and we both acted like nothing ever happened. Of course!

I woke up around five this morning. I simply had to get on the road. I've been driving like a lunatic ever since. I have only stopped for gas, the bathroom, fast food, and it's a basically drive in-and-out-back-onto-the-road routine. I have been driving like this for about twelve hours. There are empty to-go coffee cups all over the floor of my car. I'm about to leave the state of Maryland. And I feel so incredibly good to see this motel sign. I pull into the dumpy motel parking lot and pay for

a room. This is a trucker-type place and the only thing to
do here is crash. I drive the car over to the room and flop
my things on the bed.

After settling down, I dial into the 'Net and I have
about three e-mails waiting for me. One is from Caz. I
never really thought about this. The fact that there are
going to be e-mails to deal with. I must think of a way
to tell Caz that I did not bring my computer. Or that I did
something with it. The next e-mail is from the Derbigny
Clinic in New Orleans. They're telling me that Great
Granddad was last there in April, and that he only has a
P.O. box. He never discloses his home address, although,
according to some older records from a few years ago,
there is an address for him on Dumaine Street. I make a
note of all this and check the next item. It's a letter from
Les. I'm relieved and immediately I plug in and write to
him. I jokingly tell him about my crazy and frantic drive
out of New England and kid with him about his whereabouts and Pony, his girlfriend.

For a minute I want to say some stuff about Lisa, but
I don't. I want her here, damn it. I want her here in this
depressing motel room. I decide to nap for a while and
wind up sleeping like I'm about to croak. It's the kind of
sleep where you can hear all this commotion going on,
people slamming doors, people coughing in the next
room, cars starting off, and you're still completely dead-
weighted from complete exhaustion. There are no
dreams, except the nervous flickering of images bouncing around. An incomprehensible jumble of things best
left to the realms of oblivion.

I drowsily notice a faint indication of blue sky showing through the upper window. For a minute, I think that
maybe I had slept only a couple of hours, so I close my

eyes again. After a few minutes, my eyes are wide open. I look at the electric clock buzzing next to my ear. It's 6 am! The last time I checked the clock it was four-thirty in the afternoon! I jump out of bed, ready to drive another ten hours. I leap into the shower, dress, pack up everything and head out the door again. I step out into the parking lot and do a double take on my car. It's obvious someone rammed into it. Of course, I'm infuriated. I know this kinda garbage is bound to happen here and there, but this soon! I put my things in the car, and calmly walk over to the jerk sitting behind the desk.

He's a youngish Asian guy with an inscrutable air about him. Well, Mr. *Inscrutab*le shrugs and finally shakes his head and says, rather stoically, "Probably happened late last night or something. You can check the lot, but we have a pretty full house."

I walk back over to the car and re-examine it. It isn't all that bad. The back fender is pretty badly mangled, but I can still open the trunk ok. It's just a drag. I want to say that this is in no way an omen, but I can't help but feel that it is. I take out my notebook and scribble in it as the first thing in my entry for that day. I head out and grab a few things at a store to eat on the way. Of course, I drown down about three cups of coffee in the car as I sit reading these crazy maps. In about an hour, I'll be in Virginia. I pull back onto the road and head for the freeway entrance. I buzz along, listening to *R.E.M.* bouncing my head up and down like a yo-yo. Anything to pass the time and not feel lonely. And I'm a bit lonely, alright.

There's nothing but countryside, rolling hills and greenery everywhere. Everything is lush and summery beautiful. I wish I could pop out a cell phone and call Lisa over at the nuthouse. She's probably doing something pretty depressing right now. Like combing some nut's matted hair. After shock treatment or something. She's really a brave girl. I bet she's good with old people. She would've come in handy on this trip, that's all I'm going to say. It's been three days already and I haven't written to her. I started something the other night, but I got too tired and didn't finish it.

As I sit amid the pea-green walls of yet another Motel Six,
and I woo the imaginary you that's sitting there ,
I lumber towards the portable refrigerator door,
and reach for a relic of love from the night before.

I kind of lost the idea there, thinking a lock of her hair would be a good thing to find preserved among the sandwiches and stuff I had brought along with me, but then I changed my mind. It actually sounds a little gross. A lock of hair lying around in a bag of lousy sandwiches. It's a drag watching the neon lights from the tacky Vacancy/No Vacancy sign outside the window flash in these sickly blue and green colors, but as I sat there thinking about it I grew extremely depressed. I need to tell her that life is exciting and fascinating. Soon, I'll be at Brad's. And he says we'll have things to do. I know he wants me to help him do some chores because there're certain things Brad can't do because Brad's a dwarf.

I met Brad when we were twelve and thirteen. Brad is about a year older than I. We were at summer camp in upstate New York. When I first saw him, I did a double take. I don't know exactly how we hit it off, but we did. We immediately became buds. Here I was, this tall gangly kid hanging out with this dwarf. Everybody liked him, though. You'd think the other boys would've made fun of him, like roll him up into a human bowling ball and slide him down the hall or something, but they didn't. Brad had this quirky but likeable personality. Real confident and all. And, well, you could see why. His parents really liked him.

Most people say, well, all parents love their kids, but I am not saying that. I am saying that his parents actually liked him. As a person. You could see that.

It looks like I'm driving into one of the great historical areas here in Virginia. As I approach the Manassas National Battlefield, I have this absolutely nuts idea. Caz told me that her guy is into doing *Civil War* reenactments. I remembered that I had once read an article about *Civil War* buffs who get all dressed up in the original battle gear to re-enact-right down the last detail-the great battles that took place. So I guess my way of trying my hand at this is to get out the Luger and walk around, pretending I'm all geared up and ready for action. I park the car in one of the lots outside the Manassas grounds and decide to take the gun out. It's all quiet as I walk along a famous dirt road, originally a trench of some kind because there is a stone wall running alongside of it where the land drops off a few feet. I imagine that I'm running along side this wall and carrying a rifle. I'd much rather do this than go to the museum and watch a video. My pace quickens as if I'm being chased. I turn around and pull the gun out pretending I'm grabbing some jerk by the neck. I say to *"him"*: *Yes. I told them. I told them. I told them all about the surprise battle today, and yes. We stole your munitions, you ox-head* ! And I pretend I'm wrestling *the guy* to the ground and holding the cold Luger at his chest; then I exterminate him. *POW!* Of course, there weren't guns like this in those days. But it's nice to imagine what it must have been like to be a real soldier. Back then, war was a noble thing. All this technology today has ruined that. You nuke and chemically maim people. You don't even get to run out there and fight for your life. To experience the adrenaline of knowing you are risking your body, your very life for a noble cause. Instead you end up with deformed children.

I walk the grounds more and decide to return to the car and drive to a spot where I can take some time out to write to Lisa. I find a spot in a field near a cluster of trees and take out the notebook. My letter to Lisa will include my unfinished poem, except I am going to say that I wished I had a lock of her hair to touch because I find it so soft and soothing. That I would never think of sticking it in a paper bag with a bunch of sandwiches if I did have the little treasure. I put out my best romantic handwriting and swirl *With Love*, and my signature with some extra fancy touches. A little drawing of a leaf at the bottom of my florid *L*.

After I do this and address the envelope with extreme care, and place a stamp on it, I flip out the notebook again and open my letter to Boyce with : *I think I want to strangle you right now. Here I am, at a great age, and a great time in my life, and a great love back home, and I want to punch you, too.* Of course, I go into how I punched Andy and that whole ordeal.

It's about eight in the evening when I arrive at the Shenandoah National Park. The sun is still out, so I can see if it's a serene place to spend the night. I gather my things from the car and walk over to a spot near the river and spread everything out on the grass. I take the Luger out and rest it under my pillow. The sun is finally beginning its slow descent. I say, it's about time. I have a strong desire to resist any thoughts about Lisa. I seem to go through this every night. If I think about her and get into all that, I will blow it. I'd call her and end up driving back up to Connecticut and I simply can't do that. Tomorrow, I'll be arriving at Brad's and hopefully, that will distract me from doing something stupid.

The sky is all aglow in these incredible colors of orange and pink. And there's even a slight breeze cooling the grass. There isn't a soul in sight. And I feel like being nature-boy right now or something. I strip off my clothes and wade into the river, leaving my things on the bank. I eye them now and again, as I wade into the cool water and rest myself against some rocks. I swim out a bit further, the cool water running through my fingers as I float on my back and wade. The sky has softened into the oncoming shade of night, and I can see the moon and stars beginning to appear in the summer sky. And I like the way my body feels, naked in the water; that I am just a guy living in the elements, without time or reference, without identifiable demarcations of this or that generation or nationality, for that matter. I just am. A being in the physicality of life. In a place where I'm to live my spirit out for testing. For testing of a self that is forever evolving. A self that always was and will live forever on, in this or that incarnation; in disparate roles in succession, always leading to more infinite knowledge, a furtherance of co-creating with the orchestral maneuvers that spawn this great universe. It occurs to me that I'm thinking this without hallucinogens. I brought no herb with me on this trip and it's going to remain that way.

I swim back to the bank and pull myself out of the water. I use my clothes to dry myself off as I realize I forgot to grab a towel out of my car. I dress and walk over to where I have my things. I plop down and unroll my sleeping bag, fluff my pillow and checking for the Luger, which is still there, I drop into a restful sleep.

It feels like nothing could wake me up, and out here, there isn't a sound save the trees blowing slightly in the night wind. I think of Lisa, her hair feather-soft against my arms. It's too perfect here to not have a girl next to you. There's such tranquility here that the lull of the trees in the wind sounds as if it's quietly speaking to itself. You can smell the grass and the earth while a few crickets croak gently in the night. I feel as if my body is slowly dropping into the ground and the earth is rocking me, holding me as I fall into a deep, restful slumber.

****

"Yew got a registration form for that *thang*?"

I jump up, squinting my eyes at this fool, dressed like a Canadian Mountie or something, a forest ranger, I would imagine, as he's kicking the sleeping bag in an attempt to rouse me up even more. I practically jump on top of the guy. The sun is blasting all over the place, it must be eight in the morning. He's badgering me about the Luger. Apparently, it slipped out from my pillow as I was sleeping.

He asks again,

"Yew got a registration form for that *thang*?"

I tell him to check the *thing* out; that it's an original Austrian Luger made in 1912, before World War I and I'm to return the thing to my Scottish great grandfather down in New Orleans.

I point to it as it lay in his hands,

" It isn't loaded. Check for yourself."

I explain that I wanted to use it to scare somebody off in case I were attacked or something. Well, *Forest Ranger* isn't falling for it. This guy continues to give me a hard time, telling me I had illegally slept in the park and that since I look like an ok guy, he's doing me a favor by letting me off the hook. He stands here, legs slightly spread apart, a toothpick sticking out of his lips, his hair practically a slab of micro-turf it's so short. I think it's the fact that he's impressed as hell with the gun that he's loosening his stride.   He spins the thing in the air, flip-ping it around like John Wayne at the *O.K. Corral* or something, and pretends to fire the thing. The guy's prob-ably bored out of his skull that he works such a lame job, and actually, I think he should thank me for letting him play with my heirloom gun.

I don't want to press my luck, though, so I tell him about my great grandfather working for Gig Mastriani back in the speak-easy days and the like. That he's now dying and has asked the nurses in his ward about the gun. That he must have a last look at it before he croaks.

"And that's my mission. To bring it to him."

Ken, the park ranger, squints at me and asks if I would like to join him for a ride around the grounds. I leap on his horse and he begins to tell me his life story. It's probably not every day that he sees somebody close to his age hanging out around these somber, solitary grounds. He's just yacking away about this and that; telling me he works this job only in the summers and that he's majoring in law enforcement at a nearby school.

He tells me, "Thayer's some battle scenes folks do around here".

I tell Ken that I had heard that some of the famous

battlefields are haunted. Especially Gettysburg.

Ken spits and nods his head, " Thayer ghosts on all the major battlefields. All of 'em haunted, not jus Gettysburg."

He says this with a bit of pride in his voice, like he's proud that he's a Virginian and that his roots go all the way back to the early settlers. At least, that's what he's telling me. Ken is now whipping out his wallet. Now I've seen fancy credit cards with maybe a famous painting embossed on them or something like that, but old Ken here flashes—I *kid you not*—a Visa credit card completely adorned with a glossy portrait of non-other than General Robert E. Lee. He proudly flashes it my way and tells me:

" Hell, we got kin that go all the way back. They actually grew tobacco."

Is that right, Ken-boy?

And here it goes. Inevitably, whenever I shoot the breeze with a guy I just happen to meet, I must check him out. Like how smart is he? What school does he go to, if any? How much does he know about this or that? Is he better at things than I am? That sort of stuff. And, most importantly, can I tell him a good yarn about something? That's always at the top of my agenda. If I impress him, I'm in. Guys seem to do this sort of stuff and not so much with girls, as one might think, but with other guys. I'm not sure what to say about the Visa card of his, but I yack about my great grandfather knowing all these famous gangsters.

Ken and I spend some time skimming rocks into the river talking about the usual stuff, but I don't want to go into the usual topic of scoring women and the like. Lately, bragging about how you nailed some chick in a bush somewhere, like Ken's telling me, just turns me off. So I casually change the topic a bit and we spend a few more minutes chatting away about things.

Ken offers to bring me back to my car on his horse, which I don't mind as we've gone a considerable distance from where he found me.

****

I arrive at Brad's family farm about an hour earlier than I predicted. It's a long circuitous drive up to the main house, and I can see Brad riding one of his Shetland ponies. He trots toward the main house, waving his stubby arms at me. He arrives all sweaty, jumping off the pony as he walks up to greet me with an outstretched hand.

"Hey, Simon! Long time no see, man."

I bend down to hi-five him and scoop him off the ground. Like the old days. He wiggles and squirms, "Let me down, man. I'm older than you. Do you realize that?" It's true, Brad is almost twenty. About a year older than myself. He rolls out of my arms back onto the pavement, nudging his chin in the direction of my car,

"Need some help with your stuff?"

We walk over to the car and collect some of my things. Brad hates it if you don't act like he's a normal guy. He wants me to see the custom designed car his parents gave him for Christmas. It has a special, raised seat and all the controls on the steering wheel. We enter the house and lay my stuff on one of the couches in the den. I ask him how in the hell does he spend his time out here, and he tells me that he is working on his airplane model collection in the work shed. He tends the farm and tools around on the Internet.

He climbs up on one of the oversized chairs, shaking his head.

"I think *chatting* on the '*Net*'s getting a bit dangerous. I've got three girlfriends on there now. One of them says : '*You must be some guy!*' Of course, I don't lie or anything, I just don't blatantly come out and tell her I'm... well... on the short side. Instead, I tell her I know how to do all this jock stuff. Actually, they're all impressed with my propensity on things sportive and such. I'm painting quite a picture. One of them thinks I'm brilliant. I'm dying to send her a snapshot. I bet I never hear from her again. It should be one of the first things I say about myself. I was in heavy counseling for this all through high school. By the time I graduated, I made a promise that I would always just be myself...but I can't. I really can't. At least not completely. Hey, do you want a sandwich or something?"

We spend the next few hours walking the grounds. Brad shows me his airplane model collection in his work room.

He tells me, "I'm already looking at programs in aerodynamic engineering out in California. I know it's the practical thing to do, but since I won that contest, all I want to do is write comedy, Strayhorn."

I encourage him that he should follow his hunches. That it's not every guy that can win contests like that. Brad waves me off with his tiny paws and tells me that comedians are really social misfits.

" I went to a party after that award ceremony and some comedians were there. I felt like I was in a room filled with ventriloquists; you know, freaks who never learned how to socialize, having dummies say what's really on their minds. Well, these guys were no better. Next time you catch these guys on TV or somethin', keep in mind: they're all two French fries shy of a freakin' *Happy Meal*, dude. "

I don't know what comes over me, but I just come out and say it. I point-blank tell Brad that I want him to help me hunt down this guy who took advantage of my sister.

I say: "You might like this. The guy's almost seven feet tall. He's a basketball player over at your school. He's into recreating Confederate battle scenes. At least that's what Caz tells me. Got any ideas?" Brad rubs his chin; day-old stubble prickling his tiny hand.

"Sure, man. What's your plan?"

"I'm thinking of scoping the guy out, and then maybe landing some sort of attack." Brad responds,

"Well, that could be interesting. But of course, we have to be careful. Maybe we should dress like bandits or something. I have a henchman's outfit my mom made me one Halloween. I have it stored somewhere around here. It's black and has a hood and masked face. I don't know how that will really do me much good, because I'm the only dwarf I know of that attends the university. It's hard not to."

I assure him, " Brad, if you're in disguise they won't know whether you're a kid or a dwarf."

We decide to let the idea sit for awhile and to drive around in Brad's new car. We head into town and peruse the various shops and the like before driving down the street where this guy lives. We pull up in front of the apartment building and note that there are only four units. It looks like not many people are around, so I walk up to the front of the building to verify the guy's name on the mailbox. The name *Jeffrey A. Dabney* is there in plain view. We sit in the car for a while, hoping the guy will show up. We drive back to the campus and scope out the library and some of the campus hang outs for a very tall guy, but to no avail. Brad decides that if we come back later in the night, I probably could use some type of disguise as well, so we spend another hour or so discussing that, as we encircle the same few blocks around the campus. Finally, Brad has an idea. "This is awesome. We're going to freak this guy out, man. Didn't you say he was into the Civil War?"

"Well", Brad continues, "*Civil War Re-enacter* freaks. That's what you call them. They're all over the place here. I know a guy who works as a farmhand for some people who are *Re-enacters* and they actually possess some impressive Confederate uniforms, and what we'll do is borrow one of those and mess you all up, like you're a walking-dead zombie from the era, and freak the hell out of the guy. We'll think of some profound things to say like: "*Leave me alone. Stop replaying the war.. Or General Lee...*" or one of those guys, "*will rattle the graves of your ancestors and you will never live in peace. We will haunt you.*" Something like that."

I mull this over a bit and say: "I don't know, Brad, we haven't established what the guy looks like. We only know he's very tall. I mean, what if he's away somewhere on vacation? We could end up sitting in the car all night."

Brad starts the car up again and we head back to the farm. We enter the den and flop ourselves on the overstuffed chairs. Brad gets on the phone and explains to his friend that since these people he works for are out of town, they wouldn't know about our borrowing one of the uniforms for the night. There's a pause.

"Well, let's just come over and check 'em out. Okay?"

Brad puts the phone back in its cradle, and eyes me up and down. He says,

"They might be a bit on the small side. This man isn't as tall as you, Strayhorn, but only by an inch or so". Suddenly, I'm beginning to dislike this idea.

"Brad, maybe we should just approach the guy as ourselves and ask a few questions."

Brad snaps: "And take all the fun out of it? Why, man? I mean, the guy took advantage of your little sister."

I tell Brad about the note I found in Caz's room. That the guy sounds like he's married or something. That her reluctance to talk about her affair to me seems to say that she's still being protective; this is always a sign that the guy's a scab. Creeps get by with these kinds of things only because girls are hopelessly attracted to them. Brad continues:

"As long as he's her dreamboat, well, maybe you're right. The guy deserves nothing in the way of polite society. Let's get on with it."

Brad climbs the stairs to one of the upper rooms and proceeds to search for the henchman's outfit. After he gets into his costume, we head out to the farm where his friend works to retrieve one of the uniforms. We arrive at the guy's doorstep. He's freckly and has fire-red hair. He asks, "Ya'll wunt me ta cum along? Keep ya compny an all? Maybe we shuld be a brigade or somethin'."

Brad then introduces me and as we walk in, he whispers that Gordy's from rural West Virginia. "Hard to understand him at first, Strayhorn, but you'll get used to it."

As we enter the house, I show the Luger to Brad's friend. He scrunches his face, telling me that I need something more true to the era. He walks over to a huge antique armoire and pulls out a classic, Confederate rifle and tells me to *go for it*. That as long as these folk don't get wind of it, it's ok. Gordy stands here looking blank-faced over at Brad. Brad immediately shakes his large head. He tells me,

"Give it back to him, Si. You can't come along. It'll complicate things, Gordy."

I hand the rifle back over to the guy and retrieve the Luger, telling him that I didn't want to take responsibility for the antique gun his employer went through probably a lot of trouble to find. It was enough that I was borrowing the uniform. Gordy gets up from the small wicker chair in the corner and proceeds to open the armoire to show us the variety of uniforms this man's amassed over the years. It's some collection, alright. I feel like I'm in a museum or something. Gordy and Brad encourage me to put one on, but I know the pants will be too short. I feel like an idiot, but I step into the thing anyway. Gordy then hands me a fake beard. Brad says, "Si, put it on. You may as well get into it. Where are the long sideburns and slings, Gordy?"

I waive the both of them off. I'm beginning to feel a little nervous and I want to rethink things. Of course, I recall what Boyce kept telling me: to stay out of my family's business. But I can't help it. After seeing Caz so distraught and bummed out, I just knew this guy had something to do with it. Brad places the henchman's hood over his face. I pull on the beard, place the cap on my head, pull my black socks up over the above-the ankle pants, sling the rifle over my shoulder and nudge my head toward the door. "Let's get this over with."

Gordy hovers over me, inspecting the uniform.

"Yew sure look like the real *thang*, alright."

I gently step away from him and turn to Brad as we head for the stairs.

"I'm going to really feel like an idiot if we end up sitting in your specialty car and the guy never shows up, that's all I'm going to say."

Brad gingerly hops down the stairs. "If that's the case", he says, "let's just look at it as a dress rehearsal."

We turn around and Gordy's standing there, looking lanky and forlorn, his hands stuck in his jeans pocket. Brad and I glance at each other.

Finally, Brad says, "We can use a runner. You know, to scope out the hangouts. We certainly can't do that, dressed as we are." Gordy grins. Brad pulls the hood off his face as he points at Gordy's upper thigh, yelling at him, "Come on, you asshole. But you better keep that trap shut. Not a word to anybody, understand?"

Gordy vigorously bobs his head as we walk out the front door. I walk next to him as Brad leads us out to his car.

"You know you're nuts to be coming along with us. I just want you to know that. You could be doing something far more interesting than this".

As I look around the very quiet and solemn grounds of the farm, with a few crickets singing in the grass, I catch myself pondering my own remarks. This is probably one of the most exciting things this guy's done all year. What do you do when you care-take a farm? He tells Brad and me that we can come over in the next few days to watch one of the horses give birth; foal, he says. I guess this is one of the featured events of the season. Brad remarks:

"Don't we need reservations for that, Gordy?"

The guys shakes his head. "Ya makin' fun of me, again, Brad."

Yep, I would reckon so, Gordy.

We hop into the car and head back to town. Gordy tells us about how he and Brad met. Of course, Gordy is not going to let Brad completely get by with his remark. "Wuz'nt it at the Furst Congrigational County Fair? Yew bein the apple bobbin guy up thayre we wuz all thrown water balloons at?"

Brad immediately quips, "No, dumb-dumb. I was the fire-swallower with the massive tattoos all over my bicep riddled chest."

Gordy vigorously shakes his red head. " ..Nu-eh. Yew wuz the guy sprawlin' around with all them purty women unda the harem tent, that's whatchew were. A stud-daddy if there evuh wuz one. Course, I wuz stuck at the end of thu line, eatin my yo-yos..."

I can barely understand what the guy's saying, but I can tell, these two have done this routine a few times before. Brad grins. They're continuing to jive each other until I finally interject.

"Alright, guys. Can we move on to something else?"

We end up driving the rest of the way in complete silence. Brad fidgets with the controls on his steering wheel as he sails past a couple of slow trucks heading down the highway. And I think to myself as I look at his tiny body in its elevated seat. All he wants is basic acceptance. That he's a guy like any guy and he can hold his own. Run with the best of them and all that crap.

"Si, I can feel your mind cranking away. What's up?"

I wave him off, saying the fake beard may be a problem and could he please put on some music. I turn around to talk with Gordy. I tell him that I'm glad he came along for the ride and that I would be over at his farm to see the mare give birth. I always wanted to see that. Gordy nods appreciatively, but remains quiet. We approach the campus exit off the freeway and Brad suggests we drive by the apartment building to see if there's any activity in this guy's pad.

We dutifully drive over there, and of course, the place looks practically deserted with only one of the lower apartments showing any signs of life. The place is enshrouded with lush foliage and trees. Brad's talking away like a fool and I want to reach over and gently squash him back into an imagined jack-in-the-box container to shut the guy up. He has this propensity to over-complicate things. Rather than hang out to see if the guy shows up, we decide to go to the area just outside of the campus where there are restaurants and bars. Gordy volunteers to go into them to scope the places out for a guy who is nearly seven feet tall. Of course, we think this is a great idea, given that we are both in disguise with Brad looking like he stepped out of the movie, '*Time Bandits*', rather than a threatening assassin. I look like a complete fool in this uniform and I'm scratching the hell out of my face under this stupid-fake beard and sideburns. I ask Brad how long he thinks we can sit around like this.

"As long as it takes, my man."

Well, I'm glad he's enjoying it, that's all I'm going to say. Gordy steps out of the car to begin his scope-out while Brad and I bob our heads to the music of some really vintage *Faith No More*. Brad shakes his large head and places his black cloth mask back on as he proceeds to tell me that he once participated in a Civil War battle reenactment.

"Down in the Shenandoah Valley. And dude, it's real serious. You wouldn't believe the grisly details these guys go through. Every move is planned down to the *T*. I was relegated to the level of *servant* to the *officers*. Tossing out their half-eaten gruel and garbage; running behind them while they prepared their munitions. Talk about realism. I didn't take offense, though, except when one guy hoisted me up and pitched me over to some ass-hole standing around the encampment. That really pissed me off. I threatened to sue the guy and he laughed saying that back in the 1860's, dwarves were lucky to have been given favorable representation in tales by the Brothers Grimm. Forget about anything luxurious like having *rights.*"

We both notice Gordy as he walks out of one of the bars shaking his head and shrugging his shoulders at us. He points to a few of the other places up the block and across the street and we nod back. Some people are sauntering by our parked car and I tell Brad to please take off the mask to prevent any unnecessary suspicion. I say this as I yank the sideburns and beard off my face.

Brad informs me, "You're a real paranoid, Strayhorn. I'm the only dwarf I know in the immediate area, and so for me, it's wise to keep the mask on because I could be a kid for all they know, like you said. Of course, I 'm referring to the idea that people end up hearing about our little attack."

And I reply: "Yeah, a three and a half foot kid—the size of a five-year old- who sits at the wheel, blaring *Bad Religion* while he takes a drag off his cigarette. Speaking of which, can you roll the window down more?"

Brad turns the music lower and reaches up to put the sun visors down to distract any undue speculation from the people walking by. Finally, Gordy comes running over to us.

"Thayer ain't nobody in these places that culd fit the description yew described."

Brad and I grin at each other, touched by the charm of this guy. We both chime, "Get in the car, Gordy," as the car shimmies its way out of its tight parking spot. We both tell Gordy that he did a good job.

We decide to do a quick run through a fast-food fried chicken place and order some food. After munching in a parking spot for a few minutes Brad suggests we simply drive over to the guy's apartment to finish eating and to scope the place out. We find a spot under a huge Sycamore tree and gingerly munch away, our masks and disguises resting on the seat between us. Gordy enter-tains us with a few yarns about his life on the farm as we gobble away like goons.

It's practically pitch-black outside near this guy's apartment which is on a dead-end street with one faint streetlight at the end of the block glimmering away as moths enshroud the thing like a swarm of bees on a hon-eycomb. If anyone lives in this building, there's absolutely no signs of life. Unless they're all old people and go to bed before 11 pm, which is about the time right now. Brad announces that he has an idea. "We should get out of the car and stage our positions. You see that tree by the walkway? I'm going to climb it and wait up there. Gordy, since you know how to work my car, why don't you get at the wheel, I'll move my seat, and park just a few feet away. We'll just wait until the guy shows up.

Si, just wait under that bush and when we see him we'll spring our attack."

We move the car a few feet away from the building's walkway and turn off all the lights. As Brad wiggles out of his portable elevated car seat, he tosses it to Gordy to store in the back. He haphazardly puts the cloth mask with its little eyeholes back over his head and runs up the tree like a frenzied koala bear seeking its perch.

I then re- apply the beard and sideburns and place the Confederate cap back over my head. Gordy hands me the rifle and tells me again that I look like the real thing. I step out of the car to squat in the bushes. Gordy backs the car down a few feet and quietly waits. I'm beginning to itch in this heavy uniform and I can hardly see what's in front of me, it's so dark. I can hear Brad switching squatting positions in the tree. In a low voice, I tell him that maybe we should call it quits. That the guy is obviously out for the evening, probably scoping out some chick in a dive somewhere as he lures her into his trap by telling her all these yarns about his brain-power and that we should spilt. It's useless. Plus, I'm highly uncomfortable. Brad tells me to shut up. I announce that I'm now giving up. That it's over. Brad is growing furious with me and in a harsh whisper says that he has not gone through all this trouble to simply give up. And that I should stay put. We are doing the right thing, he says.

Gordy now quietly steps out of the car and approaches the sidewalk and politely chews us out. "Thayer's a car comin'. Pleeze shut the hell up!" He runs back to the car to quietly lay on the seat. A car is definitely approaching, alright, and I'm beginning to shake with leaden-drenched fear. Complete with wobbly dread. My mouth is so dry, I can barely lift my tongue. The car engine's growing more audible as it turns the corner and swings down the street. I know I'm at least covered, but I am shaking like leaves in a storm. The car is now approaching the building, as I feared, and the headlights suddenly shut off and the engine ceases its soft rumble. What to do, what in the hell to do? I peek through the shrub and notice a figure stepping out of the car. I can't make out the guy's face for anything.

I hear his steps on the walkway and they stop for a moment and then turn. I boldly jump out of my safe position, regretting for a micro-second that I am leaving it, and I blindly stick the gun at him and begin my best Alabama (Gram's) drawl. "Hurd you' is tryin to dig up the dead...Well, I'm here on behalf of the *General*, and he says ta stop. An ta stop yew from diggin' up bones best left for dead."

The guy's not saying anything. He's obediently backing up the walkway, shocked into complete silence. We approach the tree where Brad is perched, and of course, it just occurs to me why he climbed up there in the first place. Brad leaps down from the tree, right onto the guy's shoulders, scaring the hell out of him as Brad shrieks, pounding his tiny fists atop the man's head. In a creepy-sounding whisper, Brad tells the guy to " *leave her alone, leave her alone*". Finally the man says in a deep, scholarly sounding voice. "Leave? Who? What on earth are you talking about?...Ow!" Brad pinches the guy's ears. As the man reaches out to grasp Brad's head, he backs up the drive and lands on his ass. Brad quickly jumps off his shoulders and runs away from him and I quickly run backwards as I shout: "Leave her alone!" "Leave who? Who are you? What *bones*? Are you crazy? I'm just a teacher! Who are you?"

As we run across the lawn, Brad throws pine cones

at the figure squatting on the steps to the building; suddenly an outdoor light flashes on. As we run to the car, we quickly look back. I know I had a faint hint of it, but now before my eyes, it is confirmed. The man sitting there looking all baffled, with a newly arrived neighbor, an older lady, standing behind him in baffled surprise, is a black man. As plain as day. And he's a mighty average-sized guy at that. Hardly a *'Globe Trotter* seven-footer. We all get into the car and Gordy backs down to the end of the block and speeding down an alley hoping it gets us to the main road, which it does. We are all so stunned, no one is uttering a word. Our disguises are off and we are boiling like peanuts. At least that's what Gordy keeps saying.

We quietly head out of town and onto the Interstate, heading back to Brad's farm. I'm shaking my head in pure disbelief. I thought I knew Caz, but I never knew her to be...so *diverse* in her taste in guys.

"Didn't know lil' sis was into the *brown sugar*, eh, Si? They say once you taste the *brown sugar*, there's just no goin back ..."

I tell him: "Alright, Brad. We don't even know if that really was the guy."

Brad continues, "He parked in the allotted spot for that apartment. I made a note of that this afternoon, Strayhorn! "

Brad brags about how well he did in his little ambush attack and he is telling us that he would've loved to have seen the guy's face when he landed atop his unsuspecting shoulders. Ha, ha, ha. I'm sorry we did this. It was all my idea, and now I feel it wasn't worth all the trouble. He sounded truly surprised and I'm now wondering if he is just a teacher over at Caz's school. But how do you explain that note?

We pull up the long driveway leading back to the farm house and we are all tired. I tell Brad and Gordy that I want to stay out here; that it's more comfortable for me to sleep outside under the stars. If Lisa were with me on this trip, this wouldn't have happened, that's all I'm going to say.   Surely, I would've had better things to do. I lug my sleeping bag out of the house to rest in the field behind it. I fluff my pillows and slowly crawl in.

****

The sun is blaring pretty high in the sky. This tells me I must've slept ten hours or something, because from the looks of it, it's about two in the afternoon. Brad squats next to me; he's shoving a newspaper in my face with one hand, and holding an oversized mug of coffee in the other. I wave him off, but he's not letting up on me. Not one bit. He slaps my head with the rolled up newspaper. "You better read this. I think we could be in trouble, Strayhorn." I glance down at the thing, and grab the mug of coffee from Brad's puny hand as I brace myself to read the small article at the bottom part of the page. The headline reads: *Racial Attack?*

An apparent racial attack by two disguised youths shocked a popular Speech and Drama teacher, Jeffrey Dabney, 35, living on a quiet residential street just out-side the university area. Dabney arrived at his home a little after 11 pm last night after spending hours rehears-ing..." The story goes on to say that Dabney was mostly shocked at the fact that there was one tall guy dressed in what looked like a *Confederate* uniform, along with a rifle. He wondered, however, about the very short youth that leapt on top of his shoulders, dressed in a tiny executioner-style dark outfit, along with matching hood with tiny eye-holes, making Dabney a bit curious about the message of such a costume. *"Perhaps it's an ominous message of some kind toward my race. Or maybe it's something new; maybe a take-off of the usual white robes worn by the KKK."* Dabney continues to say that the taller man in the Confederate rig was giving him odd warnings. That *General Lee* will "haunt" him. Dabney found this baffling since he can think of nothing save for a paper he once wrote about the relatively unknown subject of blacks who ended up fighting for the Confederacy.

Brad and I pause looking up at each other in utter disbelief: "The *Confederacy*?!"

We both continue to peruse the news article. Dabney continues: *"That was about six years ago, when I was still in school. But you never know. The thesis I wrote was controversial at the time. I just didn't think people would bother to dig these things up after all these years."*

My head spins. Dabney hardly fits the description given by Caz. But how do you explain the note I read? Maybe Shorty here is a *former* lover. But it doesn't fit. I must've made a mistake. Maybe we should even call the guy and apologize. Brad says, "Oh, so you think this guy is going to invite us in for tea and crumpets and genteel conversation? Are you crazy? We'll end up behind bars for assault and battery. And I have no dough to bail us out and neither do you."

I tell Brad that if this is the way he feels, then I should get the things he wanted me to do over with and head back out on the road.

We're corralled in the den of the main house eating a late breakfast and discussing the best way to skirt out of this mess. Gordy's ironing the uniform I borrowed so he can sneak it back into the armoire back at his farmhouse. Brad rehashes last night's events. He can't seem to get over how he had effectively scared the hell out of the guy when he landed on his shoulders and tells us that it was a very old trick he had learned when he was a kid. Ha ha. I'm very tempted to pick up the phone and simply ask my sister some important questions, but I hesitate. I can't so readily disregard what I had agreed to with Boyce and I simply must let it go for now. Brad picks up on my mood and offers unsolicited advice.

"There's nothing worse than thinking you know someone when you really don't, Strayhorn. What if he took advantage of your baby sister?"

I don't know what to think of all this. I'm now not so sure about anything. I just need to get going. I tell Brad,

"Show me what you want me to do for you because I'm leaving tonight."

Brad gives me a sour look. "You're jumping to con-clusions all too readily, Strayhorn. I need to know if we really did make a mistake first, and I'm not totally con-vinced. Never mind the stuff I asked you to do. Gordy always pitches in. Why don't you just leave, okay?"

What in the hell did I ever see in this guy? So he's a smart guy. Maybe I feel for the guy being that he's the size of a laundry hamper. But I'm lousy when it comes to cutting off people just because we disagree on an issue or hating someone for not having the innate sense to do the right thing. Brad sits here pouting and twirling his nim-bly fingers, looking a bit pathetic to me. I suppose he wants to believe he's right and I too readily assume I made a mistake. Maybe Brad is right. And I guess I need to just move on, as he suggested. I silently leave the room and begin to collect my things still lying in the hallway. Departing now won't really upset my plans any, and actually, I like being on the road and on my own.

I step out of the front door to load up my car. As I am stuffing my sleeping bag in the trunk, I hear someone approaching me from behind. It's Gordy.

"Sure wuz nice meeting yew, an all. If yew wanna stay at the farm, I'm willin' to put yew up. Jus have to tend to sum things. Alls I have to do is tend to a birthin' mare. Folks won't be inquirin' much about yew. They mine their own business."

I thank Gordy and shake my head. I tell him I need to move on anyway. Gordy suddenly jumps toward me and tells me to hang right there, he needs to give me something. He jogs back into the house. I'm sort of hoping I see Brad wobble down the walkway, but of course, he's probably still mulling things over in his large head. I slam the trunk shut and walk back over to the front of the car to peruse my maps a bit before setting out. Gordy returns with a grin a mile wide.

"Well? Doncha know yur missin somthin' perty important an all?"

I squint my eyes at him, questioningly and remember that Gordy had the Luger. "Gosh! That's the most important thing. Thanks, Gordy. I'd hate to get on the road and end up in Georgia somewhere, remembering I forgot."

He hands it to me, all polished and glimmering in the sun.

"Hey, thanks, dude. You didn't have to do that."

It goes to show you that strangers can be a lot kinder than your buddies. Gordy wishes me luck and tells me to give me a call if I ever need anything as he hands me a piece of paper with his name, address and phone number scrawled on it. Gordy shakes his head and tells me that

Brad needs a little more time to think things through. That I shouldn't take it personally. I start up the car and wave to him as I'm about to pull away. For a moment, I look back to the house and notice a tiny figure peeping through the window. I wave at Brad and turn down the gravelly drive. In a few days, he'll probably e-mail me saying something like:

"I was just joking, man. I wanted to see if you'd take me seriously. And as usual, you did, mutton-head."

Meta...Mor...Phose

Carlin and I are sitting here at his kitchen table, an unlighted bong between us. When I arrived about an hour ago, Carlin immediately went to his bedroom and retrieved the bong and placed it on the table.

"For memory's sake, huh, Strayhorn? Hey, remember how we'd sit in the bushes in back of our house back in Connecticut? What were we listenin' to? Ted's *Pink-*"Is there anybody out there?" *Floyd* collection? Remember that?"

Carlin nudges me with his fist. "Ted's an asshole. He now works for an insurance company. He has two kids and just turned thirty-five. Can you believe it?"

Ted is Carlin's older brother. I ask Carlin about the rest of his family.

"Well, Dad, you know, the Admiral, well, he's not talking to me anymore. But, hey, he's an asshole, too. He threatened me. I had to join the Navy or else. I'm going to college next year."

Carlin gets up and gathers some scattered papers from the floor in the next room. He slides them on the table in front of me. He speaks:

"Oceanography, dude. Remember how we'd talk about all that stuff? Well, that's what I'm going to do."

I glance down at the application forms. One is for a nearby university. Another is for University of California in San Diego. I say:

"Dude, you can do it!"

As I hand the papers back to him, I notice they are water-stained and a bit dog-eared. It looks like Carlin's been hanging on to these applications for a while.

" Hey, if I don't do this, I may end up joining you out there on the rigs."

Carlin's uncle is the one who's arranged the oilrig job out in the Gulf of Mexico when I arrive in New Orleans in a week or so.

Carlin assures me, "It's all taken care of, Simon. He knows you're coming. They ship out mid-month so you have plenty of time."

Carlin's lived in North Carolina since he was sent here by his father for military school three years ago. Since then, he graduated, alright, but hasn't really budged as far as getting on with his life. He tells me:

"I quit my job about two weeks ago. All I did was telemarket old retired people out of their savings. It was hell getting them to part with their dough. *Thoroughbred*s. Five thousand dollars a pop. Everything's pooled into a general partnership. I made some money, but I found out about some *inside stuff*. There ain't no real thoroughbreds. It freaked me out. I mean, I could go legit and sell newspaper subscriptions, but the money's lousy."

Carlin decides to feed the bong with some herb. He puffs away, offering me a hit. I decline. Carlin gives me this incredulous look.

"What's with you, dude?"

I tell him I'm already worn out from the drive. Actually, Carlin looks like he spends a lot of time smoking away. The apartment stinks, and there's nothing but moldy stuff in the refrigerator. He tells me his roommate is out of town for most of the summer and he's thinking of subletting his room. We shoot the breeze for a while until I can barely keep my eyes open.

At about midnight, I tell Carlin that I must get some zz's, as he yaks away about some bozo he knows who tried to heist an armored truck as it pulled into the supermarket where he once worked. I rise from my chair as if under a spell and beeline for his roommate's mattress in the next room. I flop down as Carlin follows behind talking away. Carlin nudges me as I lie on my side. I don't know how long he sits here next to me as I trail off. Soon, I can only hear a mumbling voice that fades to nothing.

****

I awoke this morning deciding that I'm going to be peachy cool around Carlin. It seems he and I may have lifestyle differences. But he's an old friend and what can I do about it? We're driving around his neighborhood a bit before heading into the main town where he knows some people who attend the university there. We're just chatting away about things and I suddenly remember that the cash I've allotted for myself since leaving Connecticut has now run out. I need to get to an ATM. I'm just so proud I spent only a couple hundred bucks, I tell Carlin I'll buy him a lunch at *Mickey D's.* Carlin frowns.

"Dude, there's a fried chicken place I know of that'll at least give you real biscuits. That's all ya eat here, anyway. Biscuits, grits and everything fried. That *MacDonald's* stuff is like eating gauze. Gauzy bandages. Rubber bands."

I shake my head at him. " Dude! *Top Ramen* is like eating rubber bands. Have you ever bought that stuff? You can usually get 6 packages for a quarter or something. A lot of street junkies and students know about *Top Ramen.. Mickey D's* is gourmet compared to that stuff."

We pull into a shopping area, and I get out to retrieve

some cash. I pop over to the machine and slip in my card and punch in my numbers; I wave at Carlin as I wait for the screen to flash. I look back and the screen is blinking a meager sum as my balance. I do a double take and punch in the codes again, this time, requesting an account statement. As of two weeks ago, I had roughly $1,500.00. Andy had already put my *penalty* money back into my account and actually, this was exactly why we had gotten along so well the couple of times we got together before I left home. Now the screen is telling me I have all of $357.00 in my account. That's impossible! I step over to the phone and call the customer service line.

Carlin gets out of his car, shaking his head at me.

"What's up? Dude, you look really freaked."

The woman on the customer service line is going over all of the transactions of the past two weeks. Scattered throughout this period, there were several $200.00 withdrawls. And they were all done at ATM's in Connecticut. Immediately, I think of Andy. I thank the lady and get off the phone. Carlin walks over with me as I proceed to wipe out my account. Save for the fifty-seven dollars to keep the account open.

"Hey, Strayhorn. I'll buy ya some grub, okay? You may need your dough for some *Top Ramen* later down the pike, eh? Why the long face? I'm just kiddin' with ya! Come on!"

I know Carlin means well, but he's really grating on my nerves. We get back into his car and drive over to this fried chicken place. We settle in a booth by the window carrying baskets of grub. Carlin's right. Everything is deep fried.

"Look," he tells me, shrugging his shoulders as he

speaks, "Things happen. My old man, the *Admiral*, well, he would do shit like that all the time. I finally closed my account and had my girlfriend open a new one for me. You remember Sarah? She's like five years older than me. I told you how we met, eh? I went over to her house to deliver a pizza while her guy was out of town. I was her ' honey' for a while, but she's married now."

Suddenly, I don't feel so hungry. I tell Carlin that maybe I should hurry up and get down to Louisiana. That maybe once I'm there, if I have to scrape up some extra dough before setting out to the gulf, I can be better pre-pared if I leave here earlier. "Ya got a point there, Strayhorn. There's always grunt work you could do."

We continue to munch our food in silence. Carlin offers me a fried glob of something I don't recognize.

" It's a tomato, Simon. Ya wanna try it?"

I wave him off, and resume eating the hushpuppies.

When Carlin and I get back to his place, I decide to e-mail Boyce. I tell him what's going on and what he thinks might be happening. Did Andy make those with-drawls? Carlin and I spend the rest of the day talking about a lot of things. While we listen to CDs we talk about the old days. He assures me that everything's in place and once I get out on the rigs, I'll be making plen-ty of dough.

"You'll be laughing at this, Strayhorn. You make obscene amounts of cash as a rig-man and my Uncle Al takes care of all my friends. So don't worry."

I find myself glancing at Carlin's phone. I'm tempt-ed to just call Andy and ask him why in the hell he did this to me, but I clench my fist as I hold myself back.

Carlin looks up at me, "Hey, just call him and get it over with."

I wave him off. We decide to go out for awhile and play pool at one of the dives in his neighborhood. When we get back about four hours later, I check my e-mails. Sure enough, there's a message from Boyce. He says he honestly believes it would be uncharacteristic for Andy to dribble the money out in that kind of fashion. That since he had access to my account outright, then why wouldn't he have taken it all out in one fell swoop instead of in $200.00 increments in so many sessions? It doesn't make sense. He tells me he's proud of me; that I'm hanging in there; that I'll be ok and to not lose faith.

Carlin's staring down at me. "You ok, man? Want some herb? C'mon, a little bong action like the old days?"

"Naw. I'm staying clear-headed. I already told ya. I need the break."

I go into this yarn about the "huge" quantities of herb I had consumed while at Gringham. I tell him there are bongs there that would remind him of the ornate pipes the *white rabbit* smokes in *Alice in Wonderland*.

"Things with kaleidoscopic hoses, some with laser beams running through clear plastic tubes in all these different colors; huge Tibetan-like bowls, massive and round; and some rolled boils that hissed like something out of a great mystic hot spring, they were so steamy ".

I raise my brow a bit and Carlin lets out one of his famous hyena guffaws.

"Ha! Ha! Haeeeeeha! Ha!Ha! Hee hee heeeyah!! Strayhorn! I'm so glad ta see ya!"

****

After pondering things for another day at Carlin's I gave up and decided to head down to New Orleans. And I keep wondering: who's the rat who wants to undo me? I have mulled over this the entire time I have driven out of the Carolinas, into Georgia, Alabama, Mississippi and now into Louisiana. And it's a drag. I have to watch every quarter. Every time I stop for food or gas, I have to think of how much I can eke out. Of course, I'm walking around with all the cash I have left in the world, which is roughly $250.00. I sleep on the road with my great granddad's gun resting inside my chest. And the nights are barely cooler than the days.

Sometimes I wake up with a jolt, shakily grabbing the Luger to aim at a raccoon or a muskrat. It's pretty creepy, that's all I am going to say. And sometimes I cry. Of course, I get over it, and comfort myself that I can always sell my laptop, or maybe call a few friends for some spot-cash and this seems to soothe me enough to get me through the night. But of course, by morning, I'm flushed with shame that I would wimpily call my friends like a little lost kid, and I forge ahead through another day of driving. There's no way I'm going to do that. No way. I'd rather wind up a beggar on the streets of the French Quarter with a freak-show act of some kind than to do that. I try not to think of the comfortable days when I could simply pull up to a lousy Motel Six and crash for the night amid the tacky setting, neon light flashing in the room all night and all. When you're broke, a place like that looks like one of the palaces belonging to the *Sultan of Brunai*. And gone are the

233

nights that I sleep snugly and dreamily. Each night, as the sun is finally sinking into the swampy, grassy terrain, I pull out the wad of cash and count it before burying it deep in my pockets. In the morning, when I pull into a gas station, I head for the bathroom with my satchel.

I take everything off, splash water all over my body, grateful if there's a faucet with real hot water, and clean myself as best as I can. I pull out the razor and shave, wash my hair, hoping the guy behind the counter doesn't grow suspicious. Sometimes they do, and pound on the door to see if I keeled over and died or something. Of course, when I walk out, my hair is sopping wet and there's water all over the floor. After the frown or the scowl, which I have learned to endure pretty well, I step back into my dumpy car and wave at the guy figuring it doesn't really matter as I am probably never going to see him again. When you're broke, you sure do learn to endure a lot and all that really matters are basic things like if you're hungry or not. Everything else is well, gravy. And actually, some hot gravy over some miserable S*top 'n Shop* food sounds pretty good right now.

I approach New Orleans around mid-afternoon and drive directly to the lousy hostel where I can crash for about twelve bucks a day in a room full of travelling fools like myself. The place seems quaint enough, a warm-like atmosphere amid a lush tree-lined street in the uptown section of the city. I check in at the table in the entry way to what looks like a very old building. The lady at the desk seems kind enough, lots of ho*neys*, and *darlins* as she tells me where everything is. I ask her if there's a safe where I can lock up my valuables and she tells me that it'll cost me an extra three dollars a day. I figure it's worth the extra cost after pondering my dwindling wad of cash. I hand over the laptop and stuff two hundred dollar bills in an envelope for her to lock up.

I feel like I have arrived at a detention hall and at any moment, I'll be frisked and ushered to a small booth where some bozo will take a mug shot and send me off to my chambers. The lady reaches for a set of keys and waddles up an ancient staircase to a large room where there must be a dozen bunk beds. I flop myself on a lower bed near the wall figuring it would be one of the quieter spots for me to rest. There are about five guys in here, chatting away in a foreign language. It sounds either Norwegian or German, maybe Russian. They're blonde and pale in complexion. They grin over at me, as the little woman points in my direction. "This here is Simon, and he's travllin' from up North, an he's..." she turns to me, smiling politely, "...a student, honey?" I smile and tell her that I'm just down for a few months to work on the rigs out in the Gulf of Mexico and that I'm a student, but I'm not attending school right now. I tell her that my dad is from here and went to school here. "Well, now that must mean ya have sum family here and all?" I politely tell her I have some relatives here and they are old and practically ready for the *last rites* and I may be seeing them if I have the time, before something happens.

The group of foreign guys look like pretty well-off dudes with lots of American cash hanging out in their pockets. But, of course, they can't be all that well-off if they're staying in a place like this, but you'd be surprised. One of them has a pair of *Ray-Ban's*, those really expensive sunglasses, perched on top of his Norwegian blonde head, and a very expensive *Nikon* camera hanging from his neck. I walk over to the bunk bed and roll my stuff under it, taking out some of my essentials; my notebook, headset, and CDs to take along with me as I explore the area and make a few phone calls. I have only a few days before setting out on the rig and I want to roam the area and hang out and explore while I can. The lady is laughing with the group of foreigners as she turns to me and hands me a set of keys. I take them from her and slip them into my pocket as I sling my backpack over my shoulder, nodding at the guys as I walk out of the room.

This town sure has a slow-moving pace to it. It's so hot and muggy, I feel like I'm walking in water, instead of air. Treading the ground, as every move seems cumbersome and strained. No wonder you see people sitting around on porches and outdoor cafes fanning themselves as they slowly get *tanked*. I walk the leafy green streets and hop one of the streetcars that crawl down St. Charles Avenue, a pretty impressive boulevard of massive Spanish oaks and mossy entrails dangling everywhere amid some pretty remarkable architecture. Before setting out, I grabbed the Luger out of the car and tucked it in my bag. The only address I have for my great grand-father is the one on Dumaine Street in the French Quarter. My only real lead to his whereabouts and I'm hoping I find him there. Not that I am ready to do this today, but I want to approach him soon as I will be off-shore for a long time.

Carlin tells me I can make about fifteen grand in about a three-month period. You come back and a month later, you're back out there making the dough. Not only do they pay you handsomely for your back-breaking efforts, they serve meals that can feed a couple of foot-ball teams and they have real chefs making real gourmet, top of the line stuff. Like steaks, chops, spare ribs; seafood, salads, steaming vegetables. All the food I happen to be craving right now, actually.

The thought that Andy must really hate me pops in my head. He'd have to. Anybody to clean out the slender account of his only son has got to have it in for him. My question is, why?

I received another e-mail from Boyce this morning. He said that maybe I should think of someone other than Andy. That it was an act of thievery and that I should consider this. Boyce. I think of him, sitting back in his big chair, blowing smoke, scaring the hell out of some poor sucker like the fake wizard in the *Wizard of Oz*. Giving orders to not pay any attention to the little man behind the green curtain, and all the while this is a guy who once changed his son's grimy diapers. Hard for me to imagine that one. I miss that balding weirdo, though. I'm actually looking forward to e-mailing him again later.

The streetcar slowly rocks and turns into the downtown area, lazily screeching to a stop at every other street corner, picking up tourists and citizens alike as we sail amid new and old buildings bristling in the summer sun. Not that I expect to find my great granddad sitting in a rocking chair waiting for my arrival. After he split his ties with everyone in the family some thirty-something years ago, he avoided their attempts to kiss and make-up. He's probably a crabby-assed, old dude and I really don't care if he is. I'm rather expecting it, actually. I just want to hand him the gun and ask him a few questions.

I get off the streetcar as it waddles to a squeaky halt on what looks like a major intersection. Actually, it looks like I'm now in a downtown area that has seen better days. All the stores look run down and closed. I cross the wide old boulevard and enter Bourbon Street. There are grungy-looking men with scratchy voices hustling people to walk into the striptease joints and it's about three in the afternoon. Another day on the job, I guess. There's ragtime music playing in some of the places where tourists sit on barstools drinking famous exotic drinks. I walk further along, looking into shops, and actually, the strip-tease joints look a bit depressing. All the photos of the strippers out front look like they're about fifteen to twenty years old, and well, I can only imagine what these ladies look like now. Still grinding away after all these years, their breasts sagging and dragging around as they bump yet another grind for the random souls sitting around in the dark, drinking away like loons. Probably all of them lonely and alone. But loaded with excessive cash they don't know what else to do with. Something I would not mind having right now.

I find a hotel and enter its swank, marbled-floor lobby. I make headway to the phone bank and call Carlin's uncle, Al Charbonnet, at the office number I was given. A man answers. I ask for Al and he puts me on hold. After waiting about three agonizingly long minutes Carlin's uncle finally comes over the line. I introduce myself and there's a long pause. I explain that Carlin probably mentioned me to him. Another pause. He then asks me if I'm in the union. I tell him, no, that Carlin explained to me that they're always getting non-union guys on board. Carlin's uncle asks me to hold again. Finally, the old guy comes back on and tells me a crew went out a week ago, and I'll have to wait 'til late August. If I want to make that trip, I better get down to their office down by the docks and fill out all the forms to get my name on the list.

Al asks me, "He's still smokin' dat stuff, iddn't he?"

The guy sounds like some of Andy's old friends that grew up with him down in the Fauberg. It's a New York *Bowery* kind of accent very much heard among the lower classes of New Orleans.

I tell Carlin's Uncle Al, "Yeah. He's a real dope head nut and right now, I want to strangle him."

"He—heh-heh-heh-heheh-hack-hack!" Old Al continues, "Yeah. An he ain't gettin' nuttin' from me. Dat kid's always cookin' up sum baloney about sum'n an— I swahya— it's a wonda his daddy dudn't crack his head open. Kid can't even clean a fuggin *terlit*. He's de laziest of 'em. He came down heeah one summa an we had ta trow 'em outa heea. Culdn't wait ta send 'em back!! Comes from class, dat knucklehead."

Al has me grinning. I could listen to him for hours rant about my bum buddy, Carlin.

Al's asking me what brings me down this way and I tell him my dad's from here. Of course, I do my best buttering up job. I tell him he went to St. Jerome's and the guy shrieks, he's so excited.

"Yeah? I went dare. Graduated in '57."

I tell him that my dad's a lot younger than he is, and he sounds disappointed. I then tell him about the house on Frenchman Street and the guy seems like he's listening raptly. He tells me about an old butcher shop on Frenchman and some other street, I didn't catch the name, and how it was converted to a bar and a hang out where he used to play pool. The guy tells me that he's going to put me at the top of the list for the next boat out. He wants me to come over and eat with him tomorrow afternoon.

He asks me if I like catfish and hushpuppies, and oysters, and fried potatoes, and all this other stuff, and (of course I could eat anything right now) so I say I do and he asks me to promise him that I will be over there at the Ambrose St. office at 1:30 to meet him, that he wants to take me out to lunch.

There's a line of people standing behind me when I finally get off the phone. Before sauntering out of the swank lobby, I remember to visit the men's room. In places like this, there's usually extra soaps and sometimes you find men's cologne sitting on the counter. I walk in and there's a small, bald-headed black man, looking crisp and impeccable as he greets me and hands me a towel to dry my hands. The old cat looks like a pretty nice guy, alright. Here I'm thinking I can swipe a few things and the man is treating me like he wants to work me over with one of his grooming brushes. He asks me if I'm travelling: if I go to school, all the while he's smiling and nodding his head politely. People here are a trip. The guy actually wants to get into a conversation. Maybe he's lonely, though. I mean, if I handed towels to strangers all day long, I'd be pretty lonely, too. I dig in my pocket and toss a dollar bill into the little plate. He smiles and thanks me as he wishes me luck. He laughs and tells me that I must go to these places to hear music further down in the *Quarter*. I tell him I will as soon as I get some work. He runs over to the plate and gives me back my dollar. I feel like an idiot taking it back from him, but I pause, knowing that it may insult him all the more if I refuse it. The old guy tells me: "I do well here, son. Put all my kids through college. One's a lawya. They done well, mmmhuh."

Not that it's any of my business, but I have to ask

him. "How much do you rake in at a job like this?"

Guy looks up, "Oooh. Let's see….on good nights, anywhere from $150.00 to $200.00. Been doin' it for thirty years. Day all know me. Big shots. Come in here, with their buddies, get all loaded at thu bar, wid all their friens from outta town. You know... droppin' *twenties*, sum of 'em, and dey be blind drunk, sonny. Don' botha me nun a bit, yeah, aaa-huh."

Jeeeez, *I'll say*. The guy hands out towels to rich, drunken men every night and rakes it in. No wonder he seems so serene. If you ask me, if I were a black guy, I'd be thinking, as I'm brushing off some asshole's seersucker suit, this sure is one way to get *even*. Nodding and giving out *yessums* as you're pulling wads of cash out of the idiots' oversized pockets. Grinning like a cheetah as you brush 'em away. One right after the other. But I bet he doesn't do that. Probably doesn't really have to. The men that stroll in here probably feel pangs of guilt seeing this little old man standing there looking all spiffy and eager to hand them a towel, like a good subservient black guy. They probably feel like they have to tip him generously, as the old guy tells them how well the United Negro College Fund has served his collegiate kids. Or something of that order. I can just imagine.

I step onto Bourbon Street and decide to park myself at one of the outdoor cafes near the cathedral. It's lovely here. Banana trees lazily hang their floppy leaves over the tables. Lush foliage abounds. For a moment, I feel kind of sad. There are groups of people at the other tables, laughing, smiling, looking sexy and young. It makes me feel all the lonelier. I pull out my gear from my bag: the notebooks, the personal stereo. Right away,

I scribble in my journal about my disappointment in the job, and my enthusiasm about talking to Carlin's uncle. I imagine my *Lovely* is shaving the head of some maggot-infested patient at the nuthouse, so I put out my fanciest scrawl:

My Guinevere,

> *The sun descends slowly and a bit lazily in the Southern sky, perhaps a bit more so, as I approach the Equator more and more each day. Tomorrow I set out for the Gulf of Mexico. In the meantime, I'm pining away amid the verdant lushness of what seems to be a very sexy city. Of course, it pangs me that you are, perhaps, clipping the crustacean-like toenails of yet another wiry-haired loon, forgotten and neglected by a family from long ago. I wish I could touch your neck and stroke your golden hair while you're on your coffee break, but alas! Good things come to those who wait! Soon, I will be bringing in the dough to take with me when I meet up with you in a mere four months or so in the enchanted city of Edinburgh as promised.*

I close out the letter with a florid touch and remember to write out a couple of quick postcards to the family. I say everything is peachy cool and wonderful, not mentioning anything that's going on. On the one to Andy, I resist saying anything sarcastic about the stolen money. In fact, I don't mention it at all. This ought to piss him off. I jot a couple of notes off to my friends and on impulse, I write a card to Trent Chisolm at his home address in New Mexico. I pack everything up and head down Chartres Street, which will eventually take me to my great granddad's address on Dumaine.   I pay the waitress and walk into one of the charming cobblestone alleys that flank the old St. Louis Cathedral.   I proceed on to Chartres Street, remembering that Dumaine is in the lower section of the French Quarter, not all that far from Esplanade Ave, the boulevard that divides the Fauberg Marigny and the French Quarter.

My dad grew up in an old house on Frenchman Street, which is in the Fauberg as it is below Esplanade. It's now a hip area with Bohemian cafes and restaurants and some nightclubs, but when my father was growing up it was considered a neglected and run-down neighborhood. As I walk further down everything becomes quiet and almost residential in feeling. The shops become less ornate and antiquish as you walk along, and there are people here and there walking dogs and carrying groceries and stuff. I finally reach Rue Dumaine and look for the address I have scrawled on the notebook I carry around with me. It's a very old brick one-storey house with shutters and a small set of stairs leading to the doorway. I boldly walk up the steps and give a loud rap at the door. There is no name written on the mailbox, and no mail sitting in it, for that matter. I wait a while before I knock again. I take a seat on the little iron bench that sits on the porch area and write a brief note:

> *Am looking for Simon F. Strayhorn. I have something of yours from long ago and would like to return it to you. Am hoping to find you here when I try again tomorrow.*

My hand trembles as I write this and my mouth is feeling a bit dry. What if the old bastard has a fit or something? What if I return and he's a mad old lunatic cursing me because I dared to break his solitude, his solemn seal he made against the family as Andy told me. It was some thirty years ago when Great Granddad shut the family out of his life, and it probably doesn't even occur to him that he has a great grandson who's now a pretty big guy. I want to freak him out, actually, and I will be coming back, that's all I'm going to say. I decide to leave the note unsigned and slip it under the ancient door. I pause for a few minutes longer and decide to leave. It just occurs to me that I have not eaten anything since late this morning and I could use some grub.

I walk over to the next street where there's an open market. I pick up some food and head out to the Frenchman Street house where Andy grew up. I had seen it before when I was about eleven years old. It's an ancient building with a real slave quarters in the back of the main house, and there is a patio with a fountain that divides the two sections. Since Andy doesn't really talk much to his sisters, my aunts, I don't really talk to them. It's really kind of stupid, but that's the way it is. I barely know their kids, and we only see each other rarely. My mom told me that this was because my dad had the brains, talent and money-making abilities of the family, and he basically told them all to kiss his gifted ass. Seems like this kind of thing basically runs in the family.

Suddenly, I'm not so interested in walking back down in that direction. I decide to sit awhile. There are people bustling about, mainly tourists, and there are some street musicians playing horns on one of the corners across the mall area in front of the market. These kids and an old man are tap-dancing around one of the street corners. A plastic bucket stands in front of them. The kids look like they're about six to ten years old. And the old man is white. I say this because the kids are black. The old man is dancing around with an umbrella, and is wearing an old, withered-looking hat. People saunter and drop money in the bucket. The old man spins away from the tap dancers and twirls his paper umbrella as he walks up the street. He turns round and waves back at the children.

****

I've been sitting in the hostel living room for about an hour or so. New arrivals drop in and sit awhile. I try to busy myself with small talk and reading magazines. I feel so antsy, I decide I must do something, so I step out to my car and drive around a bit. I'm craving companionship, entertainment, anything to get my mind off my worries. I drive around quite a bit until I decide to check out this place where I can hear this really cool R&B music playing. When I step inside, the place is jam-packed with all these beautiful girls. Well, there are guys, too, but there's a banner behind the bar that reads: It's *Ladies' Night*! Well, this ain't so bad. I walk up to the bar and order a double shot of the house bourbon. I wander around amid the sweating arms and tube-tops, umbrella drinks and beaming smiles.

I stroll around a bit, in fact, I'm circling the same territory until a waitress looks over at me.

"Whaddya havin?" I tell her I had a drink at the bar. "There's a two drink minimum, ya know." I order another double shot and ask her to bring it over to the pool table where I'll be standing around watching the players. The waitress brings me my drink and I wander through the crowd and out to the back where there's a group of girls sitting at a table on a patio. One of them is waving in my direction. I turn around to check if there's someone behind me, and she smiles, beckoning me to come join them. I pull up a chair and introduce myself. She leans forward and braces my knee with both hands. "Don't you know Josh and Eric? You know, from the club?" I decide to play along a bit, and tell her I know too much about Josh and Eric. Only I thought she knew they were an item now. She looks a bit freaked. "You're ridiculous! Come on, where do I know you from? Josh and Eric are brothers!" Gulp. Well, I dunno. I scratch my head. I say, "Probably the club". The girl takes a sip from her umbrella drink and rolls her eyes. "Well, wherever I know you from you sure are cute!" Well, gee whiz. Company! I can see where this is going, alright. Now some of the other girls are looking over at me. "Nah. I don't know those guys. I've never been in here before until tonight." She leans on me again, but closer, and she's raising her brows at me, "Wanna get out of here a while?" Well, actually, I wouldn't mind that at all. It's kinda different when a girl is doing the picking up. Actually, it's refreshing. We weave our way through the crowd and out onto the oyster-shelled parking lot.

We step into my car and drive only a few blocks to her apartment. As we drive, I try to remember her name. I know she told me, but now I'm embarrassed to ask her again. We arrive at her building and climb several stairs to her attic apartment. As soon as we get in the door, old, *whatshername* starts in. She throws her arms around me and we start kissing like crazy. This is hot, this is really sizzling hot. And we're just going all over the place. She's unbuttoning her blouse, and I'm unzipping the jeans and suddenly, like a bolt out of the blue, I stop. I freeze and slam the brakes. I tell her, "I can't do this." She's looking at me a bit freaked. She's a babe. I tell her she's a babe.

I ask her, "What's going on?" She turns away and brushes her hair from her face. "Just leave, then. Just go, okay?" I stroke her cheek. " You're a beautiful girl. Whatever's happening, it's probably a lot of bullshit. I have a girlfriend I really like. She's in Connecticut. It has nothing to do with you."

I can't believe my own ears. My friends would think I'm nuts. Cory Banks would be drooling over the dish that's standing here in front of me in her sexy half-buttoned see-through blouse. I fasten my jeans and put on my T-shirt. As I leave she tells me I'm a nice guy. That she could see that right away. At the door, she tells me, "I was just giving you a line. I knew you didn't know those guys. I made it up!" We laugh. She offers me a beer for the road and I shrug. Why the hell not?

I climb back into my pathetic car, and drive back to the area where I had noticed another place that had live music and dancing. I park again in the oyster-shelled lot and walk a few blocks to the other dive. I walk in and just as expected, the place is even more crowded than it looked an hour or so ago. I figure this is good news. I don't know a soul here, so I start to dance around a bit, losing myself in the sea of sweaty arms and legs. A tiny black girl and a lean and rather tall black guy shimmy onto the dance floor from behind the bar where they're working. They start to dance with me, the girl waving a kitchen towel in the air as she shimmies her butt around and around; her body spinning in a circle. The guy leaps around like a frog, and every once in a while, he eyes the swing-door to the kitchen, checking to see if the boss sees him out here goofing off, I suppose. The girl seems real friendly and compliments me on my dancing technique.

She shouts, "Whooooo—-yeah! Shake it, baby. Oooooooo——yeah!"

The guy grins like crazy and says, "What's up, man?"

As the band quiets down, I chat with them a bit, and they both tell me to come over to the bar when I want to take a break and they'll give me a drink. Well, hey, why the hell not? I saunter over to the bar where these guys are back to business and I sit a while as Gary, the bartender, makes me these crazy concoctions. Well, as I'm swilling away, a terrifying thought enters my mind. *What if these guys are planning to roll me?*

I know this sounds crazy, but why are they being so warm and fuzzy? So I'm sitting here really looking at these two, wondering if they're covering up something. When I finally announce that I'm leaving, I head out the place, which is still rocking away, and charge for my car, looking back every few seconds to see if they're following me. When I realize that no one's approaching me, I feel like a lum-lum.

I walk back into the place, deciding one more drink wouldn't do any harm. They're still serving stuff and smile when I walk back up to the bar. I tell them I had to just check some things in my car. The girl asks me if I want some food. In fact, she insists that I do and brings out a platter of all this fried stuff. Seafood, fried potatoes, tomatoes, bread. I don't much care because I devour the entire thing. I slap a ten dollar bill on the bar and tell them to please take it as a tip from a grateful bum who's down on his luck. They both look concerned.

I say: "I was supposed to have a job. And now I have to wait a month, so in the meantime, I have very little to get by on."

I tell them the whole story and they both write down names of restaurants and bars where there might be some work available. Then they write down the name of the place where I happen to be and put the phone number on it. They tell me to call them the next day or so to see if they could find out about some available jobs. Who are these people? I never met people like this before. They're angels. Absolute angels. I feel so much better after talking everything out, I can't stop high-fiving them and actually, I almost cry. Right here at the bar among all these drunken fools. Sharina and Gary. As I leave, I feel like I made a couple of buds. Not acquaintances but real buds. But of course, I'm a bit drunk. And the evening's not quite over.

I manage to drive to another group of hangouts around the universities, and at two a.m. they're still rocking away. I settle for a bit at an outdoor cafe and load up on coffee and as I sit here, the Swedes that I met earlier at the hostel come rolling by. One points to me and smiles. Now they all gather around me. They tell me they're from Norway. Students travelling throughout the United States for the summer. They speak English pretty well. So we talk about music, computers, college, sports. We sit here chatting well over an hour.

I finally putter back to the hostel in my car, and as I'm gathering my things, I realize that I don't have my bag where I had some money (beside the stuff I have locked away) and the Luger. So I'm about $30.00 short of what is left of my meager till and I'm missing the gun. And now it's all coming back to me. I left the stupid bag at that girl's apartment. I remember it now, because I purposely carried the thing with me into the place because I had had everything in there and I was becoming leery of parking the car in these strange and dark neighborhoods. Why I didn't toss it into the trunk I do not know. I just wasn't thinking. And I suppose there was this vague idea about the condoms I have in there. And this is why I brought the whole bag upstairs. Even though I was a bit buzzed from the drinks, I remember the street she lived on because the street sign, *Magnolia*, was right in front of her house. That's all I know.

****

As soon as I get up this morning, I write out a sign that says: "Am in dire need of satchel bag. Has antique item that is a family heirloom. Are you the girl I am looking for?" Before I leave the hostel I tell Dini that I'm leaving instructions for the bag to be left there and I tell her it's a real important matter. She tells me that they'll be glad to accept it. No problem. I run over to a print shop and I make copies so I can post them up and down the girl's street before I head downtown. By noon, I'm done and I hope that the girl doesn't think I'm a slime for my only leaving an address where she can drop the thing off. It sounds so business-like.

I approach the building where Al Charbonnet asked me to meet with him. It's another old building with red bricks and huge ancient doors. I waltz in and there are a lot of men standing around in the hall talking and laughing. Rough-looking guys. Rig workers, I guess. Standing around waiting to get their dough. Or whatever they do. I ask at the window for Al Charbonnet. The wrinkled-faced woman takes a long suck on her lipstick-soaked cigarette; she dragon-mouths me as streams of gray smoke roll from her nostrils. She places her cig in the ashtray and points her long painted nail at the ceiling. She's moving her lips at me alright, but I can barely hear her.

She slides the glass window open, "He's upstayaz, dawlin. Upstayaz. Rum three fowrteen. Right when ya turn thugh cornah, jus keep wawkin up thugh hall, suga, and you'll see em in dare. He's thugh short fella. He's reeeel sweet. Can be kinda cranky sumtimes, but he's a doll. Really. He'll take care of ya, precious. Is dat all ya wanna know, dawlin? Or is dare anything else I can do for ya? Wanna snack, cup a cowfee, precious? Yu awright?"

This woman's a real trip. All I'm asking is where I can find the guy and she's talking to me as if I am a 10 year old kid hobbling in the door with broken limbs and a smashed head. Do I look that pathetic? Do people not talk to her? Or is she just lonely sitting in that glass booth all day long answering phones, smoking away?

I proceed up the stairs and into the long hallway. The floors are waxy clean and the ceilings are about eighteen feet high. I find the room and overhear old Al talking on the phone. I move the door slightly before tapping on it to get his attention. The guy's giving me a *who in the hell are you?* kind of look and begins to wave me away. I back out into the hallway as I hear Al finishing up his call. When he hangs up the phone I step in.

Al shakes his head and tells me: "Ya supposed ta git in line like evryboddy else. What's de name, is it on heea?" Apparently, I have caught Al in one of his cranky moods.

"I'm Simon Strayhorn. I talked with you yesterday. You wanted me to have lunch with you. But if it's a bad time, I'll just come by another day."

Al beckons to me: "Git in heea. Jeezus, it's busy taday. Sit down. We'll go in about two minutes. I'm stawvin, howboutchew?" Al's digging his paws in a crinkled, brown paper bag, looking at me with a huge grin on his face.

"Got sum things ta tell ya, Simon. Ain't lookin' good. Gotta call from de boss. We had ya application awready, an I feel like an iddyat. Don't git scayed, now. Wea gonna help ya out. But. . . hey ya wanna slice of dis hogshead cheese?"

I slide back in the chair, bracing for the worst. I want to sit up and simply say: *Cut the crap, Al.* But I don't. I sit here waiting, as his prodigious lips smack on the whatever in the heck it is he's eating.

Al continues, "I wanted ta see if we got any information on ya, so I did somthin' stupid, yestaday. I asked if we had evva received an ap from ya, and well, we did, and de boss was aroun' and well, now he knows. "

I raise a brow:

"Knows?"

"Dat stupid Cawlin, iddiyt! Didn't he tell ya dey won't take ya out dare unless ya tweny yeas old? Dat dummy!"

My heart doesn't sink. It nose-dives. What in the hell am I going to do now? Well, it's stupid. Al's holding some of the meat puppet garbage in his moist beefy fingers.

I ask, "What do you call that stuff, again?"

"It's hogshead cheese! Didn't ya daddy tell ya 'bout hosghead cheese? It's a delicacy from out dare in Acadiana. Bayou country."

Al says not to worry. He's going to think of a way to get me in. The idea is to be careful around the insurance companies. There are tricks around this, he says. Then he says there are other jobs that pay pretty well, that I could work as a cook's helper. It isn't such a bad way to get acquainted with the work. He eyes me up and down and punches my arm a bit. He thinks I've got a good build and must come from strong stock because I have good teeth and what looks like strong bones. He asks if I ever played football, basketball. I tell him basketball and that I was very active in sports in high school.

We walk down the stairs and Al stops and blows a kiss at the heavily made-up woman sitting in the smoky glass booth.

Al says, "Layta, Chooch! Gawd! Ya dawlin! Who loves ya, Baby?"

Chooch blows a smoky kiss back at Al.

I ask:

"*Chooch* ? "

Al tells me her name is *Caboose*.

"She was the *last* of seven kids. But evryboddy heea calls her *Chooch* ". We walk on. There are a couple of huge men standing around. Al grins at them both. They must be rig workers. They're gargantuan. One's about seven feet tall and is about the size of a vending machine. The other is almost as tall, his massive hands hang loosely against his side-of-beef shanks.

Al turns to me." I wancha ta meet deez guys. Hey,Yuma! Truax! Cum heea. Cum on ova heea right dis minit. I wancha ta meet da new kid on da block".

These enormous troglodytes walk over to us, nodding their huge heads at me, swallowing my hands in theirs. Next to these guys, I'm a wus. But Al's bragging about me as if I were his long lost jock-nephew. Al tells them that he wants to send me out next run, and that I could go as a junior rig-man in training or something, and work in the kitchen for starters. Yuma and Truax are saying enthusiastic things all over the place, their heads shaking, their eyes sparkling, their lips straining as they keep them from bursting out in wide scary-looking smiles. You can see it. Any moment, these guys are going to emit gigantic belly laughs and blow us out of the door, but they're keeping straight faces and nodding away, and saying "yeah, man" and keeping it all very polite and civil in front of the foreman, or whatever Al's title is. I can just imagine these guys hauling me outside and pulverizing me for having the gall to fill in a-non-union application.

Al and I head down Ambrose Street. We stop at a simple looking building with a barely noticeable sign out front. We step in and the place is filled with more huge men. This must be the land of huge men. There's cigarette smoke wafting in the air. All of them drinking beers and wolfing down massive quantities of food. We find a table in the very back away from the crowd hanging around the bar. Al tells me this is where the guys all hang out and that the food is incredible. He tells me that I can order anything I like. I'm hungry, so I order away. Actually, I'm sort of hoping this meal lasts me until tomorrow, so I am ordering all kinds of stuff. Al's telling me about knucklehead Carlin.

"He's a lazy rotten bum, dat kid. Howdja evva gitchaself involved wid a brat like dat kid?"

I proceed to tell old Al that we had been friends since our elementary school days and out of habit, we kept in touch. Al is listening raptly as I tell him that, as a kid, Carlin was a pretty nice guy. But as he grew older, he mostly spent his time in a bong. A smoky haze. A real cookout head, that Carlin. I tell him I think it's a shame. That he's actually a bright guy. Our food arrives and I plow right into the platters heaping all over the table. Al tells me that I'd love the rigs.

He leans closer to me and practically blushes, "Da food out dare is summin. De roast beef's beautiful. De sauces dey pour ova it awe so luscious, you'd die! You'd jus die! De guys had ta tell dah cooks dat dey had ta go easy. It wuz becummin dangerous. Dey just culn't take it. Dey were actually so *turned on* by de sauces, dey didn't wanna werk. Can ya imagine dat? We had a crises on our hands."

Al's is not the best-looking face to look at while you're eating, that's all I'm going to say. And he talks about food as if it were sex or something. Al looks like he had some acne problems in his youth, and his hair is gray and thinning and his face hangs down a few layers of extra chins. I tell him that the food is absolutely awesome as I swallow another deep-fried soft shell crab.

Al nods his head. "Yeah. Ya eatin' 'em right. Ya daddy musta toll ya about dese soft shell crabs. Gotta eat it whole wid de claws an all. Ya doin' it right, Simon!"

I bob my head as Al talks, realizing that I have no recollection of *my daddy* telling me *how* to eat these things. I'm just so famished, it doesn't matter to me that I'm actually swallowing a crustacean, claws and all.

I tell Al about where I'm staying, and what I think of his city so far. I tell him how much fun I've had and that

I hope I can simply find a job to hold me over. I tell him that I'll probably try to find something like a sales job. Al's lips are smacking with pleasure as I say this. He says it should be no problem to find a job right now. He asks me more questions about my family and the like and we move on to a platter of fried oysters and shrimp. He asks me what I like to do and stuff like that. He tells me that I sound like I'm more on the ball than Carlin. And he apologizes once again for my not knowing there was an age requirement for the job. Al asks me to give him my number at the hostel so he can let me know if anything comes up. He tells me that the kitchen job pays a very decent wage and that while I may not make as much money as I wanted, it would be ok as I won't have to pay for things like room and board. We talk and eat for a very long time, and old Al is ordering the beers like crazy. I'm pretty drowsy from the food and beer and I want to go somewhere and nap. I ask Al if he knows any nice place to relax, and he tells me to go to this park not far from where we are. From there, I can take a bus back into the French Quarter as I'll be returning to the Dumaine Street address in search of my great granddad.

We finish up the food and Al says, "dare's one thing ya gotta have. An it's de bread puddin'."

I politely accept and when the thing arrives it's soaked in brandy.

Al leans over gleefully and lights the thing on fire.

"Ya gotta have it dis way".

I watch the leaping flame, wondering just how long we must allow the small fire to burn.

Al says, "Stamp it out now."

I do so, and wolf down the little spongy cake on my plate. Someone has dropped some coins in the juke box.

There's an old song, "*The Things I Used to Do*", by *Guitar Slim*, blaring through the room. It's a cool song. Al tells me about the old days and the famous singers he has had the privilege of hearing. I tell him that my dad likes all that R&B stuff. Al leans over and squeezes my hand. He tells me that he's really glad to meet me. That he'll be in touch and if not, he wants me to also check in with him from time to time. Al must be a lonely guy, that's all I'm going to say. But so am I, sort of. When I think about it, I'm a *drift*er now, and well, I accept alms gratefully. I thank Al profusely. He waves me off. Says the lunch was nothing. That if I'm around, he'd like me to come over to his house for Thanksgiving. He then leans forward and tells me the way he cooks a turkey. His eyes light up and his hairy nostrils are slightly flaring.

"I take a big turkey. About a thurty-pounder. I den take a smalla turkey and stick it inside de big turkey. Den, inside of dat, I take a duck and stuff de duck inside de smalla turkey, see? Den, I take a small chicken an I stuff de chicken inside de duck! All of 'em aw stuffed wid oysta dressin', bread crumb stuffin', yu name it. It's de best!"

Sounds a little kinky to me, Al, but I'll take your word for it. Actually, it sounds like the famous chef who suggested this crazy recipe was having a nervous breakdown when he came up with the idea. Either that or he was drunk. Al tells me that it's hard for him to go back to the office after such a meal. In fact, he tells me that he needs to go across town to run some errands and offers me a ride near the park he recommended. I accept the offer, but tell him I'd rather be dropped off in the French Quarter instead. Old Al.

We head out of the parking lot and drive into a famous street that runs alongside the river. Al drops me off at the French Market area and once again, I thank him for the swell lunch. He waves his paws at me as he pulls the car away. I step onto the sidewalk, into the blaring sun. I briskly walk around the market area and out to the river walkway. There are ships pulling in, most of them huge freighters from South America. The Mississippi River is a boiling brown body of water. I walk over to the market area and back onto Decatur Street finding a tiny hangout that's dark and cool inside.

I step in and there are about three people sitting on the cushioned stools, toying with their drinks. The bartender looks like he's done time. He has missing teeth and tattoos crawling up and down his hairy arms. He seems friendly enough, though, and actually, he looks glad to see another body walk into the practically deserted bar. He slides a paper coaster towards me, and asks what I'd like to drink. I tell him that I just had this enormous meal with a few beers and what I'd like is a plain soda.

The lady sitting next to me frowns in her glass while she flicks her cigarette in the ashtray. She must be about sixty years old. Her hair is a pinkish red and her face is covered in make-up.

She leans over to me.

"Food too much for ya, huhm, honey? Ya must be from outa town."

I tell her that I am, but that I have family here. She wiggles her nose at me while taking a long drag off her cigarette.

"Yeah. Dis place is som-in, alright. De politics awe filthy. Got dat crook in de govena's seat in Battin Rouge an he's in de mafia. An dey luv em heeah. Absalootly luv dat thief, huh, Earl?"

I imagine the humped figure clad in a T-shirt and resting his head on the bar is *Earl*. Either he's passed out or napping, like I wish I were. Old Earl here doesn't budge and the woman is still talking to him, asking questions.

She turns back to me.

"Well, he's out. I toll 'em not ta orda anything. Dat it's too early fowr dat stuff. What's he drinkin', Bobby?"

The bartender tells her that he served Earl a few shots of sloe gin.

The lady wiggles her nose again and raises her shoulders, shrieking.

"Sloe gin! Dat stuff is so sweet it makes me vomit, I swear ta Gawd. My daddy gave me suma dat stuff one time and I passed out right dare unda de table".

The lady turns to me and scowls.

"Jesus gawed! Don't evva try dat stuff, ya heea me?"

I assure her I won't, and finish up my soda, noticing that's it's almost four-thirty. I tell the lady and the humped figure, Earl, goodbye and leave a dollar on the bar for the bartender.

Out on Decatur Street, I proceed down to the house a few blocks west on Dumaine. Hanging on the front door is the note I wrote yesterday. On it someone has scrawled: *No one living here anymore*. Oh, really? Then *who* wrote this? Maybe the old man's paranoid. I decide to check out the back of the house. It's a long, one-storey building, and in the back there's a quaint, walled-in garden with a fountain, I can see it through the grilled gate on the side of the building. I walk back to the front porch and plop myself on the bench. I lay my head on the chair arm and close my eyes. There's a slight breeze in the air. My legs are a bit uncomfortable, but anything is better than having to walk.

After about twenty minutes, I decide to head out for the park. Al was right. It's very pleasant here and the massive trees lessen the heat a bit. I walk over to a quaint little spot near a pond where ducks are swimming all over the place. The breeze is slightly picking up and I'm relieved to be laying here. It's very quiet with only a few people walking around. I close my eyes and think about my situation. I know I'll have to look for a job somewhere starting this weekend. And I'm hopeful. My body is heavy with fatigue. I feel it settling into the soft grassy ground, embedding itself deeply into the earth. The breeze is blowing slightly, and I feel a few drops of rain on my body, a welcomed relief from the oppressive summer heat.

Rock, rock, rock. My body is tranquil, but inside, my spirit is screaming, and I'm again, walking on a seashore. I'm anxious and seemingly alone. Someone once told me when I was a child that when you lift an abalone shell and hold it against your ear you can hear an entire oceanic universe echoing inside. And sometimes the sound can beckon you. I look up to the sky, and there's nothing but blue and gold. I look to the landscape in back of me, and there are two figures standing there. I ponder a decision and the uneasiness rising up within me is beginning to increase. My heart is pounding and my mouth is dry. I turn to the waves and lose myself in the silent lull of foam coagulating as the water rushes to shore. I can hear them now. They are approaching me, these two figures. And they're disguised as assassins and their faces are indistinguishable, hooded, veiled. I call out to them to please stop. To please stop back and watch me as I show them the hidden, bejeweled daggers I hold under massive robes of color. I'm armed, I tell them, and they cannot approach me unless they give me the answers I've come for. *I'm Simon Lazarus.* The resurrected one. If you wish to have me dead again as I once was, then you are welcomed to try. But I will fight you. I will fight you and you will be lying there in the sand having to answer me as my foot rests on your chest. I'm an apprentice to the forces that once besieged you, and you, having age, think that you can hover over me the wounds you wear as emblems, but if you are here to badger me, I will fight you off. You pose as elders, but you aren't really here to bestow any wisdom to me, you are here to shame me into silence. I have the weapons and they are here, and they are hidden and that is where I will keep them.

The two figures are standing atop a dune, and they are trembling, their knees are knocking, their teeth are chattering. They're actually frightened off and I can see them running. Running away, over the dunes, and all I'm thinking is that I have spoken for something that blew through me. It baffles and humbles me as I stand there dazzled in the light. I feel my body trembling inside as this great force heaves through me and out of me, and back out to sea like a roaming wind seeking to attach itself to its rightful owner. I look out to the blue and green waves, the sun sprinkling flecks of gold as they move in their majestic power. And I fall down to the ground and lay there exhausted, the sprays of water dancing atop my face as I feel my body sinking into the wet sand. I hear the ringing of my own voice echoing inside:

I'm Simon Lazarus, and I will wait until I am ready

*to rise and roam with new bones, and maybe when I'm
ready, I will show to the world a new heart, and the daggers will fall away; their usefulness exhausted in elimi-
nating the worn hearts of old and their hollow experience. What was good for them will not work for me. And
I will be ready . I will be ready.* As I pull my body up to
leave, one of the figures has returned. He conceals his
face as he stares deeply into my eyes. Who are you? I
cry. The figure turns away and starts running. I attempt
to follow, but my feet are like lead and there is a voice
telling me to look back to the sea, I do and for a flicker
of a second, I see my father rowing away in a boat. I
force my legs to move into the foamy waves as I yell for
him to wait for me, but he's rowing too fast.

And I'm soaking wet; a bit confused as I shake
myself awake. The rain pours over me in great sheets
and the ground I'm laying on is puddle-deep with water.
I pull myself up in a great thrust and run for shelter under
the awning of the museum building. I'm completely
soaked and I dare not enter the building since it is probably refrigerator-cold in there. So I sit here watching the
cars in the rain, their windshield wipers rigorously
sweeping away sheets of water as they slowly crawl by.

****

Since that stormy afternoon, I've been holed up here
in the hostel with a pretty bad cold. Later that evening,
I had come down with chills and a fever. Dini Hebert,
the lady that runs the joint, has been very kind to me, and
gave me a private room for a few nights for the same
$12.00 a night rate. Which floors me. While I was sick, I
had asked Dini if my bag had ever been returned. On the

day I had gone downstairs for the first time in what seemed like ages, I noticed it sitting behind the counter. I asked Dini about it, and she told me that it had been returned , all right.

Late one night there was a loud rap at the door, and some outraged creep carried the thing inside, swinging it around in the hallway, asking to meet the owner of the bag. When they explained to him that I was upstairs ill and sleeping, he threw the bag at the desk and walked out, saying if he ever saw me near his girlfriend again, he'd pulverize me. Well, it's all I needed. I checked the bag and to my surprise, everything was still in there, including the Luger. You'd think the thing would've been loaded with a bomb or something. And I was relieved to see that the thirty dollars was still in there, too. In fact, everything seemed as it was, except for one thing. The condoms were missing. I guess in the midst of his rage, the guy probably threw them at her, and then picking them off the floor, decided to keep them.

I've been wracking my brain over the want ads for a few days now, and my till is growing thinner by the day. Sharina has called me a couple of times to give me some tips as to what restaurants and bars were offering jobs but all of them were for waiter or bartending help and asked for experience. There's one notice I find, however, that asks for no experience. Just a strong pair of hands and the ability to work fast. As an *'oyster shucker'*. It's the only ad for such a position that said they'd hire a beginner. All the others are asking for *heavy experience*.

I tell Sharina, my new pal, I think this is absurd. You take a shell, crack it with a tiny hammer, and cut the oysters out with a knife. Any bozo should be able to do that. Well, Sharina pauses for a while; I can actually hear her breathing over the phone, and after a few seconds, she says I'd be surprised. That it's a tough job, especially if it's a busy restaurant on a Saturday night. I tell her that the restaurant is in the heart of the French Quarter.

Sharina lets out a heavy sigh, "Oooooooh, boy! No wonda they aren't askin' for much experience. Do you know how busy those places git?"

Well, I don't care. After meeting those tough guys over at Al's office, and considering work as a chef's assistant on the rigs, this isn't anything. It'll be just the right amount of money to rake in to keep a roof over my head, and the ad said "*immediate hire.*" All of the better jobs, like library's assistant, which I applied for, had mailing addresses, not even e-mail ones, and I can only imagine how long it would take just to get an interview. The money wasn't much better for those kinds of jobs anyway, and this one said I'd get a share of the bartender's tips.

I'm driving my car downtown today, as I told the lady, Mrs. Giangiani, that I would be down there to interview with her within the hour. The place sounds like a strip joint, but she promised me it was a restaurant with a famous oyster bar. That people mostly go there for drinks, oysters and to hear the music. Which she said, was one of the best spots in town. I manage to find a parking spot a few blocks away, and I run to the restaurant, a sign out front flashing: *Babs' Big Easy*.

I walk in and the place looks pretty swank. Shiny tile floors, a mahogany bar with polished brass railings, antique-looking ceiling fans, mirrored walls with elaborate mahogany trimming. The waiters are standing around, adjusting their immaculate, starched waistcoats, and the bartender looks like a real pro, dressed in a crisp white shirt with black bow tie and vest. The place looks like it's preparing for lunch, as it's about eleven a.m. There's music playing, and it sounds like a ragtime piano solo with a cool rhythm section playing in the background. For a minute, I am remembering this tune. In fact, it's eerily familiar to me. I look over at the bartender who is raising his brow at me. I tell him I'm here for an interview, but could he tell me who's playing this tune?

He smiles at me, and rubs his chin. "That's *The Professor. Professor Longhair.* He's dead now. Wait here. Let me get Babs."

The guy lifts the waiter's stand, his heels clicking on the tiles as he walks to the back and up a flight of stairs. I remember this tune, alright. It's something I heard at my dad's. Cat knew how to play the piano, that's for sure.

A heavily perfumed fat woman with dark brown hair and loads of eye-makeup approaches me. The bartender lingers behind a bit as he pauses to give instructions to a group of waiters. She smiles at me, a gold tooth shining at the bottom of her mouth. "The student, right? I spoke to ya a while ago?"

I nod my head.

"Well! Ya look like a big guy to me! Lemme see ya hands, son."

She runs her fingers over my hands and looks up at me. She tells me that I will need to wear rubber gloves at times, but that I'll be professionally trained. I ask her what the hours are, and the usual stuff. She tells me that I'll start with the daytime shift, and will gradually work up to the late afternoon/evening shift. The work is tougher at night, but the tips are better. Whenever a drinking customer orders oysters at the bar, I get a share in the tips. Roughly thirty percent.

Old Babs shouts: "The erster freaks only cum out at night, son, with thu rest of 'em. Ain't that right, Joe?"

The bartender nods his head, slapping a towel over his shoulder with one hand as he twirls a glass in the air with the other. Babs reassures me that, for starters, the day-shift will be enough. She smiles at me again and asks if I can start tomorrow. I'm so grateful to be getting a job I tell her I could start today. I step away from the bar as she tells me to be at the restaurant at 10 a.m. sharp. That I'll be in training all day.

I step out of the door where a couple of busboys are taking a smoke. One of them looks at me, and follows me a bit as I walk out.

"Hey! Yu thugh new shucka?"

I turn around, and the two are grinning at me.

"Nobody's goin' ta give ya nuthin' in thayr; Joe's an asshole...*brutha*."

The both of them jab each other in the ribs laughing and waving at me. They're probably right. That guy didn't exactly look like the type to share tips with an oyster shucker. But I don't care. Even if I only get forty-five bucks a day. It's still work. I wave to the busboys and shout back to them. "And don't tell me, if I'm lucky, I'll get promoted to busboy, right?" One of them shrugs his shoulders and laughs.

I walk back to my car and head uptown to the Derbigny Clinic where I made an appointment to see the doctor that performed a minor operation on Great Granddad about six months ago. I drive down the leafy-lined street in the uptown section of the city, and walk into the quaint little lobby. I approach the reception desk. A nurse smiles at me and slides the glass door open. She politely asks me to step into the doctor's office and wait in there. I'm ushered into a small, cozy-looking office that faces a patio area that sits in the middle of the complex. A tall, bespectacled man, about fifty-five-ish steps into the room holding a file, smiling down at me as he asks me to remain seated. "You must be Simon Strayhorn, the *younger?* We got your inquiries. Well, your great granddad is alive and well, alright." He smiles and then explains to me that my great granddad is a real character. That he has all of his wits and had the staff laughing the last time he was there.

The doctor leans over his huge desk as he tells me that the old man was being examined by one of the nurses and given that he seemed to have a crush on her, he refused to disrobe unless she did the same. He continues, "The whole place cracked up laughing. He's a healthy, active 91-year old. Not one senile bone in his body. And sharp. We hardly had to explain anything as he elected to consult with specialists on his own. He wanted nothing in the way of conventional medicines, either. Said he was once involved with a Native American woman and had been schooled in herbal medicines. He smokes *grass*. In fact, he commented to this same nurse that she missed her chance in joining him for a toke on the stuff earlier as we were about to perform the surgery. Good thing he told us, though. We might've over-medicated if he hadn't said something."

I'm sinking into my chair. This all sounds absolutely horrifying to me. Another *hipster*?

I tell the good doctor that I have tried to make contact with the old goat, but to no avail. He thinks that the old man is playing foxy with me and that I should persist.

"Well, he is known to keep to himself." The doctor gets up, "Maybe he'll come around. He's due for another visit..." the doctor peruses the schedule in his book,"...soon. In fact, he'll be in here Friday next. That's a little over a week from today. At 12:30."

The doctor walks over to the door, letting me know his next appointment is waiting. I thank the guy. I'm stunned and excited at the same time. I was really expecting the old man to be feeble-minded and near death. I stumble on my gun-boater *Nikes* as I walk out of the office. The doctor pauses and looks down at my feet and smiles. "He wears those, too. The kind with the blinker lights in them."

As we walk up the hallway that leads to the reception area, a nurse is standing beside a frail elderly woman, smiling at us. The doctor stops in his tracks and introduces me to her. "This is Mr. Strayhorn's great grand son, Wanda".

The nurse laughs. "You should come over and surprise him. He'll probably have his headset on. Ya can't miss him."

Headset ? It's really too much. I *hate* the guy. I hate him. He's been living well down here all these years and I didn't know anything. I'm glad I came in here, I'm relieved at hearing the truth. He's never bothered to inquire about me. He never even bothered to do the decent, Scottish thing and pick up the phone and say he wanted to talk to me. I never did anything to him. I didn't snub him. He snubbed us. Who does he think he is?

I'm not charmed by the good doctor and nurse, either. I see right through the old goat. He avoids everybody because he sits on a pot of gold. That lady shrink he shacked up with all those years made him a wealthy man, alright. My dad left all this for a reason. And here I am walking right back into it. No wonder Andy resents the hell out of me. No wonder he swiped my dough. Serves me right. While I have the time, I am going to write Boyce a very long e-mail. It looks like watershed time. If I see that old gizzard in his stupid blinking sneakers and headset, I'm going to kick his bony ass. And I'm going to aim the Luger at his old skull that's all I'm going to say.

I drive away from the cluster of medical buildings that sit in back of a hospital and head back down into the French Quarter. I'm going to shoot that old man. I'm taking the gun and I'm walking up to that porch and banging the hell out of that front door like the SWAT team. I have had enough of the Strayhorns and their perennial hipster ways! Here I was, all of my life, thinking maybe, maybe the old man had some style. Some originality. I dunno. Maybe still dressing in tails and a top hat on New Year's Eve or something. A man with something truly distinctive to offer: wisdom, experience, and the usual things you associate with aging men who were born in the old country. And what do I finally hear? I get the big news that the guy dresses like he's into *gangsta* rap.

I pull up to the house and park my car. I take out the Luger and let it rest in my lap as I observe the people walking by. I check for any activity in the house, and as usual there is none. Or there seems to be none. I leap out of my car and hop up the stairs. I cock my ear to the door and I can detect a slight humming noise. A vacuum cleaner or something. Here's my chance.

I know he's in there. Probably vacuuming the rug as he listens to *Dr. Dre* or whatever in his headset. I rap the door loudly with the Luger. And I wait. The vacuum is still going away. I knock at the door again and still there is nothing. Okay, he's probably hard of hearing and has the headset turned on full blast. I wait a little longer, tucking the gun in my jeans at the waist. I begin to pound the door and kick it hard.

"Come on out you old coward! Come on out and let's see what you're really made of you old man! Come on out and face me, ya Scottish bastard! You can't fool me with your games, your foxy little ploys. I'm named after you, you old coot!"

Finally, I hear the front door click. It slowly opens and before me is an attractive black woman wearing an old fashioned scarf tied around her head. She's actually young, about thirty-five, and she's looking at me as if I were crazy.

She waves her hands in the air and tells me to shush my big mouth. "Honey. He doesn't live here. Yu lookin' for Mr. Simon? He's ova at the othu house. Hasn't lived here in a couple of years. He rents this out, and I'm here ta fix it up for the new tenants. Whatcha so mad at, anyway? He jus an old man, son. He's a nice old man, too. Wouldn't harm anybody. Minds his own business. He's fun, you know. Enjoys himself. Here."

She steps inside and writes the address of the house where my dad grew up. I ask her how long the old man has owned the building. She furrows her brows and tells me he had always owned it.

"He likes it alot betta than the one on Colasie—uh, ah, the one in the Garden District here". She hands me the note. That rich old bastard. I ask her what else he owns and she looks taken a back. "I dunno, son. You kin to him?"

I tell her who I am and that I want to see him. "But don't tell him anything" I add, "I want to surprise him."

"I'll say. You do that, and he'll call the cops. He's a tough old man. I wouldn't fool with him any. He's seen alot, you know. Yu shuld have more respect for him. But I won't tell him anything, ok?"

I thank her and apologize for scaring her with my antics. I hear the vacuum cleaner switch back on as she gets back to her work, leaving the door ajar. I knock on the door a bit and ask her if there's a phone number where I can reach him, and she tells me that he doesn't allow anyone to have his phone number. That she doesn't even know it and has worked for him for a number of years. I don't believe this, but I let it go. I then ask her if she was the one who wrote on the back of my note the week before or so and she shrugs her shoulders. This woman is apparently under some tight set of instructions.

I slip back into my car and head for the other house. I pull up to the old building on Frenchman Street. It looks newly painted and fixed up. I tremble as I walk up to the walled gate and ring the buzzer. There's no response. As usual. I leap a bit in the air trying to catch a glimpse behind the great wall in front and as I do so, I notice broken glass strewn over the top of it. Well, that's clever. I'll be back. That's all I'm going to say. Wait a second... I run back to the car remembering the crumpled note I haphazardly stuffed into my notebook that afternoon before I got caught in the rainstorm. I return to my car and examine the two notes. Hers, with the Frenchman Street address and the other. Both are different, alright. He wouldn't just go over there to check on things. He lives there. He must. I stuff the gun back into the satchel and lock it in my smashed trunk. I look on my map for a public library and decide to drive to the main one downtown.

After spending an hour and a half dizzying my head in these street directories, the librarian tells me he thought the woman probably meant to say Coliseum Street. Here it is in plain view: the exact address and the name: Simon F. Strayhorn. It even lists a phone number. I leave the library like a crazed loon, running down stairs and back to my car. I speed uptown. I find the house, alright. And it's a beauty. A three-storey, 19th century wonder, with trees and lacey iron lawn furniture and charming clusters of flowers here and there. I approach the walkway leading up to the house and I freeze. Dogs bark as they run from the back of the house. And they are ferocious-looking Dobermans. Well, shucks. There are four of them and they're making a lot of racket. I jog backwards from the black iron gate and race back to my car. Okay, so I can't exactly do it this way. But I have his phone number. I'll just call the old hipster and mess with his head a bit. I'll breathe heavily before saying I'm Gig Mastriani, his old pal from the grave. The guy was finally gunned down in the 1950's. It'll probably give him a heart attack.

I arrive back at the hostel and Dini is standing behind the desk. I hand over my stuff and I sit in the waiting room changing my shoes, figuring the *gun boaters* should be retired. I want nothing to do with anything in the way of creating a bond with my hip great grandfather. Actually, I want nothing to do with him save my single mission in returning the stupid gun.

Dini forks over my laptop as she knows this is the usual time I write e-mails to people. I have a lot to get off my chest, that's all I'm going to say. Dini looks at me funny. "Simon, you sure are lookin' mighty flustered." I tell her that I finally got a job and that I know I have less than a week to clear out of there. Her eyes light up, "We're lookin' for a handyman 'round here. Weekends only." I tell her that I believe I will be working most weekends. She frowns and tells me that, actually, the work can be done on a catch as catch can basis, as long as it gets done. It means I could stay on here and rent one of the spare rooms at half-price. I have to remember that the spare rooms are pretty shabby. They aren't as nice as the single guest rooms, like the one I was in while I was sick. But I could use the discount. And it would relieve the pressure of having to scout for a new place to live. Dini commiserates with me a bit. She thinks it's a shame I can't enjoy myself. I check my phone messages. A couple are from Sharina.

I pop over to the payphone and take out the sheet of paper that has the phone number at the Garden District house. I dial the number and a youngish woman answers the phone. I'm shocked and I simply hang up. I call Sharina and leave her a message. I set out and drive around for a bite to eat. While waiting for my order, I try the house again.

This time, a small child answers the phone. Stunned again, I hang up the phone. What's going on here? Don't tell me. The old coot has another family. The gall. Finally, I call the number again and the woman and the kid answer the phone at the same time. The woman tells the little kid to please hang up. I point-blank ask her if I could speak to Simon. She pauses for a minute and says she doesn't know who I'm talking about. I explain to her that I am looking for my great grandfather and could she please help me. I explain to her my plight and she listens intently. After a bit of a pause she tells me that she and her husband are renting the house, that they deal with a such 'n such real estate agency. The working phone came with the place, but no one has ever actually called for the owner there. I jot down the name of the agency and thank her.

****

My first week of work at *Babs' Big Easy* has been pretty bad, that's all I'm going to say. I'm not simply an oyster shucker, I'm a seafood handler and no one comes near me after I finish my shift. I shell shrimp, I crack crabs, I hammer oyster shells after I carry huge sacks of the things from the kitchen and out onto the seafood bar area. I wear a rubber glove on one hand, while the other bleeds from all the sticks and stings I get in a day's work. Afterwards, I hose down the seafood area back in the kitchen and my limbs are killing me by the end of the day. All I can do is hobble back to the car and roll down the windows as I drive back to the hostel to shower. The other day, Dini took me aside, while pinching her nose, of course, and gave me a key to the back door, telling me I'm to use it from now on. Not to offend me or anything, but it would be bad for newly arrived guests. Well, I guess I can't blame her. Anyway, each afternoon, I take out my clothes, hose them down in the backyard area of the hostel and hang them to dry once I wash them. It's a grunt life, all right. If I have a few extra minutes, I'll get back into the car and drive around a bit.

Sometimes I drive up to the river-viewing area in Audubon Park where I watch the ships and write letters. But lately, my fingers are too sore to write for long stretches, so I keep my messages brief. Everyone in the world thinks I'm offshore in the middle of nowhere except for Boyce. I gripe a lot to him and he writes me back and tells me how proud he is of me. He warns me to not blow it with the old man. That he's worth checking out. And from the last e-mail I received from Boyce, he suggested I simply write the old guy a letter. Frankly admitting who I am and that I'm aware of his penchant for ignoring the family. So the other night, as I was sitting on my perch near the river, I wrote out this letter to him.

> *Dear Great Granddad,*
>
> *That's right. I am your unknown great grandson, and I am writing you this letter because my search for you has become most foiled and elusive. You seem to know how to get around! Your grandson, Andy Strayhorn, is my Pop. I grew up in Connecticut and I am now a college student on a very long break. I'm interested in philosophy, and I may go to medical school.*
>
> *Right now, I work as an oyster shucker. But I'm set to go offshore in a few weeks. I will be gone until late October, and upon returning, I will be setting out for Europe. I would like to meet with you someday soon. Could you please call me? Or drop by Babs' Big Easy, some afternoon? It's not far from where you live.*

I have to admit, I was pretty nervous addressing the thing and then mailing it to the Dumaine Street address, the place where I believe he really lives. I remember I walked a long time that night, and watched the sunset lighten the sky in these incredible pink and orange colors. I wondered about Andy and his growing up here, and what the old man might remember. If he had ever spent time with Andy when he was a kid and all. And maybe that shouldn't matter. I would just like to hear what he has to say. I just want some facts. Since I last wrote to Lisa, I have tried to not think of her, pretending in my mind that I am out in the middle of nowhere and unable to get a message to her. But it's hard. As for my family, I'm relieved to not have any contact with them. There have been nights when I have woken up in a sweat thinking about the missing money, but then I settle down and quietly rest my eyes as I think of my life down here as being not so bad. Sometimes, I flick on the little lamp and write in my journals, and I count the weeks I have left before setting out on the gulf.

Al Charbonnet came into the restaurant the other day and sat at the bar with a friend of his. He ordered some oysters and occasionally glanced at Joe as I hacked at the shells. He gave me a few pointers saying I was actually pretty good for a beginner, and he left me a three dollar tip, sliding the bills in my direction while Joe spun a glass in the air. From the way Al looked at me from time to time, I could see he didn't think much of Joe. And well, Joe thinks he's the king of bartenders. He's always barking orders at the busboys. Al leaned over to me and suggested that maybe Babs and Joe are an item. But I wasn't sure I believed that one. Babs is about fifteen years older, but then again, you never know. I don't even want to admit how the guy bosses me around.

The other day, Joe handed me a ten dollar bill, telling me that was my share of the tips. But it was the first time in two days that he forked anything over to me. I called him on this and he shrugged his shoulders saying that Babs should have told me that I wasn't going to be getting anything extra during training. That, actually, he was doing me a favor by giving me the extra dough. Well, I caught the guy counting the money and it must have been $130.00 just in tips. Now I should have received roughly $30.00 from that, but Joe gave me this incredulous look as he forked over a ten dollar bill. "Take it or leave it, my man." I replied, "Listen. I'm hardly your man. I'm a worker here and I get a thirty percent cut." Joe shook his head; his nostrils emitting jets of smoke from his cigarette. "Yeah, but that's only for the seafood orders at the bar. And we only get a few of those per shift. Doncha remember?"

Well, I figured maybe he was almost right, but when I sat down later and figured out the orders, I clearly saw that he gypped me out of ten dollars. I should have gotten twenty. Added daily, this could amount to a nice sum of extra cash. So I am now watching old Joe like a hawk. I can't help it, the guy's a thief. And maybe I should look the other way. After all, if he isn't shacking up with Babs, he sure is in good with her and I can't afford to lose my job right now.

So I keep the beak shut and take his piddling cash out of his slimy paws every afternoon, and walk away avoiding the stares from the busboy gang. That's right. Actually, the busboy *congress* is more like it. They all stare at me and scratch their heads as they convene outside smoking. They're unanimous in their deep dislike for Joe and ask me when I'm going to kick the guy in his ass. One of them, Tyrone Bentley, elected to help me get back at Joe by greasing the floor mat where he stands behind the bar. Every day, I'm getting closer to doing it.

****

During my off hours, in what spare time I have, I try to get myself more settled into the hostel as it seems this will be my home for a bit. So I've been making my little room cozier, and the other day something really weird happened while I was fetching some stuff out of the trunk of my car. I don't know what to think exactly, but I feel like a real lummox. As I was grabbing one of the notebooks I took from Caz's stash back home, a bit of information about that Dabney character spilled out. In the back of the notebook was a folded copy of a newsletter from Caz's school. Inside, there was a featured story about Jeffrey Dabney, being in one of the local hospitals with a broken leg. There's a photo of the guy grinning amid all these school girls standing around his bed. The article went on to say that Dabney, the drama teacher, had broken a leg by falling off a scaffold while he was adjusting the light settings during a rehearsal of some production the school was doing, and that he was regretful that he couldn't see *"his girls"* in a scene from a play that the school was performing at some regional playoff. My sister was also part of the story, saying that she was especially sorry that Dabney could not be there as she was one of the lead actors in the performance. *Blah Blah.* Well, what can I say? It looks like the note I had read was written by Dabney while he was shacked up in the hospital. It explained a lot. And, well, no wonder he was saying he wanted to see her, *"wanting to get away from this place"* and saying stuff like *" I'd tell you to go break a..."* I'm now assuming...the proverbial *leg*, or whatever corn the actor's saying is. All I can say is: *ha ha*! What a dummy I can be.

In addition, another week has passed and I have not gotten a word back from my great grandfather. I figured maybe it came as a surprise to him and maybe he's still mulling things over. Each day, I go into work to the same situation and I have become tolerant of the grungy routine of hacking shells, cracking claws and shelling shrimp. Babs seems pleased and I no longer complain to Joe when he slides me my meager portion of the tips. I actually don't know if I care anymore. Sharina and Gary stop in here and there and chat with me at the bar. Last Sunday, I attended Sharina's church, and we went out to Sunday brunch at a restaurant nearby. As you can imagine, I have developed an aversion to seafood, and I eat a lot of fries and hamburgers.

Al Charbonnet called and left a message this morning and he wants me to get back with him right away. My nerves are jittery right now, and I'm actually feeling a bit hesitant in calling him back. I have a hunch the news may not be good. He didn't sound real positive about my going out with the crew because of a seniority problem that came up with another guy who has already gone out there on several runs and is eager to get on this time because it had been several months and so, I am not expecting any good news. Why else would he call? My financial situation isn't all that bad. I do very little around the grounds here and I get a private room at half the price it would normally cost me. Plus I get freebies in the kitchen. So I'm covered for food and stuff. But at the rate I'm going, I don't think I will be able to save much if I am to take off for Europe in a few months. The cook assistant's job would definitely help as the money works out to be a significant wage. A gold mine compared to the meager wages I'm earning now. But these things are minor compared to what's reeling in my head now.

Last night, I suddenly woke up after dropping off like a dead dog on my little bed. Each evening I seem to go through a nap routine, and fall asleep at five in the afternoon, sometimes sleeping into the next morning, but lately I've been waking up around one am. I grew depressed looking around my tiny room, and decided to throw on some clothes and prowl the streets. Which was weird, because this is a very dark and enchanting city at night. It's as if the true city comes to life at night, with all its mysteries unfolding. And actually this couldn't have happened in a more appropriate setting. After swilling some coffee at a local hangout, I drove downtown and parked in the Fauberg.

I prowled around, peering into some of the nightclubs, digging the music, and I walked past the house on Frenchman Street. It looked completely abandoned, so I headed up to Dumaine Street. I paced around the front of the house a bit before walking to the back. There was faint lighting streaming through the windows that face the enclosed patio. After my eyes adjusted to the light, I noticed a figure sitting in the garden. You could hear the fountain pouring sweetly into the pool of water, and banana leaves were slightly moving in the mild wind. The moon was full, and as I stared through an opening in the brick wall, I noticed a small figure lifting himself from a lounge chair. I could hear him whispering to himself, but could not make out the words.

For a minute, he stepped into the light coming from inside, and to my astonishment, I saw that his hair was silvery and long. Like an old hippie's. I was taken aback by this, and then out of nowhere, my knees started knocking, and my lips began to quiver. It took me a while to get a hold of myself, and when I did, I tiptoed back to the cracked opening in the wall and resumed my spying number. At one point, the old bastard started slapping a fly swatter on his arms and then on the table, cursing in a rousing Scottish brogue, the mosquitoes and moths that flitter around all night. I hadn't seemed to notice any mosquitoes around me until he did this, and soon I, too, started slapping my calves here and there. At one point the old goat turned around to look at the wall. Then he turned his head back and continued to drink what looked like a cup of coffee.

I watched for a few minutes longer, relieved that I had finally confirmed that the old man actually lived there. I quietly left, tiptoeing my way down the walkway that leads to the street.

As I was driving up one of the major boulevards that leads back to the hostel, I had a profound flash of insight. I had seen the old man before. In fact, I had seen him in my dreams and there's a vague memory somewhere in an herb-toking session back at school. Although the memory is hazy, the figure had that same long silvery white hair. In my sessions with Boyce I would bring up this figure, thinking that the old man was symbolic of something. It was only when I saw my great granddad sitting there under the moonlight, sipping his cup of coffee and mumbling to himself, that it occurred to me that the figure was an actuality. He existed. I don't know why but it scares me. The charming idea of a kindly senile old man nodding in a wheelchair has been transposed by this image of a scary, all-too-alert old snake. And I see him as a sinister force that wrecked havoc through the subsequent generations of my family.

When I got back to my little room, I furiously wrote out all that I was feeling in my journal. It occurred to me that maybe the family had made up this bit about the old man not wanting anything to do with them. That the real truth was the other way around. No one wanted anything to do with the old man. Man, I'm a moron. Sometimes I am the stupidest, most naive of fools. And I'm grateful I see the truth now, that's all I am going to say. I came pretty close, though. As I scribbled away, I thought of Andy and Pap. Pap, my grandfather, died over twenty years ago-before I was born-in a bizarre fall while he was vacationing with my grandmother in Florida. I don't know all the details to that, but I wrote a lot of stuff down and I thought about things that now made sense. No wonder Andy was so vague and reluctant to talk about the old gizzard. He was the family's shame. It explains everything. And I'm no longer interested in returning the gun I carried with me down here like a thimble-head. If I do return it, I will do so by leaving a note on the door and placing it in the bushes that sit in front of the great brick wall that encloses the garden to the Dumaine Street house. This all seems fine and well until I allow myself to think of Boyce. If I tell Boyce that I'm scared of the old goat because I don't exactly like to think that he had appeared to me in these dreams, Boyce would probably go hog-wild-therapist on me. He'd tell me that I have to walk through the fire. But so far, the old man hasn't called or written me back, so maybe I'll be lucky.

****

I arrive at my job, welcoming the grunt labor that distracts me from delving too deeply into this stuff and Joe's standing there reading the morning paper, drinking coffee, a cigarette smoking in the ashtray. He's a sleazy character, alright. He brags about how well he did at the races last night, and pops out a cell phone as he calls his bookie, who comes in here every now and again. He's an enormously corpulent man and people usually have to assist him when he climbs onto the barstool. He never eats here, though. If he did, they'd have to fill one of those feedbags they put on horses and strap it onto his face. I can just imagine the guy munching away. Usually, he swills a drink or two as Joe leans over the bar looking at the pointers the guy notes for him on the racing form. I try to not observe too much. But a lot of times I can't help but notice.

The *busboy gang* is arriving now, all of them waving to me as I set up everything in my little spot by the bar. I walk back to the kitchen where I begin my haul of the burlap sacks filled with oysters and Tyrone is asking me how much Joe gave me in tips yesterday. I tell him that I'm always getting about the same rip-off amount and he asks me when I want to kick Joe's ass. What alley can we pull him into and all that. The one out back or the one where he parks his car?

This has become a regular morning ritual, this little discussion as to when and where I am going to finally do Joe in, and lately, it's getting a bit tiresome. Whether I like it or not, I still need this job at least for a while. I would love to kick Joe's ass, but I need to be in a better job, first. I try to tell Tyrone this, but he will have none of it. His buddy, Rip, suddenly shouts to another guy, one of the part-timers.

"Hey, whatchew gurin ta tell Strayhawn taday, 'bout dat man he cum in hea Sunday?"

The boy looks up at me, as I'm about to call Al Charbonnet from the phone the staff uses in the kitchen.

He says: "Thay's sumboddy lookin fo yu. An old cat. Wearin' really dawk glasses. A white, scary-lookin mutha..."

My knees are slowly turning to Jello. I look at the guy dumbstruck., and ask: "What did you tell him?"

"Toll him yu'd be heeah durin thugh week. Whatchew think I tell 'em?"

Both of them are staring at me.

Tyrone turns to the other guy.

"Why ya tell thu old man that? Can't ya see Strayhawn ain't wantin' ta have anythang tu do with that old man?"

Tyrone turns to face me. He asks:" What he do, Strayhawn? What he do to you? You look really… *white*, man. I mean, pale."

The part-time guy briskly rolls silverware into cloth napkins, nodding his head as he casually adds, "Dat ol cat wuz the *whitest*-lookin' thang I ever seen and right now, you're lookin' jus like 'em."

Tyrone walks over to me and tells me not to worry, that whatever the old man did to me, they'll kick his old ass out of there if he tries anything. I shake my head and tell them that I was just shocked. That I had written to him. That he's my aging great granddad. That I'm just surprised that he actually came to the restaurant looking for me. The part-time busboy tells me that he seemed ok. But that he looked weird in his dark shades and white hair pulled back in a ponytail. He then informs me that he thinks all old white dudes are pretty scary looking to him.

The part-time guy adds: "He had a real funny-soundin' voice. Cat had a gravelly voice. Like he dun werkin' fo de *mob*…"

He spreads a wide grin when he says this. I look over at Tyrone, who's now busying himself with setting up plates and glasses on the counter. I bragged to Tyrone one afternoon that old *Gramps* had been a runner for the mob. I guess I wanted to make an impression on my fellow workers here.

I drag the last of the oyster sacks out of the kitchen and up to the bar where I gingerly start cracking and hammering away. Everyone's impressed with how well I've learned my little job here, and the boss seems happy. Babs is flashing her teeth at Joe as she finishes up her instructions and she's now walking over to me.

She says I'll be ready for the night shift in a few weeks and asks if I want to go the full weekend round. She tells me that I'd be working with a different bartender, Eddie, an older guy I had seen in here picking up his checks. Tyrone had told me that Eddie was a mellow kind of guy. About sixty-ish, and very professional and well mannered. No one had any complaints about him, so I feel good about the news. Except I'll have to get to know a whole different work crew. And I'm beginning to like these guys. I ask Babs if I could give it some thought, and she nods her head, grinning in that fixed lipstick-laced smile of hers. I'm trying not to appear nervous as every few seconds I look to the doorway whenever anyone walks in. I keep expecting to see this ashen-faced old goat walk in and up to the bar asking for me as I, of course, scurry to the floor ready to crawl back to the kitchen. Maybe I should just quit.

I crack and hammer away like a lunatic, wishing, just wishing I could take the rubber glove off, tear away the stinky apron and throw everything on the floor and break out into a run down Bourbon Street and jump on the next boat out to the gulf. As soon as I think this, I remember that I neglected to call old Al! I quickly shell a few more shrimp and tell Joe that I have to get some more stuff from the kitchen as he schmoozes away with one of the noon-time regulars.

I walk back to the phone area and dial Al's number. After the usual pauses and such, a woman's voice comes over the phone. It's *"Chooch"* the lady I had met when I went over to see Al for lunch a couple of weeks ago. She's asking me how everything is going, and had heard that I was sick. She tells me that I am just a sweet precious to be so patient to wait another minute and begs me to please pardon her as she puts me on hold yet again. Finally, Al gets on the line. He tells me that he has some good news and some not-so-good news. The bad news is that I'm on a tentative hold for the job. That unless the other guy gets a better offer, he's going to be taking off with the crew; the good news is that they are considering having a second spot open. That the chef could use more help. He will know by the end of next week. "Oh, Si, I have sumthin heer fo ya. It's a letta. An it's from Connettacut."

I ask Al to tell me the return address. It's a business letterhead. My dad's firm. I tell him that I'll be over there at some point to get it. I thank old Al and get off the phone.

How in the hell did Andy know how to reach me? And why? What does he want? Suddenly, a wave of dread is enveloping me. I call Al back immediately, and for the first time he actually answers the phone.

I ask: "What's the postmark? On the envelope?"

Al asks me to hold and comes back to the line. He tells me it is from about four days ago. I thank him again, and Al tells me that he'd be happy to drop it off. That he's having lunch at a famous restaurant around here and will be in the Quarter anyway. I agree to it and get off the phone. I think back to when I had written to Great Granddad, and well, it looks like he had plenty of time to contact my father. I forgot to ask the old goat to keep my letter confidential, that I didn't want anyone to know about my contacting him. Well, I'm an idiot, alright. I should've just come down here with Andy. In fact, I would have been better off.

I re-enter the restaurant and return to my work station at the bar. I'm cracking away and thinking all this over. It's already a little after twelve and people are beginning to pour in. About six people approach the bar and order all this seafood along with beer and the like. I slide the oysters onto their little aluminum shells and cram the crackers and sauce on the plates. I slide the platters down the length of the bar. In a way, I'm glad to get busy. If I think anymore of this stuff, I'll flip out right here at my little spot. I'll fling oyster shells and crabs all over the place, then walk over to Joe and punch him out. When he lands on the ground, I'll whistle over to the *busboy gang* and we'll start kicking Joe's ass. In front of everyone.

At the opposite end of the bar, Joe stares at me, his

fists resting on the brass rail where he usually hangs his towel. He slowly shakes his head. Now he's walking over to me, slapping his towel over his shoulder.

He says, tooth pick twirling busily between his lips, "What in the hell's goin' on with you? You tootin' up back there in the kitchen with the boys? Huh? Oh, 'xcuse me. I mean, ya must be smokin' that crack back there with the boys? Huh? Slow down! Ya drivin me nuts. Take a break. Do somethin'. Chill!"

I shake my head at Joe's ludicrous accusation, and look toward the dining area, and right in front of us is this little man, wearing extremely dark sunglasses. And he's looking right at us. A giant mosquito; a praying mantis with pasty white skin and white hair. A tiny yelp emits from the back of my throat. Joe looks at me and then the old man, and says: "You two know each other?"

Joe turns his attention to the old man,

"What'll ya have?"

In a gravelly voice, the old guy asks for a cranberry juice over ice with three slices of lime. Joe nods his head tossing a paper coaster in front of the old man. And now the old man is grinning at me.

He says, "Well? Are you the lad who wrote to me, or do I have the wrong shucka? Heh-heh."

I nod my head like a real drooling idiot. I don't exactly know what to say. I hear a bit of the brogue, but it sounds like it's a mixed accent. *Lad.* He asks me to come closer. I lean forward. He tells me that he doesn't normally wear the dark glasses. But because of his cataract operation he'll be wearing them for a good while. He informs me: "Takes months. Get over these things takes months. But I can tell, ya look like little Freddie."

Freddie? He must be talking about Andy. Fredrick Andrew is his full name. I can't believe this. I really can't believe this. Joe returns with the drink and places it in front of the old man. Joe gives me a surly look and tells me to please get back to work. I'm staring at the old man and even though I can't see his eyes, I can tell he doesn't like what Joe just did. I walk back to my little corner and start hacking away. My great grand dad slowly sips his juice through a straw. He suddenly calls to Joe and I lean closer in, pretending I'm looking for something behind the bar where my great granddad is sitting. Great Granddad says to Joe, "So. Tell me, the Giangiani family, the owners of this place, are they still runnin' their operation out there on the old highway, lad? I believe 'tis a garment factory or somethin'? You know, their *front*?"

Joe's jaw slightly trembles. In fact, he looks a bit taken aback. He leans closer to the old man and tells him that he didn't hear him. The old man starts waving him off.

"Ya heard me. Don't give me that one. Tell Babs I say hi, okay? Just tell Babs an old friend wants to know how the pants business is doing."

As I'm cracking away and sliding the oysters onto the platters, I watch my great granddad tell Joe that if he continues to pick on me- Great Granddad nods his big dark glasses at me as he speaks-he's going to have some of his friends visit Joe in a day or two. Of course, I take this as my cue. I lay down my little hammer, pull off the rubber glove and walk over to them. I casually ask: "Everything ok, Great Granddad?"

I turn to look over at Joe and he's scared. The guy actually looks frightened. I drink this in and salivate away when I notice there's a slight presence breathing behind me.

I turn around and Tyrone and Rip are standing there grinning like fools. Tyrone is holding a rubber bucket from the kitchen as he begins to grab the dirty glasses from behind the bar, while Rip is staring at my great granddad, with this ridiculous permanent grin plastered on his face. Joe starts barking orders at them. Tyrone pauses and looks up at my great granddad.

The old man is baring his teeth at Tyrone, cocking his head in Joe's direction as he turns to pour a beer for a customer.

"Cocky bastard, iddn't he? Snied, ornery bastard, that one."

Tyrone and Rip are now shaking with laughter. The both of them are rolling around and jabbing each other in the ribs. "Ol man's cool. Cool as hell, Strayhawn!"

We all watch as Joe steps away from the bar and walks to the back of the restaurant and up the stairs. I tell Tyrone that he's probably getting Babs, but Rip tells us that Babs already left. The coward is probably calling the cops. On an old man. What a creep. But Great Granddad pipes.

"Guilty, that one!"

Rip is still staring at my great granddad.

He says: "Old man is cool. Hey, what you know 'bout Babs?"

My great granddad is tight-lipped as he shakes his head. Finally, he says that he had known the Giangiani family, in fact, he knew Babs' grandfather.

He continues: "Crooks. The whole rotten lot a them. And that bartender fronts and covers for her. I can just tell. Son? Young man?"

I stupidly point at my chest.

The old coot continues: "Quit this job. Come on. Get the hell outa this place."

I don't exactly know what to do. Tyrone and Rip are looking at me a bit sheepishly. After all, we've become a real team over the past few weeks. I can't leave these guys.

I look over at them, "Not just yet, Great Granddad. Not just yet."

Gramps leans a bit closer on the bar: "Well, can ya take a bit of a wee break, then? Go to a spot somewhere and chat."

Rudy, the floor manager, is now sliding up to the bar. He briskly glances at us and asks Great Granddad if he would like anything else, and then looks over to me in that inscrutable manner of his. All polished and sleek. Rudy informs us that Joe's upstairs for a while and he'll be taking over Joe's spot. I try not to grin too much as I tell Rudy that this is my great granddad and if I could take a break for an hour or so. He looks the old man over and then at me.

"I suppose so. But Babs won't like it. Go ahead." He steps over to my station and examines my set up.

"Looks good. Go on."

I step out with my great granddad. Tyrone, Rip and the part-time guy are taking a break outside. We wave to them as we hobble into the sun-drenched street. I'm basically speechless. I hardly know what to say to the old guy, except I'm smiling a lot. As we approach the corner, the old man turns to me. I look him over as he speaks. He has on a white cotton shirt and some plaid Bermudas, athletic white socks and *gunboaters*.

He says: "We scared the hell outa that guy. Ya realize that, lad?"

I bob my head up and down like an idiot. We sure did, *Gramps*, we sure as hell did. He looks me over, then strokes my shoulders and arms. His dark glasses flash up at me as he speaks. He says I'm a strappin' lad. This is a trip. To think that I was actually afraid of this guy. This little old man. I can't wait to tell Boyce about this. I really can't. As he points to a small cafe, I ask him if he had told anyone about my letter.

He pauses and looks at me incredulously. "Now who would I tell, lad? Little Freddie? We talk every so many months or so. I had no reason..."

We enter a quaint cafe, the air conditioning blowing like crazy. We decide to sit outside in the hot sun, under an umbrella table, figuring it may be more comfortable. My great granddad continues: "I had no reason to call your father. Why?"

Suddenly, I remember Al Charbonnet was supposed to come by the restaurant; I hope Rudy accepts the envelope for me. My great granddad is staring at me. His shiny black glasses looking hot and molten in the harsh sun.

The old man bores in: "Aye, but you're a ponderous one, alright. Just like the whole lot of us. Curse, that ability to think. I saw it in your father, I saw it in my father, what little I remember of 'em, and I see it in you. My sons? Well, I didn't know them too well, but I think they were the exception. They weren't the thinking kind. Skips a generation here and there, but you, you're a contemplative type. So you like philosophy? I studied some philosophy as a lad, and I caught up with all that later. Well before I was your age, I had to leave my schooling. Had to run the presses. My father had died in the Great War. Did you know that?"

I can hardly believe the earful I am hearing. I'm not sure if I knew that about my great, great, grandfather. "No." I tell him.

The old man continues, "Well, it was that fool, that Gilmartin bastard that ruined everything the Strayhorns had. When my father went off to the war, it was 1916. I was barely eleven years old. He died a year later, was killed in combat, and that's when the family fell into desultory times. Not that we were of extreme wealth, lad. But we were an established family of strong repute. It was Gilmartin, my uncle, my mother's brother, that stepped in and took over our business. We were a publishing family. We were well regarded, but our wealth was being depleted. We had all studied at St. Andrews, and it all stopped with me. Bad investments and crooks taking over things when we were left vulnerable. I had to go to work."

I can hardly take all this in. I'm still digesting the fact that he talks to Andy a couple of times a year, much less get into the *Great War*. I suggest to Great Granddad that maybe we should get together afterwards for a long dinner.

The old man stops talking immediately after I say this and quietly pours sugar into his coffee. I tell him that I didn't mean to seem rude, it's just that I'm so shocked to finally meet him after years of wondering what he was like.

He looks up at me and grins. "I'm a bastard. Just know that. And an ornery bastard at that. Nobody messes with me".

For a minute, I believe him. After what he pulled off in Babs' joint, I can honestly believe him.

"I got a lot to talk to you about", he says, "After I

read your letter, I spent a long time thinkin. I liked
Freddie, always did. He's the smartest of the lot of 'em,
that one. And gifted. I have his drawins. A lot of his
drawins from when he was a lad younger than you, and
the boy could do the finest details you'd ever see. They
were mean to him. You know that, don't you?"

I'm not sure of what the old man is saying here. I
knew Andy was the different one, the smart one, but
mean to him?

The old man continues: "They were stupid idiots and
I made sure he was going to be an educated Strayhorn,
like he was meant to be. Got a lot to tell you, lad. If I
worked for Gig Mastriani, which I did—I know you want
to know all about that and we'll get to that in time— I did
it because I had to. I did not come to this country in all
my Scottish finery wearin' the family kilt, lad. I was an
18-year old runaway and the year was 1924. I had to get
the hell away from Gilmartin. I know about cruelty. And
I told the lot of 'em, back in the 60's, that they could kiss
my Scottish ass for all I cared, I was not going to have
anything to do with them. I didn't like the way they treated your father especially after the tragedy. He told you
about this, didn't he?"

A hazy feeling comes over me. My head feels gauzy
and numb. I watch my great grandfather's lips slowly
move, and I don't know if it's the sun, but I have to get
up and go inside for a while. The old man is rising from
his chair and holding me by the arm and staring at me as
he nervously says: "Freddie never told you, did he?
Freddie. I should have known. He's like that. All quiet
with his sketches... I should've known. Sit down, Simon.
You have my name, alright. Sit down...where are you
goin'? Where in the hell are... what are you doin', lad?"

I'm running away, and into the street and across the next street and into the alley that flanks the cathedral and I race past the carts, and horse and buggy stands, and into Jackson Square and across Decatur Street and up to the river walk and I finally come to a halt where the Mississippi water gently meets the gravelly bank. I stand there for a moment, and proceed to barf. I'm so completely freaked and embarrassed. There are tourists looking over at me, and a man is asking me if I'm ok and all that stuff, and I'm nodding my head, and asking them to please leave me alone, and I feel so completely drained I flop myself down on the rocky bank and hang my head in my hands.

****

The air is hot and dank as I step out of the building and onto the road that leads to the St. Charles Avenue streetcar. It's been a couple of days since that afternoon with my great grandfather. And I'm perusing the messages Dini handed me as I was leaving the hostel as I walk. Al Charbonnet wants me to meet him at his office, Sharina and Gary called wanting me to go out dancing with them last night while I was already out and roaming the streets. And Great Granddad. He left a number if I feel like calling. I feel like an absolute turd. I try not to think too much of my plight even though I know I'm no longer working at the restaurant. You just don't up and leave, not show up and not even call, which is exactly what I did. I abandoned the old man at the outdoor cafe, and I feel like I let him and my buddies down back at the restaurant. After all, we were all in this thing together. I was supposed to hang around a while. So I have to deal with that, and go over there and get my check. It's just as well.

At the restaurant, Tyrone is standing outside by himself. He grabs me by the shirt in a joking manner. "Joe got all freaked, thanx ta thu ole man. Dat guy's cool, Si. Dey ain't gonna fire you cuz a sum old man. Go ahead, now. Ya still have a job."

I step inside and Babs is standing near the waiters, helping them get things in order for lunch. Babs looks over at me and smiles. As she approaches, she tells me that they have my check. They are sorry but the restaurant had two busloads of tourists the other day and everything turned into a disaster because of my absence. She reaches under the bar and slides an envelope my way and wishes me luck. I relish the opportunity to tell her that my great grandfather knew her grandfather. Her eye-make up melts a bit as a bead or two of sweat trickles down her pancaked face.

I continue, "He knows all about your crooked family and your deal with Joe. And now that I know this, I wouldn't want to work here."

I do an Andy-spin on the heel, and strut out of the restaurant.

Tyrone puffs away as he joins me in walking down the street. I ask him for a cigarette. "We gots ta git thu asshole, understand me, brutha. Make mush outa thu motherfugga."

I tell him, "Yeah. Well, Gimme your number. We'll stake out a plan, Tyrone." He eyeballs me: "Ya mean that?"

Tyrone and I clasp hands, shake, and I depart heading further down Bourbon Street, thinking of a possible way we can get to Joe. It just seems that there must be something we could do.

After walking a good forty-five minutes, I arrive at Al's office. I step into the old building and *Chooch* is sitting in her glass-enclosed space rapping away on the phone. She places her hand over the receiver as I approach and slides the little window open.

"Precious. Ya have ta check in with me when ya wanna go up thayr. We all know ya, honey, but it's a new security policy. Wanna wait heea an I'll buzz Al for ya, Suga!"

Chooch dials his number and I watch the people walking by on their way out of the building. She taps on the glass and points for me to go upstairs. I enter Al's office and he's on the phone barking orders to somebody. Probably some job seeker like myself.

I wave to him and he points to the chair that sits in front of his large desk. He reaches over to the drawer on his right,takes out an envelope and hands it over to me. It's Caz's handwriting. I open it and like a glorious miracle a check for $1,200.00 slides onto my lap. Al looks over at me as I grin like an idiot. I take out the accompanying letter and start reading. It's from Caz.

>   *Dear Si,*
>
>   *We're writing you this letter to let you know that we found out about the money being drawn from your account. Noah Campbell was practically caught red-handed! You're not the only one he has bilked. There were a string of incidents. A few of our old friends' accounts were also tapped. It became clear to me that he was snooping around the house the night of my party, and he found an old shoe box where you had had an extra ATM card on the checking account Dad opened for you before you went off to college. You had your PIN*

number in there, so Mom or Gram could make a deposit for you, I suppose and we are very sad about the whole thing. Mrs. Campbell wrote you a check. She was very upset and insisted on it. We know you're probably out at sea right now and hope that this finds you when you return to New Orleans. Dad called Carlin Graves' father and wound up speaking to Carlin down in North Carolina. He gave us the address of the company you are working for. We hope you're having an adventure down there! Please write to us when you can.

  Caz

Al's now off the phone and looking over at me.

"Watcha got dare, Simon?"

"Good news, Al. It's a long story. I don't want to go into it. It's an old matter that caused me a bit of a problem, but it's all ok now. Hey, thanks."

I get up to leave. Al is looking at me quizzically.

"I got sum news for ya, too. Sit de hell down."

The kitchen job is on. I get $12.00 an hour to start, and all accommodations are free. I will be gone for two months starting in the middle of August. I will be working forty hours a week, but there will be fifteen additional hours in overtime. That's how they do it. So I will have some dough. Not a lot, but it's better than the $5.25 an hour I was getting at the restaurant. I'm a very happy guy. I came in here like a beggar and now I'm asking ol' Al if he would like some lunch. Money is an amazing thing, that's all I'm going to say.

****

I spent a good part of the afternoon with Al talking over Mexican food and margueritas in a restaurant we came upon as we drove into the Fauberg. I told him the whole story about the missing money and how I had landed in that restaurant in the Quarter. We laughed over Great Granddad's little scene at the bar, and for a minute, I felt a pang of guilt for not calling the guy. As we talked, Al insisted that I go out and have a few nights off exploring more of the nightlife, since I had missed a lot of that due to my meager job. I promised him that I would call my new friends, well, I guess my *only* friends here, Sharina and Gary, and we would go out.

As we were leaving the restaurant, Al insisted on paying for his tab, grabbing the bill out of my hand. I took Al's advice and called Gary and Sharina and both of them asked me to meet them later at the club when their shift ended. We met around midnight and prowled all of the best dance and music clubs. I told them about my good fortune and bought drinks and stuff for all of us. We did not return 'til seven in the morning. We combed the late spots and danced at almost all of them. When I returned to the hostel, I crawled into my bed and stayed there the entire day.

Early this evening, I stepped out for a few hours to get something to eat, played pool at one of the local dives around the universities and returned around midnight. I sat on my bed, all cozy and wrote in my notebooks. I e-mailed Boyce and told him everything that had happened. I was writing away when it struck me that it had been several days since I did my disappearing act with the old man. And I had neglected to call him back. It's now after midnight and I'm fully awake from my day-long snooze. I jump off the bed, and slip into my loafers, grabbing the Luger and tucking it in my shorts as I leave the room. I remember to take the micro-recorder with me.

I drive into the French Quarter, thinking I would just check things out. When I arrive at the house, everything looks shut down and deserted. I step out of the car and walk to the back, tiptoeing in case I wake the old guy up. When I get to the old brick wall that surrounds the patio, I see him. The lamp I had noticed from the time before glows from inside the back window and Great Granddad's sitting on a folding chair, holding a fly swatter as two candles slowly burn on the table. I stand here gaping at the old gizzard, with his silvery hair tied back in a pony tail, his white beard jutting forward as he scratches the bristly whiskers. All I can think is: *man, he's really an old guy.* The mosquitoes are a bit of a nuisance and I find myself slapping my bare legs every now and again. The old man, having laser sonic ears, speaks up.

"Who's out there? Is that Dominic?"

He doesn't turn around; he continues to sit there scratching his face and flapping the fly swatter every now and again. Mostly on top of the table as he drinks a glass of tea or the like. I resume my staring number, waiting for the right moment to simply announce myself and say I've decided to pick up where I had left off.

Even though the hour may be a bit odd, I'm now ready to hear what he has to say about my dad. That after thinking about it these past few days, I realize that it's better to face these things. That even though I can't explain my disappearing act from a few days before, I'm now ready. Maybe talking with Sharina and Gary helped. And maybe going out last night was exactly what I needed. I have the micro-recorder in my shorts' pocket. For a moment, I actually like staring at him, wondering about all the memories that are crammed into his old head. I'm enjoying the sound of the water flowing in the fountain and the way the moonlight shines on his silvery, white, hair.

I'm standing here in a mesmerizing trance until a nasty mosquito sting nabs at my calf. As I pinch the thing off of my fleshy leg, I trip and slide against an aluminum bucket that's placed alongside the brick fence. This time, the old man gets out of his chair. He's speaking in a foreign, gurgling language. It's English with some other unrecognizable words sandwiched in. He now walks toward the brick wall.

"Great Granddad! It's me! Simon!"

"Ya like ta scare the bejesus out of me, lad. What are ya doin' here at one in the mornin'? Come on in...here...I'll get the key."

Great Granddad comes back, his eyes watery as he unlocks the iron gate. He says: "Eyes are botherin' me. I always get up at this time a night anyway. So come on in. I give ya some iced tea, or do ya like iced-coffee? I don't have much else here."

We settle into the canvas chairs that grace the patio and the old man lights a hurricane lamp to give us more light. He stares at me, and wipes his eyes a bit as we settle in at the table.

"What brings ya here tonight, lad?"

I settle into the chair and tell him, "I want to know about my dad. I want to hear everything you have to say. I can't explain why I did that escape number the other day, but I had to think about some things, I guess. And well, some of that is… I want to ask you some stuff. And I also have something I want to give back to you. I brought it with me from Connecticut. Do you remember this?"

The old man leans forward as I pull the gun out. He stares at it and takes it out of my hands, stroking it fondly. He shakes his head and smiles. Now he's laughing.

"I stole this from Gilmartin, the bastard. I carried this thing onto the ship after I fled Glasgow. Since he was plannin' on killin' me, lad, I thought it was only right to stay one pace ahead of 'em. An ya can't blame me, either. It was Gilmartin-my mother's own brother- who destroyed what the Strayhorns had."

The old man places the gun on the table and rubs his withered hands together. " He used our money to cover for his mistakes. The last thing for him to ruin was the newspaper, and by the time I fled, I knew that was goin', too. I found out all that he was doin' to ruin us. And he caught on that I knew. I was a scared kid. That's all I was. A kid. Barely nineteen years old. You need to understand this. I knew nothin' of bravery and honor. I was an abused kid who was numb in the memory of his dead father. You need to know that, too. They probably told you, I was tough. No, I was not. I was a...what's the word?"

I offer, "Wimp?"

"Yeah. That's right. A *wimp*. Actually, I was a little, skinny kid, with no money and an incomplete education. I had nothin', lad. When I landed in New York, I was both in awe and absolutely terrified at the same time. I went from one bad situation to another. I got little triflin' jobs, and lived in boardin' houses. I was lonely and wrote letters to my sisters tellin' them I would write for them to

302

come over when I made my fortune, but it never happened. I fell in with Gig Mastriani by chance. In fact, I was walkin' the streets of New York City with this gun tucked in my coat pocket when I befriended one of his gofers. I felt like a tough guy and bragged about how I was a spy in Glasgow. I made up all these colorful stories—of course, I had read Stevenson—one of *us*, lad."

I'm not sure what the old man means here, so I ask, "One of us?"

The old man looks like I just blurted the lowest of insults at him.

I ask again. "What, Great Granddad?"

The old man shakes his white head, jutting his bearded chin in the air as he turns his ancient face away from me.

"I may have arrived here in a shambles, lad, but I wasn't exactly a starved Irish ruffian! Shame about our Celtic brethren; the *donkeys* —that's what we called the arrivals from Cork. They did any kind of labor includin' cleanin' latrines. To think theirs was the land of leprechauns and fairies and along came the *Mother Church*. It shulda stayed that way. The Catholic church and the drink was their ruination. Okay. *Our* ruination. We are all of the same basic group. But back in New York, everyone called the police carts *paddy wagons* for a reason. All they did was pick up Irish drunks. The coppers had hauled 'em in so many times they started to offer them jobs. Heh-heh...then we get a corrupt buncha cops. But that's another story, lad!"

Suddenly the old coot pulls himself up from the table and announces to me:

"You're a *Highlander*! A noble Scot. An don't ya dare forget it!"

I take this as my cue to rise a bit from my chair, but the old man gestures for me to sit down, laughing a bit as he settles himself back into his seat.

He leans in, "You're a fine one ta mess with, lad. Heh-heh. Every Scot knows he's got a bit of the *donkey* in 'em. Like it or not. Now where was I? Well, I was this scrawny lad and dreams of adventure filled my head. And maybe the fantasies helped me get through. I know when I was hungry, they helped. Anyway, the kid got me in with Gig. As soon as I flashed this Austrian Luger at 'em, I was *in*. Of course, I never talked about how scared I really was. I kept those thoughts to myself. But, at first, Gig took good care of me. It was good money and the work was a bit risky. And it definitely had an excitement to it, but after six years of it, I had to run away. And that's when I went out west. I came down to this city durin' my time with Gig and I was makin' the dough. For a defrocked youth with nothin' in the world to claim, lad, I met your father's grandmother down here. She was a *love*. You have to know that. I ran away because I had to. I did some deals with one of Gig's competitors and he was payin' me handsomely and they got wind of it, lad, and were runnin' after me. I did a little informin', lad. Maybe it was the fantasy penchant. Here I had an opportunity to be an informer, and a deep yearnin' for more excitement flushed inside of me. But it got me in deep trouble. I caught a train out west and hid out on an Indian reservation to protect myself. I learned a lot there, too. I also fell in love. I was 25 years old. She was a beautiful soul, that woman. And not to betray the one here, I just sort of fell into it, lad. Didn't mean to hurt a soul, as I was young, you see. It was years later that I returned to New York and got a job workin' at the Yale Club. It was a nondescript little job in the library. It was the perfect hideaway. Eh? What thug was goin' to have lunch in the Yale Club? Right? So I sat there all day readin' books. I went back to educatin' myself. I wanted to read everythin'. All that I had missed out on. See how life is peculiar? Here ya are, lad, wantin' adventure and ya leave a school I would have drooled over to attend. Anyway. I studied all the great philosophers and the like. I read all of Freud. Jung. The great minds. The art history books. The Greeks. All of the philosophers. Every one of them, lad. Hegel, Hume, Bergson, Kierkegaard, Kant, Frederick Nietzsche, all those German geniuses. But my favorite reads were Alexis de Toqueville's *Democracy in America*, the complete works of Herodotus, and well, I suppose, *Moby Dick*. A fascinatin' book, lad. All the while, I would send money down to New Orleans. Your Great Grandmother well-knew of my situation and she seemed acceptin' of it. She knew I had to stay the hell away. But she didn't know about my little affair with the *sqaw*. That's what I called her. Anyways, time moved on, and there came the day that I met Dr. Renate Nordstrom. I had gotten to know some of the men who would regularly come into the club and there was one who always stopped in the library to chat with me. We would get into discussions about things, and on a chilly October day, he asked me to come to his home to attend a book group he held there. I was lonely, lad. I was nearly thirty-six years old and I didn't know what to do with myself. So I went. And it soon turned into a weekly thing. Now I was ashamed, lad, that I had not continued my education, but I had done a lot of readin' those two years I had worked in the library, and I could hold my own in these discussions. In fact, they all liked my observations and remarks, except when I'd get generous with the casual references. Heh. I remember once, I referred to *Madame Bovary* as that little tart, or maybe it was somethin' worse, but these elegant people were so refreshingly surprised, they all laughed. I cringed a bit because I knew I had come from educated stock. Back home the Strayhorns were once proud gentlemen. It didn't take much to have that all ruined. And of course, here I was a joke. But luck would have it that my life would change. I met this woman, Dr. Renate Nordstrom, at these discussions. And soon we fell in love."

The old man pauses, sipping a long swill of his tea. I tell Great Granddad that this is yet another "*love*".

I add: "As a matter of fact, your third. Great Granddad, you must've been some kinda guy, that's all I'm going to say."

The old man grins. You can tell he's really enjoying this.

"Well, lad, I learned it from a couple of those Sicilianos I ran with. They could swoon and charm and kiss the rings of popes to win a gal. But Renate was extraordinary. I think it was our discussion on the Greco-Persian Wars as told by that luminous and brilliant historian, Herodotus, that brought us together. We soon discovered that we loved the pre-Socratics and bemoaned the lost beauty of such texts, and well, we both agreed Gibbon was a bore".

I have to interject here. I can't believe what I'm hearing.

"I like the Pre-Socratics. And so does *Andy*...I mean, Dad.".

The old man nods his ancient head. "It's destiny, lad.

It's the Strayhorn stamp on the world. The life of the
mind is our territory. And I'm delighted to meet you.
And I should've known. Your father reminds me of
David Selkirk Strayhorn, my favorite uncle, by the way.
He was one of the great civil engineers. He spent most
of his life designin' these great bridges, lad, then went off
to Egypt to pursue some such esoteric endeavor. But
Freddie! He was more than a designer, he had an
amazin' artistic talent, but I will get to this, lad. To get
back to what I was sayin'...and I know what you might
be thinkin': *who did this man think he was ? All these
women*? All I can say is that I must've had a weakness
there. In the old heart matters. But I tell ya, lad, there
is nothin' that turns me on more than a beautiful and rich-
ly intelligent woman. The Indian—I know it's *Native
American* now—was extraordinary, and Jeanette, your
great-grandmother, was no lame-brain. She came from a
good French family; very decent people, lad. But they
were an old moneyed French family who sat on their
duffs for far too long. They had become soft, pliable little frogs. Jeanette's money eventually sank like a stone
for various reasons, and it was the Great Depression that
brought everythin' down to a bare-bones level. She was
a wonderful woman, lad. Educated in a convent. But
once I left, I couldn't really return. I was ashamed. At
least if I would have faced Gig's thugs, I would've died
a noble man for having the character to return to his little family. But my life had become that of a fugitive,
and I was too scared to return to New Orleans. It was that
simple. The Mafia is very big down here. That's because
of the Sicilians that poured into this city in the late
1800's. Everyone knows everyone. New York actually
became safer for me. And I have to admit that I was

enjoyin' this new aspect of my life; this world of the mind that I had missed out on and actually felt was my true place, and well, someday, I may show you some stuff I have published. I became a student at Columbia, you know. Earned a Ph.D and taught History for twenty years. And I'll get to that in time, too. Anyway, there came the day when I wrote to your great grandmother and asked for a divorce. She did not grant me one. I accepted that and told her that she could do what she wanted. I was stayin'. When Renate died twenty-five years later, I became financially comfortable, as they say. She was a bit older than I. She was sixty-four when the angels took her. When she granted her estate to me, I did not hesitate to invest all of that money. I also came back here and bought some property. I gave Freddie's grandmother a decent amount of money. Our sons were disappointments. I stupidly gave them things they did not deserve. They were arrogant thugs. Little gansters. *I* did that. And I blamed myself for years over that one. They were an embarrassment. And I suppose they were just doin' what men will do when they haven't had proper instructions from their fathers. I created that legacy by my absence and my own messed-up self. In those days, I did not know how to even talk about the things that were botherin' me. It took Renate's influence to change that, and I can say I did not finally become a man until I reached the age of sixty and made the difficult decision to set myself free entirely of the family. By then, it had all become a complete mess, with everyone blamin' each other for this and that, and yes, mainly me. The old Scottish buggar. It kills me, lad, because the pathetic news is that I was a scared kid who jumped on a ship when I escaped the clutches of a miserable idiot who beat the crap out of me from the time I was twelve years old. If you have ever read, the Brit, Dickens—a Brit, but good—you'll find that he accurately depicted the misery of life that was passed onto the lives of children when the concept of the child wasn't even heard of".

The old man pauses a bit, sipping his glass of tea. I'm transfixed in what he's saying, and I ask that he continue. He waves his old hand at me and looks up, continuing to speak.

"It wasn't so unusual to treat children as exploitable appendages of one kind or another. Kids were still workin' jobs to support their families in New York City when I arrived in '24, so many years after Charles Dickens wove his tales. *Santa Claus*, lad, is a late 19th Century invention, and that came out of the imagination of a graphic artist in New York City. The fat, jolly, red-suited *Santa Claus* was a novelty, a creation out of a variety store advertisin' department. It was invented, and it was only roughly based on what was a very skinny old man from Eastern Europe named St. Nicholas, who was unusually kind to children, a rarity. To tell you how I see the world now compared to the early 1900's is almost an impossibility, lad. I was yanked out of school at fourteen. Which wasn't so bad considerin'. I was workin' the printin' presses, until I was sixteen or so, and by the time I left at age eighteen I was in the copy room. And I did write a lot of stuff. I had the capabilities of takin' over by the time I was in my early twenties and that idiot knew it. He also knew that I would go through his desk and peruse the bank ledgers and the like and it was becomin' a bit dangerous for me to be there".

For a moment, the old man looks very sad and pensive. We can hear the crickets croaking and the pouring

water in the fountain. He looks up at me, his eyes a bit
watery again.

"There's nothin' worse than losin' your father in a
war, lad. He leaves like a noble gentleman and he returns
a dead animal, barely recognizable because half of his
face was blown out somewhere on a frozen field in a
strange, alien country, and probably bits and pieces of it
were later eaten by the carrion that hover the fields like
the rapacious scavengers they are.   I suppose I'm
digressin'. I meant to tell ya why I turned my back on the
lot of 'em. I will get to this. Freddie's dad was a disap-
pointin' man who blamed everyone for his troubles. He
was my son, but I felt he was not at all a true Strayhorn.
He blew most of the money. Well, all of it, really. He had
the *curse*. And that is, he drank. This is not unusual for
the Gaelic people, lad. Although I would hope the
Strayhorns weren't as bad as the *donkeys* . But I guess I
need to get over that, too. Drink never affected me in this
way, and yet I know my grandfather- who would be your
great, great, great grandfather- was a much-admired
statesman, but an inebriate nonetheless, who, fortunately,
gave it up when he was a relatively young man. At least,
I was told this. I only have vague memories of him."

The night has gone on like this for a few hours now,
and the hurricane lamp is almost completely out.   From
the looks of it, we are done with our discussion. At least
for the time being. Apparently, the old man has a lot
more to say, but we both decide that four-thirty in the
morning is a good time for us to bag for the evening. We
walk up the back stairs and into the house. He shows me
a couple of spare rooms where he has beds and the like.
His little body creaks around the house as he stops at the
different rooms, showing me around. His white hair, now

out of the pony tail and hanging softly past his shoulders; his pale gray eyes look up at me without their protective dark lenses. As we walk down the hall, we stop in one of the rooms and sit on the bed. He points to a chest by the window and tells me he has hundreds of photographs of the family in there. That he has a lot of Andy's drawings and sketches that he drew when he was growing up.

For a moment, he looks as though he's about to tell me something, but he stops himself and continues to talk about how he had returned to New Orleans in the early 1980's. I ask him why he wanted to do that, and he waves his bony hands in the air. He liked the relaxed and easy-going lifestyle, and he liked the cozy feeling of the French Quarter. I ask him why he did not return to Scotland, and he says that he had a few times in the '40's and '50's. That he only went back to see his sisters who had married well, and to visit with people he had left behind, but it had made him too sad. He loved Scotland, but the memories were too painful. He clutches my leg and looks into my eyes, and it scares me a little bit, but also softens me inside as well. He says,

"I spent a great deal of my life as an adult, never thinkin' about any memory of my father when he was still alive. I could only focus my attention on the dead war hero he became. It was as if I had never even had a father, lad. But Renate got that all out of me. I was near-ly forty-two years old before I could weep over it. I had never done that before. At the time it had happened, we were all too scared. When we got the bad news, I froze and then Gilmartin entered the picture with his strop. My father never did that to us, lad. He was an educated man. A gentleman. And he was very loving; a good heart. But at forty-two, I was still that frozen kid with the grief over

311

my father still stuffed inside me.   It's a feelin' I can't quite describe."

For a moment, the old man looks lost in thought. It looks as though he may even cry, but being the proud Scot that he seems to be, he soon straightens himself and looks directly at me: "Lad. I want you to get some rest. You can either stay here or go back to where you are stayin'.   Tomorrow, I'm takin' you somewhere. Don't worry. I have a car and a driver. Just let me know where you want to stay".

After he says this, he springs up from the bed and reaches for the Luger that's resting on one of the tables. He turns around, aims it at me and now walks over to put it in my hands. He tells me to keep it; I tell him I have to think about it. That I don't like the idea that my dad once tried to kill himself with it. The old man says,

"Yeah. I know about that. After tomorrow, you may look at things differently."

"Where are we going, Great Granddad?"

"A little town across the lake."

I leap off the bed and walk over to where I tossed my shoes. As I slip my feet into them, the old man asks me why I'm not wearing my *walking* shoes. I suppose he means the *gunboaters*.

I blankly tell him: "Cuz I don't want to look like you, ok?"

The old man laughs. "Aye, but you think I'm foolish, lad. But I got to tell ya: when you're ninety, ya must keep up with the times. People actually respect you for not stayin' stuck in ya generation. Besides, Rudy Vallee was an asshole. Someday, I'll take you out dancin'. I'm one a the best."

Suddenly, the image just drops in my lap. I had seen

the old coot before. When I first arrived in town and found myself wandering around the French Market one afternoon. Great Granddad was that old man I saw dancing with a parasol while these little kids tapped-danced for coins. Of course, I keep the beak shut, given the somber mood of the evening. The old man looks a bit sad as I tell him I'm going back to the hostel. If I don't, I know I'll encourage him to talk more, but at his age, he could keel over anytime. So I don't push it. As I depart, he tells me to be waiting by noon. He and the driver would come by.

****

I walk back out into the damp night air and end up driving to one of the all-night coffee houses. I sit here in a daze as I muse over all the things we talked about. As the sun begins to rise, I get back into the car and drive up to the spot where I watch the ships glide by on the river from my favorite perch in the park. I walk around a bit thinking about everything he's told me. I'm too excited to go to sleep, but after another hour or so, I reluctantly head back to my room, resting my tired body as I close my eyes. I fall asleep in spite of myself and when I wake up it's a little after twelve noon. As I gather my things for the shower, there's a light tap at the door. I open it and here's the old man, in his usual get-up of a light cotton shirt, oversized Bermudas, his dark sunglasses, the *gunboaters* (sans blinking lights) and instead of the crew white socks, he has on bright green nylon *knee-hi's*. He looks like an old grasshopper.

As he creaks in, he informs me, "When ya get old, lad, ya don't really sleep anymore. I'll just let myself sit awhile so you can get ready."

The old man's holding a magazine in his lap, the cover page flapped over his bony knee. When I return from the shower, the old man's leafing through the magazine, flipping the pages wildly as I dress. As I place my things in my pockets, the old man flashes the cover in my direction.

"Recognize this strappin' middle-aged lad?"

I'm stunned. It's a picture of Andy, and he's on the cover of *Architecture, Leisure & Form*. The headline simply reads: *Can This Man Save the Burlington*? This must be the magazine article Andy was referring to when I was back at the house a couple of months ago. I had no idea he would be on the cover of the damned thing.

I tell Great Granddad, " I can't believe this. He didn't tell me he might be on the cover. Well! "

The glossy photo is a handsome one, and my dad looks like he had on one of his sharp-looking suits. I have to admit, I'm proud of the guy. The magazine must have just come out as it's the August issue and we're still in July.

Great Granddad tells me, "I got it this mornin', lad, when I picked up the *Racing Form*. It was starin' right at me, plain as all the day. It's odd. It's odd, lad, because I'm going to tell ya some things today and we'll have his picture starin' at us as we talk. Maybe I shouldn't've shown it to ya. Come on, let's go!"

We step out into the sun-drenched day. A shiny black Lincoln Continental sits in the drive. And there's a man standing near the car as we approach. He looks like he's about fifty and he's actually sporting a chauffeur's cap, although his clothes look pretty casual.

He asks: "Ready to head out, Mister Strayhorn?"

This is impressive, alright. The old goat steps into the car like a country gent as I bounce into the seat behind him like an idiot. We slide into the cool leather seats, relieved as the air conditioning blows away. I thumb through the magazine as it shows pictures of the restoration work Andy had talked to me about. It looks very slick. There's another picture of Andy and his two partners. The article goes on to praise other work my dad's firm has done, but that this was by far, their most impressive project. It also says that Andy's firm had gained in reputation over the past few years and that it's a growing business. Actually, it points out things I didn't even know, and I'm a bit enthralled by it all. When I put the magazine down, my great granddad begins to speak. Or at least, tries to.

The driver is a character. It doesn't seem like he's been a chauffeur long, because he keeps wanting to butt into the conversation. From what I know about being a driver, part of the job is to be not only inscrutable, but gravely silent. At intervals, he slows down, and after doing this a few times, the old man looks at me and says that our chauffeur was a cab driver for about thirty years and he's still in the habit of slowing down whenever he notices someone waving for a cab. Finally, the old man says, "Ya not workin' for *United*, anymore, Dominic."

"Yeah. But it's a hell of a bad habit ta break, Mister Strayhorn."

So this was Dominic.

Great Granddad continues, "Dominic also does things for me. He helps out in maintainin' the properties and he runs errands for me. Anyway, lad. What does it say about your daddy? I always knew your father would do well, lad. On his talent. Never any doubt about that.

The first time I saw him, he was sittin' in the corner of the livin' room drawin' somethin'. He must have been about seven years old. I always admired his work. That is, whenever I got the chance to actually spend time with him. They didn't want me to visit much, so I didn't. I kept to my own business in New York, but every couple of years or so, I would visit. And every time I did so, the sketches grew far more complex and intricate. One day, when Freddie was twelve, we walked over to the cathedral, and we stepped inside. He had one of his sketch pads with him, and he opened it up to show me what he was working on. And it was a depiction of the interior of that fine church. He told me he had spent about two months workin' on it, going in there everyday for a half hour or so. It was beautiful, but I didn't know what became of it. In a later trip down here, I asked him about it. He was a little older then, and after showin' me even more incredible work, he took out the sketch I was talkin' about and handed it to me. It was a masterpiece. It was *Da Vinci*. It was so finely detailed and masterfully drawn, it broke my heart. He said he was savin' it for his portfolio for college. Now I may as well tell ya this, lad. I secretly kept some money aside for your father. I didn't want to tell my son about it. So I was quiet. By the time Andy had begun lookin' into colleges, I took him aside and told him to keep his big mouth shut. I had it all stashed away for him. His drunken father made it all very difficult for him. He would bully him and tell him that he would never make it at school because he would not qualify for a full scholarship. Well, that was true. Freddie only got a small scholarship, and he worried about this a lot. His father told him that he had already spent too much money on a boardin' school he attended for only two years and kept tellin' him he'd have to work and go to night school. Apparently, the boardin' school didn't work out for your dad, and he returned to live with the family finishin' high school in the city. His father was furious about this. And the man was a terror, lad. Both he and his wife made it clear to me to stay away from their children, and I did, but I always managed to slip in a word to your father."

We're now entering a very long bridge that crosses a major lake here. Great Granddad asks if I'm hungry and I say I am. He says we would have lunch after we get to the place he wants to go.

He says, "It shouldn't take too long. Now it may seem peculiar to you, but you will understand. I promise ya, lad. Anyways. Durin' Freddie's teenage years, I barely saw him, but when I did, we would have good chats, and I think he trusted me. In fact, I know he did. But durin' these years, your father was very troubled. He had spent a lot of time alone in the *slaves quarters* that were in back of the main house. Well, there he'd be, drawin' away for hours without comin' into the house to eat. In those days he smoked cigarettes and he drank a lot of coffee, and a lot of beer, too. Now he was the oddball of the family. The others didn't seem to have any of his talent nor his intelligence, and yet they followed suit along with the parents and were actually hostile to the lad. For some reason, they had it against him! For what, I will never know. It was an attitude they had towards him, but if ya ask me, my son was the troublemaker behind all this. Now you may be wonderin' -- *How is it that I know this business*? Well, I had my informers. One was a nice lady that came in to help out twice a week or so, and I actually paid the woman to tell me what was goin' on.

Maybe that's ridiculous, but I had to know. I sensed that there was somethin' terribly wrong in that house and that I even thought somethin' would happen to your father. Now I am not tellin' ya this to shock the *bejesus* outa you, but it seems there is an important fact that you don't know about."

The old man stops cold. And flashes his dark glasses at me. I must look like a blank-faced fool, but I don't have any idea what the man's referring to. After sitting here in the empty silence, I finally ask him. "What are you talking about? No. I apparently don't know, Great Granddad. And I have a feeling that I'm going to vomit. It isn't good. I know that much."

And, of course, there's no exit for me to take. We're flying down the causeway with the rest of the summer vacationers, and the sky's a bright azure blue. I look over to the water and stare at the few boats bobbing on the gentle waves, then turn back to the goggle-eyed, praying mantis staring at me.

And he grins as he informs me, "Of course, I am also gettin' to the point of why I finally told those idiots to kiss my Scottish ass, and I will get to that, I promise. Heh-heh. I like to see you grow impatient with me, but things come in their own sequence and what I need to tell you, lad, is this: Your father had a brother. He was a year older than he was. And he was the apple of that idiot's eye. Why? Because the kid was a bit slow, but athletic and behaved just like *my* son, that's why. He was a — what do they say—oh…yeah,—he was the *chip off the old man's block*. Is that the…? He was a good kid. Don't get me wrong. He was a kid. It wasn't his fault his pop thought he was the greatest. And he was an athlete. A very good one. Actually, they said he coulda been a *pro.* And he got all these scholarship offers. Athletic scholarships. They give 'em away like candy, lad. If ya can play ball in this country, they think that's the greatest...never mind the brains. Well, Andy was clearly the winner. But in that household, he was treated like a freak. As if he were *the failure.* He was athletic, but he had more interestin' pursuits to take up his time. Like use his brain. An unheard of occupation in that knuckleheaded household. Well, lad. It was bad enough already when the tragedy happened. And it was a tragedy. I was thrown in there along with your father as to who was to blame for this senseless thing. And it was because I came into town-as I usually would do so every couple of years-and I called the boys one afternoon and told them I wanted them to test-drive this car. It was an Italian sports car. And a friend of mine had a dealership and would let me borrow cars whenever I came down to visit. It was the late sixties, and in those days, this was *the* car to have. At least, that's what the kids thought. So when the boys came by, they were thrilled to see this car. All the insurance was taken care of and my friend assured me it would be alright if the lads wanted to borrow it. Well, I let them have it for the afternoon and evenin' as long as they promised to return it by the next day. Well, they went off and I thought that was that. I was happy to be a grandfather for the lads, but I had no idea the kind of nonsense that would happen soon afterward. It turns out that the two brothers rode around a good part of the day and evenin' until the older brother, Jim, insisted on havin' it for his date that night, and since he was the older of the two, he always got his way. The two ended up gettin' into a furious argument, and Jim stormed out of the house and never was he to return. It's a sad, sad thing,

lad. Your father was shaken when the police finally
showed up at two in the mornin' to give the family the
bad news. And my son, the idiot, blamed Freddie for it
ever since. As the months went by, this fool would punch
your father in the head sayin' things like it should've
been him and this kind a crap. And I tried to comfort
your father, lad. And I did so boldly by showin' up at the
house, not carin' how hysterical they got. I kept tellin'
Freddie that he was going to pull through by drawin' and
studyin', to make him self a master at the things he loved
and to use that to fortify his spirit, and I hoped it helped.
After gettin' myself into a fistfight with that idiot son of
mine out on the patio of that house one night, I almost
killed that numbskull by dunkin' his head in the fountain
like a drownin' rat. It was at that moment that I left for
good. And that was March of 1968. An I don't mind
tellin' ya that it was the most liberatin' thing I have ever
done in my life. Somehow after that, lad, I knew I was
free. I had tried very hard to make-up for my mess. I
worked hard at correctin' my mistakes, but when I heard
how that idiot son talked to his own child-I punched the
bugga in his *trap* and never felt sorry for doin' so. And
now we're goin' to pay a visit to James Conrad, because
it took these years for me to realize that the kid never
asked to be his daddy's little hero. Just as much as
Freddie never asked to be his scapegoat. And I think we
should pay homage to that. And maybe to me, lad. I was
not the troublemaker, rabble-rousin', calloused, bugga
they cast me as, either. I was once a scared, kid, too, and
I had my own rotten stuff to get over. Well. I guess I said
enough for now, lad."

We ride silently as the car continues down this amazingly long bridge that crosses the lake. A zillion ques-

320

tions are running around in my head, and after I get over the slight nausea, I feel like I'm entering a new room somewhere in a world I don't quite know. It's something I've maybe dreamt about, or had heard about, and now I was in it. Wandering around strange surroundings. Why hadn't Andy ever told me? Why didn't he just even casually say that he had a brother who was killed in a car accident and leave it at that? Why was he so stone-silent about it all? Was he still waiting to tell me? Wondering when it would be the time to *get into it*. I ask my great granddad, this wise old coot in the sunglasses and long white hair. And after a bit of a pause the old gizzard tells me,

"I think it's because he still hurts from it. Although he'd be the first to deny it. He keeps it hidden down deep. He really *did* believe the whole thing was *his* fault. That's the kind of person he is. He'd always blame himself for not being this or that. All the while, he was the one with genius. The one with sparkle and promise, lyin' under there. The two had argued fiercely, and Andy was always tellin' the kid that he hated his guts, as a younger brother would, and well, you can imagine the horror of everythin' after. It was bad enough as it was, but to be blamed for it and scapegoated all the more for it, was cruel beyond imaginin'. It was a wonder he could finish school after that. And he did. I made sure of that. And I got him out of that house. I let him live in a spare apartment so he could continue to draw, while he told his parents he was livin' with a friend's family. Your father never thanked me enough over that one. And maybe it's the only thing I'm proudest of. To break a spirit is the worse offense anyone can suffer. I was not going to have that happen to Freddie. And I leave it to you to tell him about our conversation, lad, because he won't be hearin' it from me. I think it's somethin' you should decide on bringin' up with him."

We finally pull off the bridge and wind up a small road off the highway. There are pine trees everywhere and the old man asks Dominic to turn the air-conditioner off so we can roll down the windows. At the end of the little road is an iron gate. Great Granddad asks me to get out and open it. I do and we ride into a deeply wooded area.

He says, "I bought this property, but gave a good deal of it to your family. Since I came to this country, I wanted to build somethin' grand. I didn't get very far, lad. The house is not in use and I never quite got around to all of the other things I wanted to do. The boys visited this place many a time when they were young. They liked it here. I had a burial area set among these trees. There have been a few others who died since then, includin' Freddie's father. And I have my plot. It's been ready for years, lad. But it won't be takin' me for another fifteen years. A psychic once told me—when I was about forty-five—that I would live to be 106. And I thought she was crazy. Now I'm beginnin' to believe her. You know what one of my doctors told me the other day? That I got a small, tight heart. Like a little drum. This is good. He also said my heart was like that of a forty-year old. Believe me, that's *childhood* to an old guy like me."

The car slowly comes to a hault and all of us step out. In the corner of the immense green lawn, a bit unkempt and weedy, stands a small tombstone. All three of us walk over and stand by it. It reads: James Conrad Strayhorn, beloved son of Anna Mae & James Andrew Strayhorn, born May 20, 1950, died November 15, 1967.

Great Granddad stands here for a while, creaking his knees as he pats his hand on the grave. Now the old goat begins to speak, "I brought Freddie's son, lad. We are both sorry that this happened to you. And I thought it only be right that you meet. He's quite a lad, this one."

When Great Granddad looks back at me, I start to cry. In fact, I really boo-hoo. I don't know where or how all these feelings come up in me, but I'm crying like I did when I was a child. Great Granddad asks me to sit next to him, that he wants to tell me something. As I'm sobbing like a fool, he puts his arm around me.

He leans in a bit as he says, "Ya cryin ya daddy's uncried tears, lad. Ya doin' it for him. Do you know that? Go on. It's alright for a lad ta cry. I don't care. Dominic doesn't care, either. See? He's walkin' over there on his own. He knows this is private. Now... lad, I'm proud of the way ya cryin'. Afterwards, we'll go dancin'. I'm not kiddin'. It's the way it's supposed ta be."

I feel all of twelve years old. And I guess if my great granddad wasn't so old, I would feel ashamed for crying. But somehow I believe what the old man's telling me. In fact, I believe every word he's telling me, because it feels damned good to do so. Although I had no idea I would react this way. I didn't even know the boy had once existed. How could I cry? But here I am. And it's going on for quite a stretch. After I finally stop, we get up and stroll the grounds. As we're doing so, gramps here begins to sing a song. A rather plaintive tune. He tells me it's a Scottish song he learned as a child, so the words are not in English nor in Gaelic, but in Scots. It has a folksy melody, and there's a haunting beauty to it. And the old coot sings it with a passion deep with yearning. I ask him what the song's about. And he says it's about a soul that wandered for its home and only found it when it finally lost itself in the sound of the Highland pipes that hover the hills. It certainly makes me think. I tell the old man that I didn't understand why my dad never really told me about him, and wisely, the old guy pulls off his dark glasses and looks at me with his watery gray, ancient eyes. Beautiful wise eyes.

"Aye. But that was to give ya the curiosity to find me, lad."

About the Author

A former advertising copywriter and TV scriptwriter, this is a first novel for M. A. Kirkwood. A native of New Orleans, the author studied with the *Jesuits* before continuing on with studies at the University of California at Berkeley and Stanford University. Kirkwood lives in Northern California.